CHARLIE
REYNE

CA CIPO Reg.#1210726; First Edition 2024

Birdsgate Publishing, Winnipeg, Manitoba, Canada
(info@birdsgatepublishing.com)

This is a work of fiction. Characters and events portrayed in this book are fictitious or are used fictitiously. Similarity to real persons, living or dead, is purely coincidental and not intended by the author.

Cover Design: BespokeBookCovers

ISBN:
eBook Edition ISBN: 9781777861643
Paperback Edition ISBN: 9781777861636
Hardcover Edition ISBN: 9781777861650

BISAC:
FIC027070 FICTION/Romance/Historical/Regency

CHARLIE REYNE

NADINE KAMPEN

Birdsgate
Publishing

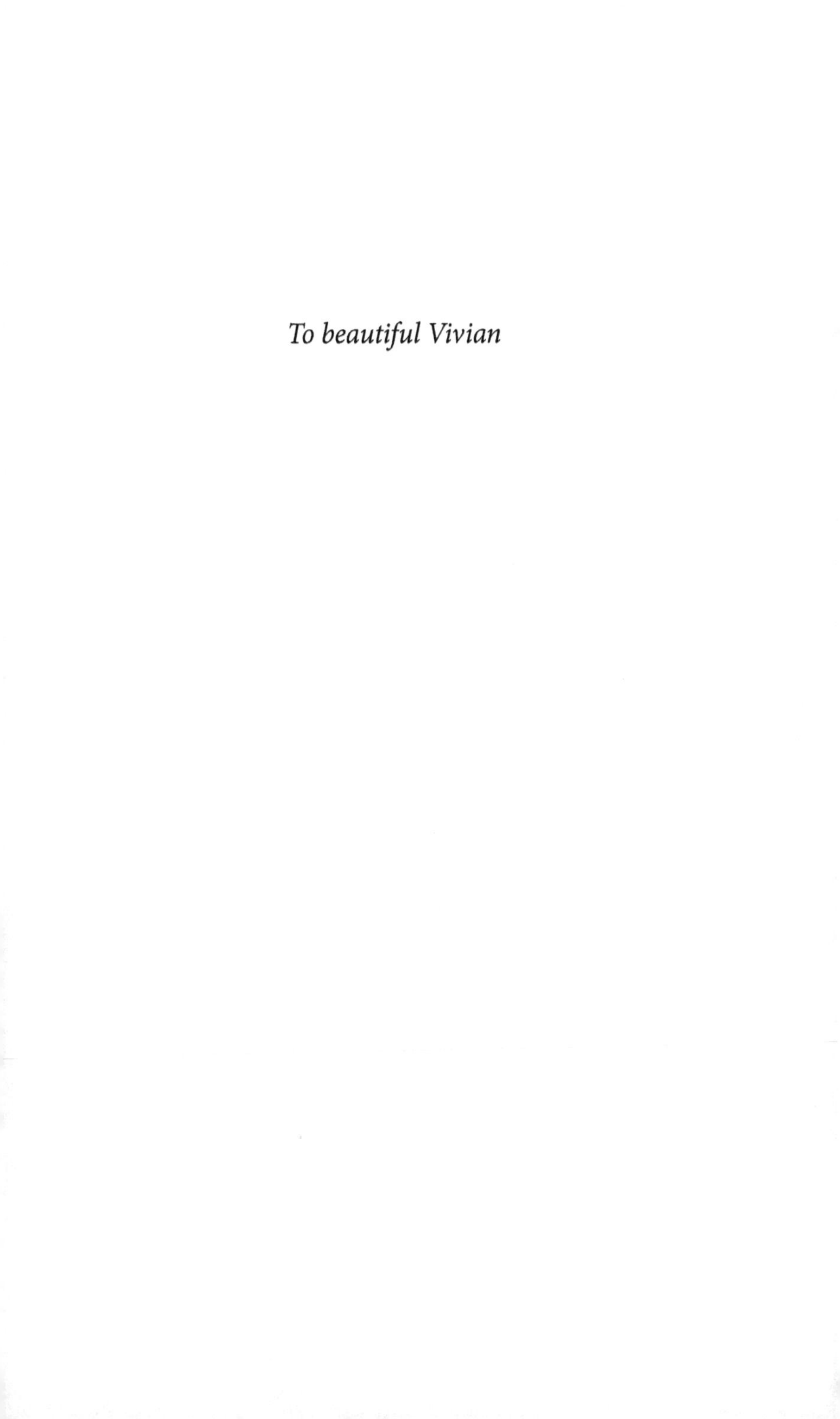

To beautiful Vivian

Part One

ONE

Behind the Drums

Charlie Reyne tucked a few loose strands of hair under her worn cap and watched nervously as the long lines of soldiers surged forward. Hearing the distant beating of the drums, Charlie felt for a moment that the rapid beating of her heart mimicked the same rhythm. She shook her head at her foolishness and listened afresh to the pounding of drums as the British and Portuguese battalions marched towards Vitoria, a little town in north-eastern Spain.

The air on the plains felt unbearably hot despite the early hour. Preferring the moisture-laden winds off the sea in Portugal to the drier air here in Spain, she hoped for a small breeze to pick up and offer relief from the intense summer heat.

Today, on the twenty-first of June 1813, allied troops stationed in the Iberian Peninsula travelled in four contingents, moving northeast along rough roads and narrow lanes towards the open plains of Vitoria. They aimed to unite along the way with rebel bands of skilled Spanish *guerrillas* to bolster their forces. The allied forces had advanced well over twenty miles over rough terrain on each of the past three days. According to Charlie's father, information had arrived during the night indicating that they were within a half-day's march of their destination. Based on their present course, they would meet head-on with the combined French and Spanish forces advancing south and east of their lines. Despite exhaustion from this latest push, most of the veteran soldiers shared an air of expectation.

Charlie fully shared that feeling. She again looked out at the men marching ahead. She felt an ache in her heart knowing what the day held for them. The soldiers in front of her were for the most part an experienced group, understanding from the pace of their march and the mood of their leaders that engagement was imminent.

The supply train surged forward. Wagons rumbled along uneven ground, churning dust into the dry air. Situated towards the rear of the supply cavalcade, Charlie waited for her turn to move forward.

'Come on, darlings,' she urged a pair of old mules, flicking the end of the long reins against their rumps. The mules ignored her. Charlie climbed down from the wagon and moved alongside the larger of the two. She blew gently in its ear. The mule tossed its head and lunged forward, pulling its partner with him. 'Thank you, dear boy,' she said, hopping back onto the wagon and taking up the reins again.

Charlie was an old hand at driving carts and wagons. An unlucky storm at sea on her journey home to England had stranded Charlie in Portugal at the outbreak of the war. Since that time, she had travelled frequently on campaigns with her father, General Sir William Reyne, and had become an experienced driver of the mule teams. Overhearing her father complaining that he was critically short of drivers, Charlie volunteered to help. While she typically travelled further back, staying with the baggage train, today she was helping with the supply transports.

'You might as well use me as a driver, Father,' she had offered the night before, spooning the last of her hot stew into her mouth. 'You know I can handle the teams as well as any of your men.'

'True,' the general nodded. He paused to consider the matter.

'I do need your help, but you have to promise me to stay well back of the action.' He reached into his breast pocket and pulled out an area map of the Spanish plain near Vitoria, laying it out and flattening the folds.

'We are to engage, then, are we?' she asked, studying his expression. 'We must be fairly close.'

General Reyne nodded, knowing he could trust his daughter to keep matters to herself. 'When we reach this area,' he tapped the map, 'the troops will move into their columns in battle formation. All going well, I want you to set up here, north of the river. You will have a clear line of vision. I want you to draw up some charts of our field positions. Can you do that for me? If we must retreat, or if you feel threatened, you and Gus and Wil are to take the mules and retrace your route. Leave everything— everything, you hear?—and go at once. Understood?'

Charlie reached for her father's glass and took a sip of his watered-down rum. She pulled her stool in closer to the table to view his map, nodding in agreement as she leaned in.

'I will give strict instructions to Gus and Wil. They will not leave your side,' said her father.

Charlie Reyne left her tent at sunrise the next morning. A hawk screeched in the cloudless sky, spiralling overhead as it swooped down and caught a small bird in mid-flight. She shuddered, shook off the image, and shifted her gaze to look around the camp. Hundreds of men were within her range of vision, most of whom had slept out in the open. She watched them, sitting in small groups eating their morning rations, pulling on their boots, or checking their weapons. How many of these men, she wondered, would return to sit another time around an evening campfire? Who would share another meal? She knew with utmost certainty that, for some, their meagre breakfast would be their last.

A tall, slender woman came up quietly behind Charlie and

touched the young woman on the shoulders.

'My goodness, you startled me!' cried Charlie, jumping up. 'Whatever is the matter?'

The woman's hands fell to her sides. She smiled gently and said, 'I just wanted to see you off. Are you ready? You must promise to do as your father has told you, *e tudo estará bem.* All will be well, little one.'

Senhora Sofia Montalto's posture and bearing bespoke confidence and elegance, notwithstanding her strange garments. Today, she had donned one of the general's shirts, worn loosely over her dress to help ward off the sun. In place of a woman's customary light shift underneath her dress, she instead wore a pair of men's trousers for ease of movement as did many of the women in the passenger train. For both personal and political reasons, Sofia had adapted to the times and her surroundings. Despite Sofia's status as General Reyne's war-time mistress, she was the only woman Charlie could remember standing in the role of a real mother to her.

The men, very few of whom had ever met the general's wife, affectionately referred to Sofia as 'the second Mrs Reyne'. Since Charlie's birth mother was, presumably, still alive and residing in England, Sofia knew there could never be a formal union between herself and General Reyne. She was a widow whom the general had met when the British joined the war effort in Portugal. Cared for by the general, adored by his daughter, and treated respectfully by his troops, Sofia was content with her situation. From a practical perspective, her relationship made her eligible for half-rations from the army's food supplies as the general's 'spouse'. Similarly, Charlie also received half-rations as the daughter of an officer. Charlie's father, fortunately a man of some means, supplemented their rations from time to time when local supplies were sufficient.

Sofia reached out and tenderly brushed away a strand of

hair from Charlie's forehead. 'Did your *papai* remind you to take your drawing case? I am sure the other officers are envious that his reports are so thorough and feature such detailed maps.'

Charlie nodded. 'I have everything ready.'

She again felt a heightened sense of nervousness, a combination of dread and anxiety that lay like a heavy cloak on her shoulders whenever battle was imminent. This time, however, she also felt hopeful. A significant campaign was underway. A victory now would give them the upper hand in this never-ending war against Emperor Bonaparte's army. Could they win this next battle? Might they return to the coast in the autumn and stay for the winter in Oporto? If luck held, and other victories followed, perhaps they could even sail to England next spring.

'I wish you were staying in the passenger train with me,' Sofia said to Charlie.

Charlie patted her hand. 'I will be just fine,' she said earnestly, wanting to convince herself as much as Sofia.

For the day's journey, Charlie had, like Sofia, donned a pair of light trousers. She knew from her father's lectures that in England she would be ostracised if caught donning a man's garments. Here, approaching a battlefield, her wardrobe choices mirrored those of the hard-working women who followed the camp. She could certainly dress to match the handful of officer's wives in camp when the occasion called for it, but today, enduring the heat and dirt of the march, she relished the comfort offered by her selections.

Sofia helped tuck in Charlie's shirt for her and surveyed the young lady's appearance. With tanned skin, dark hair rolled under her cap, and her chest bound in linen to flatten her breasts, Charlie could pass at first glance as a local Spanish lad. She and Sofia both knew that the outfit afforded only limited protection. Spanish civilians could be mistaken as friend or foe by either side; anyone British, if caught, would be imprisoned, shot, or suffer brutal injury at the hands of the enemy. What her costume offered was ease of movement, a mask for her femininity, and an opportunity for a moment's hesitation, creating the possibility of escape. As the daughter of a battle-hardened general travelling with the army, and stationed near the field of battle, she could fully expect to share the same fate as soldiers at the front.

Charlie squeezed Sofia's hands, reassuring her once again she would be careful. She finished her packing and left to join the army staff preparing to move out with the supply train. Several of the guards, recognising her, gave a friendly wave as she approached. Miss Charlotte Reyne—affectionately known as Little Charlie to the men in her father's regiment—had, by this time, been in the Iberian Peninsula for almost seven years. Her arrival had been accidental, her departure delayed, and eventually, her time there extended indefinitely due to the war.

After Napoleon Bonaparte's army, led by his brother Joseph Bonaparte, attacked England's long-time ally in 1807, the general and his troops had been freshly reassigned from India to join the war effort in the Iberian Peninsula to defend Portugal. The general had gone on ahead to the Peninsula and arranged for his daughter, visiting him in India at the time, to sail home to England with a merchant convoy. Charlie's ship, veering off course during a massive storm, crashed along the Portuguese coast. Rescued by the local villagers, the survivors remained stranded in Oporto, north of Lisbon. It was here that Charlie met and came under the care of Sofia and her sister Inês. Once the British and Portuguese forces ousted the French, the women reunited Charlie with her father. Through this encounter, the general met his mistress.

In the ensuing years, the then-twelve-year-old acquired an unusual assortment of skills. After the allied forces reclaimed Oporto, General Reyne arranged for Charlie to spend the winter months with Sofia and Inês, where she could study with a tutor and stay out of harm's way. The Montalto family's property, nestled in a small valley east of the old port town, had escaped major damage during the early stages of French occupation. It had become Charlie's occasional home base.

After two years of living near Oporto, and after the British and Portuguese forces had expelled Bonaparte's army from the area in 1809, the three ladies began alternately travelling with the troops on campaigns and working in the military field hospitals. Over four years passed in this manner. The lanky child had grown into a slender and headstrong woman who had gained respect as an experienced helper. Charlie knew the rules of engagement as well as any soldier.

This morning, as rays of sunlight diffused and warmed the darkness, Charlie watched the mules lean into their harnesses and step sure-footedly along the rocky path. Lost in thought, she suddenly realised someone was calling out to her from the wagon behind her.

'*Wir sind gleich neben dir, Charlie. Hab keine Angst!*' Wilhelm yelled in German as the supply train surged forward, telling her they were nearby, and not to worry. Gustav sat quietly beside his younger brother, scowling at Charlie. Gus was clearly unhappy that she had volunteered to drive. Moreover, he was furious with her father for assigning her to the supply train when a battle was imminent.

'*Vielen Dank!*' she called out, thanking her friends in appreciation.

True to their assurances to her father, Charlie's Prussian guards were indeed staying near her. Charlie took comfort in this. The two veteran soldiers, competent and highly skilled, had been responsible for her safety along with other assigned duties for the past three years. They had come to her aid in dire circumstances on more than one occasion.

Serving since 1803 with the elite King's German Legion, the

pair had transferred under a private contract in 1810 to work for the Reyne family. Wil had been recovering from serious wounds when their service contracts in the KGL Hussars were due for renewal. Gus, deeply attached to his younger sibling, had been loath to separate from him. Noticing the hesitation, and seizing the opportunity, Charlie's father persuaded the two brothers to work directly for him. He negotiated a transfer and assigned them at his own expense to protect vital camp supplies and munitions, which often came under attack by raiding parties, and, when necessary, to drop all other duties and serve as personal guards for the general's daughter and his mistress Sofia. This they had done with admirable fortitude.

Charlie smiled affectionately as Wil waved to her from the rum wagon. This heavy-set wagon, pulled by a team of four mules, was laden with three large vats of rum, the contents of which were closely guarded and apportioned daily to the men in prescribed rations.

Gus, still frowning, tipped his head in greeting as he urged his team forward.

No one knew precisely what the day would hold. They had, however, seen enough battles to know what to expect. What none of them anticipated was that, for Charlie, this would turn out to be one of the most disturbing days in her young life and one she would not easily forget.

'We are marshalling to the east and will unite with other battalions after we cross through this area,' her father had explained to her the night before, his finger tracing their intended route on his map.

'How strong are our allied forces?' she had asked him.

'Combined? We will number well over ninety thousand once the *guerrillas* join us,' the general replied.

The enemy camp, with roughly as many men, was known to have set up west of Vitoria. The British supply train slowed in the area not far off from where her father had predicted it would stop. Their military intelligence, conveyed by members of the Spanish rebel army, had been highly accurate and they had caught up to the enemy as hoped. As the morning light played against the low hills on the horizon, Charlie could see the allied soldiers forming their battle lines on the rolling plains ahead.

The battalions in front of her belonged to the Left Column Army. General Sir Arthur Wellesley, in full command of the campaign, had ridden into their camp late at night and instructed his senior officers to take positions north of the river Zadorra, west of Joseph Bonaparte's troops. Looking across the distant plains, Charlie could make out the allied formations. The bright red of the British infantry and the green hues of the light divisions stretched out in front of her.

Charlie and the boys, as she called them, watching the formations take shape, had set up on the outside perimeter at a distance from the other supply wagons. They had selected a slight rise of land with a few tall shrubs for shade. Occasionally, runners from the different brigades would arrive to collect supplies from the various wagons and carts stationed nearby. Finally, she heard the ominous blasts of the cannons and saw smoke rising in the distance. A loud, constant din soon arose from different areas of engagement and resounded across the plains. The three of them listened anxiously for the next hour as the distant blasts from cannons and muskets steadily increased.

Peering intently towards the battlefield nearest to them, Charlie was startled when Wil suddenly began gesturing and shouting at her.

'Charlie, *pass auf! Hinter dir!*' Wil cried in warning.

He leapt off the rum wagon and ran towards her, yelling and pointing towards a French soldier partially hidden in the tall grass behind her. Spinning around, Charlie saw a young lad lying on his stomach and loading ammunition. She swiftly ran towards him and kicked the musket from his hand.

The soldier, a youngster of fifteen years, perhaps less, had no strength to respond. He lay exhausted, prostrate in front of her, his clothing soaked in blood from his wounds.

'He is likely trying to get back to his troops,' said Charlie.

She looked at the boy as a wave of fear swept over his features. Calmly and quickly, she assessed the boy's condition. 'Wounds to his thigh and left side. *Wasser, bitte,*' she said to Wil, asking him to pass her some water.

Disagreeing with her decision but knowing it would be fruitless to argue, Wil stepped away to collect a water flask along with Charlie's medical kit. Gustav, swearing at them both, moved to the front of the wagon where he could see better and protect them from any approaching soldiers.

Wil retrieved the necessary items from the wagon, thumping his brother Gus on the back as he passed him. Turning her back to the men, Charlie loosened her shirt and unwound several strips of cloth looped around her waist and ribcage.

'What a bloody waste of linen!' Gustav yelled at them both.

Shocked that instead of being instantly killed he was being helped instead, the soldier started to cry. He reached out to squeeze Charlie's hand in thanks. Wilhelm slapped the boy's bloody hand, stepped on his wrist, and then pinned him down, all the while cursing him for his stupidity. With the boy immobilised, Charlie crouched beside him.

The boy screamed in pain as Charlie straightened out his leg, ripped apart the fabric on his torn breeches, wiped debris off his skin, and rinsed the wound. He stared in shock as she plied a long needle and rapidly sutured his thigh where a bayonet had ripped the skin and pierced him. He soon passed out.

When the young soldier recovered, he found himself stripped of his weapon and lying alone in a dip of land away from the British position. Staring up at the sky in disbelief, he lay quietly for some time, tears occasionally rolling down his cheeks. Eventually, he struggled to his knees, took a deep breath, and crawled into the nearby bushes.

While the wounded soldier had lain on his back staring skyward, the roar of battle over the plains of Vitoria continued unabated. Charlie could see the forward movement of the troops, but she was still far enough away to be out of gunshot and artillery range. Cannon fire from both sides was heavy. Her father's infantry and artillery units pressed on tenaciously. They slowly advanced their positions, aided by nearby skirmishes and attacks from their light cavalry. The noise was at times deafening and for brief moments eerily quiet while men reloaded their guns and cannons. Everyone knew the cost to individual soldiers that came with each blast of a cannon. Given the massive extent of the fighting underway in this battle, thousands of soldiers would be buried once the guns fell silent. Tears ran freely down Charlie's dusty face, streaking her cheeks. Gus, nearby, pulled out his flask and drank deeply. He tossed it to his younger brother to finish the rest.

'Perhaps it will end soon,' Charlie murmured to no one in particular.

The troop's munitions and food stations were set up north of the lines of attack, with assigned runners and a few determined wives and camp aides periodically coming and going, transporting water with rum and boxes of cartridges out to the men. In between duties, Charlie offered what medical care she could while their supplies lasted. To some, she simply gave words of comfort or closed the eyes of those beyond help. At various points over the day, refocusing on her father's request, she opened her drawing case and carried out his instructions.

With an exceptional talent for drawing and a keen eye for detail, Charlie was someone whom her father and his senior officers often asked to sketch battle scenarios and positional maps. Sometimes she drew from her observations and sometimes from descriptions given to her after the battles. Several times during the day, she pulled out a pencil and sheets of paper from her leather case and charted battlefield positions within her range of vision, intending to add better detail later.

Her drawing skill had put her perilously close to the action at times, but she had confided more than once to Sofia that she felt safer being close to the soldiers than travelling with the baggage train. Everyone who travelled with the regiment, whether soldier or officer or civilian, had experienced the carnage of war. There was no one in camp who had not hauled away bodies from the field, cared for the wounded, and buried or tragically abandoned the dead and dying. Yet being on campaign had neither inured Charlie to the atrocities nor hardened her sensibilities.

Oftentimes, it was the plight of civilians that caused her heart to ache.

'When we were coming back from the river, we found three women and an infant beside the road,' she confided to Sofia a few days earlier, her face pinched in pain by what she had seen.

Sharing Charlie's grief, Sofia cradled Charlie in her arms as though she were a young child. 'At least they are no longer suffering. Ah, sweet Charlie, you are so dear to me,' whispered Sofia. 'So very precious.'

Left alone by her mother at an early age, Charlie viewed Sofia as her closest family member besides her father. The general's lengthy service contract and his British wife's perennial disinterest had exacted a predictable toll on their relationship. The first Mrs Reyne left the family home under the guise of caring for an ailing mother, whose health proved to be robust. Weeks of absence stretched into months. Opportunities to reunite Mrs Reyne with her child ended with Charlie's departure to India. Free of familial responsibilities, Mrs Reyne remained to this day in London.

The second Mrs Reyne filled the gap created by the departure of Charlie's mother. The time Sofia and Charlie spent together during the Peninsular War felt like forever to Charlie. The pair of them had lifted each other's spirits repeatedly. They had, over the years, seen soldiers and civilians lying wounded and dying across the countryside. They had also seen countless generous and heroic acts by citizens and troops alike. Perhaps it was the practice of recording in images what she experienced, good and bad piled high and tumbled together, that helped Charlie cope. In laying down a record of events, in sketching and drawing maps and events of importance for her father's reports, she had found a way to unravel the knot of memories and sort them into something useful. She had also found other ways to be helpful: bringing water to someone; holding a hand; resting a head on her shoulder; or tucking a drawing into a soldier's pocket, offering cheer, comfort, or rest. The troops cherished her company and welcomed her at their campfires.

TWO

Eyes on Vitoria

Dusk came at last. After twelve hours of heavy fighting, Joseph Bonaparte and his senior officers recognised this was a battle they could not win. Bonaparte, commander-in-chief, reluctantly gave his officers the order to retreat.

The nearest battalions of allied troops pursued Bonaparte's retreating soldiers through and past Vitoria. With the French army's well-trained rear guard valiantly struggling to protect tens of thousands of their troops as they escaped, British troops in pursuit rushed crushingly close on their heels. Abandoned cannons, tipped supply carts, and soldiers' bodies lay strewn across fields and roadsides in eerie contrast to the peaceful hues of a rose-coloured sky.

Though they had already shifted their positions to stay closer to the troops as the battle surged forward, Charlie, Gus, and Wil remained well back from the battalions, keeping watch over their assigned supplies, and assisting any wounded nearby. Tired and hungry, Charlie unrolled a large napkin and handed out scones that Sofia had saved and packed for them.

Startled by the sound of a horse, Charlie looked up to see a rider approaching. She could tell by the man's distinctive dark blue pelisse and crimson and gold barrel sash that he was an officer of the King's Light Dragoons. He pulled his mount to a halt and looked intently at the three of them.

'My name is Lieutenant Niles, of the 15th,' he told them, correctly assuming they were familiar with his uniform. 'I am looking for Mr Charlie Reyne stationed here with the Left Column supply train. Which of you is Mr Reyne?' asked the officer.

Charlie raised her hand, sighing in frustration when this caused half of her scone to break off and fall to the ground.

'Our Lieutenant Colonel has seen your drawings in battle reports and has given orders to take you into town to record what is going on. We need to leave at once. Get on with me; I will take you in.'

'*Nein! Sie kann nicht gehen!*' protested Gus, moving quickly to block the man on the horse.

'*Charlie, bleib hier mit uns!*' Wil shouted at her, entreating her to stay with them.

'I have no idea what your problem is or what you are saying. These are orders from my commanding officer—get out of the way!' the officer yelled at them. Seeing their resistance, he pulled out his pistol.

Gus and Wil took a step back as the officer swung his arm and aimed his gun not at them but instead directly at Charlie's head. Charlie looked at the officer, shaken.

'Get the boy his supplies,' he said in a low tone to Wil. 'He is coming with me. Mr Reyne, get up behind me on my horse. Do you hear me? Move! Now!' Stunned, Charlie stepped forward. The officer reached down and hauled her up behind him.

Wil retrieved her case and reluctantly held it up to her. Clutching it to her chest, and assuring Gus and Wil she would be fine, Charlie wrapped her other arm tightly around the officer to keep herself from sliding sideways.

Pointing his pistol this time towards Gus and Wil, the lieutenant backed his horse away from the two guards and rode away.

A ride of a few miles brought the lieutenant and his charge into Vitoria. Here, they met with utter chaos. French troops had pushed through town attempting to make their escape as the British gave chase. Forced to traverse a steep and muddy lane to the northeast of Vitoria, retreating soldiers took every available horse, grabbed whatever valuables they could carry, and overturned or abandoned supply wagons and baggage carts in their train. Wagons and carts lay overturned, spilling their contents along the rutted path.

This was not a normal baggage train. The allies had overtaken King Joseph Bonaparte's main booty wagons laden with six years' worth of Portuguese and Spanish treasures stripped from the countryside, transported in haste out of Madrid, and crammed into one long train of precious cargo. Over a hundred wagons were stuck in the town, scattered haphazardly in the streets of Vitoria, blocking the main arteries of travel. Over a thousand more, some of which carried women and children or transported the sick and injured, littered the escape route and the surrounding fields.

'Stay quiet! We are going into the market district. Not a sound, do you understand? Do not speak to anyone,' the lieutenant told his charge.

Instructed to transport the artist into town rather than out along the eastern road, Lieutenant Niles rode into a narrow alleyway behind some buildings where they could safely dismount. Assessing their surroundings, he pushed open the back entrance of a three-storey shop that had already been ransacked. The shop faced the market square. To Charlie's surprise, the lieutenant led his horse into the structure with them and left it loose inside a small back room. He then barricaded both the front and back doors into the building.

Leading Charlie up a set of stairs, he found a small attic room with windows opening onto a flat section of the roof. He went through the window first and told Charlie to come out behind him. Despite the light cloud cover, the moon provided enough extra light to give them a better view of the market square and several side streets.

'Can you see well enough, boy?' the lieutenant asked, not unkindly. In getting Charlie into the town, he had accomplished the first half of his mission. His duty now was to stay with the artist and bring back the drawings. He leaned against a low gable, studying the lad, as he thought him to be. The boy's long hair straggled from his cap and curled against his dusty face. While the boy was on the small side, without a shade of whiskers, the lieutenant could tell from his posture and grip when they were riding that he was lean and fit.

'I am impressed that you have earned enough of a reputation for your drawings to trigger this request,' said the lieutenant, chagrined that his duty at this important time, while the enemy fled, was to sit idle and watch a boy draw pictures. He was curious to see for himself what the boy could do.

'Careful, come away from the edge,' he said quietly. Lieutenant Niles drew Charlie further back on the roof as the crowds of soldiers pushed and hollered below them. 'Stay low,' he cautioned. 'Someone might mistake us for a pair of enemy marksmen.'

He pretended disinterest but sat close enough to watch as Charlie Reyne sketched rapidly under the moonlight. Each pencil stroke was quick and sure. It astounded him to see how rapidly the scenes below took shape, rich with details documenting all that lay within their view. They heard the click of horses' hooves on the cobbled streets and the yells of their cavalry as riots and pillaging spread through the town. They could hear screams and cries from below. He closed his eyes for a moment, shutting out the carnage.

For the first few hours, Lieutenant Niles observed the artist drawing beside him. Exhausted, he at last slept while Charlie sketched dutifully at this side.

It was the middle of the night when the lieutenant awoke, startled by a fresh round of raucous shouts and laughter a few streets away. Charlie lay beside him. Her eyes were closed, and her head rested against his shoulder. She loosely held several sheets of paper in one hand and a dulled pencil in the other.

Lieutenant Niles pulled her fingers apart and lifted the drawings. Looking over the sketches, he was shocked to see what she had captured. He had seen much of the carnage and madness himself, but when the mayhem shifted to other areas, he had let his guard down and drifted into sleep. What had happened since to trigger these images?

Charlie's drawings showed throngs of infantry, heavy and light dragoons, officers of various ranks, and civilians in the streets below. Undoubtedly, some civilians were locals and others were likely captured from the French baggage train. Men in one drawing were strutting in women's clothing, several of them sporting high turbans adorned with hefty plumes. Another drawing showed a group of women weeping, half-dressed in gowns and soldiers' gear, paraded through the square, laden with jewellery, and draped with fine fabrics. In this same picture, Charlie had sketched a parrot sitting atop rolls of tapestry stacked high in an open cart. A pair of monkeys squatted on the rim of an open trunk.

'What in the world—' He shook his head in amazement at the boy's audacity and strange imagery, shaking his head at the outrageous drawings. 'I wonder what General Wellesley will say when he sees this,' he said to his sleeping companion. 'I can tell you now, boy, you picked a bad time to let your ideas run wild.'

Startled by his reproof, Charlie lifted her head. She stared at him with bleary eyes for a few moments. She scowled briefly, her eyes rimmed with tears, then drifted back to sleep.

While the market district was now almost empty of soldiers,

sounds of rampage still rose from distant streets. Contents from the wagons below had long been scattered or hauled away. Soldiers crowding into the square earlier in the evening had either passed out after their drunken revelry or moved on to pillage elsewhere. The lieutenant suddenly heard a man hollering. Leaning forward for a better view, he saw an officer stagger across the square holding a little costumed dog tightly against his chest, its short leash dangling beside him. In his other hand, the man held a set of reins and was leading a pony. Seated astride it was a buxom woman, wearing nothing but army breeches and a string of pearls.

'My word, these drawings must be real!' he said in shock, looking at a few more of Charlie's pictures. He shook his head in disgust.

Lieutenant Niles picked up Charlie's case and pulled out all her sketches, carefully numbered and neatly stacked. Though he was a hardened soldier, her images astounded him. Light from the moon and torch lamps below had given her a view in all directions from their rooftop lookout. Some of her drawings focused only on the looting, others on the victims and offenders. She showed jewellery, household valuables, coins, and paintings being carted off; soldiers' boots hauled away by the armful; and women paraded through the streets half-dressed, in brothel outfits and evening gowns. Treasures lay everywhere, whether taken from the town itself or dragged directly out of the wagons jammed in the streets below.

Charlie had drawn some of the uniforms in detail. Recognising the various badges, he groaned inwardly. Regimental uniforms, senior and junior, were all in the mix that passed by under Charlie's watchful eye. Details of the night's pillage, assaults on citizens, destruction, and the extraordinary haul of loot were depicted in her images of the night's madness.

'Good lord, what incredible drawings,' he barely breathed

the words. He was shocked not only by the brutality evident through the sketches but also by the artist's ability to capture the scenarios so rapidly.

Waking Charlie, he helped her get back inside the building. He half-carried her down the narrow stairs. Leading his horse back out to the street, the lieutenant noticed a shiny object protruding from the muddy path underfoot. He picked it up, brushing off the dirt to reveal a golden chain with a bejewelled peacock pendant set inside a golden loop.

'Here, boy, if it is real gold, this piece will have some worth. You can try bartering it for an extra meal or something else useful when you get back to camp. Consider it thanks for your hard work. Here, I will put it on you for safekeeping. Take care no one sees you wearing this, lest they mistake you for a girl,' he chuckled, fastening the necklace around Charlie's neck.

Riding at a steady canter, with Charlie in front of him this time to keep her from sliding off, he made it to his regiment's *rendezvous* point before dawn. He felt a strange sense of responsibility towards this young person. He was loathe to leave the little artist, but he still had work to do. With the help of one of the camp guards, he located an outlying supply tent and laid Charlie inside on a horse blanket. He stared at Charlie's features, finding himself disconcerted by his companion's girlish face and childlike frame. Dissatisfied with himself for simply abandoning Charlie, he rolled a small sack as a headrest and used a saddle blanket to provide a covering.

Something about the little artist, perhaps the long eyelashes and delicate features, made the lieutenant feel protective. Strangely, he wanted to linger here but he still had one more task in front of him. With a last look back at Charlie, sleeping deeply, and with a brief nod of thanks to the guard, he left to deliver the drawings to his commander in a camp further west.

It was an hour after dawn by the time Lieutenant Niles

returned to awaken the boy. On his arrival, a few of the men in his division waved to get his attention. They hurried to catch up with him as he marched over to the tent where he had left Charlie sleeping, chattering as they went.

'There is no one here, sir. Lieutenant, you should have seen 'em!' one of the fellows piped in excitedly. 'One of the generals from the Left arrived in camp before sun-up along with a pair of big Prussian guards and a couple of aides.'

'They came from one of the north infantry camps,' said a young ensign. 'They were steaming mad, sir. The general raged at everybody until his face turned purple. The Prussian fellows stomped around looking mighty dangerous, shouting that they had been searching for some young lady all through the night. They searched several of our tents until our boy Mallory figured out that they were searching for that artist you brought here—well, can you believe it?—that was not a boy at all! It was this general's daughter, disguised as a boy!—and they scooped her up and yelled and swore some more. They were fit to murder us all!'

Lieutenant Niles looked wide-eyed at his colleagues, dumbfounded to learn that his companion through the night, the young man, supposedly, whom he took into Vitoria, was in fact a general's daughter.

'Not a man, but a woman,' he said softly in disbelief, stunned. He felt a knot in his stomach as he thought of all that she had seen and heard in the last twenty-four hours.

'I asked 'em, politely enough, sir, how were you supposed to recognise one name out of thousands as being somebody's daughter and said that you were just obeying orders from our seniors and probably Old Nosey himself—how should we know?—in taking that artist into town. We all defended your honour fiercely, sir. Then they swore some more and took her with them and rode away.'

'Me and the boys was chatting about it afterwards,' the ensign spoke again. 'One of our lads overheard some fellows talking about the lady. Says she came over to Portugal as a youngster. She is the darling of the camps. She has been travelling with her father on campaign for years and does all sorts of tasks for him. She even sits as a hostess at officer dinners. The lads in her father's regiment have known her for so long that everyone calls her Little Charlie. That is where all the confusion comes from when they told you to fetch this Charlie Reyne person. My God, sir, and here you were, following orders and carrying all the blame for taking a woman into town, of all places! In the middle of a riot! And staying out alone with her all night!'

'If you take no mind to my saying so, lieutenant,' chirped the ensign ominously, squinting under a pair of thin black eyebrows, 'you will have the reaper to pay for this night's work; either that, or you will have to get married again, sir!'

THREE

Shore Leave

THREE MORE SHIPS had anchored near where the HMS *Pontus* lay in shallow waters off the shores of Oporto, seventy miles north of the navy's main harbour at Lisbon. Taking a deep breath of cool October air and pulling his gaze away from the sea, the captain of the *Pontus* stepped away from the quarterdeck and into his cabin. Four of his officers followed him.

Opening the leather portfolio lying on the table, Captain Henry Brantford pulled out one of several letters inside and smiled at his men. His officers looked at him expectantly.

'I know you are eager to hear the news. And gentlemen, this is indeed very good news,' he said, lifting a letter. 'I confess, we certainly deserve a short break after our victories along the coast. The Board has assigned us a five-day shore leave. Afterwards, we are to lead a convoy headed home to England. We will have enough time in Oporto to refresh provisions, repair our sails and equipment, and stretch our legs before this next assignment.'

He nodded to Mr Richard Sherrington, his first lieutenant, and waited while his senior officer handed out several sheets of paper.

'Here are your schedules and lists of duties,' said Sherrington. 'We are breaking into four shore units, each under a team of three officers.'

"I have asked Mr Norcross to arrange on-land training in Oporto,' Captain Brantford added, gesturing to his young midshipman to come forward. 'Mr Norcross assures me he has worked out something humane and he has included some afternoon games. The two notions seem incompatible, in my view. As officers, each of you is, of course, exempt from the games while on duty but I expect you to join in when you can.'

'Everyone will be keen for a bit of fun,' said the midshipman. 'I hope we can offer a goal or two of football, provided the men agree not to injure each other. On another topic, if you do not mind my raising this with you, sir, the fellows will surely be asking me if the ship remains off-limits to the ladies. How shall I respond?' He winked at the officers across the table.

'Ship rules continue in effect,' Brantford said in a matter-of-fact voice. 'Off the ship, the men may spend time as they choose, subject to standard regulations.'

'Good luck to them,' said the lieutenant. 'Another shipload of sailors in town will be great for the taverns but not much else. The place is already packed with troops.'

Brantford nodded. 'We can expect another escort unit to arrive from the north. One of the ships is bringing wounded soldiers to the Oporto hospital camp from up the coast,' said Brantford.

'What about our own sick, sir? Are they leaving the ship?' asked one of the officers.

Brantford called on Mr Elgin, the ship's surgeon, to address the issue.

'We have some sailors and a few marines needing care,' said Mr Elgin. 'Not life-threatening, but they need to recover. No fevers on the ship at present, thankfully. The military hospital camp is nearby. We are transporting our men there this afternoon for further care.'

'Do you have more details on our next assignment, sir?'

Norcross asked his captain, eager to hear news.

'I will share the Vice Admiral's brief at our next meeting,' said the captain, aiming to curb the midshipman's habit of prying into matters dealt with by more senior officers. 'Any questions on scheduling or duties? Sherrington will announce the news at six bells this morning. Gentlemen, we have had an eventful and productive period at sea. Enjoy your shore time.'

While the other officers disbursed after finishing a light breakfast, Lieutenant Sherrington lingered on for a private conversation with Captain Brantford.

'What are your plans, sir? You are overdue for a good break. I hope you will take time to relax while we are here. A few days of rest and some dry, warm air will be good for you, and for everyone. I received a post from my wife recently complaining about the rainy weather at home. It is on calm, sunny days like these that I wish she was here with me. Have you heard from your family?'

Brantford smiled in reply, confirming that he had. It was a source of deep comfort to him that his elder brother wrote faithfully to him during his times at sea. His sister Alison, too, regularly sent him uplifting letters and small gifts throughout his time away.

Brantford looked respectfully at Sherrington. A highly experienced officer, Sherrington was the older of the two men by a few years and long past due for his captaincy, in Brantford's view. Getting a later start than Brantford and lacking some of the intensive combat experience of his younger captain, Sherrington had not yet received the coveted promotion. He was, nonetheless, the type of senior officer every captain hoped to have on his ship, and Brantford was grateful for his service on the *Pontus*.

To Sherrington's deep and lasting regret, he had not been present at the Trafalgar battle eight years ago, whereas Captain

Brantford had been at the scene as a junior lieutenant. Brantford had, since that time, gained significant favour and recognition for his combat tactics as well as his defensive strategies.

Not a day went by when Brantford did not appreciate his skilled lieutenant's sound decisions and excellent skills. The two had struck a lasting friendship over their years of service together to the point where Sherrington was almost reluctant to entertain a promotion. It would mean leaving his appointment aboard the *Pontus*.

'Did I hear you correctly—are you joining me on the hospital transport? There is no need to do that. I can get our lads there safely,' said Sherrington.

'To answer your question, yes, I am joining the transport. You, however, are not. You have been working without relief for the past twelve weeks. Once you give the news to our lads, you are packing up your bag and heading ashore. I have registered several rooms at the Oporto Inn for our officers over the next five days. You, my friend, are first in line for this evening. I hope you sleep well tonight.'

Sherrington nodded his head in appreciation. 'I know there is little to be gained in arguing with you,' he said. 'I truly wish, though, that you would put yourself first now and then.'

Visiting with the Brantford family last year at the home of their father, Sherrington had taken up his complaint with the captain's older brother James. 'I have had no luck getting him to take a rest,' Sherrington had protested.

'He has never been one to let anyone take care of him,' James Brantford had acknowledged with a solemn nod. 'He would rather go without sleep than disappoint his nephews and niece if they are wanting a visit from him. If his grandmother or his sister needs anything, he is a willing slave until the tasks are complete. I will wish you success in ever getting him to change.'

Seeing Captain Brantford turning his attention back to his

letters, Sherrington tipped his hat in thanks, hoping the other knew how deeply grateful he was for the opportunity to rest, even knowing it came at a cost to the captain.

'If I do not see you with a room beside mine at the inn within twenty-four hours, I will send the press gang to find you,' threatened Sherrington. 'Truly, I mean it. You had better be there or we will come to get you.'

Travellers lined the narrow road leading out of Oporto towards the army's hospital camp. Captain Brantford and Mr Elgin sat on the front seat of a hired wagon beside their driver. Battle-injured marines and sailors with various ailments rested in the back.

As they approached the hospital camp, a long line of wounded soldiers began to stream onto the road from an adjacent narrow path. He grimaced as he saw the serious nature of the injuries and the endless line of incoming soldiers. Wounded men lay strapped across the backs of donkeys or mules. Some leaned on heavy sticks, used rough crutches, or lay across makeshift stretchers dragged by others. Wagons or bullock carts transported the higher-ranked officers. Others, heavily bandaged and walking alone, collapsed in front of the hospital camp gates, exhausted by their journey.

'What a grim trek for these poor lads,' Mr Elgin remarked quietly to his captain. 'One of the guards passing by said the injured and sick had been transported on a ship from camps along the Spanish coast. Due to heavy storms, the ships took shelter a dozen miles up the coast and an escort brought the men overland from there to this hospital camp. From the looks of it, half these men will not survive the night.'

Brantford watched solemnly as more soldiers stumbled and fell by the roadside. Even with escort troops accompanying them, there was a shortage of helpers to assist the wounded into hospital tents. A group of camp aides, mainly women and a few older children, ran down the road to assist the new patients into camp.

Noticing a woman of light build pulling a man down off the back of a mule, Brantford instructed Mr Elgin to proceed into camp and register their men while he stayed to help.

'Here, madam, let me lift him down for you,' he said, coming to assist the woman.

Hearing his offer, Charlie Reyne turned to look at Captain Brantford, assessing his size and strength. She nodded in appreciation. 'I will push him from the other side. Can you lift and brace him as he slides off?' she asked.

Captain Brantford found himself working alongside the young lady in this manner for close to an hour. While she kept her attention fully on the patients, he occasionally had a moment to observe her as they worked together. He marvelled at her unflinching efforts as she handled heavily wounded men, some with mangled limbs, without drawing back or passing the duty on to others nearby. He wondered how she and the ladies with her had come to be involved with the hospital camp. He recalled the situation back home in England. He knew from his brother-in-law's remarks that aides were in scarce supply in the hospital at Portsmouth. Even so, only rarely were ladies involved in actual patient care. He admired this young woman for her tenacious efforts. As he watched her, he noticed tears rolling down her face from time to time. She whispered gently to one soldier, squeezed the hand of another, and closed the eyes of one poor wreck of a man.

For her part, Charlie was intent on getting the soldiers into care as soon as possible. She barely took notice of her helper, except for clasping hands with Captain Brantford on occasion to jointly lift and support a patient.

'Careful!' the captain yelled to Charlie, dragging her out of the way as one of the transport mules lunged against its harness and jerked the wagon forward. Calm and collected in life-threatening battles at sea, it shocked him to feel his pulse pick up at the threat of harm to this hard-working woman, an utter stranger to him.

Charlie, surprised to find herself entangled with the captain, was quick to regain her balance. The captain released his hold on her and stepped back.

The woman's untiring attention to the patients fascinated him. Weary as he was from his own affairs, he had no qualms in using his strength and energy to ease her efforts, continuing to help until all the injured men were finally inside the gates. At that point, the hospital's surgeon waved his arms to hail the young woman and her companions.

'Are you with one of the ships taking our soldiers home?' she suddenly asked Captain Brantford.

'I am,' he replied. He was surprised that she knew this much. He had barely learnt of his assignment.

'The hospital chief-of-staff advised us this morning that there is to be a convoy,' she explained, understanding his puzzled look. 'The medical team is deciding who will go and who will stay. Your medical supplies should be ready. Our head surgeon will assist you.'

With a warm smile and a brief but sincere word of thanks to the captain for his help, Charlie Reyne left his side. Sorry to end their time together, the captain watched as she disappeared into one of the hospital tents near the camp gates.

FOUR

Hospital Camp in Oporto

'THEY ARE ALL registered now, sir,' said Mr Elgin after seeing their men escorted off to their quarters. 'The fellow at the table says we can follow his camp assistant to the central supply area.'

Captain Brantford followed Mr Elgin to another tent where they presented their lists for new medications and bandages for transfer to the *Pontus*.

'Gentlemen, gentlemen, do you have call to be in such a hurry?' asked a cheerful but tired-looking man, approaching them. 'Allow me to introduce myself. I am Dr Upton, head surgeon. I am pleased to say our cook has prepared a tasty meal. It troubles me to confess it is a rare occasion. Will not you dine with us before heading back to town? It is not often we have men from the Royal Navy here to visit us.'

'We would be foolish to refuse,' said the captain with a lopsided grin. 'Thank you, sir.'

Dr Upton led them into the camp's open-sided mess tent and invited them to join him at his table. After picking up their plates, the men seated themselves at a long table. Mr Elgin, glancing across a narrow expanse of grass towards another open-sided tent on the opposite side, gestured to where several women tended patients. One of the women held a tray with supplies. Another passed bandages to a slender young woman squatting beside a man in cavalry uniform. This woman appeared to be stitching some wound while an aide helped to calm and pin the man down. Soon finished with her task, the young lady patted the young patient on the arm, stood up, and rinsed the blood off her hands in a nearby basin.

'I was surprised to see women working in your hospital camp,' said Mr Elgin to the surgeon. 'I must say, it is a welcome sight after living on a warship for months on end. Are these women from around here or are they with the army?'

'Both,' the man replied. 'Have you been watching those three across from us? One of them is British.'

'The young lady looks like the woman I worked with outside the gate not long ago,' said Captain Brantford. Even at this distance, he could see how efficiently the team of women worked together. He watched in admiration as the ladies moved along a row of low-lying cots, tending to the wounds of each patient.

'You are lucky to have such skilled helpers, Dr Upton,' Brantford said with admiration.

'We are, indeed,' the head surgeon replied. 'We could use more like them. Most of the women are family members of officers. They usually travel on campaign. We have a fair number of local civilians and camp followers helping, as well. They are all capable workers. I am always grateful to see them return safely. With these three, I can count on their help whenever they come back to Oporto. The younger one in the apron—on her knees beside the cot—is quite special,' he said, looking with pride at Charlie Reyne. 'We would be in dire circumstances without her. God bless them all.'

'High praise, indeed,' said Brantford thoughtfully.

Fascinated by the activities around him, the captain watched the camp aides working in the opposite tent. He thought for a moment about the beautiful woman he had pledged to marry in England. He tried to picture her in such a setting, squatting beside soldiers who had suffered such horrendous injuries. Not surprisingly, he found it difficult to bring such an image to mind. His betrothed was not someone about whom he knew a great deal. Stunned by her beauty, he had proposed marriage within three weeks of meeting her. To his astonishment, after only one day of deliberation, she accepted, as did her father, approving of their union shortly afterwards. Regardless of the amount of time he had spent in her company, he could not envision her ever being in such a place as this. He was convinced that most of the young ladies of his acquaintance would faint on witnessing the gruesome realities of this crowded camp.

Momentarily lost in thought, he recalled his brief courtship and ensuing period of separation, then shook his head to clear his mind. After watching for a few more moments while the women tended to the patients, he turned his attention back to the conversation with his host.

'The two taller ladies are sisters, from Oporto,' said Dr Upton, intent on sharing further information about his helpers. 'They are both widows. Their husbands died during the occupation in aught-nine.'

Brantford felt reluctant to discuss the private lives of others. He was about to introduce another subject but found his interest suddenly piqued as the topic shifted to the woman he had personally helped earlier by the camp gates.

'The shorter lady is the youngest,' their host continued. 'She is the daughter of one of our generals. She had been with her father in India for two years and became stranded here on her way home to England. She was but a child when she first arrived in Portugal. I have known her since then.'

Dr Upton looked pensive. 'As much as I appreciate her help, I get angry and worried every time I see her,' he said, his brow furrowed. 'I have asked myself a thousand times: what can her father be thinking to let her travel on campaign with him? I would not have done so with any daughter of mine. She is barely nineteen years of age yet has seen more of this sad world than any of us would wish to see. I cannot imagine what compels him to keep her here, or her to stay.'

Brantford looked again towards the young lady hard at work in the opposite tent. He was curious about her. He almost felt annoyed that Mr Elgin chose this moment to press for more information on their supplies. He forced himself to turn his mind to matters of business.

'To be clear on the length of stay here for our men,' Brantford said, speaking of his injured men, 'they are registered on leave to recover. One of our officers will return for them in roughly a month. If any recover decently before then, you may put them to work. I trust you know how grateful we are that you have accepted some weary navy men into your army camp. And thank you, again, for the meal, sir. It has been many months since we enjoyed a freshly cooked meat pie!'

'Nigh on a year, sir,' Mr Elgin sighed ruefully.

The conversation switched back to medical matters and arrangements to transport roughly a hundred patients from the hospital camp to the harbour in Oporto.

'They will need to depart from here in three days and leave early in the morning to reach us on time to sail with our convoy,' instructed the captain. 'Mr Elgin can supply you with the details you need. Be sure to allow sufficient time to arrive on schedule. We are loading passengers mid-morning, immediately after supplies are on board.'

Mr Elgin and Dr Upton chatted for a few minutes more. Brantford, free to shift his attention where he wished, noticed that a British officer from the Light Dragoons had joined the three ladies they had recently been observing. The cavalry officer appeared to be in private conversation with the young lady who had captured Brantford's attention.

Still seated at his table at the edge of the dining tent, Brantford suddenly heard a loud snorting sound. Startled, he saw a large boar tear across the open grass straight towards his table.

'My God, the damn thing is charging us!' cried Mr Elgin, slamming his hands onto the table.

It was so entirely unexpected that Brantford needed a moment to assess what was happening. Jumping to his feet, he reached instinctively for his loaded pistol, cocking it in readiness to fire.

'Stop! Good heavens, do not shoot!' Charlie shouted at him from the medical tent. 'Chica!' she yelled out to the animal, waving her arms excitedly to attract its attention. 'Come this way, sweet girl. I am over here! This way!'

The large boar, a massive sow with swollen teats, responded to Charlie's shout and swerved towards her. Unsure of what was going to happen, Brantford kept his pistol pointed at the boar, ready to fire. One of the women nearby screeched in fright.

Smiling, Charlie dropped to her knees and held out her arms. To Brantford's amazement, the boar skidded to a stop, lowered its snout, and pushed its forehead gently against the woman's chest. She wrapped her arms around the fat creature and laid her cheek against its large head. Shortly afterwards, rising to her feet, she tugged on the sow's ear and started marching it back across the grass.

'Who let you out, frightening everyone?' Charlie scolded the animal. 'Thank goodness you found me. What kind of trouble would you be in, hmm? Where are your little ones? Ah, there they all are now, trying to find you. Time to wean them, yes? No wonder you ran away,' she laughed. She patted the boar on the head with her free hand while leading it towards a shaded enclosure beyond the tents. The men could hear her teasing and lecturing the animal as she led it away.

Captain Brantford stared after the young woman. He felt his heart pounding from worry at what might have happened to her had the boar not lowered its tusks. He looked down at his pistol, turning it in his hand.

After closing the far gate, Charlie turned towards the captain. 'You had best keep that pistol handy, sir,' she called out to him across the narrow field. 'If the camp guards find out that you almost shot our darling Chica, you will have to fight your way out of here.'

As though to soften her criticism, Charlie gave a slight wave in his direction as she walked back to her tent.

The head surgeon chuckled. 'That damn stupid sow is loved by everyone,' he said. 'Chica has produced enough offspring to feed the entire army. I must remember to get that gate repaired so her litter stays safe.'

The surgeon excused himself to return to his duties and Mr Elgin left to pick up the supplies they had ordered for their ship. Bidding his host farewell, Captain Brantford was making his way across the grassy square towards their wagon when he heard someone call out his name. Recognising a familiar tone of voice, he turned around in disbelief.

'Niles! Good grief, is that really you?' Brantford almost shouted his greeting, breaking into a huge smile.

Hurrying across the space that divided them, the two men met in a hearty embrace.

'Not in a million years did I expect to meet you here!' said Lieutenant Niles, pushing his friend to arm's length while he eagerly searched his face. 'Are you well? I thought you were about to be impaled by that fat boar!'

'I am well, as you see,' said Brantford, grinning. 'And you?' He surveyed his friend, looking over the dusty uniform and checking for any signs of injury. 'Do you have members of your division encamped here? I am surprised to see you in Portugal.

Last I heard, your battalion had been at Vitoria in June, then headed up to the coast in late summer. It has been an age since I received news from you.'

The other man's face grew solemn. 'We have much to catch up on. Are you anchored nearby for a few days? When do you leave? Let us meet up in town. I have an officer needing surgery in the next hour and I must speak to that little lady over there beforehand,' he looked solemnly in Charlie's direction. 'I can free up some time tomorrow.'

Brantford followed his friend's glance towards the woman coming back from escorting the boar. It surprised Brantford to see Niles staring at her, deep in thought.

'Are you acquainted with her?' Brantford asked.

'Yes, a little. Not especially well,' he replied, rattled by encountering Miss Reyne in camp. He had sent Miss Reyne's father a letter, but this was his first time seeing her since their time together on a rooftop during their night in Vitoria. 'What I had learnt about her initially has all been overturned. It is a complicated story. How long are you staying in the harbour? Can you meet me tomorrow? I can come to you.'

'Tomorrow is perfect for me,' said Brantford. 'There is a small inn, the only one with a dining room, near the wharf. It has a blue awning. Can you join me there? You look like you could use a proper dinner. I have never seen you this thin.'

Niles smiled. 'I will be there. It does my heart good to see you, old man!' His eyes welled up. He pushed his friend away from him. 'Get back to duty, sailor. See that you keep your word. Tomorrow it is, at five sharp, in Oporto! I will expect a hearty meal at your expense.'

Brantford nodded. He waved farewell to his friend, watching as Niles returned to the hospital tent to speak to the young lady.

'Old chum of yours?' asked Mr Elgin, catching up to him.

'The very best of chums—we grew up together. He is in the

Light Dragoons. It just so happens that my brother gave him his mount, which almost makes the lieutenant a member of the family,' said Brantford, smiling as he recalled his friend's excitement on receiving such a gift.

'Come along, Mr Elgin,' said Brantford, clearing his thoughts. 'We have stayed long enough. Our officers will wonder if we have jumped ship and gone on campaign with the troops.'

'Yes, with good Old Nosey,' laughed Mr Elgin. He raised his hand and touched his nose gingerly, self-conscious of its shape, having broken it twice. Acknowledging the shortcomings of his appearance, he sighed and picked up his pace to stay even with his captain.

FIVE

Leaving Oporto

SOFIA GENTLY FOLDED one of Charlie's linen petticoats and put it neatly alongside a delicate chemise and a muslin dress. 'Shall I pack these stockings for you, too, dearest, or do you prefer to sort these pieces first? You only have this evening left to prepare for the journey,' Sofia reminded her, placing other items of Charlie's clothing into a travel bag.

Seated in the small front parlour of the Montalto family's cottage, Sofia gazed out a small bow window while she waited for an answer. She stared dispassionately up the hill at the main residence, her former home, its shape a distant silhouette. The women had closed and boarded up the residence, situated higher in the valley, four years ago. Living by themselves with the help of an old couple, the husband who tended the garden and his wife, a part-time cook, the three ladies found it less costly and easier to keep up the guest cottage than to stay in the larger residence. Originally, the family had boasted several cottages on the extensive property, with scores of workers tending the orchards and maintaining the grounds, but most of the buildings had burnt during the fighting in 1809. Since that time, whenever the women returned to Oporto after a lengthy campaign, they lived in this outlying cottage abutting the river, surrounded by vineyards and rolling hills.

It was just the three of them in the cottage this evening. Sofia had sent her helpers home to their dwelling an hour ago, wanting to spend the evening without any outsiders present.

Sofia looked around at the worn furnishings in the small room. The quality of the fabrics and the carved wood inlays on the furniture only barely hinted at the glorious and elegant past when her home had accommodated countless family and friends. Those times were long gone, and mere memories now.

'Hurry and finish what you are doing, Charlie. Cook prepared a lovely meal for us to celebrate Inês's birthday,' Sofia reminded her. She tossed one of Charlie's gowns, freshly cleaned, to her younger sister, seated on the nearby sofa.

'Inês, will you fold this, *faz favor*?' she asked her.

'Be careful with it—that is my favourite dress!' Charlie implored from the other room. 'Inês, which birthday are you celebrating? Are you nine-and-twenty again?'

'Exactly so,' Inês chuckled. 'And at such an advanced age, you can be sure I can stuff clothing into an army bag as well as either of you. You will need to have someone press your gown thoroughly when you land. If you would like my opinion, I think you should give it away to the rag traders in Portsmouth. It has been repaired one too many times.' Inês looked sadly down at her dress, which she deemed to be in much the same condition.

'If you come with me,' Charlie said cheerily, 'I will purchase new ball gowns for both of us along with any other dresses you wish to have!'

'You are rich with promises.'

'I mean it.'

'You said I had two more hours to think about it,' pouted Inês.

'Sofia, what is your opinion? Should she come with me to England or stay here by herself? How will she fare alone once you leave for winter camp with Father?'

Sofia bowed her head to hide her face. She desperately wanted them both to leave for someplace safe, and she fervently wanted them both to stay with her here. Last evening, pacing around the property alone, staring up at the stars, she knew that what she wanted more than anything in the world was for Charlie and Inês to be out of reach of this war. She floundered for the right words to convey her feelings.

'It is high time you returned home, little miss,' said Sofia, aiming to sound nonchalant. She turned Charlie's travel papers over in her hands. 'Your father is still in a rage about you going into Vitoria. He has not recovered from it. He says it is time you lived like other young women your age.'

'That is not his real reason to send me away,' Charlie replied. 'He is concerned that people might talk about me being alone with that lieutenant for an entire night. He is not the least bit worried about me otherwise, I assure you. Yes, it was dreadful— an atrocious event in every respect. It gives me nightmares still, to be sure, yet it was not the first time I witnessed such a thing.'

Sofia scowled. None of them ever spoke about what they knew of the siege at Badajoz and, more recently, the invasion of Vitoria. She struggled to find the right words to defend some of Charlie's father's past decisions.

'What can he be thinking?' Charlie carried on. 'The solution is right in front of him. The officers in his regiment are forever petitioning him for my hand, and I am convinced that the handsome lieutenant from Vitoria feels compelled to marry me,' Charlie remarked with a chuckle. 'All father needs to do is say yes to him, or any one of them, *et voilà*, his problem is solved.'

'You know full well he wants you to find a husband in England, someone you like—'

'No, no, no. That is not his aim. He is sending me home to do errands for him—albeit important ones, and I am the best person to get these things done properly—but he does not mind if I happen to meet a single man with property while I am at it.'

'And who is not in the military,' suggested Sofia. 'He told me that you should have been let out two years ago.'

Charlie snorted in amusement. She corrected Sofia, giggling. 'You mean to say I should have come out, or been presented, two years ago.'

'Yes, presented. Instead, you are here, wilting under the hot sun and sprouting freckles. In your father's opinion, the only available suitors worth considering are a handful of unmarried officers and a few widowed ones. If you marry one of them and stay here, you will end up travelling with them or, worse, be left alone while they campaign. You are too precious to keep that up any longer, *minha menina,*' she smiled endearingly at Charlie.

Charlie was both amused and humbled by Sofia's attempts at comfort and praise. Neither Sofia's use of English nor Charlie's aptitude in Portuguese was what one would call advanced. They frequently misunderstood one another but never had they misinterpreted the care behind the words.

Charlie knew full well what her father thought about finding her a husband. He made no secret of it.

'It is about time that you married someone on *terra firma,*' her father had yelled at her, fruitlessly supposing a louder voice would convince her as it did his men.

Charlie had not been able to stop herself from chuckling. She knew full well that her father was deeply conflicted as to when, where, and whom she should marry.

'My dear father, how am I to accomplish our plans if we rush into things? Is not it better to let me manage my uncle and wait until I reach my majority before I marry?' she asked him sweetly.

General Reyne had been shocked and, indeed, terrified that she had spent the entire night in Vitoria, at grave risk of personal harm, alone with a stranger, in the middle of a riotous assault on a town, with no protection except whatever heroic action some stupid lieutenant fellow could personally offer to shield her from an unruly mob. He shuddered each time he pictured her situation. That she had witnessed the madness of that night, at great risk to herself, set his pulse racing furiously. While she remained sceptical as to her father's motives, he resolved to keep her safe and stop such an incident from ever happening again.

He still wanted to know: who was it in the chain of command who had instructed and misinformed the lieutenant? He had not stopped hunting for answers. The incident awoke him as never before to the dangers she faced while on a campaign and to his selfishness in keeping her beside him.

'Father sent a letter to my aunt and uncle,' Charlie said to Sofia, shaking off her memories of arguing with her father. 'I am certain he has instructed them to find someone for me, even if it means I cannot accomplish all the tasks he has set out for me. My relatives know that in addition to my dowry from my mother's side, I stand to inherit through my father's will. That will make it easy for them to match-make. They have no doubt shared the information quite widely already,' Charlie said dryly. 'That is, of course, necessary if they are to succeed. My future suitors will not be overly enthralled by my accomplishments and experiences in life.'

'True enough,' said Inês, urging Charlie in the next breath not to stuff her dreadfully old slippers into the same bag as her gowns.

The three women were nothing if not realistic. They understood that Miss Charlotte Reyne was an unusual candidate for the typical "marriage market".

Never mind that her manners were odd at best and a bit dull at worst. Her appearance was not going to excite the crowd. Her hair, cut raggedly by Sofia, behaved according to its own inclination. Her face—tanned, often smudged in dirt—housed a pair of dark eyes that had not the least training in ballroom etiquette and which, instead of twinkling flirtatiously at the young men, eyed them critically and shone brightest when she was angry.

Sofia ofttimes wished Charlie were not so lean, believing a bit of fat would add extra volume in the right places.

'If you were to dress like other young ladies in England, you would look just like them,' remarked Inês.

Charlie choked back her laughter. 'True enough. And if looking exactly like everyone else does not draw hordes of men to my side, I can achieve notoriety by other means. I am sure to get the clothing mixed up and wear a day dress to the ball and a ball gown to breakfast.'

Charlie rarely gave any thought to her appearance or took notice of the attention paid to her in the army camps and hospitals, notwithstanding the shortage of females.

'Truly, how shall I fare if my uncle and aunt display me in front of their friends?' she whined. 'I neither dance nor sing. I would be happy to demonstrate my stitchwork, but they would faint from shock to see the wounded men lying under my needle.'

'It is not as though you care what others think,' Inês chided. 'Your stitching skills have saved many lives, *mi amiga*! Moreover, and I say this proudly, you can draw like no one I have ever met.'

Charlie shrugged. 'You have not mentioned my music,' she pouted. 'I have a full repertoire of mournful tunes that I can perform on my *guittara*. If I tire of men laughing at me, I can make them cry.' She gently wrapped her little guitar in cloth and placed it carefully inside a large crate. 'I do believe, now that I have given this some thought, that I am equipped to play the part of a fine lady admiringly well. My aunt and uncle will be most pleased.'

'There is no point in teasing us or your poor relatives when you arrive. After all, your father is the one you must manage,' said Sofia sensibly. 'Now come, be seated for dinner, *faz favor.* Cook prepared fresh fish for us. *Está delicioso.* If Inês agrees to go to England with you, I have only three days to fatten you both up before you leave. Come, let us eat,' she said, her eyes welling with tears. Sofia had no illusions about how devastatingly lonely it would be for her to remain behind.

'Now, tell me,' Sofia coaxed Charlie as they sat down to their meal, 'what is it that your *papai* has asked you to do that he is sending you home with an armed escort? What is he up to, *o meu querido?*'

'When did my father ever do anything in a normal fashion? The main purpose of my trip, if you must know, is to transport some important items and documents. In addition, I have been instructed to purchase property,' Charlie said, deeply serious. 'Father and I have discussed this for years. I am the only one who can accomplish what needs to be done. I cannot say more; we agreed to keep it all discreet for the time being. Come, let us enjoy a taste of your excellent port whilst there are no men with us. I will be in shock in England if I am not allowed to enjoy it there. Inês, I will be so lonely for you!'

'I will come with you,' said Inês.

'Wait! What did you just say? You will? Truly? Oh, Inês, thank you! *Obrigada!* Sofia, I will take good care of your sister, this I promise with my heart and soul! Wil and Gus will be ecstatic to hear this. I salute you both.' Charlie raised her glass. 'Thank you, my beloved family. *Saúde!* To your health, both of you!'

SIX

Old Friends

ONE OF TWO inns still standing in Oporto was situated on an escarpment where the river narrowed. Seated in the dining room and peering out a nearby window, Captain Brantford and Lieutenant Niles could see the glow of the lamp lights in the village nested alongside the river Douro.

'I assumed you would be anchored offshore,' said Niles. 'Was it difficult to sail up to the wharf? How will you get out again? Will you use your own boats?'

'It depends on whether the winds are favourable. Otherwise, yes, my men can use our small boats for kedging. I am sure you know that if you get me talking about how skilled and well-trained they are, I will talk for hours. I would rather hear your news. How have you been? Have you had recent letters from family? How are Barbara and the children?'

Niles lowered his head and stared at his glass, swirling his drink.

'Barbara passed away,' he said quietly. 'She died a year ago while giving birth. Letters from her father were misdirected. They arrived a few months ago. I have not yet been home. Her parents are caring for the children at present. I fear none of them will remember me, so long have I been away.' He paused to compose himself.

'I am so sorry,' said Brantford, devastated by his friend's loss. 'Did the baby survive?'

'A little girl.'

The men sat in silence, not needing words between them.

'I recently also learnt,' Niles cleared his throat, 'that my brother Gordon has died. It was a few months back. Something was wrong with his lungs, they said.'

Aghast at hearing of the family's losses, Brantford looked at his friend with deep concern. 'I had not heard any of this. I wonder why none of my family have written to tell me.'

'I doubt they knew of it. Our family has changed residences a few times since we left Middlegate. Neither of my parents is good at corresponding unless it is on pressing matters. My father now has written to say he requires that I return home for good lest he, too, meet his sudden demise. He never cared about the dangers of my career while my brother still lived. Now that I am his heir, my importance has increased tenfold.' He gave a crooked smile and clenched his jaw.

The two friends looked at one another across their narrow table. Henry Brantford, himself a second son in a family of means, understood this last comment. While he bore no malice towards his brother—and cared deeply for his older sibling—he was not a stranger to the struggles of younger sons to adequately support themselves. Seeing his friend so shaken, he remained silent and waited quietly for him to continue speaking.

'The long and short of it is this: I am going on half-pay, Henry, albeit temporarily,' said Niles, struggling to get the words out. 'I had planned to sell out, but I have been encouraged to take on new responsibilities instead. My papers arrived last week. I am heading home. I plan to purchase some property and bring my children to live with me. I have been offered a role helping to train recruits. I have combat experience that the academy wants to utilise.'

Brantford acknowledged the news with a thoughtful nod and an encouraging smile. 'I am glad to hear of your plans. You have served well and survived with all your limbs in place. While it is not easy to leave, it is not a bad time to step away. You have responsibilities waiting for you at home and a young family to raise.'

'I am fortunate to be alive and well I know it. More times than not, it was thanks to my splendid horse that I survived. It breaks my heart to leave him behind. If he can make it through the war, I hope to bring him home one day. I am indebted to your family for giving him to me.'

'You can thank James. I had no part in it.'

While not a keen horseman like his friend, having been at sea so many years, Captain Brantford understood the deep passion shared by Niles and his brother James. He fondly remembered their childhood in Middlegate, growing up together and sharing many escapades through the years.

'But what about you, Henry?' asked the lieutenant. 'I know from several sources that your reputation continues to grow. Let me add my congratulations for your successes.'

Two bowls of hot stew arrived at their table. After dining on standard provisions for months, the pair relished the meal. Exchanging stories over dinner refreshed their spirits.

'We stay for a few days,' offered Brantford, 'but then I am to lead a convoy carrying patients and prisoners back to Portsmouth. Are you looking for a return berth? I can get you one. You need only ask.'

'On board with the prisoners?' asked Niles.

'Precisely.'

The men laughed and refilled their glasses.

'I have a berth, but thank you,' Niles informed his friend. 'Several of my men are sailing home for care, and I am travelling on one of the hospital ships with them.'

Brantford nodded. 'I am happy to say that once we arrive in England, I am scheduled for leave. We can plan to spend some time together.'

'That is good to hear! It has been, what, eighteen months since your last leave in England?'

'Do you recall the news that I shared with you in confidence?'

'How could I not? How soon before you can see your future wife? She is truly beautiful. I could never understand what she saw in you,' he teased.

'It is an odd situation, and I sometimes suspect she said yes on a whim,' Brantford replied. After all, we had only just met. Yes, I was certainly smitten, but so were ten other suitors. Why accept and then keep our engagement a secret outside of our immediate family? I feel caught in some grand scheme outside of my control. It is all fine for a lady; she can cry off anytime she chooses, whereas we men have not the same freedom. In any case, I am convinced she would be happier with someone outside the navy.'

'I understand your sentiments. Considering all that has happened, and our times of separation, I regret, for my wife's sake, that she ever married me. Poor woman. I cannot remember a time when she was happy. She deserved better.' Niles emptied his glass.

'What would you say if I told you I met someone here?' asked Niles. 'Would you think it rash of me to think of marrying again? I believe that I must marry this woman, in fact.'

Brantford looked with concern at this friend. 'You had best speak plainly.'

Niles searched for the right words. 'I created a situation where I kept a young woman with me until dawn under dreadful circumstances. She was with me through the entire night of rampage in Vitoria. Several of my men learnt of it afterwards.'

'In Vitoria! You cannot be serious!' Brantford studied his

friend's face. He had heard much in the ensuing months about the night of terror in Vitoria. He had not imagined that his friend would ever put a woman at risk. Neither did it make sense that he would land himself in an inextricable predicament.

'It stemmed from a misunderstanding,' Niles explained. 'I was told to collect some fellow and take him into the town with me. It turned out the fellow was a female, dressed like a man. I had no idea at the time. She was thoroughly disguised and looked every inch the boy. Besides, I collected her from the edge of the battlefield. Who would have dreamt that it would be a woman?'

Stunned, Brantford studied his friend's expression.

'She fooled me completely,' Niles complained. 'The issue, when all is said and done, is that I placed her in great danger by taking her into town, and I kept her alone with me for most of the night. I even gave her a necklace that I found on the street. She could have misconstrued the gift in a thousand ways.'

'You gave her a necklace, thinking she was a boy?'

'I found it in the mud. I gave it as a thank you, for her to sell or to barter,' said Niles defensively. 'Her father was livid about the entire thing.'

'I should think so. Were you able to keep her safe? Was she unharmed?'

'Yes, thank heavens. Over three months have passed, and the situation is still unresolved. I sought to meet her father several times to explain myself. He met me once to vent his anger and refused to see me afterwards. Instead of accepting my offer, he silenced anyone who knew what happened and tried to pay for my silence, as well. I finally saw her again and was able to speak to her, just yesterday, in fact. It was the first time I had seen her since that night. She was working at the camp hospital,' he explained. 'I was shocked, stunned, to find out she was there,' he added, lost in his thoughts. 'I would not have known her had not I heard someone say her name.'

Niles still resented her blunt response to his entreaties. He decided to share her remarks to him with Brantford.

'Would you like to hear what she said to me? he asked, still flummoxed by her response. 'She said I should worry less about her reputation and concentrate on my own, in case word got out that I abducted a young man and forced him to stay with me all night.'

'Well, then.' Brantford shook his head, bewildered by the tale. He took a sip of his drink to hide his smile. He wanted to laugh outright but thought better of it.

'Had I been her father, I would have sent my second at once to confirm the duel. I am at a complete loss to understand the father's lack of concern—and he is a military man, a general, in fact!'

'Is she from these parts? Did you tell her that you are leaving for England soon?'

'We only spoke briefly. She was not in the least perturbed and assures me she makes no claim on me.'

Brantford raised his eyebrows as Niles shared further details of their night in Vitoria.

'What a dangerous situation for you both. You are fortunate to have taken her out of there unharmed. She must have suffered greatly by what she witnessed.' Brantford was stunned to think how it would have been for any of the women caught in the chaos.

'I am told she is a veteran of campaigns. She has been here for years but comes originally from England. I will sort it all out eventually, but it is very much weighing on my mind at present.'

Brantford pursed his lips and nodded. He and Niles were both accustomed to performing their duties and fulfilling obligations, despite any personal issues that might arise. He could understand his friend's frustration and resolution to do what he believed was right.

'Well, you are leaving for England and will never see her again, fortunately or unfortunately, as it may be. If neither father nor daughter is seeking restitution, and she suffered no harm, it would seem you are a free man, my friend,' said Brantford.

Niles was thoughtful for a time but disinclined to respond.

Brantford, his thoughts and wishes weighing heavily on his conscience, decided to share his own feelings.

'To confess, as a man who is engaged to be married, I am rather ashamed to say that I met a young woman recently who has caught my interest,' he told Niles after hesitating to find the right words. 'Were not I already betrothed, I would certainly want to spend time with her and get to know her. I have never encountered anyone like her. She fascinates me.'

In his mind, he ran through images of the young lady in the hospital camp, picturing her tireless efforts and kindness towards the soldiers as she tended to the new arrivals. He could feel his heart rate picking up at the thought of her.

'Here I am, a man with no business thinking of anyone other than my intended, whom I am to meet in England in a fortnight. Yet some little woman with messy hair wearing a soiled hospital gown draws my eye in a foreign country. We are a pair of sad creatures, you and me. You cannot gain a lady's company for asking, whereas I am not free to ask. Come, let us plan instead for more rewarding days ahead. You have thankfully survived the war and can return to your family. I shall return to England, take my long-awaited leave, and confirm a wedding date with my lovely lady if she is ready at last to marry. Think how it will be to set foot in our homeland. Once we are back, shall we arrange a few days to go riding with James? He can supply a lively horse for you and some old hack for me. We can even get our old friend Alfred Ashton to join us if he is not in London.'

Niles nodded, breaking out of his dark mood. 'Yes, that

would be perfect. I wonder how Ashton is doing. He never writes. It will be great to get together, the four of us again, as it used to be. And I must speak to your brother on matters of business. I am commissioned to buy another dozen cavalry horses from him. The last ones he supplied were outstanding. We urgently need more. I hope to keep the animals in England for my use in local training.'

'While he is of course willing to supply horses for the war effort, I know how attached he is to his animals. I am sure he would prefer that they remain in the country. He may be more inclined to sell, in that case,' Brantford replied. 'Just remember, if you make that a promise, be sure to keep it. He will be unforgiving if you are caught in a lie.'

'A trait he shares with you,' said Niles with a smile.

'True,' Brantford said. 'Ah, they are bringing out the custard tarts the lads were going on about. But tell me more about your recent campaigns. Will the army continue to advance into the Pyrenees, do you think, or will they winter along the coast? I am longing to hear your news.'

SEVEN

Homeward

'WE HAVE LOADED the last of the cargo, Captain,' reported Mr Norcross. 'I have sent the men to the wharf with a pair of small boats for the passengers. They should be back soon. We are lucky the winds are favourable today. Will we attempt to sail out, sir?'

Captain Brantford nodded in assent. It had been three days since he shared a dinner in Oporto with his friend Niles, and four since he had met the young lady who had so captivated him at the army hospital camp. He had spent an inordinate amount of time thinking about her, and once again pushed thoughts of her from his mind.

The HMS *Pontus* ship's company was by now all on board and ready to sail. He knew that the men wanted to impress their captain and leave Oporto harbour under their own sail. Assessing the winds himself, he felt their chances of success were sufficiently high.

Within thirty minutes, the ship's small boats had returned. While the captain rarely carried passengers aboard the *Pontus*, this trip was an exception. With some of his men on sick leave in Portugal, and with soldiers on leave needing return berths to England, Brantford's superiors had directed him to transport a dozen soldiers back to England on his frigate and to accommodate, as well, three civilians.

Captain Brantford, watching the boarding proceedings, tapped his first lieutenant on the shoulder and pointed towards a young lad struggling to pull himself up the final rung of the rope ladder and over the railing. Taking his cue, Lieutenant Sherrington elbowed the midshipman, Mr Norcross, passing on the captain's remarks.

Charlie Reyne, travelling once again in the guise of a young man, this time for the journey home to England, finally clambered onto the deck, set down her travel bag, and rested for a moment.

Spying her idling there, the young midshipman yelled at her to get a move on.

'Hey there, get out of the way and get yourself below deck!' Norcross hollered. 'You are blocking everyone behind you.'

Charlie straightened up. She smiled brightly at the midshipman, all the while cursing him silently. She thumped her Prussian friends—the two heavily laden men in front of her—on their backs. *Schneller!* she cried out cheekily, telling them to hurry along.

Wilhelm scowled. Gustav, standing next to Wilhelm, looked around to see who was the one who had barked orders at their darling Charlie. He shot a surly look at the skinny midshipman and eyed the officers and the captain of the frigate standing on the quarterdeck.

In addition to the trunks that had already been stored below, plus several more trunks and crates on board another ship in the convoy, he and Wilhelm each carried large bags heavily weighted with valuables. Some of the items belonged to them personally but, for the most part, they carried the property of General Reyne who had decided to send a hefty shipment of belongings back to Britain.

Gustav, careful not to draw suspicion by showing how heavy his bags were, sucked damp sea air into his lungs. He elbowed his younger brother to straighten up and then dragged him forward towards the midship stairwell leading to the lower decks.

Charlie carried two heavy packs and wore her drawing case strapped to her chest. The larger of the bags, loaded with coins, jewellery, and other valuable items, hung from wide straps around her shoulders. She had padded everything carefully to avoid creating noise when jostled. She had also packed coins inside her boots and in pouches hidden on her body. Into her second bag, slightly smaller and heavily tattered, she had stuffed her personal belongings. Needing to catch her breath from carrying so much weight, she grabbed onto Wilhelm's jacket to keep her balance while she paused to rest.

Brantford watched this display of weakness and impertinence with amusement. Seeing the two big men mildly acquiesce in hauling the younger man along and assisting with the lad's luggage, he laughed at them all. His first lieutenant, who had not seen Brantford smile of late, broke into a grin himself.

'What is a *maid-chin*?' asked the captain, who had overheard their earlier exchange of remarks when one of the large men seemed to be teasing the lad and called him a "Mädchen."

'What the Prussian fellow said to that boy? I think it means someone with a weak chin—a sissy or a weakling, likely,' conjectured the lieutenant.

The captain chuckled.

Hearing the laughter from above, and liking the sound of the voices, Charlie tipped her head in delight towards the source and traced it to the captain on the quarterdeck. She could not see his face clearly since the light was shining brightly behind him. Squinting, she pulled her cap down over her eyes to block the glare.

'What a little sparrow,' the captain muttered, watching. The lad's face looked faintly familiar to him, but he gave it no more than a passing thought. He shifted his attention to his duties in readiness to sail and called his officers inside his cabin for a briefing.

'Final orders contain one change to plan,' he told them. 'Hanson will join us on his corvette to offer us some speed and extra protection. He will be carrying civilians and patients, but he has enough men to keep all his guns operational.'

His officers nodded in appreciation, glad to have another fighting vessel in their convoy.

'Our assignment is unchanged, and we are facing some difficult challenges. In addition to our 42 guns, our convoy is protected by two additional fifth rates with 36 guns each. Hanson's corvette carries 18 nine-pounders, we have an armed sloop with another eight, and three hospital vessels with carronades and a few nine-pounders on their upper decks. The two prisoner transport ships are similarly equipped. Essentially, gentlemen, we will find ourselves critically short of firepower to protect our convoy if we encounter any serious threats.'

'I take it we will need to put on a brave show and steer clear of any ships heading into the coastal ports,' said Sherrington. 'There may also be some privateers or French vessels attempting to sail out from France.'

The other officers nodded in concern.

'Thank you, lieutenant. The key point, gentlemen, is that while our convoy might look formidable from a distance,' said the captain, 'we are ill-prepared to engage. We will need to rely on manoeuvrability and speed to get everyone through safely. Needless to say, we are not looking to capture any prizes on the way home. We will remain in defensive formation and adapt as necessary.'

'What is our medical contingent, sir?' asked the lieutenant.

'The two frigates, *Cepheus* and *Falcon,* have no ship surgeons on board. We are lending them Mr Elgin and Mr Ridley. One of the soldiers who boarded with us has decent medical experience. That will have to suffice.'

'I see that there are some female names on the ship lists, sir,' said the midshipman testily.

'Yes, on one of the hospital ships,' the captain replied. 'The women are volunteering as aides while making the voyage home. "And for ourselves, on board the *Pontus*, we are carrying a dozen soldiers as well as two Prussian civilians and an interpreter, by special order.'

'Someone using connections, sir?' asked Lieutenant Sherrington.

Brantford paused, seeing the scowls on the faces around him. He acknowledged the silent criticism of his officers with a nod, knowing his men loathed transporting idle passengers.

'Mr Norcross, I have a special task for you,' said the captain.

'Aye, sir,' replied the midshipman, eager to hear his assignment. At eighteen years of age, Mr Norcross was older than most midshipmen. He desperately wanted to prove his worth to his captain.

'I am assigning all of the passengers to be under your supervision,' said Brantford. 'With a bit of training, the soldiers should be able to support our marines. With the three civilians, I want you to train them as gunner aides in the event we see action. I will hold you accountable for their daily training regimes.'

The captain folded his papers and looked around him appreciatively. Short of coming up in combat against one or more ships of the line or a fleet of frigates—and to this end, he would need to rely on the blockade fleets patrolling the coasts— he had confidence in the training and experience of his team on the *Pontus* to protect the other ships. 'We head to the top of the bay in one hour and will sail up the coast to *rendezvous* with the other ships,' the captain said. 'We are targeting an eight-day journey but, as you know, we are escorting slower ships and vessels. It could easily take longer. Wishing for fair winds, men. Prepare to sail.'

'Aye, captain! Good fortune on us all!' came the replies.

As the men changed shifts, Charlie Reyne watched as sailors unfurled their hammocks and hung them from the beams above the mess tables in the lower deck. Though she and her friends were admitted to travel aboard the *Pontus*, Mr Norcross informed them that they were not assigned private sleeping quarters. Gus and Wil, both former soldiers, would be treated much like marines. Charlie's role was without status; simply put, the sailors regarded her as extra baggage.

She followed Gus and Wil towards the stern and hurried to hang up her hammock between theirs, close to the hull and away from the other men. She could see at once that the lack of privacy on board was going to pose challenges to her as a female, more so than she had anticipated. Used to travelling in the company of men, she had done so within the privileged arrangements made for senior officers and those in their care—with private tents, access to officer rations and supplies, and travelling with her cot, sufficient clothing, and in the company of a small group of seasoned military women.

Disgruntled, she complained to Gus and Wil about the midshipman's whistle and the ringing peal of the watch bells. Later, listening to the rumble of snores all around her and lying pinned in her hammock between her two Prussian friends, she experienced a serious pang of regret in giving up her private berth on another ship.

'You, my dear Inês, will travel as me on the hospital ship,' she insisted before departure. 'That is the only way to get you to Portsmouth. You must pretend to be Miss Charlotte Reyne on the voyage. I have secured passage for myself on a frigate, which will be tremendously exciting. It is all looked after. I am travelling with Gus and Wil, so have no worries. We shall meet in Portsmouth within a fortnight,' she had said to her hesitant friend.

'Miss Charlotte Reyne, you will not last a day pretending to be a boy on a ship,' Gustav had lectured her worriedly. 'They will see through your disguise in a moment.'

'Nonsense!' she had objected. 'I look every part the boy. And I prepared a flawless letter of permission. You know very well that I can forge any signature in the country. How else are we to get Inês to England if we do not seize the chance now? Are you prepared to leave her behind? I certainly am not. I will pose as your translator on the *Pontus,* safe in your care. No one will suspect a thing. It is the perfect plan.'

Thus far, by luck, Charlie's plan proved successful. The convoy had been two nights at sea. They were making decent progress and had passed the north shores of Portugal and were in the open sea. She congratulated herself on her plan, rejoicing that no one had discovered that she was not a man. Since opportunities to wash thoroughly were scarce, she decided that being unkempt helped her blend in better with the men. To Charlie's great relief, their voyage occurred at a time when she was not affected by her monthly course. The sounds and smells of over two hundred and eighty men living below deck almost overwhelmed her at times. She persuaded Gus to switch places and let her sleep in the outside hammock where a shaft of cool, fresh air from an upper porthole sank along a seam to the belly of the ship. Fortunately, sea sickness was not one of her afflictions.

The British convoy continued travelling due north with the ships and vessels sailing within easy distance of one another.

Although Charlie and her friends were all assigned to the

starboard watch, Charlie had not encountered much of Gus and Wil since they had boarded. Mr Norcross, inheriting the two big Prussians as helpers, assigned them to rope inspection duties in addition to giving them training on the gun deck as the captain had instructed. Charlie smiled at their dissatisfaction with being separated from her.

'On land, we know how to protect you,' Wil protested, 'but how are we to do so on a frigate?'

'What if your father finds out you forged his signature to get on this ship?' scolded Gus. 'He may or may not discipline you, but he will certainly execute the two of us.'

The brothers were angry with her, but they fully understood her reasoning. No one could travel on a British ship without proper papers. By travelling as Miss Charlotte Reyne, Inês could travel to England with relative ease. Yet it put Charlie at risk. Travelling fraudulently aboard a warship was not only dangerous and uncomfortable but was a serious offence as well, and scandalous in terms of her reputation if discovered.

'Who knows what will happen if you get caught?' asked Gus.

'Pooh,' said Charlie. 'No one will find out. Besides, with Sofia joining my father, Inês would be left alone in Oporto. What is a little risk to us if we can keep her safely with us? This is the best solution. I can survive for a short time masquerading as your servant, but you must promise me that you will never brag about it.' She smiled cheerfully at them before they set sail and told them to stop fretting. 'The time for worry is behind us. I can feel the sea breeze already!'

Having travelled great distances by ship, she was aware of regular routines on board. She knew, for example, that she needed approval to be on deck when not on her assigned watch. She had, therefore, gained permission from the midshipman, Mr Norcross, under whose scrutiny she constantly found herself. While, for the most part, he remained civil, Charlie noticed that he took great delight in supervising her. He watched her closely, anticipating—perhaps hoping—that she would commit errors. She overheard enough to know he was working hard to impress his captain.

When she at last escaped his attention, she sat contentedly sketching images that captured her interest. From her position on the upper deck, she marvelled at the tight regulations governing the ship, the rapid changes of the watch, the skills of the sailors, and their sharp attention to duties.

All was right in Charlie's world at this moment. No cannons or muskets were blasting; the ship's company appeared to be in good health; and, for the first time in recent months, everyone around her had decent provisions and enough grog to keep their spirits high. Leaving the dusty roads and scarred landscape of the Peninsula behind her, the rolling waves and easy sway of the ship felt to her like a day's rest in heaven.

She sketched for a while in one of her notebooks, capturing through her skilled strokes the swell of the water, the ships on the horizon, and the reflection of light on the surface of the sea. Earlier, she had drawn a group of sailors busy at their tasks and another of officers conferring on the quarterdeck. Liking the captain's face, and finding his features vaguely familiar, she sketched several images of him. One picture had him standing at the railing, surveying his world. She drew several profiles of his face, with his head turned and his bicorne hat tipped against the sun.

A shrill whistle and a loud shout from above in the topsails broke her concentration.

'Ships in sight, Captain—two points starboard, sir!' a man yelled down from the topgallant yard.

Captain Brantford raised his glass and surveyed the horizon, assessing the threat. He nodded to his lieutenant, standing near him. The lieutenant signalled to their drummer, who beat loudly to summon the men to quarters.

Charlie watched in awe as an immediate flurry of activity began. Sailors moved rapidly to new positions and turned towards their captain while he continued to study the situation. At Captain Brantford's command, conveyed by his lieutenant, the call to 'come around' sent every sailor in sight rushing about in what looked like chaos but was, she understood, a well-rehearsed procedure to ready the ship for pursuit and ultimately battle. Forgetting about her own assigned duties, Charlie lingered on the top deck and crouched down by the companionway, admiring the speed and skills exhibited by the sailors. All she could see were a few specks on the horizon. To the crew, those specks were a call to action while the captain determined if these were friends or foes.

The captain and a few of his officers were behind and above her at the ship's wheel, assessing positions within the convoy and viewing the distant ships, soon determined to be French, through their telescopes. With the massive sails on the *Pontus* partly blocking her view of the horizon, she felt rather than saw the *Pontus* change its course. She looked up to see the flag signals and watched in fascination as the entire convoy shifted its formation. The *Cepheus* and the *Falcon,* the two frigates in their convoy that had been trailing to the rear, rapidly closed the gap to catch up to the *Pontus.*

She found it remarkable how quickly the ships changed formation, with the sloop and hospital and prison ships moving west to assume larboard positions to the frigates and corvette. As the distances between ships lessened, she could see that the approaching ships included what seemed to her to be two frigates, sailing west away from France. Charlie, and no doubt everyone on board, had learnt from their shipmates that two of the British convoy's frigates were not operating at full capacity. The French commanders, however, could not know this. They instead met with an impressive threat of British naval power.

The captains on the British ships, however, knowing they were short of cannons, understood that this was a battle to be won by positioning and strategy. The French frigates seemed indecisive: should they engage, or attempt to escape? As Hanson's corvette made its appearance from the south, becoming visible to the French ships, Captain Brantford manoeuvred the *Pontus*, re-positioning it in the middle of his squadron. He maintained his broadside position with cannons facing the French ships, shielding the outlying British hospital and prison ships.

'They are no doubt debating on their best course of action. With these winds, if we delay too long, they may have no choice but to engage,' Lieutenant Sherrington said shrewdly.

The captain nodded in agreement. From his position on the quarterdeck, the captain gave the signal to ready the cannons.

Charlie heard the creak as the gun ports opened. She was shocked by the deep rumbling sound of cannons being thrust forward and secured in position. The threat of imminent attack by what seemed to be a heavily armed convoy sealed the decision for the French. The British officers watched in jubilation as the enemy ships suddenly tacked and swung their prows east. They would retreat in the hope that they could avoid relinquishing their ships to their attackers.

'I suspect they will sail towards the Spanish coast, hoping to outsail us, and perhaps tuck into a cove until nightfall,' said the lieutenant. 'Should we attempt to head them towards Brest instead? We are bound to have several ships of the line serving on blockade near there.'

'They are likely aware of that. They will try to pursue a course to the southeast. It is too risky for our convoy if we conduct a lengthy pursuit. We simply need to ensure they do not circle back. Signal that we will give chase,' said Captain Brantford.

Watching the action, Charlie saw the corvette and one of

the frigates manoeuvre in pursuit while the French frigates and a pair of vessels trailing behind them rapidly retreated. Overhearing conversations on the *Pontus* and realising that it was a feint pursuit without intent to capture, she saw the enemy ships gradually outdistance their pursuers. Eventually, the British ships turned back and sailed to re-join the convoy.

It was then that one of the topmen, with a clear view from the foremast, detected another vessel, lagging and separated from the main body. Instead of retreating south and east towards Spain with the other French ships, it fled northeast into the Bay, back towards France.

'Shall we pursue?' asked Lieutenant Sherrington. 'If we can capture it, the lads will gain a little extra pay before the winter season.'

The captain raised his glass once more to survey the horizon. He looked around thoughtfully at his shipmen and a few of his petty officers nearby. With his convoy's frigates and the corvette now returning to the convoy, he decided that the hospital ships would have sufficient protection for a short period if the *Pontus* were to give chase. His ship, the fastest of the frigates in the convoy, was in the best position to capture the straggling and isolated vessel.

He nodded to his lieutenant. 'Give the word. Signal to the convoy to maintain course whilst we catch a little prize for everyone.'

'Aye, Captain,' his first lieutenant replied happily.

'Positions!' yelled the lieutenant.

Charlie clung to a nearby railing, stunned by the speed with which the ship's main and foremast sails shifted and the ship swung into pursuit.

The outstanding speed of the *Pontus* was soon on full display. Within thirty minutes, the foreign sloop was within easy firing distance while the *Pontus* remained out of danger from the sloop's lighter carronades. A chain shot fired from the *Pontus* tore through the sloop's main topsail. Another shot sliced and disabled the sloop's mizzen mast. Unable to sail, out-gunned, and out-manned, the officers on the French sloop knew that surrender and boarding of their vessel was imminent.

The sun had reached its zenith by the time the *Pontus* returned to the convoy, towing its prize. Captain Brantford's frigate sailed alongside one of the British prison ships to deposit its captives and transfer the sloop's tow line. Free of its captured prize, the *Pontus* moved to the front of the convoy amidst cheers and shouts from the nearby ships.

EIGHT

An Incident on Deck

IGNORING BATTLE STATION instructions throughout the encounters with the French ships and pursuit of the sloop, Charlie instead remained on the upper deck. Tired from crouching by the companionway during most of the action, she finally dropped to a sitting position, resting her back against the bulkhead of the quarterdeck.

It was from here that she saw the whole bizarre incident as it unfolded. One of the passengers, a weary soldier travelling home to England, came up to the open deck while all eyes focused on the transfer of the prisoners from the captured sloop. Suddenly, the soldier began climbing over the ship's deck rail.

'Jumper larboard, stern quarter!' yelled one of the topmen, catching sight of the soldier.

Startled into action, a nearby sailor managed to grab onto the soldier's trousers as the man flung himself over the side. The sailor fell forward with the older man, hanging on to him, and banging into the side of the ship.

'I have him!' the rescuing sailor yelled, locking his legs into the ropes, and struggling to keep himself and the soldier from falling headlong into the sea.

The captain, with a clear view of the incident from his position, rushed towards them from the quarterdeck and yelled for others to assist. Working efficiently, and using their bodies in place of ropes, the captain and several of the ship's marines pulled both men safely onto the deck.

The old soldier, sputtering and coughing, began yelling hysterically while the rescuing sailor, exhausted, fell to the deck. In the chaos after his rescue, the soldier pulled out a small knife and lunged forward, blindly slashing out at the unwary captain who was bent over the sailor lying on the deck. A pair of marines rushed to disarm the soldier. The captain, clasping at the slash along his side and bleeding from another cut on his leg that occurred during the rescue, staggered to his feet.

Charlie, seeing the captain stumble as he rose, rushed forward. She threw her arm around his waist and slid her shoulder under his arm to keep him from falling sideways. Appreciative of the quick assistance, the captain of the marines stepped in and shifted the naval captain's weight to himself. Charlie, free of the burden, stepped up to the soldier who had attempted to jump. To everyone's complete and utter surprise, she slapped him hard across the face.

'Stop it at once!' Charlie said harshly.

The man, stunned by the slap, stared wild-eyed at Charlie. He raised his eyebrows in disbelief. A veteran from her father's brigade, the old soldier recognised Charlie at once. Seeing the daughter of his beloved general standing before him, he instantly began to cry. The marines holding onto him, bewildered by the young man's air of authority, looked to their captain for his reaction. These were experienced and able men, well used to harsh discipline, but not one of them would have taken it upon themselves to slap a soldier across the face in this humiliating way. They did not take kindly to the lad's interference. And yet, they all saw it; the soldier responded immediately.

Charlie recognised the soldier straight away. She knew the man had lost two of his three sons tragically at Vitoria with horrendous wounds, with one son still missing. She understood his grief. Her heart ached as she watched him crumble. The man collapsed to his knees, sobs breaking from his chest. Shocking everyone a second time, Charlie dropped to her knees in front of him and this time embraced the man, pulling him to her chest, wiping away his tears while tears of her own ran freely down her face.

Astounded by the scene before him, the captain stared at Charlie, trying to piece the images into a cohesive whole.

'Shall we lock him up, sir?' asked one of the marines, furious to see their naval captain injured.

'Lock them both up,' urged the midshipman.

The captain gripped his side. 'Have the other soldiers take responsibility for him,' he said. 'You—' he turned sharply to Charlie, '—see that he gets settled with proper care, then report to me in my cabin.'

Surprised by the order, Charlie followed behind the marines as they transported the soldier to the lower deck. Worried that the old man might mumble her name if he saw her again and seeing that he was uninjured and not resisting the marines, she quietly slipped away.

Heading back to the deck, Charlie asked a few sailors if they had seen her drawing case.

'You can collect it in the captain's wardroom,' muttered one of the marines.

Charlie soon found her way to the captain's quarters. She knocked quietly on the captain's cabin door for permission to enter. Upon opening the door, she saw Mr Norcross struggling to stop the bleeding from the lengthy gash on the captain's side. Surveying the fellow's ineptitude in offering medical aid, Charlie felt certain he would only aggravate the captain's injury.

'I have considerable experience dealing with wounds,' she spoke directly to the captain. 'If you will permit me to do so, sir, I can give you proper care. This fellow will send you to your grave if you let him mess with your wound like that.'

Norcross sputtered his objections.

Captain Brantford, assessing her air of confidence, invited her forward and gave her leave to do as she saw fit.

Looking around at the small collection of materials for patient care, Charlie sent the midshipman to fetch hot water from the galley.

'I need some linen,' she said to the captain. 'Do you have a spare sheet I can use for bandaging?' Charlie could not use the linen strips bound around her chest, not under such circumstances.

'These are not the dark ages,' he replied. 'We have ample medical supplies on board. There is a kit behind you in the cabinet.'

'Yes, of course,' Charlie said contritely, retrieving it. She soon assessed his wounds. 'You require sutures, sir. I can do that for you, with your permission.'

The midshipman, arriving back with the water, stood gawking at Charlie while she worked. She looked up at his worried face.

'Mr Norcross, have you nothing else to do, nowhere to be?' she asked him. 'You are not needed here. Have you checked to see that the old soldier is doing well? How is the sailor faring—has he been looked after properly? The pair of them likely suffered rope burns. Take this salve to them. It will ease their discomfort.'

Seeing a nod of agreement from his captain, Norcross, fuming at her tone of authority, reluctantly left them. Charlie worked swiftly to stop the bleeding and suture the wound on the captain's side. He remained calm and silent throughout. She had expected this of him, as she did of her father's soldiers, but she admired him nonetheless for his self-control.

'How long have you been an interpreter for the Prussians?' the captain asked while she worked, studying her features intently. The three civilians, and this lad in particular, were an odd trio. From the orders he received, he knew a sponsor of some rank lay behind the permissions obtained to board his ship. 'Where did you pick up your medical skills? Were you at the hospital in Lisbon or somewhere further up the coast? Did you assist at one of the camp hospitals? Are you related to someone in the army?' Charlie quickly placed a large needle between her teeth and poked her head from behind his shoulder, pretending she was not able to speak at present. She pressed on with her tasks.

'I am done now,' she told him at last, knotting her final stitch. She wound a bandage around his waist and lower back and tied it off.

Seeing a heavy scrape on his upper arm, she gestured to him that she would look at that next. He presented his arm for attention.

Charlie was accustomed to men parading half-naked around the camps and she had frequently seen soldiers bathing in the rivers. This man's lean build was like many she had seen, but she nonetheless found herself admiring his taught frame. She closed her eyes for a moment, surprised at how nervous she felt, and opened them to find the captain staring at her.

'Is anything wrong? Are you feeling faint?' he asked with concern.

'No, no, just a little tired,' she answered. 'Your scrape is quite severe. I need you to press this cloth against it whilst I prepare the bandage.'

He nodded his agreement, and she moved around him for a better stance. He watched her closely, noticing the soldier's scarf unravelling from around her throat. The small figure moved almost gracefully. What an odd creature, he thought.

'You have not answered my earlier questions,' said the captain. 'I am interested to know where you gained your medical experience—did you train at the Lisbon army hospital?' he asked, returning to his original enquiry.

'I have helped in the field camps,' she replied.

He wanted to know which ones. She named several.

'You are small for an orderly. And you are how old?' he asked.

'Nineteen.'

He was lost in thought for a moment, then continued with his line of questioning. 'And how did you come to serve as an interpreter for your Prussian gentlemen?—I assume they are such. They look more like hardened soldiers. I am trying to make out how you fit in.'

'I am not free to disclose their business,' she said sagely, bandaging his arm.

'I heard you speaking to them in German,' he persisted. 'Do you speak Spanish as well?'

'I am better with Portuguese and French,' she said.

'Impressive,' he remarked. He said nothing further but watched her closely while she continued with her tasks.

When she was done, Charlie squatted to examine his leg underneath a blood stain on his breeches, her scarf drifting to the floor. As she lifted the leg of his breeches, the captain, seated above her, could see her graceful neckline, and he noticed that she wore a peculiar pendant on a thin chain around her neck. Below the pendant, he could see an edge of linen wound high around her chest.

'What happened to you? Were you badly injured?' he asked worriedly, his tone softening.

Realising he had seen the top of the binding, she felt a sense of panic. Her hand flew to her chest as she rapidly concocted a story. 'We were attacked by a raiding party some weeks back,' she lied. 'I caught the back edge of a bayonet, sir. It is nothing of consequence. I will mend soon.'

She felt her heartbeat quicken. 'Oh, stop it,' she lectured herself.

'I beg your pardon?'

Startled that she had spoken aloud, Charlie abruptly stood up. 'Your leg wound is minor. You can let that young officer practise on you and tend to it. Will you excuse me if I head off, sir?' she asked, not expecting an answer. She closed the medical kit with a snap. Picking up her leather drawing case from the side table, she took out her notebook, found one of her favourite drawings of the captain, and carefully tore it out of her book.

'You can keep this one,' she said, offering it.

'Perhaps you would like to keep it for yourself,' he said, amused. He had looked through the notebook earlier and had been surprised, and a trifle bewildered, to see so many drawings of himself.

'No, no, you should keep it. I have several more,' she admitted candidly. 'Besides, I can easily re-draw this one. Let me know if you would like me to draw you standing with your officers,' she offered, signing her initials lower on the page. 'If you have no wish to keep this likeness, perhaps someone in your family would care to have it.'

Brantford was quite speechless by this point.

Charlie, looking calm and collected, prepared to depart as the midshipman re-entered. She gave the officer a curt nod in passing.

'Stop there,' said the captain.

She turned in surprise.

'I have not dismissed you. I understand Mr Norcross issued instructions for you to report to the gun deck in the event we saw action. Is not that true?' he asked sternly. 'Instead, you stayed on the upper deck. Were you a regular member of our crew, you would be disciplined severely.'

'A dozen lashes, sir?' asked Norcross optimistically.

'No one disobeys orders on my ship. Is that clear?' The captain paused, then said, 'If those ships had been any closer, you could easily have been killed. Mr Norcross and I will discuss your discipline. He will let you know the consequences this evening.'

She tipped her head in apology to the captain, shot a look of dislike at the midshipman, and left the cabin.

'I say, what an impertinent brat. That youngster is nothing but a mere translator to foreigners and yet behaves all high and mighty. Did you see him nod like he was an earl and I his butler? I will get the lads to knock some sense into him. You know, I could easily have fixed that wound myself, sir. Let me re-wrap it for you.'

Brantford, preoccupied, brushed the midshipman's hand aside.

'There is to be no nonsense involving him or the Prussians, do you hear? They are guests on our ship.'

'Aye, captain. Take no mind. He wounded my pride, is all. I just want to scare him a little,' said the disgruntled young man, closing the captain's door behind him as he departed.

Left alone in his cabin, Brantford pulled out the passenger lists for the vessels in the convoy, which he possessed as commander of the squadron. He examined the letter of permission relating to the three civilian passengers aboard the *Pontus*, studying and comparing the documents.

For several minutes, he summoned images from his memory, recalling the face of the dedicated female medical aide in Oporto alongside whom he had worked for over an hour. Brantford remembered quite clearly that, according to the head surgeon, Miss Charlotte Reyne was her name. Scrolling through the passenger lists from the hospital ships in his convoy, he found an entry where some scribe had neatly printed the name of Miss Charlotte Reyne as a passenger aboard the HMS *Marfisa*, one of the hospital ships in his convoy. Then he looked at the signature of permission for three civilians to board the *Pontus* in Oporto. The name authorising all the passages was that of

General Sir William Reyne.

'Surely, it is her,' he said aloud, stumped by the magnitude of the woman's duplicity. Why was the daughter of an English general—and a baronet, at that—travelling aboard his ship in the guise of a male interpreter for a pair of Prussian civilians? Were the men deserters? He picked up the drawing Charlie had given to him and peered at the initials *CR* carelessly scrawled on the sheet. He tapped the paper triumphantly.

'Why on earth would she give up a private lady's berth on one of the other homebound vessels?' he wondered.

Captain Brantford scowled and paced around his cabin. He put the list down. He picked it up again, agitated. He paced around his quarters. Opening his cabin door, the captain called for his ship's carpenter. On the man's arrival, the captain laid out the tasks and put him immediately to work.

NINE

Captain's Cabin

'MR REED? WHERE are you seated? Are you in here, Mr Reed?'

Forgetting for a moment that Mr Reed was her fake name aboard the *Pontus*, Charlie did not immediately respond. Wil elbowed her in the ribs.

'Oh! You are looking for me! Here!' she said, flustered, looking up from her dinner plate towards the speaker.

Mr Norcross stood in the narrow aisle between the tables in the mess.

'Attention,' he said with a crooked smile, speaking to every-one present. 'I am here to advise that Mr Reed has disregarded his duties. Henceforth, Mr Reed will be relocated and confined to quarters. He will adhere to strict duties under the captain's direct supervision as punishment for disobeying instructions during battle action today. Mr Reed will remain under watch for the remainder of the journey. Conversation with him is strictly forbidden. Mr Reed, collect your hammock and belongings at once and follow me.'

Charlie stared at him in shock. Gus and Wil stood up in unison, protesting loudly.

'If you need a translation from Mr Reed, gentlemen,' Mr Norcross said in a mocking tone to Gus and Wil, 'bring your requests to me. Mr Reed, tell them what I just said. I will then notify the captain. He will determine if a response is permitted. Get a move on, Mr Reed. The captain does not take kindly to having his orders ignored. Take your punishment like every other man on this ship.' He cast a satisfied look around him, gloating at the looks of curiosity and surprise on the sailors' faces.

Mr Norcross waited while Charlie collected her belongings. He grinned smugly at Gus and Wil, then escorted his charge to the captain's cabin.

'Good evening, Mr Reed,' the captain greeted his guest solemnly. 'I have given some thought to your misconduct. Instead of a flogging for dereliction of duties, you are to remain in isolation for the remainder of the trip. Your new berth is behind there,' he said, gesturing towards the adjacent gunroom, in which area stood a newly constructed wooden frame with temporary canvas walls attached to its sides.

Charlie stared at him, bewildered by the change in circumstances.

'You will carry out duties as assigned by me for the time remaining at sea. You may not dine with, circulate among, or commune with my crew nor with any of the other passengers. Until you step off my ship in Portsmouth, you will henceforth dine here and remain in isolation in the berth provided.' He pointed out the makeshift canvas doorway to the small enclosure his carpenter had hastily constructed. 'You will remain in these quarters to complete your daily assigned duties, commencing with the morning watch. Do I make myself clear, Mr Reed?'

'Yes, sir,' she replied, astonished.

The captain waved his dismissal to Norcross, who overheard news of the meted punishment with clear disappointment and left with reluctance. He had hoped, at the very least, for a lashing.

Charlie studied the captain's face as he continued to speak to her.

'You have shown your proficiency in drawing. I have a set

of weather-worn maps and charts for you to replicate. I want reproductions completed before we reach Portsmouth. Use my dining table while working on these items. To maintain the required isolation, you will need to use my washstand. Keep to your starboard watch, as it is the same as your friends. You may speak to the Prussians twice daily here in my dining room. I will advise if there are changes to these rules. You are dismissed,' he said to her.

Bewildered, Charlie wondered, albeit for a moment only, if punishment with a few lashes of the cat's tail would have been preferable. She quickly dismissed the notion. The opportunity for conversation was, in any case, over. The captain retired into his private cabin, leaving her to settle in on her own. She gingerly drew open the canvas door he had pointed towards and examined the small berth.

Glancing around the space allocated for her solitary confinement, she beamed with pleasure. Seeing the support hooks in place to suspend her hammock, she installed her bed immediately. Against the wooden side wall nearest to the hammock stood a narrow desk with a bench, the perfect height for her. She placed her drawing case on the surface. There were two enclosed shelves, one below and one above the desk, where she could safely store personal items. She noticed a hook on the wall to hang her army bag. To her great delight, her room aligned with a porthole with a working window from which she could watch the waves and draw in fresh air. A chamber pot was set securely into a wooden frame at the foot of the room. Shocked to find herself in this situation, and grateful for the privacy resulting from the captain's decision, she took a deep breath and, as he had instructed her to do, she tiptoed into his cabin to wash up. She smiled shyly at him as she passed by. Returning to her tiny room, and admiring the makeshift outer walls constructed from folded sails, she fastened the canvas door and climbed into her hammock. A clean blanket lay neatly folded on the desk. Charlie picked it up and drew it across her body, savouring the extra warmth. With a last look out of her window at the sky above, Charlie blew a fond goodnight kiss towards the captain's cabin, closed her eyes, and fell into a deep sleep.

Waking ahead of the morning bells, Charlie hurried to use the captain's washstand. When done, she saw that one of the ship's boys had brought two plates of breakfast into the dining room. The captain soon entered and took a seat at his table, beckoning her to join him.

Realising that her morning meal was the same fare as the captain's, she smiled appreciatively. Charlie ate her food slowly, enjoying every mouthful. She sipped from a cup of hot tea flavoured with half a tot of rum, a rare treat from her usual cold beverages. Lifting her eyes to the captain's face, she waited calmly for him to speak.

'Miss Reyne, is it not?' he asked her.

Her eyes widened. She had already guessed that he knew she was not a man, but it startled her to hear him speak her real name. Charlie acknowledged his remark with an admiring nod.

'Do you wish to explain to me why you are fraudulently travelling on my ship?'

Charlie found his expression difficult to read. His tone was severe, his face stern. She thought he looked disappointed more than angry.

When she did not reply, he shrugged. 'If you prefer, you are welcome to explain to the authorities in Portsmouth instead.' He placed her travel document and his passenger list for the hospital ship in front of her. 'I suppose for someone with your skills in drawing, replicating signatures is not particularly challenging.'

She gathered her thoughts.

'I am waiting,' he said.

'I am bringing a foreigner to England with me, a woman,' she answered him. 'I needed to provide her with safe passage on a ship departing at once so as not to leave her alone in Portugal.'

'Had you no means of doing so without resorting to forgery?' he responded testily.

'We did not have enough time to plan. She is family to me and would have been stranded. The original authorisation from my father, intended for myself and my two Prussian friends with a berth on the *Marfisa*, is authentic. The letter for the three of us authorising transport aboard your ship is not. My father is unaware of this second letter,' she admitted. 'It is my responsibility entirely.'

'But you are of minor age, am I right? Or did you lie about your age as well? Your father is liable for your actions. You feel that your desire to bring your companion to England is justification for this gross misrepresentation and illegal charade, do you?'

Charlie could feel the pull and sway of indecision in the captain's voice.

'I do, sir,' she said.

She waited respectfully for him to speak.

'And your Prussian friends?'

'They work for my father as both camp and family guards and are here under duty to me.'

'Under duress, I presume,' the captain added.

He paused to mull over Charlie's information. He could not discern whether the names of two gentlemen had been removed from the other ship's list before being added to his. He tried to determine whether her remarks were true or if she were simply adding lies upon lies.

'With regard to legal actions relating to your false arrangements, I will let you know my decision around this once we arrive in Portsmouth. In the meantime, you will complete the tasks assigned by me over the coming days.'

He handed her several torn maps to be redrawn and

explained his needs.

'Your Prussian friends will take turns escorting you on deck twice a day,' he said. 'Do not under any circumstances speak with anyone else. Apart from these episodes, and unless accompanied by me or expressly stated otherwise by me, you are to remain in these quarters until we reach England.'

She nodded demurely and kept her head lowered until he left for the quarterdeck. She peered after him curiously.

In the coming days, Charlie made every effort to take special care of the captain's injuries, changing his bandages daily and inspecting his wounds for signs of infection.

'Are you planning to draw a picture of my scar?' he asked her one evening when she seemed to take forever to rebandage his side. 'You are staring so intently that I begin to think I have grown an extra limb out of my rib.'

'No, no, nothing of the kind,' she said distractedly. She was studying his physique and observing the muscles on his back and abdomen. 'I am simply admiring you.'

She never ceased to surprise him. He could not help smiling at her candid response. 'Are you skilled in drawing the human body?' he asked her, curious to know the extent of her talent.

'I am, yes,' she replied, suddenly self-conscious of their proximity to one another. She reluctantly drew back from him.

He said very little while she attended him, yet she could tell from his expression that he valued her help. For her part, Charlie happily cared for him and served her time in isolation. She delightedly kept Gus and Wil apprised of her light duties.

'What an interesting man,' she said to Gus on one of their daily visits. 'I am cherishing his company. He could not possibly think I would want to be anywhere else. Leave these quarters? There is not the slightest chance of that! It is such an easy schedule for me,' she said, grinning. 'I wake up early, eat with the captain, redraw a few maps, clean a little, walk about with you or Wil, take a nap, draw some more, eat again, chat with the captain in the early evening, and go to sleep. I am truly in heaven. I cannot remember when I last felt so entirely rested.'

Concerned at first about her situation, Gus felt relieved to hear that all was right with his little Charlie.

'During the day,' she continued recounting the benefits to herself, 'I am free to move about his dining quarters, except when he is meeting with his officers. He has invited me to sit at his table whenever I am drawing. My assignments are quite minimal. I rather think he is spoiling me. At mealtime, the captain never says much but it seems to me he goes out of his way not to make me feel awkward. You need not worry, Gus. I do not know why he has done me such an enormous favour as this, but I am thankful for it at every moment. And you? How are you both managing? Are you able to hide the fact that you understand and speak English perfectly well?'

'Have no worries, little one,' said Gus reassuringly. 'We already knew our duties, so we were able to carry on without instruction. Everyone simply ignores us.'

Charlie giggled and smiled happily.

As the days passed, Charlie found new ways to express her gratitude to the captain. In addition to re-drawing his maps and charts, she polished the handsome wood panelling in his cabin, sorted his books alphabetically, buffed his desk, dusted, swept, and generally did any tasks that might show how much she valued the privacy and security he had afforded her.

'I have grown rather fond of my dear Captain Brantford,' she confided to Wil. 'Do you suppose I can persuade Father to let me marry a gentleman from the navy? I am eager to gain the captain's affection, you see,' she said cheerfully.

'No, that will not work out at all,' Wil replied. 'Your father intends for you to marry someone who will remain by your side—and not be away at sea for months on end. You had best give up on that plan, miss. In any case, I can guarantee you will never see this gentleman again once we land.'

'Do you think so? How disappointing,' she pouted. 'That does not suit me at all. I cannot imagine saying goodbye to him. My heart aches at the very thought of it. Well, I shall just have to see if I can remedy the situation.'

TEN

Arrival in Portsmouth

WITH SHEETS OF rain pelting down and strong northwest winds slowing the final leg of the journey, the convoy from Portugal finally arrived at Portsmouth. They had been at sea for eleven days of travel. The ships in the convoy, arriving throughout the evening, dropped anchor in proximity to one another.

By the time the bells rang after the morning watch on the following day, those not toiling on their shift were packed and ready to disembark. Charlie, more rested than she had felt in a very long time, appeared particularly well-groomed. She scrubbed her face and hands, donned her cleanest garment, secured her hair neatly under her cap, and remained in the captain's quarters, waiting for Captain Brantford. On his arrival, she rose to her feet and stood at attention, waiting patiently for him to speak.

'Good morning, Miss Reyne. Are you well? Ready to step ashore?' asked the captain, eyeing her fresh appearance.

'I am, indeed, sir. Thank you.'

He paused to collect his thoughts, fighting an unexpected sense of regret that his time with her, odd as it had been, was at an end. He enjoyed her company more than he wished to admit. He had particularly enjoyed the one evening when they had chatted comfortably at his dining table for over two hours,

Captain Henry Brantford, disconcerted by his conversations with Sherrington, and returning from the hold, reviewed his meeting notes and waited for the officers from the other ships to come aboard. He could hear bits of conversation outside as the small boats from the other ships rowed up alongside the *Pontus*. The officers were punctual, as he expected, joining him at the appointed hour and settling down to enjoy the breakfast laid before them.

To the delight of his ship's cook, the captain had ordered extra supplies from Portsmouth last evening to supplement their breakfast meal. A hearty serving of porridge and sausage arrived from the galley oven, served with fresh scones and small crisp apples from the local market. Not forgetting his men on board, he had ordered extra fruit and fresh loaves for distribution with the morning meal.

With an excellent service record, Brantford's career had advanced steadily. At the age of seven and twenty, he was being groomed yet again for promotion. His vice-admiral informed him that he was a candidate for more senior ranks at the proper time. His role as commodore with this small escort squadron reflected his future responsibilities. A natural leader, the captain could switch between keen aggressor or staunch defender as required. His serious nature and fair-minded thinking made him a role model for younger officers. Due to the competent training his team provided to his sailors and his just management of their affairs, the *Pontus* had gained an enviable reputation. Most on board the *Pontus* were aware of their good fortune, particularly if they had served in less-than-ideal situations elsewhere.

During their meeting, the officers from the other ships in turn shared their records of events during their voyages.

The captain turned to Lieutenant Sherrington for his report for the *Pontus*.

This the lieutenant gave, closing with news about where the

patients were to be sent. 'We have been informed that Haslar Hospital, at Gosport, can accept most of the patients and will take responsibility for relocating the others. This simplifies our duties significantly. We will need the small boats from all the ships to help transfer the patients,' said Sherrington, handing out a schedule. 'By taking them across the harbour, we can save hours of land transport for these poor lads. Also, I wish to report that the prison ship proceeded into the harbour last evening as planned to transfer their occupants to the hulks. That task is done.'

Brantford nodded. 'Which brings us to our last item of business—the prize money from the captured sloop. It will be easy to calculate and awarded quickly. Due to the store of munitions and gold francs for army wages, we can expect the Navy Board to assess high value, probably close to sixteen thousand pounds. Except for the convoy's hospital and prison ships, any of us could have chased and captured that sloop. The *Pontus* happened to be the closest. I have confirmed that equal portions are to be shared among the five escort ships under standard ratios. It will offer our lads a slight boost to their incomes for this past season. Any questions?' asked Brantford.

The officers, delighted by this news, expressed their thanks.

'Once cargo and passengers are off your ships, this convoy is officially disbanded. Well done. Congratulations on a safe journey. It has been a pleasure, gentlemen.'

'That is all very well, but what did you put in this tea?' asked Captain Hanson, staring suspiciously at Brantford. 'I like mine strong, but this is robust indeed, even for my tastes.'

The men laughed, enjoying their servings of high-quality, undiluted rum, and relaxing and appreciating their brief time with one another after a successful voyage. The group chatted for a few minutes more, then disbanded, heading out to begin the day's work.

Before eight bells, the seamen on the *Pontus* steadied one of the small boats for the captain to disembark. Free at last of naval duties, he and several of his ship's company were departing for a long-awaited, four-week shore leave. Stepping onto the pier with a light step, Brantford headed towards the inn where he had arranged by messenger to meet his brother-in-law.

'If you please, sir, I have a pair of letters for you,' said the hotel clerk as Captain Brantford registered at the front desk of the Crown.

Excited to have news waiting for him, Brantford took his letters and seated himself in the tavern. He ordered a pint of ale. With an eager heart, he cracked the wax seals and began to read.

Within the half-hour, Captain Charles Sand joined his brother-in-law at his table. Brantford rose to greet him.

'It is good to see you, Henry. What has it been, eight months, at least?' asked Sand, seating himself opposite. 'I was glad to get your message. I had some business in town, so I came in last night and waited for you here. Your sister and brother will be as relieved as I am to find you well. When I sold out, I thought I would miss the service. After hearing of your heavy assignments this past year, I find I have no regrets. We are all glad you are safe.'

Sharing his wife Alison's affection for this adventurous 'little brother' in the family, Sand was relieved to see the captain looking healthy and uninjured.

'You were needed at home,' Brantford replied solemnly. 'You would have had difficulty taking your seat in the House had not you stepped down from your naval duties.'

'True, but half of the members are absent on any given day. I dare say the government could carry on. No one would have noticed my absence.'

'I doubt that. It has been an age since I have been back,' said Brantford, stretching his legs under the table. He looked fondly across at Charles Sand, a man of steady temperament with a ready laugh. Brantford had spent many nights longing for the company of members of his family. He was always glad to see his brother-in-law.

It would be hard to say who had more questions about how their lives had been in the past year. For starters, Brantford wanted to hear how Sand's three sons and his daughter were doing.

'The boys have grown tremendously this past year,' said Sand, happy to talk about his children. 'Their little sister sees herself as their master and commander.'

Brantford laughed on hearing the news. He was eager for the next opportunity to see them all.

'How is Alison?' he asked earnestly. 'Is she well?'

Sand nodded happily.

'And our brother, James, have you seen him of late?

'Indeed, I have. We were all together just three weeks ago in Middlegate. I bring his greetings, along with a monetary gift for you from the family as your birthday gift. James has given explicit instructions not to spend it on your men. Alison insists that you get fitted for a new coat so that you are not looking like a poor sailor who has been at sea too long.'

Brantford nodded. He could almost hear his sister's chiding tone in Sand's voice.

'Is my father still in Middlegate or has he settled in London for the season?' he wanted to know. 'Does he write to you and Alison from time to time? I seldom get letters from him,' Brantford complained. 'James is the one to faithfully send news. And how is my dear grandmother? Does she remember me, do you suppose?'

While they dined, Sand did his best to give Brantford an update on his grandmother's health, her deteriorating memory, other family news, and the latest political items of interest.

'You do know that my dear wife has organised your entire period of leave. I have instructions to share a few important dates with you,' said Sand.

Brantford, lost in his thoughts, stared at his two letters, and turned them over in his hands.

Surprised and disconcerted by his brother-in-law's lack of attention, Sand cleared his throat and continued his remarks.

'I know you must be looking forward immensely to your time on shore. The harvest ball in Middlegate will be held in a few days. Everyone is looking forward to your return. Your friend Ashton is hosting the ball at his home at Seton Manor this year. James has been in touch with your betrothed and her father, and they will be attending. He plans to put them up at Ben Lodge, so you can *rendezvous* there. Has she finally decided to publicly announce your engagement? If so, James has it in mind to hold a family event, a picnic was talked about, so we can gather the relatives and some old friends, and you can announce your news. I must say, Henry, I look forward to finally meeting this acclaimed beauty.'

Sand was startled by the dejected look on Henry's face. 'What is it? Is something wrong? Has she cried off?'

'No, no, though I swear it would be in her best interest to do so. I received new orders today,' he said, letting his agitation show. He held up one of the letters he had received. 'Admiral Kent has postponed my leave. I am to sail again for the Peninsula in three days.'

'No! How can that be possible?' objected Sand. He could see how crushed Brantford was by the news. 'Damn these wars,' he said.

'The only leave I can give my men is a half-day tomorrow and the next, with Friday taken up with shore duties. We sail again on Saturday,' Brantford lamented. 'The men will be devastated.'

'Can you even get them back on the ship? But never mind them. What about you? You have looked forward to this leave for months.'

Brantford shrugged, raising his hands in a gesture of futility. 'The letter from my fleet commander is clear and concise. The HMS *Pontus* with me as its captain has been re-assigned for an indeterminate period to protect supply stations along the north-east coast of Spain. General Wellesley's recent successes have them continuing their push into the Pyrenees. I have been instructed to protect shipments to the British winter encampments in readiness for the upcoming campaigns.'

'I take it no other course of action is open to you,' said Sand.

'None. The woman I am to marry,' said Brantford, lifting his other letter, 'has simultaneously written to say she has made up her mind on timing and is ready to announce our betrothal during her visit to Middlegate. As you know, we were to meet there. Now, due to my reassignment, I cannot be there. I have no opportunity to inform her of this and save her a wasted trip.'

Brantford pushed both of his letters towards Charles. He dropped his head despondently into his hands.

Sand picked up the letters and read the woman's affirmation that she and her father were by this time on their way to Middlegate to meet the Brantford family. He scowled and read her words out loud.

'Now that you are back after such a long absence,' read Sand, mimicking a woman's tone of voice, 'I feel it is a suitable time to publicise the engagement.' He glanced in scorn at the letter. 'Is this all she has to say? It is not especially affectionate,' he muttered, dissatisfied with the young lady's missive. 'Does she always write like this?'

'I have so few letters from her, I hardly know,' Brantford replied.

Sand could see that Brantford was struggling for composure. He knew that the captain had long been looking forward to a reunion and a much-needed conversation with the young lady.

'I am sure you need to discern your feelings, and hers, after such a lengthy separation,' Sand said. After a pause, he raised his eyes and looked searchingly at his brother-in-law's expression. He found it heart-breaking to watch the other struggle to cope with the sudden change in plans.

'Well, there is nothing to be done about it,' he said at last. He ordered another round of drinks. He knew, as did they all, that his father-in-law would be indifferent to Henry's change in schedule. Henry's siblings, on the other hand, caring deeply for their brother, would be devastated by this news.

'I know it has been difficult for you. I must say, Henry, I was surprised at the outset by your betrothed's decision to become engaged after such a brief acquaintance. What were her father's thoughts on the matter? Did she ever discuss this with you? Undoubtedly, she had other marriage options open to her, any of which would seem more suitable, if you will forgive my saying so. Her affection for you is questionable.'

Brantford's own opinion was similar. He had no reply to make.

'What is more,' said Sand, 'I am shocked she has suddenly chosen to announce the engagement before meeting to discuss the matter. I must say, Henry, it does not sit well with me. Surely the young lady ought to ask a few questions about your career. What if you are to be separated for another year? Why choose to announce this engagement whilst the vagaries of war keep you on active duty?'

Scowling, Brantford folded his letters and placed them on the table. 'I can offer no clarity, nor am I free to extract myself from this situation. As to her character and intentions, I think we have said enough.'

'Yes, yes, indeed. I apologise. I have overstepped. Let me only say that having earned your affection, she deserves my respect and that of the family. I am truly sorry for this troubling news, Henry, and the disappointment that it brings you.'

The awkwardness of the moment dissipated. A hot meal

and a wealth of recent memories and family news gave them much to discuss. It was Brantford who finally put an end to their evening.

'If you will excuse me, Charles, I have some letters to write and gifts to organise and send with you for the family,' Brantford explained, putting on a brave front. 'Can you meet me for breakfast tomorrow? I will pass everything along to you then.'

With errands in town the following afternoon, Charles had already arranged to stay another night at the inn.

'Yes, well, good night then, Henry,' said Captain Sand, looking at his brother-in-law with pity.

ELEVEN

A Family Gathering

CHARLIE REYNE BASKED in the luxury of having a private room at the inn. She sighed with pleasure as she washed away the grime from her travels and rang for the chambermaid to empty her basin and refresh her water supply. Sleeping deeply, she woke early in the morning and repeated her routine, this time leaning into the basin and washing her hair. After drying it in front of the fire, she donned a dress that she had laid out from her travel bag the night before and prepared to leave the room.

Gus and Wil, early risers themselves, had returned from breakfast and were at her door when she opened it. She was unable to avoid them.

'*Wohin gehst du? Wir kommen mit dir,*' Gus insisted as he entered the room, seeing that she was ready to leave on her own. 'Wherever you are going, we are going with you. You know better than to walk through the streets by yourself, especially in a port town. It is not as though you are stepping out of your tent in Spain. You are in England. If you travel alone, people will likely assume you are headed to the ships for amusement. We can go with you for your little promenade. Either that or wait until Inês arrives. You can walk about together.'

'Good heavens,' she replied, straightening her gloves and smoothing the creases in her gown, 'it is not as though we are facing enemy lines. In any case, no one will pay me the slightest heed. If I am to avoid being seen and talked about, the last thing I need is a pair of handsome, tall, blond men to walk me down the street and draw everyone's attention. I will take a short stroll by myself before I stop by the solicitor's office to set up our afternoon meeting. I need you to look after our luggage and crates. Once they unload the barges at the pier, you can arrange to move them into storage as planned. As for me, on my way back from my walk, I will see if any fabric shops are open. You will be in everybody's way there. The other customers would be sure to faint on seeing how handsome you look.'

This sugary remark pleased them both.

'Truly, this is a perfect morning for me to walk about on my own,' Charlie said, seeing she had gained the advantage. 'The clerk downstairs says there is a bakery on High Street that serves the most delectable treats. Shall we meet there at eleven o'clock this morning? Does that give you enough time? I shall be fine by myself until then. You need not fear,' she said cheekily, patting her lower leg where she carried a long army knife inside a leather sheath strapped below her knee. 'I am perfectly capable of looking after myself.'

'Must I repeat myself? You need a man with you, or a lady chaperone, or somebody, so people do not mistake you for a bit of muslin,' protested Gus. He was not sure what to say about the knife. After all, he was the one who gave it to her years ago and taught her how best to use it.

'There are ladies aplenty already headed towards the ships,' pronounced Wil. 'The sun was barely up when a large rowboat filled with women headed into the harbour.'

Charlie wrinkled her nose. 'Bit of muslin, indeed. I will pretend I did not hear you say that. Gentlemen, whichever way you are headed, I am going in the opposite direction. Do you like my pretty bonnet? It has been months since I last wore it,' she said disarmingly, swirling to show the ribbons trailing down her back.

Gus reached out to untangle the ribbons.

'Do not be late for tarts or I shall eat them all myself!' chirped Charlie as she twirled out of the room.

Walking through town, oblivious to the fact that Wil was following her unobtrusively while Gus went to the pier, Charlie basked in the heady joy of being in her homeland. Every sight and sound interested her. Coaches and curricles moved briskly along the streets, creating a noisy bustle that delighted her. She watched a pair of local shopkeepers take the wooden slats off their windows in readiness to open. Labourers and stable hands were at their jobs. Costermongers and street pedlars hurried to their favourite locations, getting ready for another busy day in town.

Charlie found the solicitor's office without much difficulty. It was situated in a solid brick building not far from the Crown Inn where they were staying. She hurried up the narrow stairwell to the third-floor office and rapped on the door bearing the title of Mr Oscar Hendridge. The solicitor had just barely unlocked his door ready to greet the morning.

'Good day, sir. I am Miss Reyne. I am come to book a time for our appointment.'

Surprised to see anyone at such an early hour, particularly a young lady coming alone, Mr Hendridge gestured for her to step into his small office. As he was shutting the door, a man's foot protruded into the room and jammed against the wood. Wil stepped forward, looking sheepishly at Charlie.

'And this gentleman,' said Charlie, scowling at Wil, 'is my companion, Mr Wilhelm Jaeger. He is in the employ of my father, General Reyne. You are in receipt of communication from my father, are you not?'

'I am,' the solicitor replied, surveying the little lady in front of him.

'General Reyne's instructions to you are clear, yes?' she asked. Slightly annoyed that Wil had followed her, but not surprised, and understanding his concern for how it would appear if she went alone, she frowned at Wil. Charlie then placed a small brown ledger and other documents from her portfolio on the man's desk. 'As my father has instructed, you are to make discreet arrangements for the private sale of these items,' she said, opening the worn cover and pointing to the first page. 'As well, you will need to deposit monies into various trust accounts that we will set up together.'

'Surely, you are not bringing all of that here!' he said, aghast, his eyes scanning the page.

'Good heavens, no. The goods that we have transported are safely stored in a secure facility until you are able to place them at auction. I think three months should be ample time for you to prepare, place advertisements, and invite suitable guests. Do you agree?'

The solicitor, annoyed at her manner in addressing him, picked up the ledger. His eyes bulged as he read the list of items she had transported to England. He did a rapid estimate of the values and stared across at Miss Reyne.

'My father's guards have accompanied me to England, and we have hired locally as well,' she informed him, letting the man suppose she had brought her very own private army to protect their property. There was no need for him to know the truth. She adjusted her gloves. I only require the use of your safe for some personal items and to protect some of our papers. It is critical that these remain safe. As stated here,' she tapped a sheet of paper lying on top of the ledger, 'my father has assigned my uncle, Sir John Tripp, to manage these funds until I attain my majority.'

'Very good,' said Mr. Hendridge, nodding appreciatively. He felt at once that it would be easier to deal with the uncle. He knew little about the young lady, other than that she irritated him beyond measure.

'One further point,' she stated, observing his satisfaction, and smiling to herself. 'You can see right here, in the third paragraph, that you are to increase my dowry account from twenty-five to thirty-five thousand pounds, effective immediately,' she said briskly. 'We will, of course, discuss these matters at length during our appointment. I am simply alerting you to a few key points.'

'Will your uncle be joining us for this discussion?'

'Not at this time, no.' Charlie passed the man a folded letter bearing her father's signature. 'My authority stems directly from General Reyne.'

Mr Hendridge sucked his lower lip into the gap in his clenched teeth.

'You are to set up one additional—and rather hefty—account immediately. My father instructs that you arrange a transfer from his account in London. Its purpose is to provide annual salaries for two of my guards and ready access for the purchase of land and planning and construction costs, hiring of staff, household expenses, and the like.'

'What an extraordinary arrangement,' blurted the solicitor, bewildered by it all. Shaking his head in shock, he made his calculations. He confirmed for a second time, and a third, that the general's signature was affixed and duly witnessed on the various documents. He gawked at the slender lady opposite him, taking in her youth as well as her surprisingly old-fashioned appearance. Never had he seen such a trust arrangement, nor such a client, in his forty-year career. He had certainly dealt with the occasional rich widow who managed her own affairs. A few owned properties and invested their funds. Never had he seen such authority, and such vast sums, wielded directly by a young woman.

'Well, then,' he said.

'Indeed,' replied Charlie. 'Does three o'clock this afternoon suit you for our meeting? Yes? Very good. Mr Jaeger and I will return at that time, along with another gentleman.' She smiled sweetly. 'And is your time free until then? I trust you will focus on searching *The Times* and local papers for advertisements of rural property to purchase. That is paramount.'

She rose from her chair and extended her hand. Mr Hendridge bowed deeply and kissed the tips of her gloves.

Leaving the solicitor's office, Charlie and Wil strolled through the market district at a leisurely pace. She stopped and peered into a milliner's display window, studying the latest stylings for women's hats. She regretted not having paper and pencil at hand to record the designs but felt confident she could easily sketch them from memory later.

As the morning passed, she saw several small groups of women hurrying towards the piers. Charlie found herself admiring the gowns of the women passing by. She realised she was drawing some looks herself. She chuckled as it occurred to her that she must seem a trifle odd-looking. Dressed in a well-worn gown in a surprisingly dark fabric, compared to the other ladies, adorned with brocade and lace in Portuguese style, and featuring an unfashionably low waistline, she decided that her attire would not rank high, if indeed it ranked at all, on the domestic fashion spectrum.

She smiled to herself. She had brought with her a trunk filled with lovely garments from the Peninsula. She was certain a good seamstress could adapt and update them to the current styles. Alongside Sofia and a senior officer's wife present in camp, Charlie had been accustomed to entertaining important guests and observing protocols of dress during official visits and military reviews. Even so, she was coming from an active theatre of war. She was, by both circumstance and nature, unschooled and disinterested in matters of fashion.

Returning to the same street as their inn, Wil and Charlie

suddenly heard a loud bray on the street. They turned, surprised to see a pair of large donkeys standing in harness and stopped ahead. Charlie watched as the driver, a boy of about thirteen years of age, left his heavily laden wagon standing in the street and darted into a doorway to make a delivery. He was not gone long and was returning just as a handsome old carriage with an insignia on its door approached from the opposite direction. Another carriage followed closely behind it. Those nearby stared appreciatively at the elegant equipages and the powerful teams of horses drawing them forward.

Rarely had Charlie seen carriage horses during her time in the Peninsula, yet she instantly recognised the high quality of horse breeding in front of her. These horses, tall and heavy, were beautifully proportioned and well-matched. The driver of the first carriage, handsomely outfitted in his livery and sitting patiently atop his box, calmly surveyed the situation.

Anyone watching could see that the opening was too narrow for the carriages to pass beside the wagon. The driver, glancing back at the carriage behind him and the light gig and a curricle pulling in further back, called out to the boy and asked him to back up his donkeys, then drive them forward again closer to the walkway.

The boy nodded earnestly that he would do so. He tried valiantly to get his pair to obey him, but his shaking hands and anxious commands confused the animals. The donkeys refused to move. The more the boy tugged and sawed on their reins, the more resolutely they stood their ground.

A gentleman mounted on a large black horse rode up beside the carriage and surveyed the scene.

'No worries, sir, I am holding them in check,' the carriage driver informed him.

Charlie, looking again at the boy driving the donkey wagon, could see the distress on his face. Gesturing to Wil to wait for her, and darting away before he knew her intention, she crossed over to speak with the boy.

'Hello, there,' she said kindly, seeing that he was trying to hold back tears. 'It might surprise you to know that I am quite an old hand at driving donkeys. Shall I try it? There is no need to worry. Slide over just a little,' she urged, climbing up beside him. She handed him her handkerchief to wipe his tears. 'Let me back up your friends for you.'

'They are not my friends at all!' cried the frustrated lad, his pride deeply wounded. He furiously dried his eyes, then shoved the crumpled cloth back at Charlie. She accepted it with a gracious nod and smiled kindly at him. He did not know what else to do, or to say, so he sat like a stone beside the young woman and watched her take the reins.

Spectators gathered in the street. Two ladies inside the elegant carriage were looking out the near-side window. The tall gentleman on the horse dismounted. With his horse standing quietly behind him, he positioned himself near the head of the carriage horses where he could better signal to the driver and calm the team. Understanding Charlie's intent, he nodded at her politely.

Seated confidently in the wagon with the reins in hand, Charlie took full control of the team. She got their attention with a smart smack on their backsides using the boy's long switch. As the pair lurched forward, she deftly halted them and drew back gently on the reins with even pressure. Feeling the steady pull on their bits, the pair obediently started backing up.

Manoeuvring a heavy wagon backwards along a narrow street was challenging, but Charlie was true to her word. She was indeed skilled at driving carts and wagons, although more often she drove with mules rather than donkeys and typically over rough terrain and rutted paths. She soon accomplished the task at hand. To create more space, after backing up, she guided the donkeys forward again and edged them neatly to the side, creating a wider corridor for the carriage and other vehicles to pass.

The gentleman gave her a nod of thanks and signalled to his driver, who drove his team neatly past the wagon, followed by the other vehicles. A sweet old woman watching from inside the carriage smiled and waved at Charlie through the window as she passed by. Delighted, Charlie smiled in return. She nudged the young boy at her side to take his hat off, which he did with a shy glance towards the old woman.

The Crown Inn where Charlie and her friends were staying was a short distance away along the same street. Charlie and Wil watched with great interest as a heart-warming family reunion unfolded involving the occupants of the two carriages as they pulled forward in front of the inn. Startled, her heart rate quickened as she recognised the captain of the *Pontus* arriving at the scene in front of her.

Captain Henry Brantford was stepping along the promenade with Captain Sand when he spied the carriage and its insignia.

Charlie heard Captain Brantford's excited greeting.

'James, is that you?' the captain called out to the man on foot who was leading his horse. 'Oh, my word! You have come all the way here! I cannot believe it!'

The captain ran across the road as his older brother turned towards him. Their faces lit up with pleasure. The two men embraced one another heartily.

'Henry! Hey, little brother. Let me have a good look at you!' said James Brantford enthusiastically, surveying the captain at arm's length. 'I have worried for naught. You are safely in England, thankfully, and the picture of good health—perhaps a trifle thin, but otherwise looking hale and hearty!'

'I am well, indeed, I am. My word! How did you know—?' Henry Brantford looked questioningly at him, then across at his brother-in-law, standing quietly beside them.

'Guilty as charged,' said Sand. 'I sent a messenger. Fortunately, James arrived at our place last night so was close enough to get here.'

'Who is in the carriage?' asked Captain Brantford excitedly, leaning forward to see inside the first carriage.

From a distance, Charlie watched the older brother open the carriage door and assist the dearest little old lady Charlie had ever seen to climb down. Next to step down from the carriage was a pretty woman, appearing to be close to Inês in age. From their affectionate greetings to one another, Charlie supposed that they must all be close family members.

There were plenty of hugs and tears among them and squeals of excitement from the second carriage as four young children and a pair of adults spilt out onto the pavement. The family gathered around excitedly. Theirs was an unexpected reunion, organised rapidly by Captain Sand for the family to visit with Henry before he returned to duty.

'Is there anyone else inside?' the captain asked eagerly, looking into the front carriage in the hope of seeing another passenger.

James Brantford shook his head.

'It was too far for them to travel. Miss Westcott and her father are, in fact, by this time travelling south to Middlegate from the Lake District. They are due to arrive a few days after I return. But take heart, Henry. I will take excellent care of them for you during their visit. Your assignment will not delay your reunion beyond a few more months, I hope. After that, if we must kidnap you to get you home for your wedding, we will make it happen,' said James encouragingly.

The captain acknowledged his brother's enthusiasm with a solemn nod.

'And Father?'

'He is in London.'

The distance between London and Portsmouth could be travelled in one day. No one commented on this point.

Though disappointed by his father's absence, Henry rejoiced that his family made such an effort to be with him.

'I am shocked you made this journey on such short notice,' Henry said warmly, looking from one dear face to another. 'And you have come for such a short period! I sail again in two days' time! My word, it is grand to see you.'

From her position nearby, Charlie could see how overwhelmed the captain was to see his family in front of him. She dabbed at her watery eyes and watched the captain's broad grin as he twirled one of his younger nephews and propped him on his shoulders. He tightly clasped the hand of his little niece whilst the other two boys clung to his breeches.

'Come, let us get you settled into your rooms and order refreshments for everyone,' said Charles.

'I simply cannot believe my good fortune that you are all here!—Hey, rascal, let go of my shirt,' Henry laughed, swinging the small boy into his father's outstretched arms, tucking his niece's hand into his sister Alison's, and taking the outstretched hands of his other two nephews.

'Grandmother, you look wonderful,' the captain said to the small woman. 'Did you travel well? How are you feeling? Are you tired?' He leaned over and tenderly kissed her on her cheek. 'Come in, come in, we can visit better inside!'

'My dear little Henry,' the silver-haired woman murmured to her grandson, melting into his wide chest. Her eyes brimmed with joy. 'How glad am I to see you! I have missed you so.'

'Little Henry,' James guffawed, quietly mimicking their grandmother. Slightly taller than his younger brother, he enjoyed repeating the phrase.

'Fortunately, the wagon did not scrape against your carriage, Grandmother. What a steady piece of driving,' said Henry, waving in thanks to the Brantford family's skilled carriage driver. 'And that was decent work done by the young lady in moving that wagon,' he added admiringly. Henry looked across to where the young miss stood across the road beside the wagon. He waved to her in thanks.

Flustered to see Captain Brantford looking towards her, Charlie pulled down the brim of her bonnet and acknowledged his wave with a quick nod. She hoped he had not recognised her.

'What an exciting bit of fun,' Charlie said to the wagon driver at her side. She followed the boy's look of longing towards the carriage near the inn. 'Do you want to drive four beautiful horses like that one day? It is possible, you know, but you will need to grow older and gain some weight! You must be famished from all of this activity,' she said, patting him on the shoulder and commending him for his good efforts. 'What is your name, young man?'

Charlie had to lean in to hear his faint whisper.

'Well, Master Percy Winthrop, I am very glad to have met you.' Charlie pulled out two shillings from her reticule and pressed them into the boy's hand. 'Buy yourself a little something when your work here is done.'

Shocked by his good fortune, and with his cheeks rosy from being addressed in such a pleasant manner, the boy clutched the coins tightly.

Worried that if she stayed longer the captain might indeed recognise her, Charlie bid farewell to the lad. She glanced back longingly once more towards the Brantford family, cherishing what she supposed would be her last glimpse of her dear Captain Brantford, for this he had become to her. Watching him on his ship, observing his treatment of her and seeing how his men valued him, she had measured his worth and found nothing wanting. She sighed, gestured to Wil to join her, and hurried away.

TWELVE

A Suitable Piece of Land

Gazing out the window from the little bakery shop, Charlie absentmindedly passed the plate of sweet tarts to Gus.

'Will you have more of these, or would you like to try the little lemon cakes? How do you like the strawberry ice? Is it not divine?' she asked. 'Now, tell me in detail again about the warehouse and the guards you hired, as we discussed,' Charlie remarked.

'Well, it just so happened that while I was waiting for the crates to be unloaded, Lieutenant Sherrington approached me,' said Gus. 'He and his marines were overseeing the area and making sure nothing disappeared as there had been theft at the dockyard and from several of the warehouses of late. He asked where we were taking our crates and strongly recommended that we use the same company used by the Navy Board. Their warehouses are inspected regularly and monitored closely. He said there was space in the naval warehouse he was using where our property could be stored safely without any worries. He assured me this would be as good as any bank vault. He did say, though, that we cannot retrieve our property for ninety days, as the navy is shutting down access whilst the Board develops an adjacent building. I told him that the timing suited us perfectly. Everything was to our advantage, so I accepted the terms. The lieutenant even arranged transportation of the crates and took me with him to the warehouse. Everything is safely locked away.'

'Excellent. It is all looked after. I must say, it was very good of the lieutenant to assist you so thoroughly,' said Charlie, mulling over this turn of events. 'Wil, I assume you approve of this plan?'

'Gus is confident the guards are well trained, and the warehouse lies within a stone's throw of the dockyard offices. Everything should be secure there.'

Charlie nodded approvingly, saying to Gus, 'As you have signed the contract and our crates are now in storage, then that is the end of it. I applaud your decision. We can focus on other matters.'

After paying the clerk and meandering through a few shops in the main market district, Charlie and her friends turned in the direction of the solicitor's office.

'We had best get to our appointment. Come along, boys!' she said to them.

She met with a stern look of reproach from Gus. While Gus certainly looked younger than his forty years, he was over twice Charlie's age. It irritated him when Charlie called them her boys.

'If you would stop dressing like a little old lady or some vagabond boy, you could have a husband walking beside you instead of the pair of us boys,' he said sourly.

Charlie giggled. 'Do hurry. I want to get our papers looked after so we can proceed with our plans.'

The solicitor, eager for the commission that awaited his completion of duties, had placed several documents on his desk in readiness for Miss Reyne's review.

'I have good news for you,' he said solemnly as he welcomed them into his office. He settled his guests around a large teak table. Opening his local newspaper, he pointed to an advertisement. 'There is at present a large tract of land offered in an estate sale in a neighbouring area, roughly twenty miles to the north and west. It is slightly under a three-hour drive if you wish to inspect the property. It comprises a large house that could lend itself to renovation, a decent-sized stable, and several outlying buildings, apparently in good condition. It has in total over seven hundred acres of arable land and forest. If your uncle approves, you can be in possession within the month.'

'What excellent news!' cried Charlie, clasping her hands excitedly. She picked up the various documents. 'We will need to inspect the estate at the earliest opportunity. Do you happen to know of a reputable architect who can accompany us?' she asked. She opened her sketches of the buildings and showed them to the solicitor.

'I do know someone, yes,' he nodded. 'I see here that your purpose is to add on to the house as your living quarters, but what of these drawings for other buildings? Is this a guest house of sorts? It seems overly large. I am not understanding the drawings for these other buildings. They are rather odd. What is it you intend to do here?' asked Mr Hendridge.

'This building? It is indeed a guest house. It will serve as a recovery centre for members of my father's regiment. We will keep the lads here for a time on their return to England as they regain their health and await their pensions.'

'Really! That is an ambitious undertaking. Your father or your uncle has a contract with the military, I take it.'

Charlie sidestepped the question. 'Everyone agrees there is an urgent need for housing for injured soldiers returning from service.'

'What about the navy?' asked Mr Hendridge, who had a son in the marines. 'If my boy is injured, can you keep him here to recover?'

'Possibly, sir, if the local hospital does not have room for him. Likely you have heard that the naval hospital at Haslar is the largest in Europe. That would be your first choice and a fine one, I think.'

'Hmm,' came the response. 'For what purpose are these ware-houses?'

'Storage.'

'Storage! I see. And what will you be storing?'

'Port.'

'I beg your pardon?—did you say port?—are you setting up in trade? To sell liquor?'

'Oh, good heavens, no. Not me personally, sir. How would that look, do you suppose? What would a young lady of good family with no experience in the world be doing setting up a business selling liquor? No, no, it is all being done on account of my friends in Portugal. They will supply and ship the liquor to us. We will simply receive it and send it away again for them. We will store some of it for a little while, and then perhaps sell a bottle here and there, perhaps to the navy, and to the right families, like your own, sir, where people appreciate the quality of a fine product. To be sure,' Charlie looked innocently at the solicitor, 'my friends do not intend to sell to every little tavern in the country.'

He stared at her, trying to decide if she had just made fun of him. He was at a loss to know.

'And what of these cottage-type drawings?'

'What a wonderful eye you have, sir, to understand so very well at first glance. I daresay you could have made your fortune as an architect. We are constructing cottages for people to live in, sir. In one more minute, I am sure you would have guessed it. The residents will live close to one another in a little sort of village, right where the road curves, where the residents can take care of themselves, enjoy good meals, keep a few little gardens, and help in the warehouses. The ladies, sir, will have special tasks to occupy them. They are military wives and widows coming home from the Peninsula, so you can be sure they are used to working from morning to dusk. It would be an insult to their very natures to expect them to sit about idly. The women will make hats, sir.'

'You are selling hats!'

'Not me personally, sir. I assure you. This is merely a bit of facilitation that will occur for friends. Some ladies, and perhaps men, too, will do the plaiting. Some will package and ship the hats to foreign markets, and others will sell the hats to a few local places here and there. My role is merely to enable other people to benefit from the art and craft of fine millinery.'

'My wife likes hats very much,' said the solicitor, distracted by her manner of speaking.

'Dear sir, you must let her choose one of the latest designs we will be offering. I will have her favourite made up especially for her as a keepsake. Do promise me that you will bring her to tea later,' urged Charlie, 'and I will present it to her in person.'

Gus observed his darling Miss Reyne with a thoughtful expression. Never had he known someone capable of hiding such a massive share of determination behind such quirky charm. He had watched her survive the trials and hardships of war. He had watched her grow from a stubborn and precocious adolescent into a capable and determined young lady. She had hounded him relentlessly to help satisfy her thirst for knowledge. He, in turn, rounded up books endlessly. She read them diligently. If one needed to know about local and migratory birds in Portugal, Charlie could speak endlessly on the topic. Curious about the flint mechanism used in the Baker rifle? Charlie could explain it to you. Recently, glowing with excitement, she had become a learned student of the art of basket weaving and hat plaiting.

What irked her most, and entertained the Jaeger brothers endlessly, was to be caught without an answer when queried on something unfamiliar. She invariably made up a fictitious response, in part to entertain herself and in part to avoid admitting that she did not know the answer. Gus recalled one such conversation that occurred recently in Portugal. Precious little occurred to bring about a laugh during a war, yet their dear Charlie had the knack of drawing out a chuckle from her friends in the oddest situations.

'I decided it was high time to sew up that very large gash in the sergeant's side,' she had explained to the head surgeon stationed at the Oporto hospital camp, just a few days before their departure. 'The man was screaming endlessly that some demons had come for him, and he wanted to leave this world for another. I gave him a clear choice. We could abandon him near enemy lines to have his demons exorcised there—he could not recollect that we were nowhere near enemy lines in Oporto, poor soul—or we could give him something else to scream about,' Charlie explained. 'The reason is, sir, I found him rummaging through supplies hunting for laudanum but, you may rest easy, the boys and I caught him at it. After I gave him a generous serving of gin and sewed a mile of stitches along his backside, his demons completely disappeared. He slept very well afterwards, I assure you.'

Listening to Charlie as she spoke, Gus looked with pity at the solicitor. The man was bent on determining if Charlie was making fun of him or speaking earnestly of her situation.

'I pity that bewildered soul,' he whispered to Wil.

Wil, amused at first, soon became bored.

'You can stay with Charlie,' he said quietly to Gus. 'I will go to the loading docks and wait for Inês to come ashore. Some fellows said that the small boats from the hospital ships were shuttling patients across the harbour and the ships' passengers had to wait. Once Inês gets off her ship, I will bring her to the Crown. In the meantime,' he grinned, 'I can watch the fine ladies stroll near the wharf whilst they wait their turns to be rowed out to the ships.'

THIRTEEN

Happenstance

GUS AND CHARLIE soon concluded their business at the solicitor's office. On their departure, Mr. Hendridge ushered out his guests and sat down happily at his desk, eyes bright and shining. Having suddenly come upon a windfall late in his business life, the gleeful old gentleman rummaged through his papers one more time.

Heading towards the Crown Inn, Charlie and Wil turned a corner onto the main road and came face to face with a group of gentlemen. Before them, as surprised as they were by the encounter, stood Captain Henry Brantford, his brother Mr James Brantford, and Captain Charles Sand. An officer in cavalry uniform stood further back, partially shielded from view.

'I say, are not you the young woman who moved the wagon this morning to let us pass?' asked James Brantford, his tone warm and friendly. 'You handled the team beautifully. Well done, indeed, miss.'

Surprised, Captain Brantford surveyed the neatly dressed little woman in front of him. It took him a moment to recognise his 'Mr Reed' from whom he had parted the day before.

The officer at the rear wanted to see what was going on. He leaned forward eagerly to see the young lady being greeted.

'Miss Reyne! My word, is that truly you?' exclaimed the officer in shock.

'Lieutenant Niles!' sputtered Charlie.

Captain Brantford, stunned by their being acquainted, looked back and forth between them.

'Good grief! When did you arrive?' Niles asked her, stepping towards her. 'Have you moved back to England? We only just parted in Oporto! Why did not you say you were coming to England when we met in camp? Are you on a visit? Did you arrive on the convoy?' he asked, shooting a look at Captain Brantford. 'I travelled aboard one of the hospital ships, the *Marfisa*.'

Captain Brantford, preoccupied with studying Miss Reyne's appearance, was barely making sense of the conversation. Only once had he seen Charlie in women's clothing, wearing a grimy hospital tunic with an oversized apron at the military hospital camp in Oporto. It took him a few moments to connect the pieces and digest the fact that the pretty woman standing in front of him was both the woman from the Oporto camp hospital and the woman dressed as a young man on his ship. The recent memory of their journey together on the *Pontus* lay fresh in his mind. And what had his brother said, that she was the one who had moved the donkey wagon out of the way? He needed a moment to gain his bearings. He rapidly concluded that Miss Reyne was a woman of many facets.

Determined to protect Miss Reyne's identity and travel circumstances, Captain Brantford felt that avoiding conversation with her would be the best way to do so. Upon recognising her, had it not been for Niles claiming an acquaintance, the captain would have walked away immediately. As the seconds passed, he had time to take in her present appearance. On this occasion, she was dressed neatly in a somewhat foreign-looking gown. His eyes swept from her sturdy walking shoes to the worn brim of her simple bonnet. He was so busy examining her appearance that the sudden commotion and loud noises in front of him caught him completely off guard.

'*Mach Platz!*' cried Gus angrily, pushing his way through the group, provoked by the sight of the man who had taken his little Charlie into the mayhem in Vitoria. He shoved past the Brantford brothers towards Lieutenant Niles, unsheathed the short sabre he wore at his hip, thrust the tip against the lieutenant's chest, and bellowed at him in German.

The other men could not make out a word of what he was saying. What was all this the tall Prussian was shouting, some long string of foreign syllables followed by some general's name?

James Brantford, not understanding the man but being the person standing closest to him, and rightfully alarmed by the threatening posture and tone, pushed their friend Niles backwards out of harm's way. Captain Brantford took hold of Charlie's arm and pulled her towards him. Gus stepped forward again, straining to keep his sabre trained on Niles.

'And who might you be?' asked Niles, bewildered.

'Restrain yourself, sir,' said Mr Brantford to the armed Prussian. 'You are standing on British soil. We have just brought this man safely home from the war. Put your weapon away! Do you understand me?'

'Here, here, at ease, sir. What is this about?' asked Captain Sand, stepping in as well to help calm the situation. He shoved the flat side of the blade away from the lieutenant's chest. 'Are you daft, man? Whatever your issue, you are no match for the four of us. Come, this fine fellow that you are threatening has just disembarked a ship to return to his family. What can possibly be more important? Let us sort this out like gentlemen.'

Charlie stepped forward and laid her hand on Gus's arm. She spoke to him quietly in German. To everyone's surprise and relief, after scowling at the young lady, Gus reluctantly dropped his arm to his side and sheathed his weapon.

Quickly gathering her thoughts, Charlie swung around to

face the group. She laughed disarmingly. 'My dear gentlemen,' she twittered, 'what an odd Prussian tradition this is for greeting military colleagues. I have always thought it so strange. It scares me half to death to see how these Prussian army men brandish their weapons and put on a great show when they greet old acquaintances.'

Keeping up her gay chatter, Charlie stepped up to Lieutenant Niles. She tucked her arm into his, drawing him towards her. 'Sir, it is very good to see you! Mr Jaeger and I have just recently been speaking about our time together in the Peninsula—and how you and Mr Jaeger met one another at Vitoria, where our troops achieved such an important victory. I hope you have been well since we parted in Oporto. What a surprise to see you here in England! Do you bring greetings from my father? When did you arrive?'

'I came ashore late yesterday,' Niles replied to her, keeping one eye on the Prussian. 'You made no mention of your plan to leave Portugal. It is barely two weeks since we parted,' he complained. With Miss Reyne's mention of Vitoria, Niles had pieced together that the Prussian was one of the guards who worked for Miss Reyne's father. He recognised the man now. He admired Charlie's ability to confuse the others about why a Prussian gentleman in Portsmouth had threatened an English officer just returned from Spain. He then caught sight of the jewellery she was wearing, and his wits utterly failed him.

'I say,' he sputtered, 'is that the necklace I gave to you? It looks very pretty on you—far better than it did in the dark!'

The men looked from Lieutenant Niles over to Miss Reyne. All eyes were on her.

Captain Brantford scowled and strained to see the pendant. The mention of the jewellery disturbed him greatly. He had not expected this. He disliked hearing details of such a close connection between Niles and Miss Reyne.

'Why, yes, it is!' Charlie said sweetly, touching the necklace he had given to her. Her eyes narrowed and glinted dangerously. 'How could not I keep it on me always to remember our evening together? What an unforgettable night. Ah, dear sir!' she said, turning and smiling brightly this time at Captain Brantford. 'Am I right to think that you are the brave captain my dear cousins mentioned?'

Charlie gestured towards Gus and Wil. 'They speak highly of your prowess aboard the *Pontus*. Mr Jaeger, who has been showing off his fine sabre, has bragged to me endlessly about witnessing how you captured an enemy vessel whilst they travelled aboard your ship. How exciting it must have been! I was quite envious of them. I dare say my trip was very dull in comparison. I barely left my cabin for days on end and spoke to nary a soul. My cousins and I were just this moment discussing what to do about the loss of their annoying interpreter—I understand the youngster misbehaved on your ship. The troublesome boy has run off, you see. I find myself in the role of interpreter for the moment. Not that I mind, of course. My friend, Mr Jaeger, who comes from a little village near Hanover, speaks enough English to order his next meal, but that is about all. What good fortune it is that I speak German.'

'Miss Reyne, I seem to have completely forgotten my manners,' apologised Lieutenant Niles. 'May I have the honour of introducing my party? Permit me to do so now: Captain Sand, Mr. Brantford, and Captain Brantford. Gentlemen, this is Miss Reyne, daughter of General Sir William Reyne, whose name you may know, and Miss Reyne's companion, Mr Jaeger.'

Charlie clasped her hands excitedly.

'Ah, I had thought as much! You truly are all one family! Then you are the captain's brother,' Charlie enthused sweetly, 'and you, his brother-in-law! It is such a pleasure to meet you!'

'The pleasure is all ours. I am delighted that we meet again,

Miss Reyne,' said the captain, startling everyone with his claim of a prior acquaintance.

'I beg your pardon?' she asked, alarmed by Captain Brantford's remark. She shot him a surprised look. Why was not he following her cues? Why, she wondered, was he claiming to know her? Had he changed his thinking, and was now inclined to expose her?

'Do not you remember?' asked the captain. 'We met briefly in Oporto at the camp hospital. I had transported several injured and sick men from my ship. I worked alongside you for a time, helping you carry injured soldiers into camp.'

'Ah, well, that is such a long time ago, I can barely recall.'

'Does it feel so to you? Two weeks has not dulled my memory in the least,' he pressed his point in claiming her acquaintance. 'I observed you tending to the patients and then almost had to rescue you from a charging boar. In fact, Lieutenant Niles and I unexpectedly met at the camp as well.'

Following their conversation, it was Lieutenant Niles' turn to be surprised. He glanced back and forth between the two.

'Rescue me!' she scoffed, rising to the bait. 'Had you been reckless enough to fire your pistol, I would have shot you myself! I am sure you heard me warn you at the time to keep your weapon at hand for your protection when you left the camp!'

'Ah, so you do remember me. I am reassured that I had not invented such a memorable encounter. My dear Miss Reyne, how fortunate it is that you have arrived safely in your homeland, despite having a tedious journey getting here,' the captain remarked dryly.

Captain Brantford gave a slight bow. He thought the charming Miss Reyne looked very much like a feral cat with its back against a wall, ready to hiss and spit. The image made him smile to himself.

Lieutenant Niles was not alone in being fascinated with

the turn in the conversation. The others, listening and watching attentively, exchanged confused glances. James Brantford cocked an eyebrow. Charles Sand crossed his arms. Gus scowled at all of them.

'How very curious,' said Sand quietly to James Brantford, his voice barely audible.

'Indeed,' replied the brother.

'My dear sir,' interjected Charlie, casting a nervous look towards Captain Brantford, 'I have long forgiven you for attempting to shoot our pet boar. How could I still be angry about such a small incident, when you have safely transported my dear friends to England? And did I say the journey was tedious? I am sure I did not. Each day was interesting beyond measure. My, my,' she said, pretending to brush away an insect. Looking away from everyone, and glancing up at the sky, she pursed her lips and said, 'That is such a pretty wisp of a cloud. What a delightful morning this is turning out to be. Who knew I would be meeting old friends and new on this fine day?'

As she intended, conversation with the captain came to a halt. A brief conversation ensued between Charlie and Lieutenant Niles while the others waited politely. She was distractedly mulling over the close resemblance between the two good-looking Brantford brothers when a happy shout reached them. Charlie turned to see Inês and Wil, laden with heavy travel bags, trudging along the pavement and waving at them excitedly. The pair rushed up to join them.

'Charlie!—I mean, Miss Reyne! From a distance, I could not be sure it was you! Look how shiny and clean you are! Oh, my goodness! And you are in a dress, too! Did you have hot water for your bath?' Inês asked excitedly in broken English and Portuguese. 'Oh, I am so grateful you are safely on land!'

'Hello, dear Inês,' Charlie embraced her friend. 'You must be exhausted from your trip and carrying all this luggage!'

'Not at all. It is an easy distance from the dockyard,' said Inês.

'Why are you carrying these heavy bags yourself? Could not you hire transportation? Come, let us hurry and get you over to the inn! I daresay you are in need of refreshments,' Charlie said, drawing her forward. 'Gentlemen, please excuse us whilst we take our friends to the inn.' She smiled in farewell.

'Oh, my goodness!' cried Inês, noticing Lieutenant Niles and giving him an embarrassed nod of recognition. 'I did not expect to see you again!'

Inês looked utterly dismayed. 'We were on the same ship,' she said, loud enough for all to hear.

Straining to smile, and almost covering her friend's mouth with her hand to prevent her from saying more, Charlie leaned in and told her not to talk about which ship she was on.

'Do not, for heaven's sake, mention under what name you travelled, or call me Charlie, or mention men's clothes, or women's gowns, or anything else of the sort,' she scolded her. 'Hush, not one more word!'

Inês stared at her, bewildered.

Thankfully, Captain Brantford understood their situation. He resumed conversation with the men in his party as a distraction for the ladies. 'I say,' he started, 'is Mr Jaeger's short sabre a variation of a Scottish dirk, do you suppose, or is it a Hanoverian type of weapon, or is it classified as some other short sword modelled in the Indian style?'

Glad to have met up with Gus and Charlie on the street, and with the men occupied in discussing sabres and dirks, Wil took the opportunity to speak to his friends.

'It was not the walk over here that fatigued her,' he said, speaking loudly in perfectly understandable English, albeit with his heavy German accent. 'She is worn out from leaning over the railing and losing her dinner for days on end.'

Wil suddenly noticed that Captain Brantford was part of

the gathering. He looked awkwardly at his friends, realising that he had spoken to Charlie in perfectly understandable English.

'I must commend you,' the captain remarked dryly, overhearing his comments. 'You seem to have expanded your language skills considerably during your voyage aboard my ship.'

'Indeed! Wil, your English is coming along brilliantly,' Charlie praised him. 'Such an accomplishment! I admire you for making admirable progress in so short a time. I see my days of interpreting are coming to an end. What a blessing.'

In a rather unladylike fashion, Charlie thumped Wil on the back and gave him a sheepish grin. The captain thought she looked more like a mother bear cuffing her cub than a lady issuing a gesture of admiration. Watching her, the captain recalled seeing her the first time she boarded his ship, thumping the two Prussians on their backs as they boarded. Remembering her odd quirks and habits, he could not help smiling at this waifish, self-reliant child-woman whose every action bordered on strange and outrageous.

Charlie, not understanding his smile, nonetheless felt relieved. She knew this was quite probably her final farewell with the captain, and perhaps also with Lieutenant Niles. She could not bear to leave them both on uneasy terms.

'Gentlemen, how good it has been to see you. Such an unexpected pleasure. We wish you all the best. I hope you will excuse us, as you see we need to let our friends settle in at the inn. Come, Inês, let us quickly get you over to the Crown for something to eat. Then we can arrange a hot bath for you as soon as possible,' she said, crinkling her nose. She smiled at everyone, nodded in fond farewell to the captain and the lieutenant, and curtsied in a sweet, bob-like movement that made the others almost laugh aloud.

No one would describe Captain Sand or Mr James Brantford as lacking in cleverness. Bemused by the entire conversation, they had easily observed the telling glances and awkward relations between and among the others and found the undercurrents intriguing.

'We are headed there ourselves,' said Sand. 'We shall accompany you. Here, let me assist with these bags. Niles, lend the young woman your arm, will you?' He gestured towards Inês. 'My word, these bags are rather heavy!'

'What a strange bit of fate that we should meet up with your friends today, Henry,' said the brother to the captain as the group walked towards the Crown. 'What a strange coincidence, and how very interesting, that you met Miss Reyne in Portugal at the camp hospital, and that she is known to Niles as well, and that he met her Prussian friends in battle, and that you carried these same Prussians on your ship, along with transporting the ladies in your convoy, and, furthermore, that this is the same young lady who was such a great help with the donkeys on our arrival. I have not had such an interesting morning in eons. Now, here we all are, meeting and greeting one another again this afternoon on a walkabout. Your paths all seem to be continually converging. Is it fate, do you think?' James Brantford cast a friendly, sideways glance at this brother and tipped his head towards Lieutenant Niles and Miss Reyne, walking together slightly ahead of them. 'If I am any judge of matters, they seem very well known to one another. Would you agree?'

Troubled by the implication, Captain Brantford followed his gaze. He scowled at the pair in front as he let his brother's meaning sink in. While they walked to the Crown, the captain glanced up several times, frowning at Miss Reyne. In the occasional moments when he was not watching her, he found himself studying the other woman, the newcomer to the party, with interest.

They had not far to walk to reach the inn. The two parties soon arrived, and within minutes were bidding farewell and parting ways in the lobby.

'Miss Reyne—' said the captain as they prepared to separate. 'Do you have a moment? Might I have a word with you—in private?'

'Yes, of course,' responded Inês.

'Certainly,' said Charlie, simultaneously.

'With the real Miss Reyne,' the captain said quietly to them both.

Inês looked with alarm at Charlie. Charlie patted her reassuringly on the arm. 'He knows. I will explain later,' she said softly, shooing her friend away.

Charlie and the captain stepped into the Crown's small foyer near the front stairwell.

'I had not expected to meet you again off of the ship,' said the captain. 'While I mean no slight in saying this, I regret that we are crossing paths in public. It poses a serious risk of discovery for you. However, you handled the encounter well, I must say. You avoided any missteps during our conversation. Might I add, it is heartening to see you dressed as a woman. It rather suits you.' He could not help admiring her lithe figure. 'I wanted to let you know that I am to return to duty. I leave for the Peninsula the day after tomorrow. This is truly to be our farewell, Miss Reyne.'

'On duty! What about your leave? Was it cancelled? Oh, what a shame! You have been longing for time ashore! Dear captain, if you are going back to the war again, I shall worry for you immensely, and miss you very much!' Charlie blurted out.

The captain looked at her in surprise.

'Promise me you will not be reckless,' she urged. 'I hope, I very much hope, that you will stay safe and return soon. I will be thinking of you constantly. I even left a few surprises for you in your library on the *Pontus,* thinking it would be some time before you returned. I hope you enjoy finding them. Goodness, how disheartening that you are going back to sea! What of your engagement? You must be devastated by this news. I am devastated for you. Well, then, dear kind sir, I suppose this is truly goodbye until we meet again.'

Bewildered by the warmth of Charlie's tone and deeply moved by the sincerity of her good wishes, the captain reluctantly drew away from her. He was discomfited to find her attention claimed immediately by another.

Lieutenant Niles, standing near the foot of the stairwell, had waited impatiently for his friend to step away. Surprised to discover that he and the captain and Miss Reyne were all acquainted with one another, the lieutenant anxiously pulled Charlie aside for a private conversation.

'How delighted I am to see you in England! I have longed to speak with you again!' he whispered to her, sorting out his thoughts.

'Whatever about?' she asked, annoyed with him. 'Let go of my arm before you have Mr Jaeger's sabre at your chest again. You apologised to me in Oporto for taking me into Vitoria. I do not know what further needs to be said.'

'Do you know your father's current whereabouts?' he asked.

'You can simply address your letter to him by name and the military post will deliver it. It is not a complicated matter.'

'Well, I must write to him again and let him know I have returned to England and have met you here. I expressed my views to him before, and to you as well. My opinion remains unaltered. I feel strongly that you, and he on your behalf, should accept my offer of marriage. I urge you to do so as soon as possible. How can you possibly recover your reputation once word gets out of your masquerade and our night together? And surely it will if the story has not already spread.'

'You were the one to mention the necklace,' she scolded.

'I can name half a dozen men who are aware of what

happened,' he said, ignoring her point. 'Yes, they took your father's money, but that does not guarantee their silence. By the way, I am curious to know, where did you first meet my friend, Captain Brantford? Was it at the hospital camp in Oporto? May I ask, of what were you speaking so secretively just now? I must ask which ship you were on in the convoy. I did not see you coming off the shore boats from the other hospital ships. I travelled on the same hospital ship as your friend. And why, of all things,' his tone took on a sharp tone, 'was your friend using your family name on board? I said nothing of this earlier, wanting an explanation from you, but I am at a loss to understand matters. Why did not you travel together on the same ship?'

'Dear sir, I fail to see how it is your business to query so thoroughly after mine,' she said haughtily.

'Were you on one of the other hospital ships, then? It is improbable that you arrived on the prison ship, although anything might be possible with you,' he laughed.

She made no reply.

'Surely you did not come back to England on one of the frigates. Tell me you did not!' He watched her expression closely. 'No. That is unbelievable! Have you gone mad?' he asked incredulously, guessing at the truth. 'Tell me, please dear God, you did not do what I am thinking.'

It was obvious to anyone observing their animated conversation, and several were doing so, that the lieutenant and the young woman were certainly more than mere acquaintances. There was a familiarity, almost intimacy, in their manners with one another. The captain, still in the hallway, watched them with what surely felt like jealousy. He began piecing together all he had heard from Niles about some young woman dressed as a man in Vitoria, and giving her a necklace, and negotiating with her father, with what he now observed.

The lieutenant's persistence in seeking out the young lady,

the animated conversation, and the expressions of concern and aggravation on their faces quickly led everyone watching to conclude that there was certainly some sort of relationship between these two individuals.

Captain Brantford knew enough and had seen enough by now, to confirm his suspicions that Miss Reyne had been the young lady artist that his friend Niles had taken with him into Vitoria. While he had guessed at this earlier, he still felt physically ill now at the thought of all she must have witnessed.

Captain Sand frowned deeply as he watched Lieutenant Niles in conversation with Miss Reyne. Much as the young lady was charming, he was highly dissatisfied. He wanted a word with his friend.

When they reached the upper halls, Captain Sand rested his hand on Niles' shoulder and said to him in private, 'You must excuse me for speaking my mind. It would of course be a good thing if someone suitable were to gain your interest. You deserve a loving companion, and your children certainly would benefit from the guidance of a caring mother. Alison is most excited—perhaps even determined—to assist you in finding such a wife. She has drawn up a list of eligible ladies she is wanting you to meet. I beg of you, Niles, do oblige her. Keep my wife happy and set your future course wisely. Bide your time, my friend. You have only just arrived home! Promise me you will not rush into anything with this young woman from Portugal. Why, she is barely out of the schoolroom.'

'I fail to see how this is anyone's business but my own,' Niles said sternly.

'Yes, yes, of course, but take your time, dear fellow. Have you known Miss Reyne long? Where did you meet? Did you travel together on the hospital ship? That would explain the matter.'

'We met in Spain and again in Portugal,' Niles muttered, attempting to put an end to conversations about Miss Reyne.

'I see. Well, for one thing, I am sorry you had to travel on a hospital ship. That must have been a bitter pill not to travel on Henry's frigate. It is a good thing you did not catch a fever along the way. It is good to have you back home, Peter.'

'Come, now, gents,' Sand said to his group. 'Shall we relax awhile and then go up and dress for dinner? I have booked tables for the entire family in the parlour. We are to dine at seven.'

FOURTEEN

Family Dinner at the Crown

'MY DEAR SWEET Charlie, I am so grateful to be off that dreadful ship! I barely ate at all, yet I have never been so nauseous in my life. I am looking forward to my first meal in England, on land,' said Inês, linking arms with Charlie as they went down the stairs and into the small lobby. 'I am famished!'

'Let us hope we do not meet up with the Brantford party. What would be the use of seeing them again?' asked Charlie cheerfully. 'It is bad enough that Lieutenant Niles knows that you travelled under my name, but the clever captain knows my real name and he also knows that you used my name on the hospital ship. We really must avoid them, dear heart. The captain's guests are all leaving Portsmouth on the morrow, and he leaves the following day. We can be free of worries after that. I heard that the family's main property is in Herefordshire,' she explained to her three friends. 'When I asked him, the young clerk at the front desk said that country people like to dine earlier than people who live year-round in the towns and cities. They will have already eaten and left the dining room by now.'

Entering the inn's large dining room, she was relieved to find that the room was indeed nearly empty. 'How fortunate!' Charlie said to Inês. 'They are nowhere to be seen.'

Charlie asked that their party be seated towards the back

of the room, offering an extra degree of privacy with only two other tables near theirs. They were seated for perhaps ten minutes when, to Charlie's chagrin, the entire Brantford party arrived in the room. The grandmother entered first on the arm of her grandson James.

'Good grief! Their table is next to ours!' Inês whispered.

It was impossible for the two groups not to take notice of one another. As the family members passed by Charlie's table, polite nods and gestures of acknowledgement were inevitably exchanged. Lieutenant Niles, delighted with the situation, stopped to exchange a word of greeting with Charlie. Captain Brantford contented himself with a polite nod towards Charlie and the others in passing.

Gus and Wil, disgruntled to see the lieutenant again, barely acknowledged him as he passed by.

Charlie, however, having done her best to avoid the present situation, now felt a tinge of excitement. She had not expected one more opportunity to see the captain before his departure. As much as she knew it was best to stay apart, she nonetheless relished seeing him again. She took delight in watching him and his party more closely.

'How splendid they all look!' said Inês, admiring the elegance of the women's gowns and the handsome appearance of the men.

Captain Brantford pulled out a chair for his grandmother while the older brother lent his arm to seat the diminutive lady.

'Oh, how delightful! I love her pretty *fichu*,' Inês whispered, admiring the lace draped elegantly above the elder woman's bodice. 'It takes ten years off of her age.' She looked down at her chest, wondering if the time had come to adopt that approach.

Charlie laughed at her friend's expression. 'You look wonderful,' she assured her.

Captain Sand and his wife followed next. Captain Sand was walking with a slight limp that Charlie had noticed earlier. His wife's arm intertwined snugly with his. Two other members of their household, the carriage driver and two middle-aged women, perhaps a governess and lady's maid, Charlie could not tell, took their seats at an adjacent table with the Sand youngsters in their care.

'How sweet that their children are dining next to them,' said Charlie quietly. 'At that age, I usually took my meals alone.'

The eldest of the three Sand boys, likely nine or ten years old, caught Inês's attention. His every action mesmerised her. A look of grief settled over her face.

Charlie, seeing her expression, squeezed her friend's hand. 'You must miss your son terribly,' Charlie said warmly.

Inês blinked hard and bit her lip.

'Will it be five years this spring?' asked Charlie solemnly.

Inês nodded, her face pale. 'It feels like it was yesterday.'

Inês and countless others in Oporto had lost family members in March of 1809 during the assault by Emperor Bonaparte's army. The death of both her husband and son on the same day was not only a personal tragedy for Inês but one shared by countless others. Along with the villagers and militia escaping from the invading army, her husband and son had tried to retreat across the river Douro. Crowds of fleeing citizens surged forward in panic, pushing everyone in front of them. As the central portion of the pontoon bridge sank, civilians were swept into the river. The middle section twisted and sheared away while people continued to shove and push from behind. Inês's husband and son had perished in the churning water with thousands of others. Events of that awful day were seared into their memories.

Tears streamed down Inês's face as she watched the children's table. Gus pulled her chair closer to his own and placed his large hand gently over hers. Wil, who rarely showed his feelings to anyone, studied the *fleur-de-lys* patterns imprinted in plaster along the outer edges of the ceiling. While he regained his composure, he wished with all his heart that the war was at an end.

After a few minutes, Inês regained her awareness of the others. She smiled sadly, mindful of their attentiveness to her. She picked at her meal and from time to time looked over to watch the Sand children, but now with a calmer demeanour. As the evening wore on, she even seemed to gain a sense of pleasure watching the little ones.

Charlie, too, found her glances wandering, but hers rested on the adults in the Brantford party. Watching the family members chat and laugh with one another made her feel deeply happy. She desperately wanted to hear and be part of the conversation. Apart from a few childhood memories of relatives in England, she had no recollections of large family dinners like this one, shared with loved ones. Mesmerised, she watched with a sense of longing and delight.

'The young lady we met earlier is staring at you, Henry,' James Brantford said in an undertone to the captain. 'Do you wish to change seats? Then I can block her view.'

'No, James, you have it wrong,' said Sand, overhearing them. The four men, seated closest to Charlie's end of the table, kept their voices low. 'There is something going on between Niles here and that young woman, I swear. No, no, it is true. I am not blind, you know. But there is no need to be concerned,' he remarked, elbowing the lieutenant, seated beside him. 'I will talk Niles out of it.'

'After all,' said Sand, 'There is no point in making a romantic connection to someone, almost a foreigner, at the very moment of returning home to us.'

James Brantford chuckled.

Niles and the captain exchanged looks, each uncertain of what the other was thinking.

'If you are finished painting your unlikely scenario,' said Captain Brantford, 'I think James is the one we need to be quizzing.' He turned towards his brother. 'James, I nearly fell off my chair when I read your last letter advising that you had met someone of interest. What was her name—Miss Vincent? You have never mentioned anyone by name before. Are we to congratulate you soon? Charles, have you met this lady?'

'No, I have not yet had the pleasure. James is reticent to speak about her,' said their brother-in-law, peeved.

'Well, do not mention her name to Alison or that will be the end of my chances,' said James. 'In any case, things are not so far along as I would wish. I cannot determine if she returns my feelings.'

'Did I just hear you say that you are lacking confidence in this matter?' laughed Sand. 'Well, justice has been served. When I think of the lovely young misses whose affections you did not return over the years, it is high time you put in a little effort. Truth be told,' he said to Henry, 'James has some serious competition for the lady's favour. It is not all clear sailing for our dear brother. It is unfortunate, as he is quite smitten.'

James gave him a sour look.

'I confess,' James said quietly, 'that I would choose her company over any female of my acquaintance. She is, quite simply, the loveliest woman I have ever met. Unfortunately, I have had no chance to meet her father or her closest family members. Apart from meeting some distant cousins who live not far from us—Henry, did you ever meet any of the Stancroft family in Finstead? They are Miss Vincent's relations—we have no connections to bring us together. Thankfully, Ashton has invited Miss Vincent to his ball in just a few days, the one we hoped you would attend, Henry. I hope to see her there.'

'Well, this is a first,' said Sand, surprised by James's openness in disclosing his feelings.

James, watching his younger brother closely, understood how distressing it must be for Henry to be absent from the upcoming gatherings. He said sadly, 'I am so sorry you cannot join us in Middlegate, Henry. It must be so very wearisome for you to postpone your leave, and not be home to welcome Miss Westcott into the fold.'

The captain nodded and took a deep breath. 'Unfortunately, James, I will not be able to meet your special lady. Well, never mind. My absence is for a few more months only. If you have found someone at last who makes you truly happy, then I am well pleased for you, dear brother. I will cheer you on from afar.'

'Shall we aim for a double ceremony?' asked James playfully.

'Perhaps not,' replied Henry. He was neither sure of his feelings nor highly confident of the plans of his bride-to-be.

Overhearing some parts of the conversation among the men at the Brantford table, Charlie sat despondently for several moments. She adored the captain. She needed to adjust to the news of his pending marriage. She wanted to leave the room and be alone, but the next remarks from the adjacent table caught her attention.

Captain Sand had raised a topic that keenly interested her. Gus, Wil, and Charlie all leaned forward, intent on listening.

'Niles, what was all the chat we heard from the officers about some huge wagon train of King Joseph Bonaparte's war booty being stolen in Spain? The news was all the talk in London and out into the country over the summer when word of the battle and chaos at Vitoria reached our ears. You were there. Are the rumours true? I heard that there was enough cash and treasure stolen to fund the whole army in the Peninsula for another full year and that it was our fellows who took most of it. The Navy Board issued several alerts to watch for anyone transporting valuables back to England. Henry, you received those notices, I take it?'

Henry nodded. He glanced towards Charlie, and finding her looking his way, briefly met her gaze. Then he spoke more loudly than before.

'If the situation warrants it, captains and lieutenants in the fleet have the authority to search and seize baggage on our ships. It is not an active process we follow on the frigates since we only carry government specie and shipments or captured prizes of our own. We conducted searches on two occasions since the summer, one of which was just this week. All our ships continue to be on high alert for stolen goods. The French train had been loaded in Madrid and was carrying six years' worth of valuable cargo back to Paris.'

'Niles, as I said, you were in Vitoria when the looting took place and saw it yourself,' interjected Sand. 'You mentioned that someone made drawings for you. Is it true that those images, along with first-hand accounts, helped the army recover some of the goods?'

'Yes,' responded Niles, lowering his voice, and glancing sideways towards Charlie. 'General Wellesley's officers conducted extensive searches in the days following the battle. They recovered some of the property. Still, it was nothing in comparison to what disappeared.'

Exchanging surprised glances, Charlie and her friends sat perfectly still, straining to hear his every word.

'The army's inquiry is still underway. It has been extremely hard to track where everything went. There were thousands of French, English, Portuguese, Spanish, and Prussian troops, as well as civilians, with access to the baggage train. Part of the train was ransacked right in the town but most of the wagons and carts were abandoned along the roadways and fields. Which wagons had the most valuables, who took everything—the locals, the army, our people, or the enemy—it is impossible to know. How can that scenario possibly be reconstructed?'

'Well, I heard that the drawings showed the chaos in town that occurred among the victors,' said Sand. 'The information helped General Wellesley address the lack of discipline and get back some of the goods. Well done on your part, Niles. But what a shameful night, in countless ways. I shudder to think of anyone trapped in the town. For the army to stop their pursuit to ransack and steal, with the enemy so near at hand—what a disastrous breakdown. There are occasional stories of that sort in the navy, but it is rare,' Captain Sand said reflectively. 'We have a strict formula for sharing prize bounty. I think the army could learn from us on these matters. Do you agree, Henry? By the way, I heard the news that you are sharing prize revenue with some ships in your convoy. That is rather generous of you. Your men did not mind?'

Captain Brantford shook his head. 'Not at all. That is standard practice. We were acting as a unit. The only opportunity for the *Pontus* to pursue the prize was due to the other ships protecting the convoy whilst we engaged. The revenue rightly belonged to all of us.'

'Well, you are one of a rare few who think that way. But in terms of the army, I hope some of the lost bounty from Vitoria can still be recovered to pay for expenses. If this war lasts much longer, our British taxpayers will be the next ones to rebel.'

'And yet, if I may say so, those stolen treasures originated in the Iberian Peninsula,' said James. 'If some of it fell into Spanish or Portuguese hands and remained inside the country, how can it be considered theft from the British army when the property was taken from museums and private homes in the first place?'

'What are you boys chatting about now?' asked Alison, returning from the lady's room to her seat beside the grandmother. 'I am told the desserts here at the Crown are quite delicious. Shall we order a round of custard and fruit?'

Charlie was grateful for an end to the conversation about

Vitoria. It made her nervous to think about the searches conducted on board one or more of the ships. She shuddered, as well, to think of that night. It made her feel unwell.

'Thank goodness we were able to get through with all of our bags and crates,' Wil whispered to Gus and Charlie. 'It sounds a bit like a mad hunt is still on to recover items.'

'Charlie, could we please go back to our room?' asked Inês, worn out from her emotions and from the journey just completed. 'I am tired from sitting on these hard chairs. Do you mind if we retire? Let the boys have the evening to themselves. They deserve a night on the town after all they have been through.'

'Go, leave us,' said Gus. 'We have all eavesdropped on everyone's conversations long enough.'

'*Guten Nacht,*' said Wil, wishing the ladies a good night, excited with the prospect of an evening off duty to enjoy himself.

'*Bis Morgen,*' Charlie replied. 'Until tomorrow. But remember, we are getting fitted for new clothes. I want you looking handsome. Try to get at least an hour or two of sleep.'

FIFTEEN

Another Farewell

THE DOCKYARD BUSTLED with activity. Several ships, arriving overnight and anchoring at Spithead, were continuously sending boatloads of cargo to shore. The ships' boats along with the town's small boat operators were constantly ferrying sailors and marines, the occasional civilian passengers, and supplies to and from the various ships and the shore.

With increased traffic and movement through the streets, a bit of startling news began to circulate among the townsfolk and added to the excitement in town. Purportedly, several prisoners quartered on the Portsmouth prison hulks had escaped during scheduled land exercises and were hiding in the vicinity.

'The locals are warning one another to watch for any signs of them,' Gus advised. 'There is nothing for us to worry about. They are probably unarmed and likely too sick to be dangerous but stay alert and stay away from the alleyways just in case they are roaming in the streets,' Gus said to the Charlie and Inês. The ladies were sitting on the edge of Charlie's bed. They had purchased some little cakes and fruit on their early morning shopping excursion and had just set the food out on a tray.

'I hope they manage to get hold of something good to eat before they are captured,' said Wil. 'Some of those poor soldiers have been holed up in the prison hulks eating stale hardtack for a decade. I would rather have died at the end of a bayonet.'

The four of them thought alike on this point. They were no strangers to the struggles and deprivations of soldiers.

'Let us hope they will enjoy at least one day of freedom, then, before they are caught,' said Charlie optimistically, moving to peer out the window beside her bed. 'I am surprised we have not seen anyone from the Brantford party yet. I wonder how they are spending their day.'

As though in response to her enquiry, Charlie spied the two Brantford carriages shortly afterwards pulling into the courtyard. With a clear view of the action below, Charlie watched with interest while servants at the inn brought out the family's luggage. The family members soon came outside and milled around the carriages.

'How very sad,' Charlie said quietly. 'They are saying their goodbyes. I cannot bear to watch.'

'Indeed. That is why you are staring at them so fiercely,' responded Inês, leaning in beside Charlie at the window. 'Is the lieutenant fellow leaving as well? I am sorry I will not get to see him again,' she said. 'How long will the captain be at sea?'

'I heard him say three months, possibly more,' Charlie replied, her brows furrowed.

'Yes, and you also heard that he is engaged to be married on his return,' Inês said pointedly. She had never seen Charlie show serious interest in anyone before now. It startled her to see signs of infatuation in her young friend. She, too, had overheard the conversation at the Brantford table last evening. It appalled her to think that Charlie might remain in a state of denial on this matter. 'No doubt he will be anxious to return for his wedding,' she added.

'I see what you are about,' said Charlie coolly. 'I am sure we can agree that there is no reason to dislike a man just because he is engaged.'

Inês nodded agreeably. 'True, but there is not much reason to develop an affection for a man who is,' she countered, drawing back from the window.

'I feel sorry for the captain,' Charlie said.

'I am sure you do,' said Inês.

The Brantford carriages below were soon fully loaded and ready for departure. Charlie could see two sets of carriage horses being brought around and secured into the traces. Mr James Brantford climbed into the saddle on the large black horse that she recognised from the day before. Lieutenant Niles swung himself up into the saddle of a second horse. Niles, following the flight of a pair of swallows dipping through the courtyard, suddenly looked up towards the second floor. Whether he could see Charlie watching them leave, or merely suspected that she was at the window, she could not tell. With a wave of farewell in her direction, he and Mr Brantford rode out in front of the carriages.

Charlie could hear the gravel crunching under the wheels as the vehicles rolled onto the street. Captain Brantford, standing in the courtyard to see his family off, followed the direction of the lieutenant's gaze and looked upwards for several moments towards the window where Charlie stood watching. She felt frozen in place.

He gave her a nod of recognition, then lowered his head and walked away.

'Have they all finally left?' asked Gus. 'I am glad of it. I am not fond of that impertinent lieutenant fellow, I can tell you that. I should have run him through when I had the chance.'

'Dear Gus, I have explained it all to you. It was not his fault that I went into Vitoria.'

'He held a gun to your head,' said Gus, curling one of his hands into a fist.

Charlie ignored this. 'Besides,' she said, 'though he did

keep me with him all night, he also kept me safe. He apologised profusely to Father and to me. Silly man, he is convinced he should marry me. Father is keeping the whole affair quiet. I find it all rather insulting—as though some lone soldier minding his business and doing his duty could compromise me. And now he is trying to track Father down to change his mind. How sweet is that?'

'Very sweet,' murmured Inês.

'Well, at least the lieutenant did not lock you in a room for a week as that overbearing captain did,' muttered Wil. 'If I were you, brother, and had a yearning to spear someone, I would mark the captain as the better target.'

Gus was not in any mood to talk about either of these men. Seeing his expression, Wil stuffed a lemon cake into his mouth to stop himself from laughing.

Inês looked at Charlie, her expression deeply earnest. 'Charlie, tell us truly. You spent a week with the captain in his private chambers. During that entire time, based on what you have learnt since, he knew you were a woman. Speak truthfully. Did he behave as a gentleman?'

'Very much so,' said Charlie. 'He built a small room for me away from all the men. The captain ensured I was well-fed. I had very little work to do and had time to draw to my heart's content. I also learnt a great deal about ships, perhaps even more so than Gus and Wil,' she said teasingly. 'You need not worry about what happened. We have days and days ahead to chat. I will tell you every detail. But right now, we are heading over for our fittings. Afterwards, Gus and Wil can see about getting us some transportation to visit the property Mr Hendridge mentioned. I hope you do not mind, Inês. You and I will stop in at that little milliner's shop. It is further out, a little off High Street, but not difficult to find. We can all meet back here for dinner.'

With a last look out of her window on the futile hope

of seeing the captain once more, Charlie and Inês set out on their errands.

It was to be a memorable day for all of them, though in vastly different ways.

Gus and Wil, after eight years of service in the British army, were enjoying their first full day off duty in a country where there was no imminent threat of attack. Their stomachs were full, they were rested, healthy, and spending time with two women who were dearest to them in all the world. To make their day complete, they were being outfitted as gentlemen, of all the unexpected things for two former Prussian military officers to do in a bustling port town in England.

'I regret to say, when these are ready, they will not be the best suits you will ever wear—my father says we must get ones made in London for that—but they will certainly be an improvement over your worn-out uniforms,' said Charlie.

The day, for Inês, was one of mixed emotions. She wondered how her sister Sofia fared at home in Portugal. She worried about Charlie, who at such a young age oversaw everyone's care and well-being. She was thrilled to be fitted for new gowns and she loved peering in windows as they meandered through town. She liked Portsmouth. It reminded her of Oporto before the war, before its buildings had been ransacked and burnt. She liked the little cottages that reminded her of her own home, though hers was in the Portuguese countryside, on a hill over-looking the river. People she encountered here on the streets were busy with their daily lives. They reminded her of people she left behind. This was her first day in her new home away from home. Instead of rejoicing, she wanted to curl up and cry.

Charlie, in her typical style, was carrying out five tasks at once. She carried a detailed and lengthy list of items for them to accomplish. She focused on what she needed to do next in arranging for their future abode in England. It thrilled her to think that the property they were soon to inspect might be ideal for their needs. She had, for the first time in her life, sufficient time to do what she needed to do, and ample resources to buy what she needed to buy. She was, more than anything, thankful for the company of her dear friends.

'We must both be fitted for some new shoes,' she told Inês. 'Also, I need to buy gifts to bring for the visit to my aunt and uncle. Gus, I think the haberdasher is down this street. When you and Wil are done with your fittings, please remember to arrange our transportation to view the property. See what sort of coach might be available for our use. Inês and I will meet you back at the inn when we are done.'

By late afternoon, most of their errands were completed. The women looked up at the changing sky as the sunlight faded from the day.

'Do you mind stopping in here so that I can purchase an umbrella?' asked Inês. 'From the looks of it, we will need one soon.'

'Whilst you are doing that, I will stop in at the jeweller's further down the street to find gifts for my uncle and aunt. We are close to the inn. Do you mind heading directly back towards the Crown from here so that you can pick up some sweets on the way before the shops close? I still need to buy a few more items. I will see you at the inn once I am done.'

'Promise me you will not tarry. You are not supposed to walk alone here.'

'Yes, yes, fine. I will hurry, but we both still need to pick up our items. There is no need to tell Gus. I will see you soon.'

Within the half-hour, coming out of the jeweller's shop with gift bags dangling from her arms, Charlie felt a few light sprinkles of rain. Seeing an overhead awning on a corner window facing an alleyway, she stepped around the corner to stand under the awning. She was startled to see two men lurking further back in the alley with a third man lying on the ground at their feet.

'Hello, is the gentleman hurt?' she called out, moving towards them. 'I say, is your friend injured?'

The two men swung around to face her, blocking her view of the man on the ground.

'Mind your business and walk away, miss. Nothing here concerns you.'

'You are mistaken, sir,' she replied, instantly understanding the gravity of the situation. 'A man is lying on the ground requiring help. What is your intent?'

She recalled the news shared in the morning that some prisoners had escaped. Were these two men from one of the prison hulks? She thought for a moment about the man's reply to her. His accent was not that of a foreigner.

'What have you in those bags, little miss?' asked the heavier of the two men, taking a step towards her. 'Set your bags on the ground, if you please, so we can have a little look at what you have brought us.'

Looking past the two ruffians, Charlie saw the dark stains of blood pooling under the man on the ground.

'Certainly,' she said. She put her bags behind her and reached down, pulling out the long knife from its sleeve strapped to her leg.

'Whoa, there, missy, that is rather bold of you.'

'I suggest you leave at once, so I am not forced to use this,' she said sternly. 'Leave the injured man in my care and we can part ways here.'

She watched the men intently, waiting for one of them to rush towards her. In her opinion, it is what any sensible robber would do. Gus had taught her a great deal about defending herself. It is unlikely that either of these men ever had someone from the King's German Legion as their private instructor in wielding a knife. Charlie stood at a slight angle to the men, her weapon raised. The men at first remained perfectly still, then slowly backed further into the darkened lane. Suddenly, they turned and ran away.

'Good heavens,' she muttered. 'What a pair of cowards!'

She heard a step behind her and spun around, eyeing the pistol aimed at the departing men.

'Captain Brantford! Ah! That is why they ran away so fast!' She smiled and laughed, thoroughly delighted to see him.

'What on earth are you holding in your hand?' he asked, putting his pistol away. 'Is that a knife? Good heavens, woman, did you mean to use it?'

'Of course not. I was preparing to dash away at any moment, but there was no need to do so. Your pistol has won us the day. How fortunate you happened to be nearby, and how good of you to assist. Come, let us see what is wrong with this poor man.'

Charlie tucked away her knife and hurried towards the injured man. She picked up his hand and felt for his pulse.

'He has been badly beaten,' she said, stating the obvious. 'Besides this wound on his head, he appears to have injured a rib or two. He is struggling to breathe.'

'I will stay with him. Go to the top of the alley to see if anyone is about who can help us,' instructed the captain. 'We will need to move him.'

'I am not leaving you,' she said. 'What if those men should return when you are here alone?'

He looked at her in astonishment. 'Is your memory so short? I have a pistol,' he said dryly.

'Yes, but you would only have time for one shot. Do you intend to use your pistol as a cudgel?'

'I am a naval captain. I did not reach that rank without knowing how to handle myself.'

'True enough. Well, I will come back as soon as I can,' she promised, scowling as she hurried off to find help.

When she returned, the captain felt gratified to see she had enlisted the help of two shopkeepers and a fruit monger who pulled an empty cart behind him. The helpers soon had the man lifted onto the cart and were talking with the captain, discussing where to take the fellow.

The injured man opened his eyes. '*Merci,*' he said softly to Charlie, his voice quivering.

'Ah. I thought so, you poor soul. I am sorry your one day of freedom has ended in this horrible way. Try not to speak to anyone. If fortune smiles on you, you may yet survive to see another day. *Comprenez-vous?*' Charlie asked, hoping he understood her.

The man nodded his head slightly.

'We are done here,' said the captain, coming to her side. 'These men say there is a surgeon living half a mile down the road who might be of help. I have paid them to see that this man gets care this evening and a hot meal in the morning. They will keep him safe for the night. I will investigate this matter later. Come along. I will take you back to the inn.'

She smiled gently at the man on the cart. '*Courage! Ça va aller mieux maintenant,*' she encouraged him softly, squeezing his hand in a gesture of promise that all would be better now.

SIXTEEN

An Evening Stroll

THE CAPTAIN PICKED up Charlie's bags containing her purchases and walked briskly out of the alley towards the main street. She hurried to catch up to him. Most of the shops had closed for the day and the streets were quiet in this part of the town. They walked along in silence for a time. He stopped suddenly and turned angrily to face her.

'Explain this for me,' he said. 'How is it possible that you ended up in a back alley, unchaperoned, entirely alone, in the company of two thugs and an escaped prisoner? And why on earth were you armed with that monstrous knife? Where are your Prussian friends? Where is your companion? What can you be thinking? Do you ever consider your own safety? You could have been badly harmed!'

The captain was an even-tempered, rational, slow-to-rile sort of man. He was struggling to understand why she caused him endless worry. He glared at her, completely perplexed.

'Were you anxious about me?' she asked, delighted by the notion. 'You need not be. If they had come any closer, I could easily have run away. I am quite fast, you see.'

'Give me that knife,' he said to her.

'No,' she replied. 'This one is my favourite.'

'It is not too late for me to file a report to the Navy Board about your masquerade on the *Pontus,*' he said petulantly.

'Go right ahead. I shall tell them you forced me to stay alone with you in your cabin for an entire week. Your men are already probably wondering why you confined a young man so near your private cabin. Then, if you are not sent to prison for it, and it becomes known that I am a woman, you can compete with Lieutenant Niles as to which of you will marry me simply because you spent time with me alone. Good heavens, is every woman in England treated as chattel?'

Charlie noticed the captain's clenched jaw. She smiled sweetly at him.

'I am teasing you. Please accept my thanks,' she said most earnestly. 'You cannot know how grateful I was to see you standing behind me with your pistol aimed at someone other than me. I am so very fortunate that you arrived when you did. It pleases me that we have grown to become such good friends.'

'Good friends! Is that how you would describe this strange relationship?' he asked, exasperated.

'Ah, so you acknowledge that we have a relationship. Come, let us take a short stroll and discuss the matter,' she said sweetly. 'Then we can at least claim to be more than mere acquaintances. After all, we did live with one another in your quarters for over a week. I am quite in shock from the excitement in the alley. A walk will help to calm my nerves. How far out is the *Pontus*? Can she be seen from the east pier? Do you still set sail at noon tomorrow? I should like to see her one last time.'

She nudged him in the direction of the waterfront and resumed walking.

'I wish we were related,' she told him chattily as they approached the harbour. The sun was setting, and soft light played across the water.

The captain blinked in surprise, wondering what she would say next.

'Then you would be at liberty to write long letters to me whilst you are gone and tell me of your adventures,' she continued. 'I hope you will think of me from time to time; perhaps when you are looking at your maps, or when you find the pictures that I have hidden in your library for you, or when you are staring at the hooks you installed to construct my little room. I will certainly be thinking of you. I shall pray fervently, every day, for your safety.'

'What an endearing speech,' said Captain Brantford. He truly meant it. He stared in confusion at the unusual woman at his side, astonished by his unquestionable attraction to her and the emotions churning inside him. Beyond his immediate family and a very few close friends, he doubted very much if anyone else gave much thought to his well-being during the continuous series of engagements taking place at sea.

Captain Brantford carried her gift bags on one side. Charlie held his other arm and walked contentedly at his side. It embarrassed him endlessly that he had no free hand to wipe away a tear that rolled down his face. He raised his shoulder to dry his cheek against the fabric of his greatcoat.

It caught him completely off guard to see Charlie looking at him adoringly and smiling happily as they walked towards the waterfront.

'How long will you be away on this next mission?' she asked him. 'Will you be sailing across the sea to join the war against the Americans?'

'No, that is unlikely. I have been assigned to *reconnaissance* and patrol duties, mainly in the Bay of Biscay. It is possible that I will sail to Lisbon and Oporto once or twice. I cannot be sure at this point.'

'Will you go ashore in Oporto?' she asked excitedly. 'Will you kindly take a letter for me, and send it to my father with the military post? He will be somewhere along the northern coast of Spain. Perhaps he is near San Sebastián by now if all has gone well.'

Her awareness of the current campaign surprised him. 'The winter camp details are not widely publicised. But yes, that is the area where I shall be,' he replied. 'I will personally see to it that your correspondence reaches your father.'

The captain's face looked sombre as he spoke. He had already decided to pay a visit to her father. He looked away from her, not wanting her to see his eyes and guess at his thoughts. 'Headquarters for the military post have been relocated—for the time being, correspondence is being handled directly out of San Sebastián to be closer to General Wellesley's army. But I suspect you know all this. You are amazingly well informed,' he said respectfully.

'Well, I am a general's daughter, you know,' she said simply. 'I have been involved as support in some capacity in most campaigns after our troops arrived in the Peninsula. Perhaps Lieutenant Niles has informed you of this. If you are still wondering, I was indeed with him at Vitoria. We stayed together on a rooftop in town for most of the night, resting under the moonlight.'

She saw the captain's affirmative nod and felt compelled to explain.

'I was stationed with the supply wagons that day, to the northwest of the battlefield. Many of the officers either knew me or knew my name as someone who made drawings to record the battle positions and location of supply stations for the official reports. The men in the battalions led by my father have known me for years, and some since I was twelve. They call me Little Charlie, rather than Miss Charlotte. Not surprisingly, someone thought the name Charlie belonged to a man and gave orders to take Mr Reyne into Vitoria to record what was happening there. Lieutenant Niles was following orders—the mistake was by no means his fault. I did not correct his intelligence. The responsibility for being there was mine. We were both performing our duties.'

The captain placed Charlie's bags on the ground and gripped her shoulders, turning her towards him. Deeply concerned for her well-being, he stared intently into her eyes.

'I am so very sorry this happened to you,' he said. 'What an ordeal you have endured, and over many years, repeatedly. Have you recovered from what happened? Are you well, little sparrow?'

Charlie was utterly taken aback by his sympathy and his use of such a sweet name. She had seen countless battles and fatal wounds and had witnessed more than one town being ruthlessly destroyed. Rarely, if ever, had anyone asked her afterwards how she felt. It was not due to a lack of concern. It was for the simple reason that all those close to her shared the same experiences. They were all intimately acquainted with atrocity and death.

'Yes, perfectly, I am, thank you,' she lied. 'I could not see everything that night, you know, just—' she shuddered, '—just some of the things. Beyond the market square, away from the lamps, it was difficult to see beyond the first few streets.'

Struck by his unexpected care and grave expression, the images from the night in Vitoria poured into her mind. Her bottom lip quivered. Her eyes welled with tears. Suddenly, to the captain's surprise and concern, Charlie raised her hands to cover her face.

'Forget what you saw, let it go,' he spoke to her softly. 'It is all behind you now.'

He embraced her as she cried, holding her close. She nodded as her tears flowed. She drew in a deep breath and curled her shoulders against his broad chest. Several minutes passed as she rested in his arms until, at length, she regained her composure.

Charlie pulled away from him with a sigh. 'I am so very sorry. I have spoilt your coat. I suppose my eyes are all red and swollen now. I must look hideous.'

'Not more so than when you were on my ship,' he replied. He dug into his coat pocket and pulled out his handkerchief, pressing it into her hand.

'Well. That was uncharitable of you. You must agree, I cannot go back to the inn looking like this. Mr Jaeger—my dear Gus—will slay you. Do you mind staying out a little longer with me?'

Taking his silence as tacit agreement, Charlie took a deep breath and stepped away from him towards the quayside.

'How beautiful to see the ships in the harbour. Which one is the *Pontus*?' she asked.

'You cannot see the *Pontus* from here. She lies further out at Spithead,' he informed her. 'We will have a better view if we move further along. These ships you see here are laid up and are likely being decommissioned. Most are destined for the drydocks.'

'You must find it sad that these ships have reached this end, after all of their adventures at sea.'

'Yes, I do,' he replied, surprised that she would think of such a thing. He and his friends in the navy were rather sentimental when it came to parting with a battle-hardened ship.

'And the *Pontus*?'

'She has another decade, all going well for her.'

She wanted to ask him another question, but he had moved away and was speaking to a young lad passing nearby. Afterwards, the captain pressed a coin into the boy's hand. She stood quietly, waiting for him.

'Your friends at the inn will be worried,' he explained. 'I have asked the boy to let them know that you are with me and that I will accompany you back shortly.'

'Have you! That is very thoughtful,' said Charlie, her respect for him deepening. 'Thank you, kind sir.'

As the boy turned to leave, she caught a glimpse of his face.

'Oh, my goodness! Wait! Just a moment!' she cried out to the lad nearby. 'Are not you the driver of the wagon with the donkeys? Master Winthrop, is it not? Do you remember me? We have met!' she said, rushing cheerfully towards the boy. 'Look at you, all dressed up and looking neat. Here, let me give you a little extra to thank you for your efforts.' She handed the boy a coin and waved to him as he hurried away.

Charlie and the captain soon reached the end of the walk-way. Charlie looked with pleasure at the moonlight reflecting off the surface of the water. 'There is no wind to speak of this evening,' she said. 'The harbour looks so calm and peaceful. We can almost pretend, just for this evening, that the war is over,' she said wistfully.

'What are your plans once you leave Portsmouth?' he asked, his interest in her growing with every moment. 'Will you go back to Portugal again?'

'Not immediately,' she replied sadly. 'And perhaps not for a few years. My father and I aim to purchase property not too far from Portsmouth, but not too close, either. We want something in the country, within a day's journey, so perhaps twenty to thirty miles away. We need to be reasonably close to the port but is too busy to stay here in town. Once we buy the property, I will oversee the renovations. My friends are involved and helping me with our little project.'

He was puzzled by her remarks. 'Do you have family nearby?' he asked. 'Will not you live with them? You are rather young to start your own establishment.'

'My father's sister and her husband live north of Portsmouth. I plan to stay with them for the next few months, just while our project gets underway. Once we are ready, my friends and I shall move to the new property. It is partly for my father's purposes and partly for my own,' she said.

'You make it all sound rather mysterious.'

'Do I?' she laughed. 'How delightful. We are keeping our cards close to the chest, as you men would say. There will be a great deal of construction, and comings and goings. There is no point in unduly alarming the neighbours beforehand. My uncle tells me we need to conduct some research around the poor law legislation and how the act is applied within each parish.'

He pondered on her choice of words. In what sense would the redevelopment of an old property disturb the community, and how might this relate to legislation? He longed to ask her this but felt it rude to question her so closely. In any case, Charlie was looking preoccupied at this point. She had fallen silent and was smiling to herself.

Captain Brantford found himself wanting to prolong their walk, but he knew their time together must end. He caught himself admiring her profile more than once and had to remind himself that he was not a free man. He had made a solemn commitment to someone else.

Charlie's line of thinking followed a similar vein.

'I happened to overhear your conversation at dinner last evening that you are engaged to be married on your return,' she said, taking her customary direct approach. She smiled kindly. 'I hope your bride will not be kept waiting too many more months.'

'I am afraid the timing is outside of my control,' he said, finding some small relief in her knowing that he was engaged. 'I hope to return on leave early in the new year, or by spring at the latest.'

They stopped at a stone parapet and leaned against it.

'There is a good view out of the harbour from here. Do you see those ships on the horizon between here and the Isle of Wight? That is where the *Pontus* lies.' He pointed to a grouping of ships faintly visible in the distance.

'And what a beautiful ship she is. I shall remember my trip on her always,' said Charlie, her eyes glistening. 'That was a glorious week, and a restful one for me, sir. The air was fresh, the winds filled the sails, and the sea seemed vast and shining.

I felt spoilt in your care. I cannot remember a time when I had so few duties and slept so well. I am grateful for every kindness shown to me. It felt like I had gone to heaven.'

He smiled, enjoying her exuberant expressions. The feelings she expressed just now were ones he had experienced many times at sea. How often had he stared past billowing sails when gliding across wide stretches of water, while pillars of light lit the sky or stars dotted the black canopy of night?

'I am happy to hear it,' he replied. 'It is an unusual woman who confesses pleasure in sleeping in a hammock and sharing rations on a warship.'

'Am I the first woman on your ship to do so? What a rare privilege. If you invite me, I will come again,' she promised.

'In that unlikely event,' he laughed, 'I should be glad of your company.'

'I am happy to hear it,' she mimicked his playful tone. 'I shall hold you to it.'

The skies were darkening, and the wind was picking up. They both understood that their final goodbye was imminent. He was to sail back to the Iberian Peninsula in the morning; she would forge ahead with a new life in England. He had his duties and responsibilities and was engaged to be married on his return. She had people relying on her and a great deal to accomplish in the months to come.

The likelihood of being with one another in the future, and in such intimate settings as they had experienced together to this point, was remote. The circumstances of their meeting and travelling together were moments in time that each would remember and cherish.

'If we stay here any longer, I shall cry again,' she said bluntly, feeling overwhelmed with sadness.

'Your Prussian friends will take me to task if they suspect me of causing you any grief.'

'Indeed,' she giggled. 'You and the lieutenant can act as seconds for one another.'

She waved farewell towards the *Pontus*, possessively taking the captain's arm for their return journey to the inn.

The captain looked down at the little woman beside him.

'I am sorely tempted to take a stowaway back to Portugal,' he muttered softly.

'I beg your pardon. I could not hear you.'

'You had best leave your letter to your father at the front desk tonight. I leave the inn early in the morning to run some errands, and I need to check on our patient before I leave. I board the *Pontus* at nine.'

'Aye, aye, Captain,' she said, smiling at him sweetly, her dark eyes meeting his. 'I will do as instructed and complete my letter tonight.'

Captain Henry Brantford was not a man who spent an abundance of time thinking about feelings. His duties occupied most of his time and attention. On occasion, to be sure, in the silence of his cabin, waiting for sleep, he thought about his pending marriage at some unknown date in the future, but never had he yearned for his future wife's company in a way that made him feel downright ill, as he felt now in preparing to part from Miss Reyne.

It dawned on the captain that he was smitten with this remarkable woman. He had met her unexpectedly and known her only briefly, yet in such intimate circumstances. He memorised her features as the light played across her face, storing every detail. He knew in an instant, with heart-wrenching regret for past decisions, that the memory of this woman would occupy his mind and twist his spirits in the lonely months that lay ahead.

Part Two

SEVENTEEN

The Tripps Entertain

'I MUST SAY, we are glad to see you safely back in England,' said Lady Tripp, pushing open the door to the small guest room she had prepared for her niece. 'It has been over seven years since you left. We had no certain conviction that you would come back. But here you are. This will be your room whilst you stay with us. You will be comfortable here.'

Lady Tripp had last seen Charlie when she left England to live with her father in India. After Charlie left Bombay, they had no news of her until she was reunited with her father when the British troops pushed into Portugal and forced Bonaparte's troops to retreat. Within the family circle, the father and his daughter both seemed like strangers to their relatives. Eyeing her niece, Lady Tripp decided that time abroad had not been helpful to the young lady's prospects.

Lady Tripp frowned as she examined her niece's slight frame. Most unfortunately, she noticed, the girl's skin was tanned from the sun. Her thick hair was neatly coiled but not in a stylish manner by any stretch.

'I trust you have other clothing with you and can appear in a suitable gown for dinner. You are my niece, after all. You will need to dress the part.'

'I am not understanding you.'

'How am I to take you anywhere if you do not look like a niece of Lady Tripp?' asked the aunt peevishly.

'I have only just arrived at Greydon Hall. Why would you be taking me anywhere? I am simply coming down the stairs to the dining room. And what do you mean about looking the part?' asked Charlie, looking innocent and wide-eyed. 'If I am in London, am I to think people will look at my dress and say to themselves, "Ah, I recognise the style. She must be the niece of Lady Tripp." Anyone reaching that conclusion would be a frightening sort of person. Dear aunt, you are confusing me by all this talk of dressing the part.'

Lady Tripp grimaced. She remembered her niece had been stubborn as a youngster, arguing about one thing and another and not knowing when to be silent. Unsure if her niece was making fun of her or was simply a dull-witted child who said senseless things, she decided to let the topic drop.

'We dine in two hours,' the aunt said primly. 'Your uncle expects you to arrive at a quarter of an hour in advance of the guests so he can introduce you before the meal. Unfortunately, you have not brought a lady's maid with you. How long will it be until the Portuguese woman arrives to help you?'

'She is my friend, not my maid. And, Aunty, do not you remember? I mentioned she is staying in Portsmouth this extra week purchasing things we need for our new property.'

'You left her there by herself?'

'She has already hired an attendant and a few servants for us and will have more company than she wishes.'

'I see,' said Aunt Tripp, dissatisfied for several reasons, the least of which involved the lady friend or maid or whatever she was. She was perturbed on a more important matter. She could not understand why her husband had consented to sign for the purchase of her brother's property so near to their own. It will put them within the same social circles, she had complained to her husband. She wondered if he had thought this through sufficiently.

'I will send one of my maids up shortly to help you change,' she said to Charlie. 'Do not linger in your room, my dear. It will not do to be late.'

'Thank you, Aunty. That is very kind of you to send help. I shall do my best to look and dress so that everyone present will recognise me immediately as your niece. It will be such fun to see if I am mistaken for someone else. What a laugh we shall have between us. Shoo, shoo, I need every moment to accomplish this feat.'

Charlie ushered her aunt into the hallway, swung the bedroom door shut, and hurried back across the room. She threw herself onto the bed with a muffled laugh.

It did not take her long to select a gown. Since the maid arrived more quickly than expected and was striving to be helpful, Charlie sat patiently for ten minutes while the young woman dressed her hair.

'That is fine,' Charlie said to her at length. 'No one will recognise me if you do anything further.'

Picking up the necklace Lieutenant Niles had given to her in Vitoria, she fastened it around her neck. She sat quietly for a moment, closing her eyes, and twirling the pendant between her fingertips as a reminder, not of the lives lost, but of the challenges ahead facing the survivors. Then, she stood up, smiled at the maid, and preened before the full-length mirror.

'You look lovely this evening, miss,' said the maid, admiring how well the gown suited Miss Reyne's neat figure.

'You have made me look rather smart,' she praised the young woman. 'Thank you. It will not do for my aunt to disown me just yet.'

Feeling rather pleased with her appearance, Charlie made her way down the stairs.

The Tripps' dining room could easily accommodate two dozen people but today the large mahogany table was set for a party of fourteen. The fact that there were guests coming at all annoyed Charlie exceedingly.

'We have only been in England three weeks and have just arrived from Portsmouth,' she complained to Gus earlier in the day. 'Surely, they would wish to have some private conversation with me to enquire after Father and discern the purpose of my being here, before entertaining their neighbours. Have they no interest in knowing anything at all?'

Naturally, Gus had no answer for her. Charlie would, as she usually did, sort matters out on her own.

Seats at the dinner table were reserved not only for Charlie but, by her insistence, the two Jaeger brothers who accompanied her. Sir John Tripp was unsure of what to call these two men.

'Gentlemen seems an unlikely term,' he had complained to his wife beforehand. 'They look more like hardened soldiers. How am I to determine by their so-called Prussian officer ranks whether I should treat them as gentry or not?'

'Dearest, then how shall I arrange the seating?' Charlie's Aunt Lydia had queried her husband. 'I have not the slightest notion where to seat these two Prussians amongst our guests.'

Charlie's uncle snorted disgruntledly and raised his newspaper to block his wife from view. He had no desire whatsoever to seat these rough-looking men at his table. Charlie, however, had tenaciously insisted they were not to dine with the servants.

'They are decorated military officers. My father assigned me as their interpreter,' she told her relatives. 'How shall I explain the matter if they are shunted aside?'

Charlie won the argument.

With visitors already arriving, introductions were underway.

'How am I to remember all of their names?' Charlie asked Gus distractedly.

'Who are those people? They look familiar,' said Gus. He stared at the open doorway. 'By gosh, it is the couple that stayed at the Crown in Portsmouth!'

'Indeed, it is! Captain Sand! Mrs Sand! How delighted we are to see you!' cried Charlie as she rushed to greet them. Her doing so caused a moment of confusion. Mrs Sand's only awareness of Charlie was from being seated near one another in the dining room at the Crown Inn, and, consequently, she was slow to remember her. Captain Sand, however, recognised her instantly. The change in Charlie's appearance captivated him, much to the consternation of his wife.

'I had not thought we would meet again, Miss Reyne. My word, you look charming in your new English gown.'

She laughed prettily at his backhanded compliment.

'Do you think so? Personally, I prefer the Portuguese styles. I find the fabrics here rather pale. I like the darker colours commonly worn in Portugal. However, I am glad you approve of my appearance.' She made a playful curtsey to him before turning and warmly greeting Mrs Sand.

'How are your children, Mrs Sand? They were all so well-behaved in the dining room at the Crown. They captivated our hearts. How wonderful it is to see you again. You are Captain Brantford's sister, is not that correct? I am one of the captain's chief admirers. I met him at a military field hospital near Oporto.'

There was little more Charlie needed to do to begin a friendship with Alison Sand than to express respect for the woman's beloved brother and to praise the woman's darling children. Forever defending her lively youngsters from the barbed comments of their neighbours, Mrs Sand was eager to claim an ally. She looked appreciatively at the young lady and nodded politely on being introduced to the Jaeger brothers.

'*Guten Abend!*' she said to them, dredging her memory

for her schoolroom German lessons and how properly to bid someone good evening.

The brothers bowed deeply, approving of her civility.

'After all, it is not Mrs Sand's fault that she married a friend of Lieutenant Niles,' Gus said privately to Wil and Charlie before heading to the dining room.

As the clock chimed, true to Aunt Tripp's warning, they were promptly escorted to their seats at the table. Charlie, separated by a few places from Gus and Wil, admired her Prussian friends.

'My dear boys,' she chimed before they were seated, 'you are looking handsome and distinguished in your new clothes.'

If anyone were to ask Charlie who her first love had been, she would have unabashedly responded. Whether she viewed Gustaf Jaeger, who was twenty years her senior, as a father figure, uncle, brother, kindred spirit, friend, or unrequited love interest, she adored him beyond measure. Her affection for him was rivalled only by her adoration for Wil, whom she regarded as a most beloved brother.

'Excuse me, Miss Reyne,' said Mr Jack Weyburn. The Weyburn family were neighbours, residing on a property a few miles east. The young man, son of Sir Reginald Weyburn, was seated opposite her at the table. 'My sister and I are wishing to know about your adventures abroad. I understand you only recently arrived from the Peninsula. You must tell us how you fared in your journeys, and how it felt to run wild in Spain all these years.'

Charlie paused. She looked at Mr Weyburn, bemused. 'Ah, to run wild in Spain,' she repeated, smiling sweetly. 'I suppose you mean free from constraint. I must speak plainly, sir. To run wild in Spain would be an invitation to disaster. One might certainly say that we ran with utmost exertion, many times, to avoid being shot or captured. But that has a different connotation than running wild in Spain.'

Mr Weyburn, due to inherit his father's baronetcy at some unknown future time, and not knowing that it was a title also borne by the young woman's father, felt all the superiority the title conferred upon his family. Not understanding the edge in Miss Reyne's tone, he persisted in his attempt at conversation. He tried to engage her with another question.

'Your foreign friends are Prussian mercenaries, are not they?'

'Shall I ask them that question for you?' she responded.

Disconcerted, the man shrugged his shoulders.

Charlie smiled politely at Mr Jack Weyburn and spoke to her friends in German. After another pause and dabbing at the corners of her mouth with her napkin to hide her smile, she turned back to address the young man.

'I cannot recall your name,' she said matter-of-factly.

'Mr Weyburn,' said he.

'Mr Weyburn, sir,' she repeated. 'I am sure in your studies you learnt that Kings George the First, Second, and Third, and our own Prince Regent, future King George the Fourth, are members of the House of Hanover. They are royalty of Prussian descent.'

The conversation around the table ceased as everyone looked towards Lord Tripp's niece. Mr Weyburn cocked his head, bewildered by what seemed to be a random change in topic. His father, Sir Reginald Weyburn, seated further along the table, lay down his fork and knife and listened attentively.

'If, as I suppose, you are aware of the royal family's heritage, you likely know some aspects of our military structure as well,' she continued cheerfully. 'You will have heard of the King's German Legion—the KGL, as they are commonly known. It comprises German-speaking regiments and battalions under service to the Prince Regent, by virtue of his Prussian lineage. They are considered extraordinarily effective and lethal in battle. The Jaegers, my uncle's guests, are former officers of the King's German Legion. They have retired from service.'

Charlie tilted her head at Mr Weyburn to indicate that she considered the topic closed.

The young man pounced triumphantly on her words. 'Retired, you say? Then what is their present status? I rather suspect they have sold out as mercenaries, or hired guards, if you will. Why else would they be here whilst England is still at war?'

Charlie looked towards Gus knowing that by now his fingers had curled around the hilt of the curved sabre at his hip. Wil, watching his older brother, had a worried look on his face.

Charlie caught Gus's eye and smiled calmly. Speaking in German, she asked his opinion. '*Herr* Jaeger, will you permit me to amuse myself for a few moments more or would you prefer to take him out back and spear him in the stomach after we have dessert?'

The guests, not understanding the exchange, looked on. Gus muttered under his breath. Wil choked on his food. Gaining reluctant agreement to manage the matter in her own style, she chose her next words carefully.

'What would be your response,' she asked Mr Weyburn, with a tip of her head at his younger sister seated beside him, 'if you were walking with Miss Weyburn and someone accosted her. How would you react?'

'As any brother would do,' he said, puzzled by her question. 'I would protect my sister.'

'I am glad to hear it,' Charlie replied.

He was not happy being led along but he waited for her to disclose her point.

'These two gentlemen are my family members,' Charlie said emphatically. 'If anyone were to cause me grief, or threaten to do so, they would step in to address the situation, much as you would do for your sister,' she smiled patiently at Mr Weyburn and Miss Weyburn seated near him. 'And as I would do for them.'

Captain Sand and Mrs Sand, seated opposite the Jaegers,

took a keen interest in the conversation. Surprised by the young lady's manner of speaking, the couple exchanged amused glances with one another. Captain Sand joined in the conversation.

'Friends of mine have first-hand experience serving along-side the King's German Legion,' he stated, nodding his head respectfully towards the Jaegers. 'In 1809, several battalions of the Legion supported our British troops in Portugal. The KGL helped them claim victory, saving the lives of both countrymen and local civilians.'

Mr Weyburn, conscious of the attention on him, and the looks of disapproval aimed in his direction, including those by his father, realised it was time to let the topic drop.

'Did your group travel with one of the recent convoys arriving home from Portugal, Miss Reyne?' asked Sir Weyburn. 'I understand from Mrs Sand that her brother recently led a convoy home to England.'

Charlie's face turned pink. 'Why, yes, my friends and I arrived with the convoy.'

'I am familiar with some of the ships. On which did you travel?'

'We were on different ships.' Charlie struggled to gather her thoughts and recall the names of the hospital ships. 'My friends the Jaegers had the good fortune to travel aboard Captain Brantford's frigate, HMS *Pontus*,' she offered.

'And what did your Prussian friends think of their journey?' asked Sir Weyburn. 'I have heard from Captain Sand that his brother-in-law runs a tight operation with a well-trained crew. They even captured a prize *en route*. I would have preferred to travel on Captain Hanson's corvette. I understand that most of the ships were carrying patients or prisoners and that one of the vessels ran into difficulties. Did you hear any news of that?' he asked Charlie.

'A little, yes. Sea travel can be so unpredictable,' Charlie responded vaguely. 'I heard that one ship blew off course and needed to be located. What a worry it is for family members who are longing for news every day. Uncle Tripp and dear Aunty, you must have worried endlessly about me, to send a carriage for me after I arrived in Portsmouth. I confess it has been years since I travelled in anything but a cart!'

Mr Weyburn laughed outright. His sister giggled.

'How fortunate, then, that we are neighbours,' said young Mr Weyburn disingenuously. 'We must take you on a carriage ride to experience the luxury of travelling the countryside in horse-drawn vehicles.'

'I should enjoy that immensely,' Charlie replied politely, pleased to have successfully steered the topic away from discussion of the convoy. 'Would you permit my friends to join your party? It will be thrilling for us to see the local sights. Is tomorrow suitable? We are early risers.'

She smiled demurely and sampled the roasted venison on her plate. 'Mmm, this is very tasty. Aunty, you have offered us a wonderful meal this evening. Once I consume everything on my plate, I am sure to feel truly British again. I have been running wild in Spain for so long that I have forgotten all the finer tastes of home.'

Appreciating the young lady's pluck, Alison Sand lowered her head to hide her smile. When she raised her eyes to her husband, the two of them exchanged a merry glance. She had wanted on many occasions to give young Mr Weyburn a set-down but being close neighbours of his parents, and schooled in strict decorum, she had not done so. This evening, the little lady had done it masterfully.

At the close of the evening, having reached their home after leaving the dinner party at the home of the Tripps, the Sands retired to their bedroom and the comfort of a warm fire in the hearth.

'What a delight to meet such an interesting new neighbour!' Alison Sand declared to her husband, standing on tiptoes to untie his cravat. 'I am almost sorry that my brother Henry is betrothed, and James is so smitten at present. Yes, yes, James thinks I am not aware, but I am onto him, you know. I could use a little sister like this if one of them should take a liking to her. We should get along famously. Perhaps Lieutenant Niles will take an interest in her. That would keep her in the family circle, at least.'

'Yes, but that would be a complete turnabout from all your plans for him. Do you think she would be ready to be a mother to three children?'

'Who can know? I was already mother to one son and pregnant with the next by this young lady's age.'

Captain Sand turned down their bedsheets and gestured to his wife. 'What say you, my love? Shall we consider adding another?'

'Aye, Captain Sand. What a grand idea,' she laughed.

Charlie's uncle looked up from perusing his newspaper as Charlie came into the breakfast room the following morning. The Tripps' daughter Mary, visiting from town with her husband George, entered soon after.

Freshly washed and neatly dressed in one of her new morning gowns, Charlie impishly announced to her cousin that if she were to meet any strangers this morning, they would surely recognise her as the niece of Lady Tripp.

'I am not understanding you,' said Mary.

'My *ensemble* says it all! Do not you see? It is clear proof that I am your mother's niece. Everyone will know it at first glance,' she stated triumphantly.

Aunt Tripp, already seated at the breakfast table, pursed her lips.

Charlie settled into a chair near her aunt and smiled cheerfully, helping herself to a piece of toast. Uncle Tripp sliced a hard-boiled egg and laid it alongside a fillet of baked fish, fresh from the morning market.

'I met Sir Weyburn this morning whilst walking along the lane from the village. He had heard the news that the Sands received a visit from a messenger in the very early hours of the morning,' announced the uncle, savouring his meal.

'Oh? And what might that be about, my dear?' asked his wife, pouring herself a cup of tea.

'Mrs Sand's father suffered a serious accident yesterday in London. The family is on their way to London this morning.'

'Oh dear. I hope the matter is not too serious,' said Aunt Tripp. 'Will they be staying away long? We need them here to make up a table for whist next Thursday. Well, let us hope they are back by then.'

'Indeed,' the uncle replied. 'Tell me, niece, what are your plans for the property your father has purchased? He did not offer any explanations in his last letter.'

'You cannot be surprised by that, Uncle. He is an army man and legendary for being secretive,' Charlie said apologetically. 'Please do let me thank you once again for inspecting the property with me last week and signing the terms of purchase.'

'Yes, yes, you have showered me with accolades. It was by your father's instruction that I have done so. I hardly see how my opinion affects things,' he said peevishly.

'Father would be filled with remorse to hear you speak so. He relies on your good judgement. Surely, you agree that the location of the property is ideal. It is not far from your home, which must appeal to my father, yet not too close, which undoubtedly satisfies others. It was sensible to conclude the matter with the greatest dispatch. Do you have time this afternoon to review the architect's drawings? There is much to be done to ready the property for occupancy. After your review, I shall take matters in hand. I certainly feel more confident in doing so with your support.' She gently patted the back of her uncle's hand.

Her aunt, taking a sip of hot tea, snorted in frustration. 'Incorrigible child,' she said to no one in particular. Recalling her niece's conversation at the table the night before, she eyed her husband.

Uncle Tripp rolled his eyes in response.

'What great times we have ahead of us. How wonderful it is that we shall live in proximity forever more. It is fortunate we all get along famously!' Charlie beamed at them.

The aunt dropped five lumps of sugar into her tea, picked up a piece of charred toast, and smeared it with butter and jam.

EIGHTEEN

Visit to Chellisbury

'Inês, I hope you have dressed warmly enough for the drive,' said Charlie. 'November weather is unpredictable. You are not accustomed to these cooler climates.'

Ten days had passed since Charlie had welcomed Inês to Greydon Hall. By staying longer in Portsmouth, Inês had completed many of their errands and had helped move along their plans to transform General Reyne's new property at Chellisbury. No shortage of tasks awaited them now that they were united.

Today, Charlie and Inês planned to visit Chellisbury in person to see how construction was coming along.

Inês scrunched her hands inside her mittens. She tightened her scarf and gestured at her leather boots, warm coat, and woollen shawl layered on top.

'I am thoroughly shielded from the autumn air and well prepared to endure the ride in this silly open wagon. Now, tell me again why we must suffer in this contraption when your uncle possesses a perfectly comfortable covered carriage?' she asked, lightly poking her friend in the arm as she spoke.

'You know exactly why. I have only just purchased these donkeys and I need to train them in harness. Do you remember me talking about Master Winthrop, the young lad whose wagon

I drove in Portsmouth? Gus found him for me in Portsmouth and gained permission from the lad's father to hire him. He will move to Chellisbury next month and train as one of our drivers. I am so excited for him—eventually, he will learn to drive a full team of donkeys and even a proper carriage. But for the time being, I am the only one here who knows how to do so. They shall do perfectly well as a means of transport for us to deliver these baskets for the tradesmen.'

Charlie clicked at the young donkeys. 'Walk on, my sweeties,' she said, urging them on with the long reins.

Inês watched with amusement as Charlie chatted cheerfully on, encouraging the plodding donkeys, and commending them excitedly as they broke into a trot.

'They are such darlings,' Charlie enthused. 'They are so reliable, and strong, and good-natured. I cannot imagine how we would have fared without them on those long treks in Spain.'

The women fell silent, each reflecting on the hardships endured through so many years. The minor discomfort of the moment was, in every respect, insignificant.

'I shall be grateful once the kitchen at Chellisbury is in working order,' Charlie said after a time. 'Here, dear heart, keep your knees and feet under the sheepskin.' Charlie tucked in the edges of the heavy hide to keep it from slipping off their laps.

'This, my dear,' she smiled at Inês as she pulled out her army flask, 'is to warm our insides. It is your very own family port.'

'No!' Inês cried in delight. 'You are teasing me. How is that possible?'

Charlie tapped her flask. 'Genuine Montalto Port. Sofia sent it.'

'What about the boys?' asked Inês excitedly, taking a sip. 'We should share this with them.'

'When they left for London this morning on their little holiday, I sent along a bottle for them to enjoy during their stay.

I will miss them horridly, but we will see them again within a fortnight,' she smiled warmly at her friend's crestfallen face. 'Gus will be thinking of you every day whilst he is away,' she said reassuringly.

'Nonsense,' said Inês, flustered.

The wagon lurched along the narrow path through a grove. 'Do you know, I had not thought I could be happy here,' Charlie confessed. 'Of course, I do miss Father and Sofia and our troops immensely, but with the four of us here, together, I am faring much better than I expected. And you? How do you find staying with my relatives?'

'It is not what we are used to, in terms of hospitality, but they are civil enough towards us,' said Inês thoughtfully. 'That is enough to ask of them, I think.'

'Yes, I agree,' said Charlie.

'They have been gracious to me,' Inês continued. 'I will be happier, though, to settle at Chellisbury. I think I make your aunt uneasy. Perhaps she is cautious of foreigners in general and is worried I will break into the silver closet after dark. Did you see her expression when you announced that I was to be your chaperone at Chellisbury? They are expecting you to install their old aunty, Mrs Ravenstone, and take her off their hands.'

'It startled them to learn that you are barely thirty and widowed.' Charlie patted her friend's mittened hand. 'Do not mind them. They have no understanding of what happens during a war. As for the great-aunt, I do not mind at all if she comes to live with us. We can make a place for her. But I will make it clear that you are to be my chaperone, and she is our guest.'

The women travelled in silence for a time. The distance from Greydon Hall to the Reynes' new Chellisbury estate was roughly seven miles, and mostly along good roadways. If Charlie could get her donkeys to trot part of the way, they would reach their destination within the hour.

'I am getting stiff and will need to stretch soon,' Inês remarked as the time passed. Can you stop here? Look, is not that Chellisbury in the distance? What a lovely view from here!'

Charlie pulled up her team and the ladies stepped down from the wagon for a better look. The land was relatively flat in this region, but they were coming over a low rise and had good sightlines to the estate. To the west, hay lay stacked across the open fields. Opposite, the main house, impressive for its tall chimneys and massive windows, was under renovation and expansion, with timber and materials piled neatly on the large lawn. The stables, situated to the rear, were only partially visible from this angle. To the east stretched several new buildings in the early stages of construction. The scene resembled a new village rising in the autumn landscape. A small stream, not visible from their vantage, wound around the buildings on the south side. Also to the south, a large, square building was being erected. Tall elm trees growing near the buildings partially blocked their view.

'How long have we waited for just this moment, to see it all coming together, hmm?' Charlie squeezed Inês's arm. 'Father dreamt of this layout for many years. Now it is becoming a reality. Inês, do you mind waiting just a few minutes?'

Seeing her friend reach for her drawing case, Inês nodded in agreement. Charlie sketched quickly, outlining the location and progress in constructing the various buildings.

'I will add the details later. Then I can send him a sketch in my next letter. He will be thrilled to see how well everything is progressing,' she enthused.

Inês nodded, scrunching her nose to hold back tears. She embraced Charlie. 'I wish Sofia were here to see this with us,' she said. 'She would be ecstatic.'

They stood in solemn silence, taking it all in. Reluctant to give up their view of the property, they finally climbed back on the wagon.

As the women approached the grounds, several nearby workers caught sight of them. Cheers and cries of welcome sounded. Fully half of the workers on the site at Chellisbury were former soldiers, no longer able to serve in active duty due to lingering injuries or loss of limb but relishing the opportunity to work on a project such as this. Without exception, they all knew and adored Miss Reyne. Although Inês—Mrs Alvares to them—was not in their circle of acquaintance, word circulated quickly that she was the sister of Sofia, the second Mrs Reyne. In any case, she was Charlie's friend. That was all the introduction they required.

Soon after, the ladies had set out the contents of their baskets and waited for the men to take their break. The soldiers and other workers gathered around them, invited to partake of an array of beverages and cold meats and baking brought for them to enjoy. Told that the architect had just arrived back from his inspection of the outlying cottages, Charlie left Inês to host the gathering and went in search of the man.

'Welcome back, Miss Reyne,' said Mr Marshall, smiling politely at his young client as she approached. 'Have you been here long? Shall I take you on a tour? I trust you will be pleased with our progress.'

'From what I have seen thus far, I am bursting with pride,' she responded, surveying the massive undertaking. 'I must commend you. Your designs are coming to life and your helpers are performing admirably. You have hired capable staff, it seems.'

'I could not have picked better,' he replied.

'How very fortunate. You will be pleased to hear how well-regarded you are in this region. Neighbours of my uncle, Captain and Mrs Sand, spoke highly of your talent. They mentioned that you have designed renovations to a home for their brother, Mr James Brantford.'

'Yes, the elder brother has an expansion underway for his

residence. His property is in the Cotswolds. Are you acquainted with the Sands? Their opinion is somewhat biased,' he said humbly. 'I am, as it happens, a distant cousin of Captain Sand's. That is how I came to be recommended to the Brantford family.'

'My dear Mr Marshall, you are too modest,' said Charlie. 'One need only see your drawings to understand your talent.'

He was taken aback by this comment. He was not new to this business and was immune to cajolery and flattery. He doubted very much that this young lady understood his drawings. 'Where shall we start your tour?' he asked her.

'I am eager to see the warehouse. Do you mind waiting here for a short time whilst I bring over my companion? She is not far. That is her standing over by the house. Then we can get started. I will not be long.'

True to her word, Charlie returned with Inês within minutes. Charlie watched with interest as the architect, shepherding them along a worn path, fell in step beside Inês. When he stopped for a moment to speak with his foreman, Charlie arched her eyebrows teasingly at Inês.

'Stop it!' Inês whispered, mortified. 'You will embarrass me no end if he catches you winking and grinning. Behave yourself, I beg of you.'

'When I tell Gus about your newest suitor, he will surely be perturbed.'

'Gus will care nothing of it. Besides, this gentleman has known me for all of five minutes.'

'That has been long enough to draw his interest,' insisted Charlie.

'If anything were to draw ire from Gus, it would be hearing you speaking such nonsense. Stop smirking. You are impossible.'

Mr Marshall and his foreman opened the doors to the warehouse and the foursome entered. The building was two storeys high. The front part of the space was open to the ceiling while the rooms on the second storey, intended mainly as storage space, wrapped around the walls in a horseshoe shape. Framing for several offices and workshop areas on the main level was nearly complete. Wide loading doors were already in place.

'May I ask what will be stored here, Miss Reyne?'

'I will tell you, but you must keep this to yourselves,' she said, waiting for them to agree. 'We will be installing large vats here, and stacking barrels, to hold our liquor,' she said, her cheeks dimpling.

'Liquor! My word,' said the foreman, 'you cannot be serious.'

'Montalto Port, to be exact. The very best quality, imported from Oporto. If our contract is approved, and we have no reason to think otherwise, our facility here at Chellisbury will sell supplies to the Navy. The remainder will be stored here on the main level. We will use the upper levels to store items produced in the Chellisbury workshops and cottages. The Montalto family's plan, and we will assist, is to distribute their port in Britain, and export from Portugal to Brazil, and perhaps Upper Canada at some point.'

Startled by this unexpected information, the gentlemen exchanged looks. Mr Marshall stared at the ladies with keen interest. This was a novel experience for him. From his correspondence before meeting Miss Reyne and judging from the planning and construction costs of the Chellisbury project, he had expected his client to be excessively rich and somewhat elderly, like some of his past well-to-do spinster clients. On meeting Miss Reyne in person, he had been forced to adjust his thinking. Although young and unmarried, she held the authority to make decisions. It became evident that her uncle, Lord Tripp, was a figurehead only with little interest in the actions of his niece. Mr Marshall wondered anew how the project would unfold with a young woman managing the wallet and holding the keys to the property.

'You need have no concern regarding payment, Mr Marshall,' said Charlie, guessing at the direction of his thoughts. 'This has all been properly planned. The final payment for you and your crew will be issued by our solicitor upon completion. The Reynes always carry through on our commitments, I assure you.'

'Of that, I have no doubt,' he replied honestly. 'I am simply surprised at the boldness of this undertaking.'

It was Charlie's turn to be surprised. Inês could see that her friend was about to launch into a lecture. She tapped Charlie's shoulder to distract her but to no avail.

'Boldness? There is nothing bold in this venture at all,' Charlie said dismissively. 'My father simply had enough funds to purchase a property. Then on his behalf, we hired people to develop it, and under your services have sufficient goods and labour at hand to accomplish the job. I see nothing bold in any of this. If you wish to see true boldness, Mrs Alvares and I will take you to the Iberian Peninsula. We will introduce you to our lads in the army and navy, the shopkeepers in Oporto, the local herdsmen, and countless civilians who put their lives at risk every moment whilst we chat and stroll around these grounds.'

The men gawked at her.

'Come, let us see the village next,' said Inês, pushing Charlie towards the back door, hoping to diffuse the situation. 'I am eager to see how it is taking shape.'

'We can go out this door,' said Mr Marshall icily. Scowling, he led them along the path behind the warehouse towards the nearby housing development. The foreman decided this was as good a time as any to step away.

The women followed Mr Marshall. Within minutes, Charlie was again commenting enthusiastically about progress. As with their earlier arrival, a group of former soldiers stopped working as they recognised Miss Reyne, shouting her name and calling out their greetings. The architect was fascinated by the adoration shown by the workers.

Amidst the loud shouts, men tried to gain Charlie's attention, asking excitedly about friends and relatives under General Reyne's command. Charlie answered each question patiently, sharing what she knew. She spoke guardedly when the news was less than positive. Suddenly an old man pushed through to the front. The other men fell silent and pulled back to make space for him.

'Miss Reyne. It is me, Sergeant Wally Jones, ma'am.'

'Dear sir,' Charlie replied, tipping her head in respect. Before her stood the old soldier, the desperate man from aboard the *Pontus* who had attempted to pitch himself from the deck. Her eyes were instantly misty.

'Thank you, Miss, for forgivin' what I did on the ship that day when I tried to—when I went overboard.' He bowed his head humbly by way of apology. 'I got your letter. I keep it here in my pocket,' he said, tenderly patting his chest near his heart. 'Thank you for invitin' me here, miss, and lettin' me know that one of my boys survived and may be comin' home.'

Charlie approached him and held his hands in hers. 'We all share your heartache, Mr Jones,' she said kindly. 'I am sorry for the loss of your two older sons. They are heroes in our eyes. I have heard that your youngest son, Mr Benny Jones, should be well enough to travel home soon.'

The old soldier nodded in grateful affirmation.

'Have you recovered your health, sir? Are you doing well?' asked Charlie.

He replied that he was.

'Do you remember meeting Mrs Alvares in Oporto? When your son arrives, we will invite you to share a meal with us. Will your wife come and live here as well?' she asked him.

'No, the old dear passed on some years back. I have written my Benny to tell him about Chellisbury, that it is all you promised it would be. I told him that we could share a cottage and keep a little garden. He hopes to marry his sweetheart and bring 'er here, with your permission. She is a sweet girl and takes no mind that he is missing an arm and has a few scars. She is eager to gain a bit of work herself, miss, if you can take her.'

'What is her name? We will see what we can find for her to do,' replied Charlie. She pulled out a little notebook and pencil from her reticule and jotted down the woman's name.

The tour continued in much the same manner, with waves of affection and greetings from former soldiers as the women inspected the grounds.

'Marry me, Miss Reyne,' one of the young soldiers shouted.

'Be my queen,' said another. 'You will reign forever in my heart!'

The men nearby laughed and cheered.

Charlie smiled and gave them a friendly wave.

By the time they reached the house, Mr Marshall felt with the utmost certainty that these women were unlike any he had ever met. While most eyes were on Miss Reyne during the tour, he fixed his looks on Mrs Alvares. He wondered what part she played in all of this. Was her role simply that of a chaperone, or something more? He had expected, with her being a widow and the elder of the two, that the decisions would be hers, but it seemed to be a complex arrangement.

It was clear that the soldiers adored Miss Reyne. Mrs Alvares, he noted, was the young lady's quietest supporter and keenest admirer. Miss Reyne, in turn, clearly respected the other woman and consulted her frequently. He could tell from their mannerisms that the friendship between them ran deep. The relationships between women in his circle were polite and cordial but rarely seemed to arise from deeper connections. He had not seen this type of bond among the women he knew.

'Now that I see the building, I wonder if we ought to add a

few more rooms to expand the infirmary. Sir, will you unroll the plans for us to view?' Charlie asked. The women leaned over and studied the drawings. Charlie glanced at Inês, waiting to hear her opinion.

'Perhaps it will seem crowded at times, but that will resolve itself. Rather than make this area larger, what if we house the men in other wings if too many arrive at once?' Inês suggested. 'We can use this room,' she pointed to an adjacent space on the drawings, 'for temporary accommodation.'

'Yes, I think you are right. That will work satisfactorily,' Charlie nodded.

Fascinated, Mr Marshall leaned against a framed wall, arms crossed, listening to the exchange between the women. The immensity of the project was taking shape in his mind.

He still thought the idea a bold one, notwithstanding the young woman's fit of temper dismissing his remark, and more so since the neighbouring gentry were sure to object to so many injured and retired soldiers coming into the parish. Had she and whoever had supported the project done their due diligence to interpret and address the local taxes under the Poor Law? He hoped so. He understood why the women had insisted on keeping their activities private. He was certain they would need a squadron of private guards if they went ahead with their plans to bring so many unemployed men into the neighbourhood, and, even more surprisingly, to store large volumes of liquor at Chellisbury. He was concerned that news of what was inside the warehouse would attract all manner of thieves and vagrants to venture onto the property.

They continued their tour. The kitchen in the main house, into which they now entered, was equipped to prepare meals for large gatherings. The dining hall could seat eighty people. The large size of the room puzzled him at first, but now, having heard their plans, he suggested that it was perhaps too small.

'The dining hall is not intended to seat everyone at the same time,' Charlie clarified for him. 'Some of the men will take their meals in the infirmary, and our staff will serve in two shifts whenever necessary. But if you think the kitchen itself is too small, then perhaps we should adjust our plan. Are you able to enlarge the kitchen without moving that outside wall?'

Mr Marshall affirmed that he could. He listened appreciatively when Miss Reyne concluded their tour with praise for his efforts.

'Everything is coming along splendidly,' she said earnestly. 'Now, I need to remind you of our agreement. Please also remind your foreman, and instruct your apprentices, to attempt to teach the soldiers basic skills. Most of these men will need to supplement their army pensions once they recover and leave Chellisbury. Ideally, since your team is training them, you will gain the confidence to hire them yourselves. Can you reach out to your connections? Any work arrangements we can manage from here will be a gift to these soldiers.'

'Charlie, we ought to leave soon so we are not travelling back in the dark,' Inês prodded her.

'Yes, of course. Thank you for the tour, Mr Marshall.'

Mr Marshall exchanged farewells with the ladies. He had a sudden yearning for them to stay, talk to him, and look over the plans again. The scope of the project astounded him. He watched, intrigued, as two soldiers harnessed a pair of donkeys to an open wagon.

'You arrived in that? With a pair of donkeys?' he asked, surprised. 'It will take you two hours or more to reach your destination.'

'The journey here took us just over an hour,' replied Inês. 'These animals are eager to get back to their stable. It will be faster going back.'

Charlie's eyes twinkled. She patted one of her donkeys,

gave it a little scratch behind the ears, and then climbed into the driver's seat on the wagon.

'Shall we head home, little dearies?' she said to her team. 'The next time I bring you, this will be your new home. You are going to like it here, I can tell.'

By the time Inês broke off her conversation with Mr Marshall and climbed onto the wagon beside her friend, many of the soldiers had gathered around to bid them farewell.

'Remember me to the general, miss,' shouted one.

'And me to his pretty missus,' yelled another, laughing gayly. 'Come and see us again soon, ladies! The food you brought was delicious. Thank you!'

The women waved goodbye to the workers and Mr Marshall as well. Mr Marshall raised his arm in response. As he listened to the affectionate farewell shouts from the soldiers, he wondered what it was about Miss Reyne that the men adored. He had initially viewed her as an impertinent little rich girl doing her father's bidding. Considering what he had seen, his opinion was rapidly shifting.

He re-rolled his drawings and walked over to his foreman, ready to resume work while the autumn light was still available.

NINETEEN

Meeting the General

'Here, sir, let me help you with that,' said Captain Brantford's aide, stepping around the table to help change the bandaging on the captain's upper arm. 'It is a good thing we had some wind to shake up that sharpshooter, or he would have got you square on.'

'Do you think so?' asked the captain. 'I am inclined to believe that was the only reason he grazed me. He needed some luck on his side.'

The aide chuckled.

The captain winced as the bandage came off. It was a superficial flesh wound, but still tender. He felt a sense of weariness run through his body. It had not been the pursuit and battle that fatigued him. It had been the foul weather that followed that had exhausted him and his crew.

Three days prior, the *Pontus* had given chase and blocked an ill-equipped enemy frigate in a small inlet. During the boarding skirmish, with both ships in close range of one another, a zealous marine on the other ship had let a shot fly after most had dropped their muskets, nicking the captain on the arm. While there were injuries on both sides, Brantford's marines took possession shortly afterwards without further incident. Gale winds and high waves on the Bay of Biscay then kept both ships shore-bound for another sixty hours. It was only this morning that the *Pontus* had sailed into the port at San Sebastián to deliver the captured ship and deposit their prisoners at the allied garrison.

'Get along, lad, it is just about two bells,' said the captain, waving off his aide with thanks. Brantford changed into a clean shirt, carefully tied his cravat, and donned his heavy cloak. Tonight, he was heading ashore to an important meeting. He had fortunately arrived back on time for a scheduled *rendezvous* with Miss Reyne's father, General Sir William Reyne. Arranging the meeting had been difficult, and the timing and location were far from convenient for the captain. However, in his view, it was necessary that the two men meet, and he had therefore taken the initiative and time to make the arrangements. They had much to discuss, man to man.

Six weeks of exchanging correspondence had passed, beginning with the delivery of the letter that Miss Reyne had sent to her father in the captain's care, bypassing the military postal ships and using the captain's ship as the first stage of the transport.

In recent weeks, General Wellesley's troops had forced the French army to retreat from their coastal positions after losing contests in key forts and encampments. The retreat of Bonaparte's soldiers back into France opened the allied lines of communication along the northern Spanish shoreline.

The *Pontus,* anchored near San Sebastián, was laden with captured equipment and cannons, ready to transport further east for use by the advancing British troops. General Reyne was to begin his march tomorrow, bringing his troops forward to join with thousands of other soldiers under Wellesley's command heading towards mountainous passes through the Pyrenees.

Understanding that Captain Brantford had news of a serious nature to share with him, the general invited him to meet at his make-shift camp. He and his troops had taken a position several miles inland from San Sebastián. The general sent a mounted guide and an extra horse for the captain's use in making the trek.

The captain and the general were to meet within the hour. It was not an ideal night for either of them. The sky was overcast, and the path was rough, strewn with rocks and debris from fallen trees. Feeling the northwest winds picking up strength, the captain knew he had to move quickly to avoid being stranded on shore away from his ship. Fortunately, the distance from shore to the general's camp itself was not great.

'Here, Captain, let me hold the reins steady whilst you mount up,' said Sergeant Briggs, the junior officer sent to escort Brantford. 'One of our cavalry fellows purchased this plough horse from a farmer. He is a tad skittish with a saddle.'

The young man chatted endlessly while they rode together. Asking the captain questions, and unperturbed by the curt answers, he shared stories about their latest campaigns.

'It is a rare occasion for our general to meet with a navy man,' he said, his curiosity surfacing. 'Are you bringing news of our next campaign?'

'I am here on a personal visit,' said the captain.

'Is that so? Then do you perhaps know any of the general's family? We are hoping to hear news of his daughter. She has left us and gone home to England. Me and the lads are missing her greatly and are anxious for news. I suppose there is not much chance of you knowing her.'

'I am acquainted with Miss Reyne,' said the captain.

'Are you indeed?' Sergeant Briggs cried excitedly, leaning over the neck of his horse. 'Then you have met the woman I want to marry, if life will only treat me kindly!' he boldly announced. 'I hope that by the time this war is over, I have risen enough from my current station to convince the general of my merits. I have decent connections, you know. Perhaps you can put in a good word for me,' he said, smiling brightly at his guest. 'Remember, Briggs is the name, sir. How is Miss Reyne liking England? Is she well? It seems very odd not to have her here with us. She and I arrived in Portugal the same year, you know. We have travelled together for years. I knew her beforehand as well, from our time in India.'

The captain listened with close attention while the soldier, who was perhaps within a few years of Miss Reyne's age, regaled him with stories of Miss Reyne's close escapes, her inimitable talents, quirky habits, antics over the years, and her refusal to marry anyone thus far. 'She has had dozens of proposals, but says she is waiting for just the right one,' the sergeant confided.

When they finally arrived at camp, the soldier led Captain Brantford to a tent in the middle of a cluster of tents in a small field. Light from a lantern inside glowed against the canvas walls. As the captain stepped inside, he appreciated the warm air emitted from a small metal stove inside. Chilled from the damp autumn air, he was glad to gain shelter.

'I will let the general know you are here,' said the young man, stirring the embers in the stove's metal cylinder and throwing some broken branches onto the embers. 'When you are done, I am assigned to ride back with you to the harbour. I will see you after your meeting.' He saluted the captain and disappeared between the tents.

It was not long before the general appeared. Brantford took in the older man's appearance. He had anticipated a resemblance between father and daughter but was surprised to find very few similarities in appearance. He expected the general to be on the shorter side, like his daughter, and about fifty in age, given the daughter's age. In contrast, the gentleman was a man of medium height, close to the captain's size in height and weight. He looked to be in his mid-sixties. While the daughter had dark hair and deep brown eyes, the captain found himself met by a silver-haired man with hazel-coloured eyes. In all, it was disconcerting.

'Good evening, Captain Brantford,' said the general.

'Sir.'

'Let me pour you a refreshment. Will you join me?'

'Certainly.'

The general poured two generous servings and gestured to the captain to sit opposite him. There were no chairs in the tent. The young soldier had set out a pair of empty wooden crates for their use. They sipped their drinks, assessing one another.

'You have come a long way this evening, Captain. From the tone of your letter, I suspect you have not come all this distance to exchange pleasantries and have a little chit-chat. How may I be of assistance?'

The captain raised his head, his expression grave.

'I wish to tell you in person, sir, that your daughter forged your signature in order to travel on my frigate when she returned to England.'

The general scowled. 'That is a serious accusation. You are quite mistaken, young man. I signed papers for her and two guards, her companions if you will, to travel on a hospital ship. She is skilled in working with war injuries. There was no talk of returning on a frigate.'

'A woman by the name of Mrs Alvares travelled under your daughter's name on the hospital ship. Your daughter has admitted to producing false documentation enabling her two Prussian guards and herself, dressed as a boy and ostensibly hired as their translator, to travel aboard my ship. Are you, or are you not, aware of this?'

The general was trained in the art of war. He made a counterattack.

'Can you explain to me how you navy fellows allowed a young lady to bunk in with a shipload of drunken sailors for what, ten nights, and nobody knew who she was? And that your hospital transported a Portuguese widow over the age of thirty using my nineteen-year-old daughter's name, and no one was the wiser for it? Good God! Has everyone gone mad?'

The captain placed his hands on his knees while he mentally composed his reply.

'Let me first address your primary concern. I assure you that your daughter travelled without incident. Her masquerade was not discovered by anyone other than me. I was able to transport her safely to her destination. Once I discovered what she had done, and it was two days into our voyage by that time, I fully protected her privacy. She is unharmed. The key point as it concerns you, sir, is that she forged your name on a government document. Has she told you nothing of all this?'

'I learnt of it after the fact,' admitted the general, glaring at his guest. 'She told me in the letter she sent earlier in your care.'

'My purpose in coming here is to let you know the important details. For a variety of reasons, some of which you can easily discern, I chose not to report her behaviour. The matter, as it stands currently, is to remain private between us. You realise, I am sure, that you and I are therefore both complicit in her actions.'

The general rose to his feet, warming his hands over the stove.

'You are wanting money, I suppose,' he said.

Disgusted and angered by the general's response, the captain made no reply. He waited for the older man to turn back to face him.

'Let us talk about money,' said Captain Brantford. 'When your daughter's entourage was due to disembark, my men were moving their luggage. One of their crates had been damaged. It was highly apparent, visible through the gap in the side, that they were moving coins and valuables. This was witnessed by one of our marines and reported to me by my first lieutenant. It will not surprise you when I say we were therefore compelled to investigate. As you must be aware, both the military and naval authorities were alerted that the baggage trains at Vitoria had been looted by allied troops and civilians. Any items from Vitoria found in the hands of the soldiers were to be confiscated and returned to headquarters, and disciplinary measures were in effect. To date, the army has recovered only a minor portion of the estimated value of what was taken. It is a travesty that most of the valuables disappeared that night.'

'What has that to do with my family?' asked the general.

'You and your daughter and your Prussian guards were at Vitoria. And I, as the captain of one of His Majesty's ships, am subject to the dictates of common decency as well as governing regulations. I have transported your family group to England under illegal pretences. On board my ship, your family members carried Spanish and Portuguese coin and valuable items of unknown origin. It looks rather suspicious from my perspective, sir. I require an explanation.'

'And you shall have one,' the general replied, moving to the flap of the tent. 'Briggs!' he shouted. 'Get here!'

The young officer who escorted the captain to camp came running from a nearby tent.

'Bring Mrs Reyne to me at once. Tell her to bring me my brown ledger.'

'Yes, sir,' the man replied, disappearing into the dark.

Clasping his hands behind his back, the general stood by the tent flap, waiting.

'Mrs Alvares, the woman who travelled using my daughter's name, is my wife's sister,' the general said in a matter-of-fact tone, as though that point would make things sufficiently clear. 'I suppose I should tell you, for your awareness, that I am not married to Mrs Reyne. I am separated from my wife in England.'

Perplexed by their conversation, Captain Brantford stared at the general in frustration. How could this man be related to the delightful Miss Reyne, who occupied his thoughts all too often? Had it not been for the mention of this so-called ledger and the captain's faint hope that he would learn something from the general that would make sense and allay his duty to report the matter, he would have terminated their meeting at once. He needed proof that Miss Reyne had not transported property stolen from the British army. He felt ill thinking about what might happen to her if her actions became known.

'Ah, here she is, my beautiful wife.'

TWENTY

A Necessary Conversation

THE SECOND MRS Reyne was, indeed, a beautiful woman. Her age and appearance caught the captain by surprise. His first impression placed her age as being a little older than his sister Alison. He supposed her to be in her mid-thirties. To his surprise, mainly because they were in the middle of an army camp that was packed and ready to depart in the morning, she was elegantly attired. Her hair was neatly coiled into a high *chignon*. She had the look of good health about her, and her figure was lithe. Her sister, Mrs Alvares, very much resembled her in looks.

The general's wife arrived empty-handed at the tent. On being introduced to the captain, she said to him earnestly, '*Obrigada*. Thank you for safely transporting Miss Reyne and my sister and our friends to England and thank you for not reporting her illegal passage aboard your ship. We are deeply appreciative of your discretion.'

'My wife was aware of the goings-on at the time, but did not share this with me until later,' complained the general.

The captain, liking the situation less and less, let out an exasperated sigh.

'Where is my ledger?' asked the general curtly. 'Did Charlotte take it? Did she leave us with a copy?' asked the general.

'She has it with her. There was not sufficient time to write it all out, my love. But she did write to say that it is safe in her care.'

The general turned to the captain. 'The ledger records the origin and ownership of the valuables transported to England,' he explained. 'Every item is listed there with its source. It will be obvious when you see the ledger that the goods are mainly from Portugal and gathered over several years of travel—some even from India—and are unrelated to the Vitoria incident. Any items from Spain are the property of my soldiers, obtained through barter, or harvested after battle, or otherwise obtained during war. Is it likely there are a few odd pieces from Vitoria? Perhaps, but I cannot see how that would have been possible, considering the timing and our location away from the town. In any case, I hardly see how that should matter. If one individual stole from the train, and bartered to another for a hot supper or a pair of boots, who are we to take pearls from a barefoot soldier? And why should my men have their rightful property, accumulated over years of hard battle, confiscated simply because of the fiasco in Vitoria, which did not involve them? Where would be the justice in that? Whilst it is difficult to prove to you conclusively, I give you my word that my men did not abscond with items from the trains, at least, not in any direct fashion. They never got close to the trains. They were hauling bodies off the field and burying them. I ask that you place your trust in me and my daughter. We have moved valuables out of Portugal for purposes that I need not defend to you.'

The captain mulled this over. It could be true. The explanation was plausible enough. Both the general and the captain knew that the existence of the so-called ledger, while helpful, would not definitively prove anything. A talented individual with expert abilities could easily make a fictional record look real. It is not something the captain wished to say aloud. It implicated the daughter in a more perplexing situation than he had envisioned and would leave her without any means of defence.

Sorting through the decisions that faced him, the captain repressed his anger.

'There is something particularly troubling me. Can you explain to me, sir, why you felt it prudent to send a fortune in valuables home to England in the care of a young woman with so little protection? And at a time when the authorities were searching for valuables taken from Vitoria? What if your daughter had been the target of an attack to take these items from her? Where is your concern for her well-being?'

The general and his wife laughed at him.

'Come now, you are getting excited about something that never happened. In any case, all the valuables were supposed to be transported on a different ship. That my daughter diverted some of the goods to your ship was not part of the original plan.'

The captain's temper rose further. The other man's calm demeanour exasperated him.

'Consider that on arrival in a port city unknown to her, surrounded by strangers, and unaccompanied by any family with intimate knowledge of her situation, your daughter was tasked with storing a small fortune, some of which was shipped to her hotel room, or inquiring about a safe holding space, and transporting the goods to another destination.'

'I fail to see your issue. Besides, that is not what happened. She stored a crate of rocks in her room to fool any would-be thieves, and the valuables are stored in secure premises in a navy warehouse under the watch of hired guards,' replied the general resentfully. 'In fact, I am told your lieutenant recommended this particular location.'

'I am aware of that,' the captain said curtly. 'He did so under my instruction.'

The captain's comment and tone caught the general by surprise, but he carried on with his rant.

'In addition, she was under the personal protection of her

own men. I must add, we are talking about two highly trained men of excellent character in the company of one immensely resourceful young lady. Furthermore,' he paused, looking ashamed and yet proud at the same time, '—and you have yet to learn this—there is no talking my daughter out of an idea once she makes up her mind to do something.'

The captain found it difficult to continue this conversation. He rose to his feet and fastened his cloak.

'I had hoped for some reasonable and irrefutable explanation to account for your daughter's illegal behaviour. I admit to being further confused by what you have shared. I confess I am appalled by all that she has gone through, for the sake of whatever plans you have concocted. Her health, her safety, and her reputation have been sorely tested, and all of this under your guardianship and oversight. Regarding your ledger, I will delay my decision on the required actions until I meet with your daughter and review your documents. In the meantime, I must inform you that I am in possession of your goods. You are correct in your information that my lieutenant guided the selection of a warehouse for longer-term storage. However, the guards are under the pay of the Navy Board itself. If all appears to be as you claim, unconnected to Vitoria, I will release your valuables and let the matter pass. Otherwise, I must warn you, that I will be obliged to disclose the whole, including our daughter's transport under a false identity. I trust you understand matters.'

'Indeed, I would expect nothing less,' the general concurred, recovering from the shock of hearing that their valuables were in this man's custody.

'You do realise I could accuse you of theft of these items from me,' countered the general, 'which I will certainly do if they are not returned in due course.' He studied the captain's face. 'I am, nonetheless, glad to see that you take your responsibilities seriously.'

The captain found every aspect of their encounter frustrating.

'Had I been diligent in attending to my duty, sir, your daughter would have been called to task six weeks ago and the two of you would be facing charges,' the captain said dryly. 'What has saved you both is that I witnessed your daughter's generosity and kindness on more than one occasion. I find it hard to believe that she is capable of malicious intent.'

'We can, at least, agree on that much. It seems, Captain Brantford, that we find ourselves in a situation requiring mutual trust,' said the general calmly. 'You have assured me that my daughter's voyage on your ship was without incident, notwithstanding that she stayed alone with you in your chambers for most of the voyage. She advised me that you did not harm her, and I trust this to be the case. Further, you have taken property from us that you say is safely in your care. I expect this will all be returned. For my part, I assure you of my own and my daughter's upright intent and I affirm that the valuables onboard are the accumulated property of soldiers and friends, removed from Portugal and Spain for protection against confiscation and theft, and to help people begin anew after the war. Only through trust between us can we leave this meeting with any degree of confidence.'

'I could not agree more. I will discuss matters further with your daughter. I believe we are done here, sir. Can you call for my horse?' the captain asked.

'Will not you stay for a meal, Captain Brantford?' asked Sofia, having listened quietly to their conversation. 'You have come a long way this evening.'

'No, ma'am. I must return to my ship.'

'My man Briggs will see you back,' said the general. 'I do appreciate that you came to me in person for this conversation, captain. You have set my mind at ease on several accounts. When next you see my daughter, please give her our greetings.

Tell her,' he paused, his eyes getting misty, 'tell her that the second Mrs Reyne misses her, and everyone else does, too. Tell her that I do not doubt her decisions in the least. She has my full support.' He nodded at his guest. 'Until we meet again, Captain Brantford. Oh, but wait—do you mind executing a small favour for me? I have correspondence to be dropped off at the military post in San Sebastián. Will you do that for me? This is a letter for my daughter.' The general pulled out a tightly folded sheet from his coat pocket.

'It will be too late this evening to connect with the depot in San Sebastián,' replied the captain. 'I will have no opportunity to come ashore again. If you wish, I can take your daughter's letter with me. We sail east first but will return to England afterwards.'

'That will do perfectly well. Thank you.'

'Dearest, do not forget about your other letter, the one you wrote to that reckless officer who has been wishing to pay court to Charlie.'

'Yes, yes, I nearly forgot about it. Here it is. Do you mind taking this other letter, too, then?' asked the general, handing Captain Brantford a second letter. 'Some officer has been highly persistent in pleading his case,' sighed the general dismissively. 'He will be eager to hear from me. I am not certain where he is staying, now that he has left service, but he did provide me with the address of his family seat.'

The captain took the letter. He shook his head in disbelief as he noticed the individual's name on the folded letter.

'Lieutenant Peter Niles,' The captain read the name out loud, raising his eyebrows in surprise.

'That is correct. I suppose you are going to tell me next that you are acquainted with him,' said the general, laughing at the notion.

'I am, indeed. He is a close friend of mine, sir. I can deliver this to him in person. I will be seeing him shortly after I arrive in England.'

'A friend, is it? Well, well, that adds a new wrinkle. That is most interesting,' he chuckled.

The captain did not appreciate hearing mention of his friend—a man recently widowed, of excellent character and high repute—being spoken of condescendingly as reckless, with a reputation as a man importuning a lady. As much as it bothered him to hear his friend's name coupled with Miss Reyne's, it irritated him more to hear his friend being belittled.

'I must say, sir, there appears to be some sort of misunder-standing. Lieutenant Niles is not someone possessing a reckless nature, nor are his circumstances such that he would need to plead his case. Any woman gaining his affections would be fortunate indeed, both as to character and stability.'

The captain tucked the letters inside his coat and bowed respectfully. The wind caught the tent flap as he opened it. He stepped into the cold air and peered into the dark, noticing the soldier standing nearby beside a pair of horses. He climbed into the saddle of his mount. With a final look back at the general and his wife and puzzled by how unexpectedly cheerful they looked standing together in the tent doorway, he urged his horse forward and into the darkness towards the coast.

'Well, what do you think of that young captain?' asked Charlie's father, warming his hands over the stove.

'I rather like him,' said Sofia, smiling at the general. 'He is quite protective of our dear Charlie. I appreciate how forthright he is in expressing himself. He is, however, a naval man. That counts highly against him.'

'Yes. He will be forever at sea whilst his wife waits ashore. In any event, Charlie says he is privately engaged to someone. Perhaps it will come to naught. We will have to wait and see how it all turns out. And then there is this persistent lieutenant fellow. He has been rising in my estimation, and the captain's defence of his character now has me leaning in his favour. What is your opinion on this matter? Come, sit here, my dearest, there is still some warmth in this fire.' The general pulled the two crates close together and patted on the seat for her to sit beside him. 'Stay with me for a short time and chat. Shall we enjoy a sip or two? We face a long march tomorrow and I am loathe to leave your side.'

It was well past midnight when the captain stepped off the ship's tender, the small boat he had used to transport him to shore and back again to the *Pontus,* and climbed up the ladder to the deck. He removed his mud-covered boots on the quarter-deck and returned to his cabin. His aide had left out a serving of cold meat and cheese for him in his chambers. The captain lingered over his meal, sorting out his thoughts. What in the world, he wondered, possessed a father to submit his daughter to such trials? What horrors had this young woman seen and endured in her young life? He shuddered to think of her time in the Peninsula and the many campaigns in which she had participated at great personal risk. It dismayed him utterly to dwell on her journey home to England in the company of two hardened soldiers, transported on a warship, surrounded by an entire ship's company, and without any female companion. Her survival to the age of nineteen, seemingly unharmed, astonished him. That she appeared to undertake her trials willingly, and even relish in them, shocked him. Her life had been anything but easy.

The captain lifted a leather portfolio from his desk drawer and opened it, extracting the drawings he had discovered on his journey back to Spain. Miss Reyne had tucked slips of paper into various hiding spaces, leaving him to find a significant collection of images. He leafed through the drawings, amazed anew by her ability to capture the essence of a scene. Most of the images were of himself, which made him smile. She had also drawn a small self-portrait, which he found endearing. The set included drawings of his seamen completing various tasks. He held one showing two of his topmen balanced high on the yards. Other drawings, on small rectangles of note paper, showed minute details of life at sea—a plate of food, ship boys swabbing the deck, marines on watch, and one fine drawing of their pennant flapping atop the main mast, fully extended by a heavy wind. Even more surprisingly, she had left him a series of mazes, drawn for his entertainment, along with several riddles of her own making for his amusement. He understood that this was her expression of thanks to him. It touched him deeply.

Brantford took the two letters given to him by the general out of his coat and placed them securely inside his top desk drawer. Then he picked up his last letter from his betrothed, one of only a handful written in the past two years. In frustration, he read once again her brief remarks sent to him at Portsmouth. He had received no word from her since. Despite his regular correspondence, she had not yet written to him about her visit to Middlegate and her time spent there with his family, nor about the accident suffered by his father. Her disinterest in his affairs in general and in keeping him informed of her activities was painfully and glaringly obvious.

He sighed deeply and crushed her letter in his fist.

TWENTY-ONE

The Christmas Ball

CHARLIE KNOCKED LOUDLY on the door to Inês's bedroom at Greydon Hall. Without waiting for a response, she pushed it open and walked inside.

'Are you almost dressed?' asked Charlie. 'Shall I fasten the back of your gown for you? If the men are ready before us, they will complain that we have become soft and have forgotten how to keep pace with soldiers.'

'Well, it took me ages to decide what to wear,' said Inês. 'I could outfit an entire village with all the new clothing in my closet.'

'Yes, but my aunt believes that you will need every piece. Why ever did you pick something with all these buttons? I am surprised, you know, that Sir Reginald and Lady Weyburn are still going ahead with their ball in December,' said Charlie, struggling with the little pearl-shaped buttons on the back of Inês's gown. 'My aunt says they delayed it twice. Why not cancel it altogether? I am inclined to stay home in weather like this, but Aunt is determined that we attend. And do you know why? She is obsessed with finding a husband for me. Even though I am not properly out in society yet, she wants me to attend every function within fifty miles. I would much prefer to sit by the fire where it is nice and warm.'

'Your aunty says there is a thick fog settling in. Shall I fear for my life on the way?' asked Inês.

'We have use of my uncle's carriage. I expect we shall be quite cosy. My cousin Mary and her tiresome husband are taking my aunt and uncle in their carriage. Provided our driver can remember the route to the neighbours' house, we will arrive in grand style.'

'Try not to pop off the buttons, dearest,' said Inês.

Charlie smiled happily. She had moved to India with her father at a young age, yet she still recalled the glamour and excitement in earlier years when family members prepared for assemblies and balls. Getting herself ready this evening, she felt much like the young child who had eagerly watched her mother put on her jewellery and twirl in her gown, so many years ago.

After a short journey to arrive at the ball, with Gus and Wil arriving on horseback beside them, the ladies stepped down from their carriage, drawing glances from more than one nearby gentleman.

'I must say, you both look beautiful this evening,' said Gus, his gaze lingering admiringly on Inês. 'Mrs Alvares, may I claim the first set?'

Charlie laughed at him.

Inês curtsied. 'You shall indeed have it,' she told him.

'You do look very pretty,' Charlie said to her friend. 'If I were a man, I would ask you to dance myself. And you, gentlemen, will be busy all evening fending off the fathers wanting to introduce you to their daughters. My word, you are handsome gentlemen when you are cleaned up, looking so fine in your new attire. I do miss seeing you in your full uniform though. You will be in such demand that I will have to find my own dance partners.'

With a cheerful smile at her friends, Charlie picked up the folds of her gown and hurried up the steps, leading the way inside.

Her three friends, coming into the hallway behind her, smiled to themselves. Miss Charlotte Reyne undoubtedly had no notion of how lovely she looked this evening, nor would she notice any of the stolen glances aimed her way.

Her hair, grown longer now and styled by her cousin's experienced maid, lay bound in a loose roll at the nape of her neck. Dark curls framed her face and her deep brown eyes sparkled with excitement. She wore a pair of dainty earrings that looked perfect with the exotic necklace given to her by Lieutenant Niles in Vitoria.

With their coats and shawls removed and handed off to the butler, and accompanied by their handsome escorts, the women's appearance quickly drew the attention of other guests. Inês, with her brunette hair, hazel eyes, and mature good looks, seemed almost exotic in her darker fabrics. She moved gracefully amidst the men and women around her.

Gus and Wil, outfitted in fashionably close-fitting coats from a renowned London tailor, were, in Charlie's and Inês's opinion, the two most attractive men in the room.

With her three friends beside her, Charlie entered the ballroom and paused in the doorway, happily taking in the merriment of the occasion. The array of lights and festive decorations fascinated her. Nearby, several gentlemen interrupted their conversations to stare at her.

The impression Charlie created was not that of your typical society miss. She was very pretty, certainly, and she had an inkling of that herself. But more so, she was unusual, and almost elusive, despite her friendly smiles. In stature, she ranked on the shorter and thinner side. She carried herself with an almost athletic grace. To her Aunt Tripp's chagrin, she did not in the least resemble a sweet young lady not yet formally out in society. With her good looks, confident posture, and delicately styled gown, she quickly became an item of interest.

Charlie Reyne commanded attention without the least awareness she was doing so. Her friends affectionately watched the effect she had on others. They viewed her as a one-of-a-kind treasure—special, precious, and unique.

'Everyone is staring at you, Inês,' Charlie whispered. 'You will certainly be on the dance floor for every set this evening.'

Inês smiled at her. 'Darling, it is you who draws interest.'

'Well, if that is the case, I will tell you why. They are thinking to themselves, "Ah, look at that gown, will you? There goes the niece of Lady Tripp. I would recognise her anywhere."'

'Stop it!' Inês laughed. 'Your aunt might hear you!'

'Where is she? I will tell her so myself.' Charlie grinned at her friend and marched off in search of her aunt. Inês, left on her own, stepped back towards Gus and Wil near the refreshment table.

'Is she on a rampage?' Gus asked.

'Up to mischief, yes,' Inês replied.

'Speaking of mischief, I hear they will be dancing the waltz later this evening, fresh out of the ballrooms of London. Shall we twirl about together? I danced the waltz in Berlin some years ago and memorised the steps. Not everything is invented in London, you know, and certainly not the waltz.'

Inês raised her eyebrows at him.

'Of course, you of all people know that,' he admitted, smiling fondly. 'Come, I have not had any exercise in days. I am eager to dance. Wil, do you plan to stand there forever? I am claiming Mrs Alvares. You will need to find our Charlie.'

'I will meet you on the dance floor,' said Wil absentmindedly. 'I am going to enjoy some of this delightful punch first.'

Charlie, in making her way towards her aunt and uncle, soon found herself standing face to face with someone she knew.

'Lieutenant Niles!' she said, surprised and excited to see him.

'I am sorry, have we met?' he asked, looking confused.

'It is me!' she said, annoyed with him, lifting her necklace to help him remember.

'Miss Reyne! Ah, I am merely teasing you. Of course, I recognise you!—I was just this moment searching for you and found myself admiring the prettiest woman in the room. And here it turns out to be none other than you.'

The lieutenant stood back, admiring her. 'I had to ask myself, is this fine young lady the same Miss Reyne I knew from before? Is this really 'Little Charlie'? You look beautiful this evening.'

'I think so, too,' she nodded. 'I must appear a little different from when we first met. You look dashing, sir. Are you well? How is your family? Your children are healthy, I trust? Do they travel with you?'

'Yes, fine, yes, and no.'

She tipped her head, puzzled.

'You have asked so many questions, I scarcely know which one to answer. Are you wanting to dance, or do you have a moment for conversation? Shall we find somewhere less crowded?'

'Yes, yes, and yes.'

Lieutenant Niles chuckled as he led her to an adjacent room.

They noticed a sofa near the fireplace in the parlour and seated themselves comfortably, content in each other's company and pleased to sit and watch others in the room and those passing by in the crowded hall.

'I find it disconcerting to be away from the war and back in society,' said the lieutenant. 'I have wondered how it must be for you, having lived away all those years,' he said. 'Do you miss your father?'

'Yes, of course. Although we have been separated many times, I have mainly been at his side throughout his time in the Peninsula. I often fear for his safety and wonder when I will see him again. His troops are in their winter camp close to the border. They will be engaged again soon, or perhaps they are fighting at this very moment.'

Lieutenant Niles nodded.

'I have written to your father again,' he said solemnly. 'I have asked him for permission to marry you.'

Startled, Charlie turned to face him. 'Whatever for?' she asked. 'Surely, you are not still worried about our night together in Vitoria! First, no one will ever know about it. Second, a war necessitated our being together. I assure you: you are not the only man with whom I spent the night in the dark countryside in Spain. That is no cause for marriage.'

'I understand how you might think so. You did not grow up in England and are not familiar with the rules of society. My reputation would remain intact. Yours, however, would be ruined.'

'These people are all strangers to me. What do I care of that?' she asked him, appalled that it should be a consideration for either of them to entertain. 'I can return to Portugal if need be.'

'It is not so very different there, and you know that. Your father has replied to me.'

Charlie fussed with her gloves, stretching out the fingertips.

'My letter had a speedier route than usual. The *Pontus* was on an urgent trip back to England last week. Captain Brantford brought your father's letter for me. He was in touch with your father recently himself. He was escorting supply ships east of San Sebastián, towards the camps.'

He saw that he had Charlie's full attention.

'Captain Brantford was just here, and you saw him? How did he come to have a letter from my father?'

Niles shrugged.

'I have received a letter as well, but it came by regular delivery. How is Captain Brantford—is he well?' Charlie asked with concern. 'He and his poor men must be frozen to the deck in this icy weather.'

'Do not you wish to hear what your father wrote?' the lieutenant asked gently.

'I know very well how he replied to you. He wished you good luck, said that you would need a great deal of it in your dealings with me, more so if I accepted, and wrote that he would wait to hear from me after you have made your suit. If and only if you have my happy consent, then you may raise the matter with him at an appropriate time. Am I right?'

Dumbfounded, the lieutenant let her words sink in. She had quoted almost verbatim what the father had written to him.

Charlie smiled sweetly.

'I know him better than you suppose,' she said. 'He is used to commanding troops, but when it comes to his daughter, he is at a loss in knowing what to do. I am not the most obedient daughter. Mercifully, he is wonderfully pliant and the perfect father for me.'

Charlie patted the lieutenant on his sleeve.

'My dear sir, do not be so easily fooled,' she said to him, chuckling. 'He wrote to me as well. He repeated word for word what he wrote in his letter to you. I simply memorised it and have quoted it back to you.'

'Ah. I see.'

'Yes. You should know that I am not planning on marrying any time soon. If I find myself in the middle of a societal uproar, and people pull out tar and feathers and attack me, we can discuss the matter again. But you, sir, need an opportunity to find someone you care for deeply, and who is ready to look after your young family. I do not fit your requirements. All your friends will tell you so.'

'Have you no interest at all?' he asked, disconcerted by her straightforward remarks.

'Come, sir, let us be honest with one another. I will never marry a man forced by circumstances to ask for my hand. It is considerate of you but unnecessary. Truthfully, I am not even thinking about marriage. I have quite a bit of work in front of me related to a project with my father and my friends. If, at some future time, we find ourselves drawn to one another, then we can think about these things. In any case, I must tell you, my affection lies elsewhere. I am the sad victim of unrequited first love. Perhaps it will pass. In the meanwhile, I hope you and I can be friends.'

He looked at her with admiration. 'I shall be honoured, if you would call me such,' he said sincerely.

They sat quietly, both lost in thought.

'You asked me how the captain is doing,' he said next.

'I did,' she murmured. She looked at him shyly.

'He was here on a special mission, delivering urgent correspondence for the Navy Board. Captain Sand alerted me to his visit. We saw him for barely an hour. The *Pontus* headed back out to sea the same day to escort another supply convoy leaving for the coastal encampments. You will be pleased to know he met your father.'

Charlie listened intently. 'I confess, that is a bit worrisome.'

'How so?'

'I will tell you another time. It is a long story.'

'Captain Brantford asked me to give you his warm regards.'

'That was kind of him.'

'He said to tell you the second Mrs Reyne—have I got that right?—and your father send their regards. He appreciated the drawings that you left for him in his cabin.'

'Did he?' she asked excitedly. 'Oh, I am so glad. I placed them where he was sure to find them. I should have been disappointed had not he discovered at least a few.'

Watching her, the lieutenant knew with a sinking heart that it was his friend the captain who had captured her interest. He felt saddened for his own sake, and deeply sorry for her due to his friend's circumstances.

'I met his betrothed last month when I was visiting his family in Herefordshire, near Middlegate,' he said, wanting to be sure she understood the situation.

'Did you? I am sure the captain wishes he had been there as well. I am sorry he could not see her. Is she a beautiful young lady?'

'She is exceptionally lovely.'

'I tire of sitting,' said Charlie, uncomfortable with their conversation, and rising suddenly to her feet to put an end to it. 'The heat from the fire will scorch my skirt if we sit here any longer. Sir, will you rescue me from my aunt's scolding for sitting out the dances, and instead let me practise my steps with you?'

He rose and tucked her arm into his.

'Shall we, my lady?'

'Indeed, good sir.' She giggled at him. 'Are you certain about dancing with me? I have only just learnt the steps and am sure to make mistakes. You will need to help me.'

The lieutenant smiled continuously through the first two dances with her. Where she ought to swing left, she went right. When the group stepped forward, she retreated. While others might have died from embarrassment, she laughed gleefully, like a youngster on a delightful adventure.

Despite Charlie's poor performance on the dance floor, she never lacked a partner for the rest of the evening and was the centre of attention off the floor as well as on it.

'Do you suppose they have heard by now that she is wealthy?' Inês asked Gus as they surveyed the young men vying for her attention.

'Her relatives will not have made a secret of it,' he replied.

'I hope her head does not swell from all this attention.'

'Perhaps it will, a little,' Gus replied warmly. 'I am not overly worried. She will figure it out in time. After all that she has endured, she deserves to shine brightly.'

Charlie looked towards them at that moment. She beamed at them and winked.

'I knew it!' Wil said proudly. 'She is not fooled for a second. These men are just little boys in her view.'

After watching Charlie, Gus noticed that Inês was no longer standing with them.

'She is over there,' said Wil, following his brother's look. 'She is dancing with that architect fellow. What is his name again?'

'Mr Marshall,' said Gus glumly.

'My, my, it does appear that Mr Marshall enjoys the company of Mrs Alvares,' Will stated quietly. 'What say you to that, dear brother? If you do not take better care, you will be spending your old age, should you live to see it, entirely by yourself.'

Gus tipped his glass, emptied the contents, and walked away.

'Where are you going?' asked Wil.

'I am fetching Mrs Alvares a beverage. She will be thirsty after the dance.'

'Good job, brother,' Wil muttered. 'Wait, I am coming, too. I could use one myself.'

'Me, too,' said Charlie, suddenly coming up beside him. 'Wil, I need you to dance with me so I can get away from all these young men. Do you see that tall fellow with the yellow waistcoat? He is twenty-three years old and boasts that he spends all his time at parties and clubs. The others are hanging on his every word. We should ship them all to my father so they can learn a few useful life lessons.'

Wil took both of her hands in his and squeezed them.

'Promise me something,' he said.

'What is it, dear one? Have I offended you somehow?'

He shook his head emphatically.

'Promise me that you will never change.'

Charlie burst out laughing. 'Silly man. I cannot promise

you anything of the sort.'

'Then promise me that you will think things through and not rush into any decisions.'

'Well, then I would be changing, and you asked me not to do that.' Charlie saw that Wil was being deeply serious. 'I promise that if I decide to change, I will perhaps seek your opinion.' She looked at Wil fondly. 'I will not forget who we are, and where we come from, and I will not forget that you are my family,' she assured him. 'You are so very precious to me, dearest Wil.'

'I accept your promise. Come along. The lieutenant looks like he is waiting to speak with you again. Do you see that? Gus is speaking with him and already has his hand on the hilt ready to challenge. Shall we converse with the fellow anyway?'

'Yes. Lieutenant Niles is in my good books.'

'Then he is in mine as well. But do let us be quick. It is not wise to leave the two of them alone. Gus has not forgotten what happened in Spain.'

'But shall we get you your beverage first? What did you say you were drinking?'

'It is a rum punch of some sort. Shall I get one for you? Can you handle it?'

'Am not I the daughter of General Sir William Reyne?'

'You are indeed. Poor man, he must miss you fiercely.'

TWENTY-TWO

The Winter Months

'I MUST TELL you, Charlie, nothing you have said over the years about your homeland has prepared me for my first winter in England. What a dreadfully cold country this is. I am used to cyclical storms and torrential rains along the coastal towns in Portugal for brief periods during the winter, but this feels worse.'

'I could not agree more,' Charlie nodded. 'If it is any comfort, everyone says this is not a normal winter. While it has been many years since I lived here in my childhood, I cannot recall any winter like this one. I have never seen ice and fog and snow to this extent. Are you sorry for your decision to come home with me?'

'I am indeed,' said Inês, pulling her shawl tightly around her shoulders and picking up her sewing to head for another room. 'Wil says the fire in the parlour is throwing off good heat at present. If you need me, you can come and collect me there.'

Charlie and Inês were not alone in their dissatisfaction with the weather. None of the guests in the Tripp household were ready to head outside to brave the bitter cold in the days and weeks that followed the Weyburns' ball. An almost impenetrable fog had settled over most of the country and most heavily in southern areas closest to the sea. No one was able to leave the house and safely navigate the roads. The Tripp household was filled with friends and relatives unable to travel. It seemed to Inês that everyone was attempting to claim the warmest chairs by the fire in the large parlour. The windowpanes, with their frosted web patterns and opaque glass, appeared as though they would shatter if anyone so much as touched them.

'It would be far more pleasant had my cousin Mary and her annoying husband gone home when they had the opportunity,' said Charlie. 'I have never met such a complainer as he is. Did you hear him last night? The cheese was too sharp, the bread too crisp. Apricots ought to be ripened more before they are cooked. He likes his meat very well browned, thank you. Oh, my heavens, he is a tiresome man.'

'I am in full agreement,' grunted Gus, looking up from a newspaper he had picked up to pass the time, looking for the latest war reports.

The celebration of Christmas itself, with its twelve days of festivities that ensued, offered enough food and pastimes to placate them all. The Tripps were experienced in entertaining, and their kitchen staff at Greydon Hall knew how to satisfy their guests.

Not everyone, though, was easily pleased.

'How much longer before we can move to our new place in Chellisbury? I need some distractions, some active work to occupy my time,' Wil confessed to his friends.

'Eight weeks, possibly ten,' replied Charlie. 'You will need to find some activities in the meantime to occupy yourself. The servants are saying this is the worst winter they have ever known. Even the mighty Thames is frozen, for goodness' sake. And the snow on the main roads to the north is higher than the tops of the carriages. No one is going anywhere. You can be sure there will be no progress in construction at Chellisbury until the weather improves. For our amusement, my aunt and uncle are holding a little *soirée* once they can send out their invitations. They will include a few of the neighbours and some friends from nearby. We can look forward to fine meals and games, and perhaps some music and country dances. There might even be a few pretty ladies for you to meet, Wil.'

'I am not interested in these pale English girls who are afraid of the sun. Once the war is over, I will marry some lovely *Fräulein* from Prussia.'

'Someone who sings for you?' laughed Inês. 'Suit yourself. Who knows how long you will be waiting?'

For Charlie, though they remained housebound due to the weather, the weeks of January passed pleasantly enough. She struck up an uneasy friendship, more like a truce, with the Weyburn siblings Jack and Elspeth and a few of their cousins who had been staying with them over the Christmas season. The young people, braving the cold and ice, made the short trek to Greydon Hall a few times to visit the Tripp household.

Evenings were often spent playing cards or writing letters. From time to time, to everyone's delight, Charlie brought out her guitar to play and sing tunes for her aunt and uncle and friends. Even cousin Mary and her hard-to-please husband seemed to enjoy listening to music to break the tedium of the dark winter nights.

Inês, skilled with her needle, spent time adapting her English gowns to resemble more closely the Portuguese stylings that she preferred. Gus and Wil, finding the Weyburn crowd too young, and the Tripps' dispositions too formal, browsed through the family library for anything of interest. They broke up their days with short morning walks, cleaned their guns, sharpened their sabres, polished their boots, and performed other tasks that brought a sense of structure to their idle days.

Of them all, by the end of January, Charlie was perhaps the most restless. She longed to get moving, to pick up their crates from the guarded warehouse in Portsmouth. She wanted to order supplies, purchase linens, dishes, and furniture, and move their belongings to Chellisbury. There had been little advancement of late in any of these tasks. She was eager for progress.

Charlie was lounging in her room in the afternoon in early February, sketching dozens of images of her friends, and looking over several of her drawings of the gallant Captain Brantford, when her aunt's maid knocked on her door.

'Lieutenant Niles is here requesting a moment of your time, Miss Charlotte,' said the young lady.

Charlie hurried to the parlour where her aunt and uncle were chatting with the lieutenant. Her aunt cast a knowing glance at her husband as Charlie joined them.

'It is not every day we get a gentleman caller,' she said sweetly. 'How good it is of you to stop by for a visit.'

'Thank you, ma'am. I am afraid I cannot stay long. I am leaving the county and wish to bid all of you and Miss Reyne farewell. As well, I have some news that you will wish to know. You will hear of it at some point, I dare say.'

'Oh? Do not keep us in suspense then,' said the uncle.

'Your friends, the Sands, send their regrets that they have not contacted you or any of the neighbours since their return from town. Captain Sand asked me to advise that there has been a tragic death in his wife's family, and they are in mourning. They thought you might have heard since they returned before Christmas, but the Sands asked me to inform you in person. They are not receiving guests and are leaving again on an extended trip. The Sands will return to Mrs. Sand's family home afterwards, along with their brother. Miss Reyne, you met their brother, Mr James Brantford, when we were in Portsmouth together.'

'Yes, I remember him very well,' she said, concerned. 'What of the captain?' she asked in a worried voice.

'He has been informed by letter,' said their guest. 'It was his father who passed away.'

'Oh, my, how very sad,' said the aunt.

'I am sorry for this news,' said Charlie. 'The Brantfords are like family to you. You must be grieving this loss yourself.'

'It is the family I am concerned for now,' he said, intent on keeping their details private. 'Their situation is unexpected. I prefer not to speak more of this for the time being.'

'Well, thank you for informing us of the reasons for their absence,' said the uncle. 'You said you came to bid farewell. What are your plans for the remainder of the winter, sir?'

'You may have heard from Miss Reyne that I retired from active service and am currently in a new position. I am engaged with the Sussex Yeomanry at present, but I must return to my barracks in the north. We are bringing in new horses for training and welcoming some recruits. Before I leave the area, I wanted to say farewell to all of you, and to Miss Reyne. I regret that I am not able to stay longer. I am afraid my schedule is tight. I have left my horse standing at the front of the house with your groom.'

'I see,' said the uncle. 'Well, niece, perhaps you would like to escort the lieutenant to claim his great coat and see him out. Visit again, lieutenant, when you are next in the area. We are always glad to welcome friends to our home.'

Lieutenant Niles and Charlie stood together on the circular carriageway at the front of Greydon Hall. Sensing that the lieutenant wished to say more to her, Charlie dismissed the stable hand and stood patiently, searching her friend's face, waiting for him to gather his thoughts.

'I did not wish to say this in front of your family,' Niles finally said, 'but I know your concern for the Brantford family to be sincere. I felt that you would wish to hear first-hand from me. It cannot long remain a secret. In addition to grieving the loss of their father, the family is facing serious repercussions from his death.'

To Lieutenant Niles' surprise, Charlie merely scowled

and nodded.

'This is the father who did not bother to travel eight hours from London to see his entire family, including his mother who had come down from the north, and his son, whom he had likely not seen for nigh on a year. He chose instead to stay back. No doubt he ensconced himself at his club and gambled away his fortune.'

'Have you already heard the news from someone?' asked Niles, shocked at her accurate description.

'Heavens, no. What other kinds of serious consequences might you have meant? Apart from a secret love child to disrupt the family line, gambling would be the obvious vice. I have heard the troops speak endlessly of their family affairs. Changes of fortunes are far more customary than one might anticipate.'

'I see.' He paused, worried that he had disclosed too much.

'You need not worry,' she immediately assured him. 'I will not discuss this with anyone. I am deeply sorry for the family. It is bad enough to deal with the loss of life. Trust me, I know this from experience.'

'Do keep them in your thoughts. A great deal of upheaval lies ahead for everyone. I cannot be sure how it will go for any of them,' he said sadly, shaking his head.

'How fortunate the family has you and other friends and family to lean on at such a time. You are dear to them and are like a brother to them both. I have seen friends pull together at the most difficult of times. It makes a world of difference to the ones who have suffered most.'

'It is different on the battlefield,' he said, knowing she would understand him. 'Men go out knowing full well they could be shot or lose their lives that day. It is a risk they face daily. None of what happened here needed to happen. Their losses could have been avoided. Now the entire family suffers due to lack of judgement and deceit, all around,' he said, clenching his fists in anger.

Charlie picked up one of his hands and held it lightly in both of hers. She stood with him thus for over a minute, standing quietly with him while he regained his composure.

Watching from inside their home as the couple said their farewells to one another, Charlie's uncle and aunt found themselves diverting their looks, and stepping back from the window. They did not know what had been said between them but felt the compelling urge to offer them privacy.

On the seventh of February, a letter arrived at Greydon Hall addressed to Mr Gustaf Jaeger.

'Now, that is a rare event. How exciting for you, Gus. Is it from Father?'

Gus turned over the letter and examined the seal.

'Did my uncle pay for the delivery?' Charlie asked him. 'It is a very odd system. Letters go all the way to London for sorting and then come back here, rather than coming straight away, and you then pay for all this back-and-forth travel. You must ask about the cost and reimburse my uncle, so he is not feeling put out about it.'

Gus ignored Charlie's remarks. He broke open the dark wax seal and unfolded his letter.

'It is signed by Lieutenant Sherrington, from HMS *Pontus*,' he said, his voice edged with surprise. 'He writes to say that the construction in the warehouse quarter will be completed within two weeks and the warehouse where we have stored our belongings is scheduled to reopen in March. He says, however, that the warehouse has now been re-assigned as part of the expanded naval depot, and we will therefore need him present to sign his permission for us to remove our crates. He will meet us there, he writes, in said building, on March the fourth, at two in the afternoon.' He stopped, looking puzzled, and glanced at Charlie.

'What is it?' she asked.

'He invites us to bring an interpreter, to avoid any misunderstandings, and he also requests the presence of Miss Charlotte Reyne to represent her father. He asks that you bring your father's brown ledger, for purposes that will be made clear on our arrival. He and Captain Brantford have booked rooms at the Crown during that time, should we need to contact them.'

'Let me see the letter,' Charlie demanded, surprised and agitated. She snatched it from his hands and read it for herself.

'Well, of all the nonsense. Why did not he write to me directly? You do understand his meaning, I am sure! They have taken our shipment into custody, that is what they have done. They suspect we have transported stolen property. That can be the only reason to ask for the family ledger. How do they even know I have it with me?'

Charlie paced behind the sofa, marched in front of it, and finally threw herself into a large chair, knocking a small stool on its side. Her eyes were bright with anger.

'There is no need for any of you to come to the warehouse. I will go alone,' she said with icy calm. 'I will meet with this Lieutenant Sherrington gentleman and show him the ledger. You can wait at the inn. I will arrange for us to pick up our crates the following day, get the items sorted and delivered to the bank, and pay another visit to the solicitor with items for auction. Then Inês and I can finish any final purchases for Chellisbury. We can pick up medical supplies and dry goods when we are in town and bring them back to Chellisbury ourselves. I will ask to borrow Uncle's carriage for a few days, and we can bring our wagon. If all goes well, dear friends, we can be ready to open Chellisbury by late March or early April. Lieutenant Sherrington's timing could not be better.'

The friends listened in silence. They knew at once that

Charlie's cheerful tone was a mask, not unlike others she had donned over the years they had known her. Not one of them was a fool. If these officers of the navy determined that the goods were stolen from Vitoria, they would take everything. Moreover, Charlie's actions would be laid bare for all to know.

Maintaining an outer appearance of calm, Charlie's stomach was churning. Confiscation of their shipment would be disastrous financially, but she had a worse situation on her mind. On a personal level, by her actions, she was guilty of forgery, impersonation, and, if they ruled against her, illegal transport of stolen goods on a naval warship. Sailors and soldiers faced execution for less.

'When was this letter sent? How likely is it the captain will attend our meeting with the lieutenant? Do you plan to see him if he is in Portsmouth?' asked Inês, not quite grasping the whole situation.

'He is questioning my integrity,' said Charlie, deeply perturbed, her mind on a different path.

'Who is, dear?' asked Inês.

Charlie ignored her question.

'I have put you all in jeopardy. If it does not go in our favour, you must be ready to leave Portsmouth at once.'

Charlie stood up. Her worried eyes locked on Gus.

'Come now,' he said, rising to steady her. 'There is no need for panic.'

'I am not panicking. I am angry.'

'I signed the warehouse contract. Under no circumstances are you going into that meeting by yourself,' Gus said. 'Wil and I are both coming, and we will be in full uniform.'

'I am coming, too,' said Inês firmly. 'Sofia gave me her little pistol. It tucks very nicely into a reticule.'

'Are you listening to me?' asked Gus, squeezing Charlie's shoulders. 'We are all coming with you, and we are not leaving without those crates.'

'Are you going to wear your handsome hussar busbies?' Charlie asked him, dabbing her eyes.

'We will indeed. It is high time Colonel Jaeger and Major Jaeger showed their true colours.'

'We do look rather intimidating when we are in uniform,' offered Wil.

Charlie looked around at her dear friends. 'You are so good to me.'

'You are not going to cry, I hope,' said Wil. 'Your eyes get puffy. It makes you look quite dreadful.'

Delivering his little barb, and worrying more deeply than he cared to show, Wil picked up a recent copy of *La Belle Assemblée*, a women's clothing magazine that Charlie's cousin Mary had left behind. He flipped through it, pausing in delight to examine the drawings depicting the latest styles in ladies' nightgowns.

'Ah,' he said, studying the images intensely, 'finally something worth crying over.'

TWENTY-THREE

A Fond Farewell at Greydon Hall

'CHARLOTTE, HAVE YOU forgotten anything? Where is your shawl?' asked Aunt Lydia, fussing. 'It is at least a three-hour drive to Portsmouth. You cannot be halfway there and discover that you have left things behind. We can bring whatever you have forgotten when we come to visit you in Chellisbury, but that is not for a few weeks. Are you sure you have everything?'

'Yes, dear aunt, I have everything I could ever possibly need, and then some,' Charlie said with a gentle smile. 'In fact,—'

'In fact, you are so well dressed, everyone in Portsmouth will know you are my niece. Now let it be. I rue the day we had that conversation,' chided her aunt.

'I was going to say, everyone will know I am your niece because I am so very intelligent,' said Charlie.

Her aunt burst out laughing.

'Brat.'

'Aunty, you are just like my father. You would have made an excellent officer. The men would have followed you into any battle.'

'I doubt that very much.' She paused, glowing from the rare words of praise from her niece. 'I confess, I have come to see that we are not so very different in our ways. Dear child, I will miss you. Promise me you will not be a stranger to our home.'

'Goodness, we are in Portsmouth for five days only. Once we

are back at Chellisbury, we shall be a mere fifteen miles away. I will come back to Greydon Hall so often you will wish me at Jericho.'

'None of your army cant here,' said Lord Tripp, coming out of the door with Inês on his arm. Gus and Wil had already said their goodbyes and were mounted on their newly bought horses.

'If you gentlemen had told me earlier that you like to ride, I would have outfitted you,' Lord Tripp called out to them. 'Join me for a hunt, during the season. Or I can meet you partway and we can ride towards the Downs. Charlie, if you take the time and learn to ride like a proper lady, you may come along. I am not opposed to that sort of outing.'

'My dear uncle, you will be embarrassed beyond measure to see me on a horse. I have no aptitude for it. I would rather sit comfortably and drive a pair of sweet ponies.'

'Mules or donkeys, more like,' Wil piped in.

'True. Look how handsome they are. And you, young man— even more so,' she said, smiling at Master Percy Winthrop, the wagon driver, seated happily behind her donkeys.

'Compared to this wagon, Uncle's carriage is considerably faster,' she said to Master Winthrop. It had only been a matter of weeks since he had arrived at Greydon Hall and begun his training. 'Once we are past the turnpike,' Charlie warned him, 'we will be travelling at different speeds and may become separated from one another. If so, we will meet you at the Crown. We have booked a room for you there. The clerk wrote to say they could stable our donkeys for the night. They have room to store the wagon behind their courtyard until we need it.'

Her uncle handed her a small packet. 'The letter for the solicitor is inside, and another for my man at the bank, in case you need it. I have written to the owner that over a dozen crates are arriving. As we discussed, they will be safer there than with the solicitor. The bank has enough space and will hold whatever items you bring whilst the solicitor arranges for the auction. I will plan to meet you in four days. You will need me to sign for you. There is a letter here to be sent to your father as well.'

'Thank you, sir. I can set my mind at ease with these arrangements.' Charlie stood on her toes and kissed her uncle on the cheek. 'I shall very much miss our card games. You are a formidable opponent, sir. I shall have to improve my skills and practise on Wil before our next game.'

'To teach him how to beat me as well, no doubt. Get in, get in. Watch your step. Inês, you go first. Charlotte next. We will see you all soon. Remember to take my watch in for repairs. I am lost without it.'

'*Auf Wiedersehen,*' said Gus.

'Farewell, dear family,' Charlie waved from the carriage. 'We miss you already!'

'Go, go,' cried her aunt.

Her uncle called out to Master Winthrop. 'I heard the roads are wet and muddy. Watch out for the ruts once you head south. Keep your animals calm and in good control when another carriage passes and you shall be safe, lad.'

Lord and Lady Tripp stood on the stairs in front of Greydon Hall. They waved at their parting guests and stared down the narrow lane long after the carriage and wagon rolled out of sight.

'It is going to be rather dull here now,' Lady Tripp said despondently.

'Far too quiet,' agreed her husband. 'I never thought I would miss seeing the backs of that crowd. By George, I have surprised myself.' He guffawed and snorted. He dabbed his eyes.

'Here, my love.' Lady Tripp passed him her lacy handkerchief.

Lord Tripp blew his nose and handed it back.

'There is still some toast and jam in the breakfast room. I will ask cook to brew more tea. Come along, then.' He tucked his wife's arm in his and patted her hand. 'A little sustenance will do us both good.'

'I miss my brother,' she said, finding a dry spot on her hand-kerchief to dab her eyes. 'She is just like him.'

'Much worse.'

The couple laughed and walked together across the wide empty hallway of the house.

Arriving three days in advance of their meeting, the friends had sufficient time to accomplish the lion's share of their tasks. They were staying once again at the Crown, but in more luxuriant rooms than on their first visit. Charlie had booked a suite with a small sitting room for herself and Inês to share and additional rooms for the men.

As they went about their errands in town, each took on the responsibilities relating to their new roles.

Experienced in managing her own home in Portugal, Inês took charge of procuring household supplies and hiring servants for Chellisbury. In terms of preservation and storage of goods, Inês was highly attuned to issues arising in hot climates. The weather here, however, presented new challenges. She had asked Charlie's aunt for help in understanding domestic management in England, and in doing so she had gained an ally through her efforts in their four-month stay at Greydon Hall. When it came to estimating and ordering quantities of food required for feeding large groups, she consulted with Charlie.

The challenges of setting up their import business also fell to Inês, again due to her experience. Before the French and Spanish invasion and the burning of Oporto, the Montalto family had been renowned for its production of fine port. Inês's father and his brothers had been successful merchants, supplying their finest products to the Portuguese and Brazilian markets and providing a suitable brand for the Portuguese navy. On getting married, Inês's husband had invested in the Montalto family business and had spoken on many occasions about their trials and successes. So, too, had Sophia's husband, a distant cousin who shared the Montalto family name and who also owned part of the Montalto vineyards. The girls had been in and out of the family vineyards and warehouses as children and as wives and understood a great deal about the processes of making and selling the family brand. Fortuitously, a section of the vineyard had been unscathed by both enemy and allied fires. One of her uncles, surviving the war thus far, continued to maintain the family vineyard with help from his neighbours.

Since the time of the ladies' first visit to Chellisbury, Gus had inserted himself as the liaison with Mr Marshall for all things construction-related. His decision in part stemmed from his interests and abilities, and, in part, his prudent aim to intercept conversations Mr Marshall might wish to strike up with Inês. His role gave him authority over shipments coming onto the property, storage, tracking of supplies, and oversight of all the outlying buildings.

Wil took on the mantle of 'Mr Mayor.' He would see to the settlement of the soldiers first into the infirmary, and then, to those staying on for employment, into the cottages encircling the small market square that formed the new village. His role was to train staff to work in the warehouse and to schedule soldiers for guard duty throughout the property.

Charlie's role, as always, was chiefly that of the planner and overseer. She was to set up the millinery workshop and find someone to run it. She was the impetus and spark that made things move. Apart from the quiet influence of Gus, her superior in age and experience, her leadership in all their activities was otherwise tacit and unchallenged. Her friends looked to her for a signal, a go-ahead indicator, before embarking on a journey. Hers was the first word of encouragement and the last word of thanks. Charlie controlled their budget and bore the weight of decision-making.

Yet today was different. She continued to insist that she should go to the naval warehouse to deal with the matter and defend herself alone. No one was paying any attention. The men, looking distinguished in their military attire, had come to the ladies' hotel suite, and waited patiently for them to be ready.

'Gus, should I wear my sabre or just bring my musket with the bayonet?' asked Wil, calling out from the sitting room.

'Bring your sabre,' instructed Gus.

'Heavens, we are not going to fight our way out,' said Charlie, plopping herself onto a chair while she tied her shoelaces. 'If they keep our crates, I fear there is little we can do for the moment. We will take them to court.' It pained her to say this. The captain's kind face came to mind, and she gave her head a shake. The order to meet at the warehouse had come from his lieutenant but she felt sure the captain was behind it all or, at the very least, fully informed.

'Their decisions may waver if they see that we have come prepared to take what is ours,' Gus replied.

'That is unlikely. However, I will pack my knife.' Charlie tucked her weapon into its sheath and strapped it on her leg.

'Inês, leave the pistol here,' said Gus firmly. 'If it goes off, it is just as likely to hit one of us or blow your toes off. Just bring yourself.'

Inês left her bedroom and joined them in the sitting room. The other three stared at her, speechless.

Inês, Charlie's beloved friend, the widowed Mrs Alvares, sister of the second Mrs Reyne, the darling woman who had long captured the heart of Mr Gus Jaeger, was today the daughter representing the interests of the Montalto family of Oporto and the townsfolk who were struggling for their livelihoods.

'You look stunning,' said Charlie, smiling tearfully. 'I have never seen you in your traditional dress. I saw you sewing pieces of it and applying the brocade, but I never dreamt you would look so beautiful.'

'Inês, *minha querida, estás linda!*' said Gus, praising her beauty. He picked up both of her hands and twirled her around. 'You have done your hair differently,' he said softly. He was reluctant to release her, but Wil elbowed in.

'Look at you, pretty lady. If Gus does not hurry up and marry you, then I shall.'

Inês seemed to barely hear them. 'My ancestors will not sleep if your government keeps our belongings,' she said with utmost sincerity. 'You must promise me we will not leave empty-handed.'

They nodded determinedly at one another and marched out of the room, drawing stares from other guests as they made their way to the front and out the doors of the hotel.

'Charlie! The ledger! Where is it? Tell me you have not lost it!' cried Inês as they were about to step into their carriage.

'Oh, my word!'

Charlie tore back into her hotel room while everyone waited anxiously. Breathless, she rummaged through her belongings. Grasping the tattered brown ledger that she and her father had carted around the Peninsula for six long years, she clutched it to her chest.

'I have it!' she cried, waving the ledger in the air as she hurried back, her heart racing. 'I cannot believe I almost left it here. Have I forgotten anything else? No? Then let us go and meet with this Lieutenant Sherrington and his naval colleagues.'

Their carriage and wagon stood ready in front of the inn. Optimistically, they had emptied the wagon of purchases and supplies in readiness to load their crates and bags. Charlie took a deep breath. She listened to the cries of gulls circling overhead and turned to shield her face from the damp harbour winds.

TWENTY-FOUR

Inspection at the Warehouse

THE FOUR FRIENDS climbed into Lord Tripp's carriage. An anxious silence settled over them as they travelled to the warehouses near the dockyard.

'Is this the building?' Charlie asked Wil.

'The larger one, next to it,' he replied.

Two armed marines stood at the doorway. The guards opened the loading doors for them to enter. Charlie's group had to squint momentarily to adjust their eyes to the change in light.

Inside, Lieutenant Sherrington sat at a table at the far end of the space. Their stored crates and bags were neatly stacked to one side. Beside the lieutenant stood a burly marine.

'That marine chap is an officer from the *Pontus*,' whispered Wil. 'I remember him well. *Jawohl, er ist ein beleibter Mann; he is a stout fellow*—not someone to cross swords with if you can avoid it.'

Charlie looked around the room. A second table had been set up perpendicular to Lieutenant Sherrington's table. Captain Brantford sat there alone. He rose to his feet as the party entered.

The naval officers, watching the new arrivals, could not fail to be impressed as the party of four advanced. Had this been a full military or naval review, their appearance could not have been more suitable.

The Prussians—freshly shaven, boots shining, equipment polished—looked distinctive in their fur busbys and regimental colours of the 1st KGL Hussars. In their blue-laced jackets with red and gold sashes and fur-trimmed pelisses, they looked every inch the Hanoverian officers they had been for over 15 years of service. Mrs Alvares, elegant and stunning in a red gown trimmed with black lace and gold brocade, brought to mind images of a former lifestyle in the Iberian Peninsula. Though the royal family had long departed from Portugal, she would surely have passed for a woman of the court in former days. Her gown and decorative headpiece reminded them of a vibrant culture in a foreign land.

Walking between the men was the diminutive Miss Charlotte Reyne.

'What has happened to my plain little sparrow?' the captain wondered, looking at the smartly dressed young lady. His heart swelled as he watched her approach.

The *couturier* recommended by Lady Tripp had taken a liking to Charlie. She had been pleased to meet Charlie's request for a gown featuring military motifs currently popular in women's clothing. This one suited Charlie to perfection. She wore a dark blue pelisse, tightly fitted to the high waist, with double gold buttons set down her chest and at the cuffs of her sleeves. Her white muslin gown fell in simple lines over an underlying sky-blue shift. She seemed to float towards the officers, stepping daintily in her leather slippers. On her head, she wore a pert blue hat with short black feathers. Golden braided straps swung from one side. She was, in the captain's eyes, the most charming and beautiful woman he had ever seen, eclipsing anyone in his memory.

'Good day, Captain Brantford,' said Charlie as her group reached the tables. She forced herself not to rush towards him. 'Will you do us the honour of introducing our two parties?'

There were only three chairs provided for them to sit, as Mrs Alvares' attendance was unexpected. The men remained standing through introductions as the marine collected another chair from the front office.

'It is a pleasure to meet you. I am here representing my father, General Sir William Reyne. As well, I will serve as the interpreter for the officers,' Charlie said. 'Colonel Jaeger and his brother, Lieutenant Jaeger, speak English quite well, now that they have been in England for some time. However, I will assist as needed.'

Charlie studied Lieutenant Sherrington's face, wondering if he would recognise her from her journey aboard the *Pontus*. He did not, nor did the attending sergeant of the marines. Captain Brantford's efforts to protect her identity while on board had proved successful. With the passage of time and the dramatic change in her appearance, anyone in the ship's company would find it challenging to connect this pretty young woman with the small lad on board the *Pontus*. Charlie set her worries aside in this regard.

'I suggest we proceed with this interview. Please be seated,' said Lieutenant Sherrington. 'Captain Brantford is here as an observer.' He cleared his throat, looking at his superior.

'Last October, in preparing to unload our ship in Portsmouth, our marine sergeant, Mr Miller here, noticed that one of your crates had been crushed along one side. Some of the contents had fallen out. He felt obliged to repair the damage, at which point it became apparent that the crate was filled with silverware, including utensils, candlesticks, and such, and various other items of high value. He reported this to me as being suspicious, and I informed our captain. He agreed with my suggestion that we offer to store your supplies for you while we conducted our research. An investigation subsequently ensued. Under the provisions of naval regulations published in early August, shipments of valuables potentially originating near Vitoria in Spain are subject to inspection. By such regulations, I am undertaking an examination of your crates in your presence. We will do so now. Should we determine that these items were taken from the baggage trains at Vitoria, be advised that the authority to confiscate your goods is invested with us. Any involved military personnel will face disciplinary action. Civilians are liable to prosecution. Am I clear?'

'You are, indeed,' Charlie replied in a steady voice, pursing her lips.

Inês, likewise, outwardly appeared calm, but her cheeks were red. She stared furiously ahead. Gus and Wil sat perfectly straight and still.

Charlie's group took comfort in the fact that the shipments aboard HMS *Marfisa*, the hospital ship on which Inês had travelled, were already in their possession. They had safely stored many of their items in the bank or the new warehouse at Chellisbury. The crates being examined today were largely those under General Reyne's and Charlie's care and management. Several also contained items that originated in Oporto.

Sergeant Miller and his assistant opened each of the crates and undid the fastenings on several tightly packed army bags. Occasionally, the sergeant or his helper exclaimed in surprise as the valuables became visible to the group.

Lieutenant Sherrington spoke quietly to the sergeant, who left the room. He reappeared in five minutes with four more armed marines who stationed themselves inside the loading doors.

'Captain Brantford, may we speak?' Charlie rose to her feet and took her ledger to the captain, laying it on the table in front of him. The captain replied that the lieutenant, as the officer investigating and reporting on a possible infraction, should receive it first. The captain said he would review the ledger afterwards.

'As you wish,' she said curtly, withdrawing the ledger and pinning it tightly against her chest. She bit her lip, surprised and hurt to realise that the captain intended to remain impartial and not interfere with proceedings.

'Shall we start here?' She beckoned to Inês and walked to the first crate. 'These contents belong to the extended Montalto family, long-established merchants from the Douro valley. The enemy burnt their homes. Most of the men in town were killed or, if they served in the military, transported to serve as part of France's foreign legions on the Russian front. Mrs Alvares, will you explain the contents, please? Gentlemen, these are listed in a separate section towards the back of our ledger, where we have grouped items that are being shipped and sold. The earlier entries pertain to items belonging to our soldiers. I will keep the ledger here for the moment, to consult as we proceed.'

Mrs Alvares picked up a large silver carving fork and searched in the crate for the matching knife. She held these affectionately in her hands and said, 'We last used these in the autumn of 1807 at a large family gathering before *Monsieur* Bonaparte's army and his Spanish troops crossed our border. The table was set for twenty-four of our relatives.' She paused and drew a deep breath, remembering the faces of family members whom she had not seen since. 'Would you like me to write down the names of those who attended our dinner?' she asked in a sarcastic tone.

'That is unnecessary,' replied Lieutenant Sherrington, shaking his head.

Inês rummaged deeper inside the crate, lifted out a silver candlestick, unwrapped some utensils, and laid out an elegant silver place setting on the captain's nearby table.

'The silverware and all the contents of this crate are the rightful property of the Montalto family. The letter "M" is engraved on the flatware, here, and here,' she said, pointing out the elegant carving on the handles.

'What purpose does it serve to transport these items to England, Mrs Alvares?'

'I intend to sell them at auction,' she replied. 'With the assistance of Miss Reyne and her relatives, we are gathering resources to help restore the Montalto property and restart my family's business in Oporto. No one there can afford to buy these items from us. We have no benefactor to lend us money. It makes no sense to keep the silver in storage whilst we struggle for revenue to rebuild our business and manage the vineyards. For over two decades, my family held contracts to supply port for our Portuguese fleets and later the merchant vessels heading to the colonies. Those days are behind us. The men in our family are deceased or missing. Along with my sister, presently somewhere in Spain, I will seek a contract between the Montalto family and the British Navy. We are optimistic this can be negotiated at the right time. Selling our family's silver will help to set us up for success.'

No one expected this. Captain Brantford instantly felt as though a huge weight had been lifted from his shoulders. He had desperately hoped the general had not lied to him and had not been complicit in theft. This explanation, though relating to one crate only, dispelled any doubts and gave him the assurance he sought. He unclasped his hands and looked encouragingly towards Miss Reyne.

The lieutenant and the marines listened with full attention, half fascinated and half in disbelief. The sergeant lifted the lid on the next crate. Inside were small bags, each filled with strange assortments of jewellery and personal items. Charlie lifted out one of the small cloth bags and opened it. She handled the contents gently, withdrawing a worn diary with a folded letter tucked inside, a miniature portrait in a small wooden frame, a man's handkerchief, some heavy brass buttons, and a pair of women's earrings.

'Ah,' she said with a sad smile towards Gus. 'This bag belongs to Mr Haynes. I have not looked at this in ages.'

Charlie slapped the sergeant's hand away as the man leaned in to pick up the next bag. 'Step back, Sergeant Miller. I will pass things to you. Take care not to mix things up.'

She turned to Lieutenant Sherrington and spoke again of the contents of the first bag. 'This is the property of Mr George Haynes, who is deceased. His belongings are in my care, to be delivered to his wife. We do not know her address. It will take some time to find her.'

She opened the next bag filled with an odd assortment of jewellery, a large collection of men's rings, and Portuguese coins. Charlie looked at the point where she had stitched the number two-hundred and eighty-six neatly alongside the bottom seam of bag. She placed her ledger on the captain's table, turned the pages carefully to keep the sheets intact, and traced her finger along the line of entry opposite the matching number.

'You will not be pleased with how this collection was acquired, Lieutenant Sherrington, but it is a common practice on the battlefield. These rings were removed from corpses and collected by two brothers and a lady who followed the baggage train. The soldiers are members of my father's regiment, first battalion. They asked me to sell these on their behalves and hold the proceeds until after the war, in hopes they might survive to claim it. If neither return, we will attempt to find a relative. Their lady friend, unfortunately, died a few years ago, during a retreat.'

Their process of examination continued, with the sergeant randomly selecting bags for inspection. After examining a few dozen, they opened a bag filled with teeth, listed under the name of a highly ranked officer. Charlie explained that the officer was "sending them home for his brother's use".

The lieutenant, disturbed by the nature of the contents, ordered them to proceed to the next crate.

TWENTY-FIVE

Resolution

THE AFTERNOON'S INVESTIGATION, diligent and meticulous, wore on in this tedious fashion, with episodes of examining and explaining, consulting the ledger, and naming the owners according to the lists. There were hundreds of odd and unique listings and an almost monotonous repetition of types of valuables. Some packets had no monetary worth whatsoever and were purely sentimental; others had astounding resale value.

Midway through an examination, the lieutenant again bade them stop. He exchanged a few words with the captain. 'We will break for refreshments. We have no tea available, but perhaps you will take a glass of wine,' he said to the ladies. 'Gentlemen, we can offer you some ale, generously provided by the front office.'

The group milled around, forming small groups for conversation during the pause in the work. The marines present in the warehouse were from the *Pontus,* and several recollected meeting the Prussian gentlemen during their travels aboard the *Pontus.* They asked them what they intended to do with the collection of Prussian sabres that had been carefully bundled and stored in one of the army bags.

'They belonged to our friends and were issued by our army in Hanover. They are not the property of the British army,' Gus said solemnly. 'If Prussia ever regains Hanover, I will take these home to their families.'

Seeing Charlie standing apart, lost in her own thoughts, Captain Brantford moved to her side. He believed there was nothing he could say to restore the feeling of friendship between them. Selfishly, he merely wanted to stand near her, keep her company, and listen to her if she wished to say anything. To his great surprise, she spoke to him almost immediately after he came to her side.

'Did you find my drawings in your cabin?' she asked him shyly. 'I tucked the smaller ones into your books. You should have about thirty of these once you have them all. I hope you liked them.'

'I did, indeed,' he said, startled that this was what she wanted to say to him. 'Thank you. I especially appreciated the small portrait you drew of yourself in the guise of a German interpreter. It was wise of you to limit the drawings to those known to be aboard my ship. Anyone might have discovered the pictures, had not I found them.'

Her mind was occupied with other matters.

'I recently met with Lieutenant Niles at the home of my uncle,' she said hesitantly. 'We had much to say to one another.'

'Did you?' asked the captain, unexpectedly jealous.

'He mentioned to me that someone close to you had died,' she said, blinking back tears. 'I told him that if I were to see you soon, I would ask you if the letters of this person's death had reached you.' She dared not say more, in case he was not yet aware of his own father's death.

'I see. You speak of my father. He died in November,' he said, touched by her remarks. 'I have received several letters since that time relating to his death and family matters. You need not be worried for me in this regard.'

'I am so relieved to hear it! May I offer my deepest condolences, and those of my family?'

'Accepted,' he replied.

He had no wish to speak to Miss Reyne, or anyone for that matter, of his strained relationship with his father or the chaotic circumstances of Mr Brantford's death and family affairs. He saw her troubled expression and said, 'Truly, you need not be anxious on my account. I have had time to connect with family members and to reflect on my father's life and our relationship. Due to my choice of career and time spent away, I barely saw him over the past decade. His passing naturally affects our family, but I confess I was not close to him. I grieve most for my brother, the eldest son, who shoulders responsibilities for us all.'

She patted his arm, her face scrunched in sympathy.

'I am grateful for your interest. I am surprised you are on speaking terms with me at all,' he said quietly. Her concern warmed his heart.

'How so? You are simply doing your duty. It was your marine sergeant who discovered our wares, and he reported to his lieutenant, who then brought the matter to you. I fail to see how it could not come to this. Your hand was forced. I am familiar with that concept.'

He looked at her, filled with respect. He felt grateful, for the sake of their time shared together and for his own feelings that deepened each time he encountered her, that she chose not to blame him for the present situation. As the captain of a ship in His Majesty's service, and someone who by nature treated people fairly, he could neither ignore naval regulations nor overlook the legitimate findings of his own men, much as he had wished to do so in this instance. He nonetheless held final say in the matter and retained the ability to intervene if circumstances called for it. Yet, believing his instincts would not prove him wrong, he let the investigation proceed. While he had learnt not to believe everything Charlie Reyne said, having witnessed her spinning some truly remarkable lies, he had seen first-hand her endless compassion and pure motives. Everything he had supposed, everything he knew about her, was holding true.

Lieutenant Sherrington spoke again, directing them back to their positions for the investigation to continue. Three more crates remained to be examined. They opened the heaviest of these next. To the lieutenant's surprise, it was stuffed with family diaries, cookbooks, atlases, accounting books, and novels, all in Portuguese.

'I did not realise we were transporting the Oporto Library. Mrs Alvares, why did not you leave these in Portugal with your friends?' asked the lieutenant, bewildered.

'My friends are no longer there, sir. I have no certainty that my family home will not be ransacked again, or burnt, with scavengers and deserters rampant in the country. Our home is presently standing empty whilst my sister is in Spain. These books are precious to us, so I brought them with me.'

'I see. And in this box?' he gestured to a marine to open one of the smaller crates. Inside were a young girl's dress, tattered and faded, and a small pair of shoes. Among the children's items, the marine lifted out a variety of belongings—a childish drawing of a fat hog, a bag of marbles, a slingshot, and an Indian baby-doll tightly wrapped in tissues.

'Those belong to me,' said Charlie, gently picking up the toys. She caressed the doll's broken-off fingers and smoothed its hair, half of which was missing. 'My father stored these items in Oporto at the home of Mrs Alvares's sister Sofia. He insisted I bring these back to England with me. He said I might need them one day.'

Wil burst out laughing. Gus snorted and elbowed his brother.

'Let us see the last crate, thank you, Sergeant,' said Lieutenant Sherrington dourly, gesturing towards a large box behind the others.

Charlie felt sure everyone could hear her heart beating as the marine uncovered the contents. This was the most important crate in Charlie's mind. Herein lay the real treasures. These were the items they desperately wanted to transport away from Vitoria. Once word got out that the senior officers were reclaiming valuables that might have been taken from the Vitoria baggage train, she and her father knew at once that the belongings of their soldiers would be searched. Their immediate aim was to get the troop's most valuable property—all of which the soldiers had collected over several years, was in some cases designated to fund operations at Chellisbury and was unrelated to the Vitoria incident—into safe custody and protected from the search. The final crate brimmed with expensive jewellery, specie of high value, and, most precious of all, a large wooden box, inlaid with mother of pearl, full of letters from soldiers.

'I must explain this one for you, sir. You are in the navy. I understand that when you capture ships, your seamen share prize money according to a strict ratio. The army follows similar principles, but according to our soldiers the process is not well organised. I have heard them complain that their officers often keep most of the valuables for themselves. Over the years, the men brought their treasures to me, awarded after battles and in the capture of enemy supplies. I recorded their items and stored these for them. We had two options: bring everything with us while on campaign or store it someplace to reclaim later. On two occasions, the soldiers lost all their valuables during a sudden retreat when we abandoned our passenger trains. Over time, when it was the enemy's turn to flee after major battles, the troops gained new items. Some gained treasures through bartering, acquiring a gold ring or other jewellery in exchange for food or a pair of worn boots. Yes, the battalions under my father's governance were present at Vitoria, and proudly so. Yes, these items would be regarded with suspicion. No, our troops did not go into town, nor were they anywhere near the fields beyond the town. Our men were stationed in the rear and employed after the fighting in bandaging the wounded and burying the dead. The contents in this crate did not originate in Vitoria. We removed them as quickly as we could from the vicinity to prevent them from being confiscated.'

The officers listened carefully to her account.

'Miss Reyne, our records show that your father sent you from Vitoria almost immediately after the battle and with an armed escort. Rather than travelling northeast towards the coast of Spain behind the troops, you went west first, and eventually arrived in Oporto with your crates. Can you explain why you left so suddenly on the heels of such a clear victory? I understand these officers here accompanied you.'

'We were part of an armed escort taking patients to the nearest camp hospital, which lay to the west, as well as accompanying Miss Reyne for her personal protection,' said Gus, taking umbrage with the insinuation that they were fleeing with stolen loot from the train. 'San Sebastián was at that time still in the hands of the French. We were a vulnerable entourage. There was no safe passage to the coast at that time.'

'I am an experienced medical helper,' added Charlie. 'It was natural that I should leave immediately to assist with our wounded. As well, my father was doubtful as to how far the French forces would retreat. They are renowned for their skill and determination. They had just lost their entire supply train and a priceless baggage train from Madrid laden with valuables from six years' occupancy in Spain. It was entirely possible that they might double back with reinforcements. We could have been under counterattack within hours or days. My father determined that I should leave at once. I convinced him it was wise to take the soldiers' belongings with me. My father then directed that I should come home to England. We agreed that it was time for me to do so.'

'How long have you been gone from England?'

'Do you mean in Portugal? Close to six years, roughly. Prior to that time, I had been in India for two years. I spent many months travelling from India home to England. Then I became stranded in Portugal when my ship crashed ashore.'

Captain Brantford bowed his head, quietly envisioning the endless trials the young woman had faced. The lieutenant, also shaken by her remarks, tried to understand how this lovely young lady could possibly have been accompanying the soldiers during active conflicts over such a long period. How had she survived? He beckoned the captain to join him. The three officers stepped away for a private conversation. They were gone for close to half an hour. When they returned, the lieutenant spoke.

'I would like each of you to explicitly affirm, in clear language, that you are not transporting valuables stolen from Vitoria. Please rise and state your name as you do so. Gentlemen, we will begin with you.'

They stood in turn and made their testimonies.

'Sign here.'

'Miss Reyne, you are next. Are you transporting goods stolen from the French army's baggage train in Vitoria?'

Charlie was about to say no when she realised she was wearing her necklace from Vitoria. Her hand rose involuntarily to touch the pendant given to her by Lieutenant Niles, lying against her chest. She seemed on the verge of confessing this at any moment. She was struggling to take off her necklace, and searching for words to explain the matter, when the captain rose from his seat and came up behind her.

'Has your clasp come undone, Miss Reyne? Here, let me help you with that.'

He lifted the hair curling against her neck. He pulled her

fingers away from the fastener, his large hands firmly gripping both of her small hands in his for a moment then releasing them as he slowly refastened her necklace.

'What a unique pendant,' he said, admiring it, speaking loudly enough for all to hear. 'Be careful not to lose it. How disappointing if it should slip off here in this large space. One of us would likely step on it, and that would be the end of it. I daresay it is special to you.'

'It is. Thank you, Captain.'

His movement, his words of support, and his steadying hands had given her the time she needed to collect her thoughts. Her cheeks were pink. She could still feel the warmth of his hands against her neck.

'Let me assure you, Lieutenant Sherrington, I have not stolen any property from Vitoria,' she said, looking straight into his eyes. 'None of us have. Mrs Alvares was not with us at the time. She was in Oporto assisting at the camp hospital. These crates were filled over many years, and long before the Vitoria engagement. As I explained, we were personally involved at the time in the battle and afterwards in the care of the wounded and injured. We did not open and add anything new to any of these crates. The items in these crates did not originate in Vitoria.' She, too, affixed her name to the document signed earlier by the Jaegers.

The officers conferred a final time.

'Thank you for your time. We find your explanations reasonable and have reached an agreement not to confiscate your items. This matter is closed. You may remove your crates. I am told you have a large wagon and a carriage with you. My men will help you load,' said Lieutenant Sherrington. He passed his dossier on the case to the captain and saluted. The captain placed a hand on his shoulder.

'Thank you, Lieutenant. I appreciate your diligence, as always.'

'Miss Reyne,' said the captain, turning to speak to her and

her party. 'Do you stay at the Crown? We are there ourselves this evening. Perhaps we can persuade you to dine with us, to atone for your loss of time this afternoon and thank you for your patience in this matter. Are you free to dine at six?'

Charlie looked pleased. Seeing no signs of objection from her friends, she said, 'We shall be delighted, but do you mind delaying until seven? We must deliver some of the crates to the bank first.'

'Seven it is. Here, let me get this for you.' He picked up her doll on the table, placed it carefully back into the crate of children's items, and carried it out for her to the family carriage.

TWENTY-SIX

Accidental Disclosure

Gus GOT OUT of the carriage in front of the Crown and steadied Mrs Alvares as she stepped down. He let go of her hand reluctantly as Charlie bounded out behind her.

'My word! Look who is here! Uncle John!' cried Charlie, staring at Lord Tripp who was standing near the front door of the inn. 'Good heavens,' she called to her uncle, 'we were not expecting you to arrive until tomorrow. And Aunt Lydia! You have come all this way! How delightful to see you both. I cannot believe you are here!'

'When your uncle said he was to meet you at the bank tomorrow, I said to him, if you will but come one day early, I will accompany you and we can make a little pleasure trip of it. We can dine together, said I, and do a little shopping, and see our niece and friends before they leave for Chellisbury. Your uncle agreed that it would make for a lovely outing. So here we are.'

'Well, we are happy to see you,' said Charlie. She enthusiastically hugged her aunt, squeezing the air out of her. Inês, beside her, steadied Lady Tripp to keep the slender woman from collapsing under the exuberance of Charlie's embrace.

Lord and Lady Tripp were astonished to see how well-dressed everyone was for an afternoon purportedly spent on chores and errands.

'You have worn such finery today,' said the uncle, his glance travelling appreciatively around the group. 'Gentlemen, I have not seen you in uniform before. You look very striking, indeed.'

'Mrs Alvares, did you bring this gown from Portugal?' asked the aunt, oblivious to the steady handwork done over several weeks by Inês in gathering and adding lace, embroidering golden rosettes, and preparing her extravagant headpiece while staying at Greydon Hall. 'I daresay you will set a new fashion. And, Charlie, you look positively charming in your fine clothes.' It puzzled Aunt Lydia to hear that while appearing so resplendent they had only been to a warehouse and a bank. 'Have you made plans for the evening, then?' she asked them. 'We are hoping to dine with you.'

'We are just about to meet in the dining room with some friends, a few naval officers. They stored our crates for us when we first arrived, and the captain, in fact, led the convoy that brought us home to England,' explained Charlie. 'I hope you will join us, if you do not mind dining with a larger party.'

'Not at all,' said Lord Tripp.

Moving to the back of the carriage to access the luggage rack, Gus and Wil lifted down their army bag filled with Prussian sabres to take it up to their room. Lord Tripp, fascinated to see the styling on the sabre hilts protruding from the bag, was full of questions to ask the men.

'Are you settled in your rooms already? Aunty, come with us whilst we drop off a few items. Uncle can visit with Gus and Wil. We can meet in the dining room at seven. Come, I am dying to get out of these tight little shoes and put on something else. Our room is on the second floor at the rear. This way, dearest.'

They were at last, after chatting and freshening up after a long day's activities, seated in the dining room. Lord Tripp looked down the table at his niece and her friends. Lady Tripp, opposite him at the end of the table, chatted with Wil on one side and Lieutenant Sherrington on the other. Charlie, seated to her uncle's right, was delighted to have Captain Brantford at her side. Across from them, pleased with the arrangement, Inês and Gus had an animated conversation in German and Portuguese, occasionally breaking into English as common ground.

'Lieutenant Sherrington,' said Lord Tripp in his deep voice, 'I understand you offered our family and friends secure storage space upon their return to England last autumn. I have heard there has been a great deal of theft from the warehouses. How very considerate of you to provide access to a guarded site.'

The friends and the naval officers, suffering varying degrees of awkwardness, looked at one another. Each was inclined to let the remark pass without comment.

'Let me thank you,' Lord Tripp continued, 'on my brother's behalf, for your kindness. And Captain Brantford, I understand we are to thank you and the lieutenant for the safe transport of the convoy that brought everyone home last autumn. They are all now enjoying some peace away from the noise and dangers of war, I am sure.'

'We were simply performing our duty, sir.'

'Were you acquainted with our niece and her friends before today, Captain?' asked Lord Tripp, wanting to see how the man would answer. His brother-in-law had written him to say he wanted to find out more about the man's background.

Charlie replied before the captain had an opportunity to speak.

'Yes, we have met several times,' she informed her uncle. 'Do you recall meeting Lieutenant Niles at the Weyburns' ball? Well, he is a close friend to Captain Brantford and his entire family. Who would have thought it? Mrs Alvares and I met both Captain Brantford and Lieutenant Niles in the military field hospital outside of Oporto. Here in Portsmouth, we met one another along the promenade, and our two parties were introduced. Then, we were seated near one another at dinner here at the Crown and saw each other again the following day. You may tell my father that we are almost old friends. Wait, never mind, he already knows this. I asked Captain Brantford to take a letter to Spain for him, and he kindly brought one back for me.'

'Did he, indeed?' Lord Tripp listened to this account with interest, watching his niece's expression. He then shifted his target and studied the captain's face. He looked down the table at his wife, who was listening to this exchange and smiling knowingly from the far end. She was privy to the letter from the general to her husband. She had heard about this handsome captain and had taken a keen interest in meeting him.

'My niece forgot one of her notebooks at Greydon Hall,' said the aunt. 'It is a sketchbook filled with images of some captain aboard his ship. Are those images of you, then, Captain Brantford?'

Charlie looked in shock at her aunt, her cheeks turning bright pink.

'Where is my book? Did you bring it with you?'

'It is in my room. I will give it to you after dinner.'

'Dear Uncle,' Charlie said sweetly, 'Mrs Alvares and I travelled on one of the hospital ships – the *Marfisa*. Do not you remember my saying so? The Jaegers were the ones aboard the frigate.'

'It is as you say, of course,' interjected Uncle Tripp, 'but your aunt showed me drawings of some captain on board what looks like a warship. I suppose all captains look somewhat alike. How did you get such a close look at the inside of a frigate, when you were travelling on a hospital ship?'

He looked suspiciously at the captain, finding the resemblance to the man in the drawings to be particularly strong. It was not as though there was only one drawing. He counted fifteen or more drawings of some gentleman looking very much like this captain. It puzzled him immensely.

'Uncle, do you remember me mentioning that I regularly drew battle positions for my father to include in his field reports?'

He nodded.

'When I have not been to some location in person, as was often the case for these reports, people would describe the situation to me. I then drew pictures based on what others observed. The Jaegers were on board the captain's and the lieutenant's ship, which was a frigate, and they told me all about it. I simply drew what they described for me, as a kind of keepsake for them.'

'I see,' he said. He bent his head and added so only she could hear him: 'And so you provided them with multiple images of a captain's handsome face. How very fortunate for them to have such memorable recollections of their voyage.'

The letter that Uncle Tripp had from his brother-in-law not too long ago stated that some Captain Brantford chap, if his circumstances changed, and having taken a shine to his daughter, might come around to see her. If so, the uncle was tasked with finding out what sort of man he was and letting the general know whether he thought him to be a good prospect. From the looks of his niece and the captain, chatting happily to one another and captivated by each other's company, the general was right to take an interest.

'It must have been complicated to find my wife's brother in Spain and to meet with him. That would have taken some effort, you being a naval man, and him stationed on land in the middle of who-knows-where.'

'While we encounter occasional delays and misdirection, our communication systems are nonetheless excellent. It was not difficult to locate him. We met briefly, in early December,' the captain replied. 'We were guarding supply ships in the harbour near San Sebastián. General Reyne and several battalions under his command were encamped nearby, preparing to march east to join General Wellesley's main forces. Their camp was not far from shore. I was able to deliver Miss Reyne's letter in person and exchange greetings with the general. I found him to be well,' he said, turning to Miss Reyne. 'He was preparing for an early departure. By the way, Mrs Alvares, I met your sister whilst I was at the camp. I have heard good news of this latest campaign. There have been endless skirmishes and battles along the Spanish coast and into the mountains in the past eight weeks. According to the latest report, our troops are making steady progress. We received a bulletin yesterday describing recent allied victories in the north of Spain. The most recent battle in the report was almost two weeks ago, so the news should appear soon in the London papers, perhaps today or tomorrow. I trust that your father remains in good health, Miss Reyne. I hope that he and his men were able to take a few days to regroup after these events.'

There was a tone of optimism in the captain's voice. Everyone had been following the news of successful battles in Europe and the Peninsula, hoping that the day would come when Emperor Napoleon Bonaparte's *Grande Armée* would no longer be a threat on the continent.

Lord Tripp listened attentively to the conversation and watched his niece closely. He had no difficulty ascertaining his niece's regard. Her feelings of admiration and respect appeared sincere; she made no effort to dissemble. Unabashed, she hung on every word spoken by the captain.

'She completely and utterly adores the man, this much anyone can tell,' he said to his wife later that evening, shaking his head. 'She could not take her eyes off him.'

'Yet, he is very circumspect,' replied his wife. 'It is no wonder since he is leaving again so soon and cannot spend any time on land with her at present.'

Lord Tripp liked the man. He detected care and concern towards his niece but saw nothing that was flirtatious or secretive.

The captain's conversation, while spoken for all to hear, was intended mainly for her ears. The extra attention he paid, turning to her, including her, reassuring her, was in Lord Tripp's view rather heart-warming. Knowing she would be worried about her father and his troops, the captain's tone was set to reassure her, where that was possible.

To everyone's surprise, before dessert was set out for them, the waiter arrived at their table carrying a tray of glasses.

'Ladies and gentlemen, will you do me the honour of joining a toast with me? I wish to congratulate a remarkable gentleman here with us this evening,' said Captain Brantford. On acceptance by the guests and a nod of permission from the captain, the waiter placed a glass in front of everyone, offering a choice of white wine or lemonade.

'Congratulations, Lieutenant Sherrington—or rather, our newly promoted Captain Sherrington! A more upright, honest man, a better friend, and a finer sailor, I could never find. You have long been exemplary in fulfilling your duties. At last, you are to be rewarded.'

His colleague looked at him in shock, surprised to see the captain passing him a letter from inside his coat. The letter bore the seal of the Navy Board.

'It arrived today,' Brantford said, smiling. 'Since the admiral is away for a few more weeks, I gained the privilege of delivering this news to you on his behalf.'

'Everyone, please join me in congratulating Captain Sherrington for his promotion. To you, good man,' said the captain proudly. 'In a few weeks, you will take command of HMS *Falcon*. It is an honour well deserved and long overdue. Well done, Captain!'

Sherrington coughed and straightened his cravat.

Lord Tripp's quest to discern the relationship between Miss Charlotte Reyne and Captain Henry Brantford was, by this unexpected announcement, temporarily put aside. The conversation shifted towards the new captain's exploits, well described by his colleague, and supported with votes of approval by Wil and Gus, who testified to the man's skills and abilities as witnessed by themselves.

'I only doubted you once,' said Wil, 'and that was when our Miss Charlie stopped that man from jumping overboard on the frigate. You and that midshipman fellow—what was his name, Norcross?—got upset with Miss Charlie for slapping that old soldier. But he served under the general's command, and knew who she was, and held her in the deepest respect. That is why she could calm him down in that way. It is a good thing he was half out of his mind, or he would have given away Miss Charlie's identity any moment.'

The room fell silent. Everyone stared at Wil. Inês gasped. The captain gaped at him in disbelief. Gus put his head in his hands. Lady Tripp looked bewildered. Lord Tripp and Captain Sherrington, moments later, looked in confusion towards Captain Brantford.

Charlie burst out laughing, snorting through her nose.

'Oh, this is too good,' she cried, wiping her eyes. 'We have successfully protected this information for four and a half months and after one pint of ale and a glass of wine, you have blurted it out to everyone. Dearest Wil, you are so precious.'

Charlie laughed so hard she had to hold her sides. She was trying to suck in air to breathe. Inês started giggling. No one else thought it was the least bit funny.

'I do not understand at all,' said Aunt Lydia.

'Of course not,' said Charlie, barely able to speak.

The captain waited for a moment for Charlie to gain control of herself, then laid his hand on her arm.

'That is enough,' he said sternly. Oddly, he felt like laughing along with her, so bizarre was it to hear this disclosure from her good friend. The matter, however, was far too serious. This was no time for levity.

'Miss Reyne,' said Captain Brantford, taking control of the situation, 'if you and the others would excuse us, I would like to speak in private with Captain Sherrington and Lord Tripp. Do you mind leaving us to our conversation? If not, and you wish to linger here, I am sure we can find a quiet corner in the tavern further down the street.'

'No, no, stay, by all means,' said Charlie, taking a deep breath, trying not to laugh. 'We will leave you. Come, everyone, let us give these gentlemen some time alone. Dear Aunt, may we see you to your room, and have a word with you?'

She looked with smiling eyes at Gus and Wil and grasped Wil's sleeve.

'Do not worry yourselves. We are in the captain's good care. It will feel better to have it out in the open, amongst family and this small group of close friends. Come, let us leave them be. Aunty, do you mind if the men join us for a visit as well?'

As they left the dining room, the captain could hear Charlie's laughter down the hall. Once they were gone, the captain arranged for Charlie's uncle and the new captain to be seated at a smaller table in the furthest corner of the dining room. No one questioned his reasoning. They were deeply troubled and anxious to hear what the captain had to say.

'It is a long story,' he informed them, ordering refreshments for the table. 'I hardly know where to begin. Sherrington, do you recall when I got cut by the old soldier and the young interpreter came to my aid? As you just heard that boy was, in fact, Miss Reyne. I did not know it at the time, but that was the moment when I first started to suspect she was not some young interpreter boy at all, but someone in disguise. But let me go back a little and tell you about my first encounter with Miss Reyne, and Mrs Alvares also, in Oporto. It will help you understand how and why Miss Reyne came to be on our ship. Captain Sherrington, I hope I may trust your discretion as a friend, and colleague, and you, Lord Tripp, as her guardian. If you do not agree with my decisions, I will understand and accept that you need to act in accordance with your own principles. But hear me out first. Sherrington, do you like this red? Is it too dry? Perhaps I should have ordered white,' he said apologetically.

'No, no, this is fine,' said Sherrington, encouraging his friend to continue.

The captain swirled the liquid in his glass.

'It was while we were in the Oporto harbour. We stayed there a few days to reload supplies and give our men a much-deserved rest. Sherrington, you will recall I went with our surgeon to take our lads on sick leave over to the army hospital near there. That is where I met Miss Reyne. She dressed as a woman at the time,' he said, smiling in reminiscence, his tone softening. 'I learnt a great deal about her and about other women helping in the army camps overseas. I can assure you, gentlemen, you can be very proud of our English ladies who are in the Peninsula.'

The men listened intently. The candles in the wall bracket burnt lower. They talked long into the evening about Miss Charlotte Reyne and her remarkable friends who had dined with them this evening. Lord Tripp shared what he had heard about the plans underway at Chellisbury, about turning it into a recovery home, complete with a distribution warehouse for the Montalto family business, the humble beginnings of a new village, workshops to generate revenues for the residents, and the group's dreams and hopes for future developments.

'I thought at first my brother-in-law had lost his wits and was building a massive new home for himself to inhabit on his return,' said the uncle incredulously, absorbing the new information. 'He already has a sizeable estate. The plans for Chellisbury, and the way it is organised, are extraordinary. It is completely outside the usual order of things. And it is all managed by this young slip of a miss who, with no experience in these matters, has everything in perfect order. She continually puts the affairs of her father and his troops before her own, or perhaps her interests are inseparable from theirs. I hardly know. I have never been so shocked in my life to see what they have built, nor have I ever met anyone so generous with energy and time as my niece. I daresay her friends are similar in character.'

During their conversation, Charlie's unwavering commitment, deep sense of purpose, unusual and often flawed reasoning, hot temper, and wild and frequently childlike antics became better known to them all.

Captain Sherrington, thinking of himself in his friend Brantford's position, could find no other solution than the one Captain Brantford had arrived at to protect the young lady. He wondered if he would have had the courage to make the same decisions as the captain had done. It amazed him to think that Brantford had not asked him to overlook the luggage incident and supposed his friend's confidence had been high in achieving the outcome he expected. Sherrington admired his friend the more for it. He fully understood the risk Brantford had taken, putting his career at stake to protect the general's reputation and Miss Reyne's dignity while shielding her from the ramifications of such reckless behaviour.

'Good lord,' Sherrington said, 'no wonder you disappeared into the forest in the middle of the night in San Sebastián. You felt it imperative to meet with her father!'

Much to his surprise, Lord Tripp had come to cherish his niece in the few months she had lived with him and his wife. Never had his home felt so alive and filled with joy and energy as it did in these recent times. He felt a huge sense of relief that it was this captain, this reasonable, thoughtful man, who had discovered his niece's behaviour and not someone who would have turned her in without any regard for her well-being. As he watched the men converse, his respect for these naval officers grew. He understood that those who risked their lives together protecting others shared a tremendous bond. He felt a small twinge of envy at the close friendship between them.

For a moment, he wished his life had had a fraction of the camaraderie and excitement in it that these two shared. He was not, however, a man to fool himself. He was not the type, and well he knew it, to have given up his role, his advantages, his position in society, to take on a life of adventure and danger, regardless of the financial reward for which these men were eligible in their chosen profession.

'Who is aware of all that you have shared with us?' asked the uncle.

'Only a few. Miss Reyne's father and his lady friend, her friends who are here with her, Lieutenant Niles, whom you have met, and now yourselves. Miss Reyne will have told her aunt by now. I trust that is everyone. There are ramifications and consequences far beyond those Miss Reyne already faces should this information extend beyond this group. May I count on your discretion?'

They assured him of their silence.

'Heaven forbid we should any of us blurt it out as Mr Jaeger managed to do this evening,' said Sherrington. 'Once she recovers her senses, she will be ready to shoot him!'

'Indeed,' said Captain Brantford.

They looked at one another. Captain Brantford lowered his head and covered his mouth. Even so, they could see his broad smile. When he looked up, the men were enjoying the recollection just as he was.

'Do you know, were I not already a married man,' Sherrington murmured, 'I would be half in love with this niece of yours, Lord Tripp. My word, she is an adventuresome and resilient lass. The experiences she has faced, and over such an extended period, are simply incredible.'

Captain Brantford fell silent. Her path in life was not one he would have chosen for her.

Lord Tripp sensed that Captain Brantford was highly conflicted in his feelings towards his niece; or, at least, in whether he would drop his reserve and actively pursue courtship. More than once had he watched the captain during dinner time, sitting next to her, with his lingering looks and wistful expression. Lord Tripp looked at the man in sympathy.

'From what I have seen and learnt about her, my niece is not an easy young lady for a man to know and understand. Let us hope some gentleman comes to appreciate her one day and can bring her some well-deserved happiness.'

Captain Brantford clenched his fists under the table.

'What is next in your schedule, Captain Brantford? Are you and Captain Sherrington sailing back to the Peninsula?'

'We leave in three days. We are escorting supply ships for General Wellesley's troops and some smaller merchant vessels headed to Lisbon. I take solace knowing that I have Captain Sherrington at my side for a short time until he takes command of the *Falcon*.'

Captain Sherrington nodded, his pride and his joy in receiving this recognition evident in his expression.

'Since you are here for a few days, if you have time, gentlemen, perhaps we can share another meal. I can speak for our party in welcoming the opportunity. During dinner, I overheard you discuss a leave planned in May,' Lord Tripp said to Brantford. 'Will you stay in this vicinity for any length of time? If so, my wife and I will be pleased if you will visit us. Also, we are to host a spring ball at our home. Everyone takes a turn at these things. Our friends and neighbours are indicating that we should be next. Miss Charlotte has never had a proper coming-out ball.

May we count on you to grace our event, in her honour, and wish her well?'

'Thank you,' said the captain, bowing his head. While he could not announce it, he knew that when he returned and his leave began, he would be seeking the company of his future wife to discuss arrangements for his wedding. 'I am not able to predict my schedule this far in advance. My last leave was cancelled. Right now, the navy is needing every available ship and every able sailor on duty.'

'I will send you a formal invitation closer to the date. You can reply and join us as you are able. You and your wife are welcome also, Captain Sherrington. It would be an honour for us to welcome you. Let us see how your schedules look by then. Who knows, perhaps this war will cease one of these fine days. Let us hope so. It has been a relentless struggle. How many more lives will be lost, I wonder, before this war ends?'

TWENTY-SEVEN

News along the Front

STANDING ON THE quarterdeck of the *Pontus,* Captain Henry Brantford shielded his eyes from the mid-afternoon sun. He stared across the prow, surveying the sea, assessing wind conditions, and determining their best tack across the turbulent waters of the Bay of Biscay.

The *Pontus* was known for her speed. Today, with her sails tightly trimmed, she was travelling between ten and eleven knots. Certainly, the ship's design reflected a critical emphasis on both speed and stability. Yet Brantford was a firm believer that the successes of his men hinged only partly on attributes of the ship. Moreso, he admired his sailors for their ever-improving skills and efficiency, adding layers of excellence to how they functioned as a team. Their reputation for success was no accident.

In conjunction with transporting military supplies, Brantford had for his past two trips been specially tasked with conveying military messages between naval and army headquarters and outposts. Communications could not be left to chance. They had made good time in sailing from Portsmouth. Strong winds propelled them rapidly towards the port at Pasajes, east of San Sebastián. From here, the military dispatched communications to its troops across the border in southern France.

Seeing Captain Sherrington step up from the companionway

onto the deck, he beckoned his friend to join him. Prior to the missive arriving from the Navy Board, this was to have been their last voyage together before Sherrington assumed his captaincy on another ship. The events of the last three weeks, however, completely upended their plans and missions.

The hoped-for, longed-for, news of peace had come at last. War with France and its allies was at an end. In the captain's cabin lay new directives—a mission for which his heart rejoiced. The allies had marched into Paris. The process for Napoleon Bonaparte's abdication had begun. Great Britain, Russia, Austria, Prussia, and France, as well as Sweden, Portugal, and Spain, were assigning delegates to meet in Vienna. Together, they would articulate anew a peace treaty to conclude this war. Their new role on the *Pontus* for the remainder of this assignment was to restore peace and order in the Bay of Biscay.

It had been exactly eleven days since he said farewell to Miss Charlie Reyne in Portsmouth. Before leaving, he had waited patiently to meet with her one last time in the courtyard behind the Crown Inn.

Charlie had come running down the back steps of the inn on the day of their parting, calling out his name. He could still remember the tone of her voice.

'My dearest Captain, I am over here!' she had cried out, holding down her bonnet with one hand and raising the other in greeting as she ran, her skirt billowing out behind her, sunlight glancing off her shoulders.

He stared at the little woman who had captured his heart and whose path in life had so strangely intersected with his. He supposed she had been awake all night writing to her father. Her eyes looked weary. Her hair, pulled back into a rough knot, needed a few more pulls with a hairbrush to make her presentable. Her shawl dangled awkwardly from her shoulders. He wanted to laugh, yet his eyes misted at the sight of her.

'Miss Reyne,' he replied to her greeting, waiting for her to reach him. She carried a letter in her hand.

'I was too tired to finish writing last night. Here is the letter for my father,' she said, picking up one of his hands and prying open his fingers. She placed the folded letter flat against his palm and closed his hand using both of hers.

'You cannot lose this. It must reach him as soon as possible,' she said.

Everything this woman said, did, threatened, or promised to do fascinated him beyond measure. It pained him to leave her. He wished he could shake off the feeling.

'I can take it as far as Pasajes,' he told her.

'Thank you. I hope my father is well,' she said worriedly. 'Would you perhaps be able to meet with him in person?' she asked, her eyes pleading with him.

'It is not likely,' he replied, regretfully. 'I will not be anchoring and going ashore at any point along the coast. But I will have other communications going to Pasajes, and I can send your letter safely to shore in one of the liaison boats. Our military postal service will direct this to your father wherever he might be encamped.'

She stood quietly, looking up at him.

'You must realise, this time it really is our final goodbye,' he told her reluctantly.

'Why? Do you plan on getting shot?' she asked him, tipping her head, bird-like. 'Will not you return to England after the war? Have not we, in some small way, become dear friends? If so, then surely we will meet again,' she assured him.

'I cannot entertain that hope,' he said grimly. He had not been able to quell the surge of feelings in his heart. His situation was unchanged, his future spoken for, his departure at that point imminent. On his return, he would honour his word and marry someone else.

At sea these past months, amid the duties and scenes of war, it had been thoughts of her that sustained him. 'What is it that draws one person to another?' he often pondered. Remembrance of her quirky expressions, sweet smile, and boundless energy occupied his mind, but only partly explained his attraction to her. Whether he was standing at his guard rail surveying the rough seas or resting in his cabin perusing the drawings she left for him, she occupied his thoughts. He guiltily carried the self-portrait she had drawn for him inside his pocket watch and found himself staring at it whenever he longed for her company.

'Captain!' Norcross called loudly from midship, breaking into the captain's reverie. Norcross raised his arms skyward, pointing to signals from the topman on the mizzen mast. 'Ship ahead, north-three-quarters-east,' yelled Norcross, this time pointing across the bow towards the horizon. 'You had best look, sir!'

The shrill sound of the watch whistle pierced the air as Brantford raised his spyglass to his eye, squinting to discern the cut of the ship's sails and the shape of its hull.

'Either Dutch or French,' stated the captain. 'Get Sherrington for me. We need to ensure this ship has news of the terms of peace. Inform our drummer to beat to quarters, Mr Norcross.'

Had Charlie been on board, she would have marvelled anew at the incredible speed with which the seamen took up their stations as they prepared to catch up with the other ship. Winds were blowing hard on the Bay of Biscay. The sails on the *Pontus* were already taught. How much more speed could they gain?

On the Quartermaster's signal, the seamen changed tack. It took an hour to come in close enough to communicate with the other ship. Atop the main mast, his signal bearer rapidly manipulated a series of flags, conveying news of France's surrender. The captain waited with an air of expectancy as signals arrived from the frigate, now known to be French.

'Signal that we are acting as an envoy and that I wish to

board for official communications and discussion,' instructed Brantford. 'Assure them that, while our cannons are battle-ready, we will not fire on them unprovoked.'

'Aye, sir.'

With his officers well-informed and experienced in their operations, the captain stood on deck, relaxed, hands behind his back.

Their signals were transmitted according to international standards, leaving no room for misunderstanding. Receiving acknowledgement signals from the other ship, the captain moved towards the steps coming down from the quarterdeck. Below him on the main deck, the captain of marines marshalled a small team of guards in readiness to board the frigate.

Perhaps it was thirty seconds later, perhaps sixty, when a nervous marksman on the topgallant yard of the French ship's main mast fired a shot. Astonished, the captain heard the sound at the same time as he felt himself being spun around. He stared into the eyes of Sherrington and watched in stunned surprise as his hat flew off, floating in the air. He wanted to say something to Sherrington, to ask him to relay a message to Miss Reyne and tell her that he was sorry about all of this. None of his words came out. The hard planks on the deck seemed to suck him down and pull him into the dark wood. He could hear Sherrington's voice calling his name.

Brantford wished he could remember what it was he wanted to say. Something about the war being over? No, something else, more personal. He wished he could remember. He tried to push out some words, but his lips were not moving. Captain Brantford squinted up at the sky, his vision blurred. Had he closed his eyes? He hardly knew.

The sky turned dark and swirled around him.

TWENTY-EIGHT

Mission Fulfilled

Six weeks had passed since the allied army marched into Paris in March of 1814. Following the signing of the Treaty of Fontainebleau on April 11, the withdrawal of British troops from the Iberian Peninsula commenced. Sick and wounded soldiers, including those under General Reyne's leadership, began reaching Portsmouth by the boatload. Tens of thousands of soldiers were either on the way home or waiting in southern France and northern Spain for transport ships to arrive.

Charlie and Inês walked arm in arm down the long hall at Chellisbury and entered the infirmary. Camp cots were filling up rapidly with yet another arrival of wounded soldiers home from the war. To accommodate the expected influx over the coming weeks, they converted adjacent spaces into temporary infirmary wards. Additionally, they set up cots in the main dining room and the hallways.

On entering the infirmary, Inês let go of Charlie's arm and gently pushed her into the room. As Charlie walked between the beds, some of the newly arrived soldiers waved in gratitude and held out their hands in greeting. Others cried, nodded, or cheered, as their abilities permitted. Tears streamed down Charlie's face as she recognised familiar faces amongst the new arrivals. Many of the men hailed from her father's regiment.

Others had served in battalions under General Reyne's command at some point during their postings. Most of them remembered and adored the troop's beloved Little Charlie.

Charlie walked the full length of the room, greeting and consoling the men. She paused beside a soldier with bandages covering parts of his face and shoulder. He was missing an arm, and his face and abdomen were covered in bandages. She lightly touched his shoulder.

'Mr Benny Jones,' she whispered to him softly. 'Dear Mr Jones, is that truly you?'

Opening his eyes, the man blinked to clear his vision. He was the youngest son of the old soldier who had tried to jump from the *Pontus*. He stared up at Charlie, confused.

'A special young lady is coming to visit us soon who is eager to see you,' she told him gently.

The young soldier sobbed quietly, turning his face away from her.

'She is to arrive in three days and will move into your new cottage with your father whilst you are recovering. She writes that you are to hurry and get well. We plan to train her as an aide to assist the patients. She hopes to help look after you. Will you welcome her here?'

The young man nodded, his head bandage becoming damp with his tears.

Charlie dried the unbandaged side of his face with her handkerchief. 'She has waited a long time to see you. You must get well; do you hear me?'

He nodded, his eyes speaking volumes.

Several weeks earlier, Charlie had hired a renowned local doctor to stay on permanently at Chellisbury and care for the patients. He came now into the room behind her.

'Gentlemen,' she said to the soldiers, 'this fine man is Doctor Ingram. He will be looking after you during your stay, assisted by our orderlies and helped by our aides—the women who are wearing blue aprons. Most of our team have not worked in an infirmary before. Please do your best to encourage them as they learn to care for you. Welcome home, dear friends. We are so glad you made it back.'

Choking up as she spoke to the men, Charlie cleared her throat and left the room. Inês, giving Charlie time to compose herself, joined her in the hallway and handed her a heavy shawl and a pair of leather gloves.

'Wil is waiting for us,' she said with a gentle smile. 'He says we should hurry.'

Charlie chuckled. 'Did Master Winthrop harness the team for us?'

'Yes, yes, and Wil praised him and says the wagon is ready to go. He says to tell you that Master Winthrop is a fast learner and doing very well. Come along. I have waited all morning for my lessons.'

'I cannot understand why you want to learn to drive the donkeys. It is needless, you know. We can get you a little one-horse gig to get around the property.'

Even so, Charlie was pleased to teach her friend. Waving farewell to Wil and thanking the boy for bringing around the wagon, the two of them climbed up behind Charlie's donkeys, now expanded to a team of four, and proceeded down the long avenue.

'We will go up to the main road so you can practise driving amongst other vehicles. Are you ready to try? I will switch places with you on the main road. Do you see how I hold both reins in my left hand? Remember, the switch always stays in your right.'

The women reached the main road and exchanged seats. Charlie fell silent as the wagon rattled along at a steady pace on the muddy road north of Chellisbury. Once they reached the toll road and passed the turnpike, she encouraged Inês to push the team to a trot.

There had been a smattering of cool rain the night before, with temperatures still lower than normal for a morning in early May.

Charlie took a deep breath, savouring the rich, earthy fragrance of spring. The women were continuing to enjoy their morning ride when suddenly they heard a loud crashing sound ahead of them and a mix of horrific cries.

'Can you see what has happened?' asked Inês, holding on tightly to the reins, and unable to see around a curve in the road.

'Take care! Keep our team under control,' Charlie instructed her as they rounded the turn.

Startled with what they saw, Inês pulled the team to a full stop. The women stared in horror at the scene in front of them. A phaeton lay on its side, its back wheel dangling loosely. Opposite, a coach lay tipped on the road, its front wheels in the ditch. Its horses, wide-eyed in fright, struggled and twisted from the drag on the harness. Several people lay on the ground. Luggage spilled behind the coach. Surveying the scene, Charlie saw the coach driver trying to get up off his knees. He seemed dizzy, as though attempting to sort out his thoughts amid the chaos. A teenage boy who had been riding in the imperial rack atop the coach came to his side, lending him his shoulder.

'Young man, release the horses!' yelled Charlie to the boy. 'Can you manage it? Do it at once! The driver will tell you what to do. You, sir,' she yelled to the driver, 'stay with those two women, beside you in the ditch.'

Charlie and Inês set to work at once, prioritising their tasks. The driver scrambled over to where the women lay, then slumped down beside them, unable to remain on his feet. After freeing the horses, the young boy ran over to assist two men who were lying near the phaeton, one of whom was not responding.

Inês and Charlie pried open the coach door from the

uppermost side and began assisting those who were able to climb out. The situation inside the coach was worrisome. Passengers had fallen against one another. One of them lay pinned on the bottom. Grateful for the help of an able passenger inside, the ladies were able to pull and lift out two others. Lowering them to the ground was time-consuming and difficult.

They could hear the crunch of gravel as another carriage rapidly approached from around the bend. Charlie hopped down and ran towards the curve in the road, arms outstretched, to stop the oncoming horses. The driver, skilled and alert, pulled his team to a stop. At first swearing at the young woman on the road, the driver quickly saw the vehicles beyond her and understood the bedlam that awaited them had they not stopped on time.

'What is going on?' a deep voice called out. A large man stepped out of the carriage.

'Captain Sand! Oh, thank goodness!' Charlie cried. She looked in surprise at the second man climbing down.

'Lieutenant Niles! Well, I am very grateful to see you both!'

"Miss Reyne? Are you hurt?' asked the lieutenant.

'No, no, I am fine. Please, we urgently need your assistance.'

With the help of the newcomers, they were able to carefully extract the remaining passengers, freeing Charlie and Inês to assess and deal with the various injuries.

Under Charlie's and Inês's skilled hands, with help from Lieutenant Niles who had sometimes treated wounds on the field, the passengers were eventually bandaged, braced, and solaced. Several patients, for they had become so by this stage, were wrapped in makeshift bandages from a petticoat taken from one of the women's luggage. They carefully lifted a man suffering an injury to his ribs and laid him on the bench in the back of Charlie's wagon. Lieutenant Niles and Captain Sand helped several other passengers into the back of the wagon.

In releasing the horses from the mail coach, the young boy

inadvertently let two of the team run loose. As well, the pair of horses from the phaeton, once unharnessed, slipped free of the boy's loose knots and were grazing in the nearby field. Captain Sand's driver, after ensuring his team remained calm and secure, marched off into the tall grasses beside the road to retrieve them.

'What happened?' asked Captain Sand after they had performed the more urgent tasks. He scowled suspiciously at the young men propped against the tipped phaeton.

'It is as you suppose, sir. They seem to have rounded the bend at a full run and swiped the side of the mail coach. That young man,' Charlie pointed into the distance, 'is your own and my uncle's neighbour, Mr Jack Weyburn, out for a little fun with two of his cousins. You cannot see from here, but that is a double-seated phaeton. The larger man in the blue coat was the one driving. The other man, lying on the ground, took a knock on the head. We will need to watch him for a few days.'

Lieutenant Niles and Captain Sand took in the scenes around them, impressed by the work done by Miss Reyne and Mrs Alvares in handling the chaos and injuries from the accident. The heavily loaded mail coach had carried five passengers plus the driver and two lads on top. Including the phaeton passengers, most had fortunately sustained cuts and bruises. Three of the travellers, however, required more serious care.

'We will take them to Chellisbury for a closer assessment and to give everyone a hearty meal,' asserted Charlie. 'From there, we can notify the mail service. Are you able to leave your driver here with the mail and all this luggage until they send a replacement coach? We can send some men back from Chellisbury to deal with the two vehicles. Do you agree?'

'Where and what is Chellisbury?' asked Captain Sand. 'And why go there? We are five miles from my property. Surely it is preferable to go there than to some unknown place.'

Charlie was about to answer when Mr Jack Weyburn, able to stand at last, ventured to join the conversation.

'I could not agree with you more, Captain Sand,' said their neighbour. 'I have heard a great many rumours about the goings on at this Chellisbury place—and none of them good. I am told it is owned by some immigrant merchants who are trying to peddle their liquor in England. There are all sorts of riffraff wandering around the property. They even have a pair of one-armed ruffians guarding the entrance to the property. I fail to see why that would be your destination. I am all for going to Captain Sand's house,' he said, laying his hand against the carriage to keep himself upright.

Charlie raised her brows. 'Dear Mr Weyburn, you are welcome to go wherever you wish. We are taking everyone else to Chellisbury,' said Charlie emphatically.

'Chellisbury has an infirmary,' Inês added, seeing their puzzled faces. 'It is but three miles from here. We can transport almost everyone in the wagon. Mr Sand, if you can take the others in your carriage, that would be helpful. As you can see, the back wheel on Mr Weyburn's phaeton is broken.'

Their affairs were soon sorted out: who should stay back with the mail and luggage, who should travel in Captain Sand's carriage, and who in the wagon.

'Which of the lads is your driver, Miss Reyne?' asked Captain Sand, not able to spot a likely candidate. 'Do you need one of us to take a seat on the wagon?'

'No, no, we are fine. You will need to follow us. Be careful not to miss the turn-off after we leave the toll road.'

Amidst much moaning by the injured passengers, they set off for Chellisbury, with the two ladies from the mail coach travelling inside Captain Sand's carriage. The Weyburn cousins and other passengers from the mail coach travelled in the wagon with Charlie and Inês.

There was little conversation, beyond some weak excuses made by Mr Weyburn's cousin for his reckless driving. Inês travelled in the back of the wagon next to the patients, attending to their comforts as Charlie handled the team, driving them at a rapid trot. As they approached Chellisbury, two guards stepped forward to open the gates at the top of the long avenue and had a brief conversation with the ladies. One of them, nodding at Charlie, disappeared along a path into the woods. Niles, who had seated himself beside the driver of Captain Sand's carriage to create room inside for the women, watched in keen interest. Though the guards were in civilian clothing, he could tell from their general air of confidence, and as a clearer indicator, from their army-issued boots, that these men were soldiers. He was curious and eager to see what lay inside the Chellisbury gates.

They soon arrived at a cluster of buildings, the main one being a large three-storey house with long, one-storey wings extending outwards on either side. Charlie drove her wagon briskly past the front doors to a side entranceway. Lieutenant Niles instantly noticed Charlie's two Prussian friends coming out to meet them.

Gus and Wil, chatting briefly with Charlie and taking in the situation, issued a set of commands to others inside. Several orderlies came out to help people down from the wagon. A pair of men brought a stretcher to lift down one of the injured passengers. Inês disappeared inside beside the stretcher.

Lieutenant Niles hopped down from the carriage and waited while Charlie approached him. Captain Sand and the others were soon standing on the lane at his side.

'Welcome to Chellisbury,' said Charlie. 'This is our home. As well, it is a recovery place for our soldiers. Those ruffians at the gate,' she turned, speaking in a reserved tone to Mr Weyburn, 'are celebrated former soldiers from my father's regiment. They are two of our heroes who recently returned from the Peninsula.

The immigrants you mentioned are my friends: Mrs Alvares, who bandaged your head, along with Mr Gus Jaeger and Mr Wil Jaeger, whom you met last autumn at the home of my uncle. They were honoured guests at the ball at your parents' home. Do not you remember meeting them? Ah, speaking of my uncle, here he is now.'

They all turned, astonished to see Lord Tripp emerging from the house and coming towards them.

'Captain Sand! Lieutenant!' he nodded in warm greeting. 'My, my, what a surprise to see you here. Mr Weyburn? Good heavens, this is an unexpected visit. And two more Weyburns! You have all accompanied my niece home, I see. Come inside. Our guards brought instructions to arrange a meal for everyone. In the meantime, you can relax in our humble abode.' He led them up the wide front steps and through the heavy front doors of Chellisbury.

Charlie excused herself and summoned an aide to help move Mr Andrew Weyburn to the side entrance where the other injured passengers had entered.

'Lady Tripp, my dearest, we have company!' Charlie's uncle called out cheerfully to this wife. 'Look who is here to join us for a meal! Our neighbours have arrived. They are a long way from home, and rather worse for wear! Charlotte has beaten us to it and has invited everyone over to see the new property. We shall have to make do with what we have on hand, in terms of provisions, eh? My dear, will you see if cook can conjure up some sandwiches and cakes and perhaps tea for everyone? We will keep our guests comfortable until the next mail coach retrieves them. Gentlemen, come, you must be famished. Welcome, welcome here. Follow me!'

TWENTY-NINE

At Home at Chellisbury

THAT A TRANSFORMATION had occurred in the lives of the Tripps was clear as day to Captain Sand. Lord Tripp, the man for whom one boring day followed another, had suddenly taken an interest in life. No, not an interest—a passion. Unlike past occasions, where he seemed to feign interest out of a sense of social duty, today the man sat forward in his chair, back straight, eyes bright, and feet squarely planted on the floor.

Typically lazy and rude, Lord Tripp surprised them all by rising to his feet as Mrs Alvares joined them. He even stood up, miraculously, for the entry of his wife. The Jaegers, too, received his warm greetings. Lord Tripp gestured to the chair closest to him for Gus to be seated.

Captain Sand wondered what had happened to the man to cause this astounding shift. Captain Sand had been away of late, spending time with his wife's family to the north, in the company of his brother-in-law, James Brantford, in Herefordshire. He was not someone who paid attention to all the daily gossip concerning the lives of his neighbours. Having been absent and preoccupied with important family matters, his awareness of local news was even lower than usual.

As for Lady Tripp, she was someone whom Captain Sand and his wife often avoided. She was notoriously curt and snobbish towards the neighbours. The woman was, on this day, gracious and welcoming to all. He had never seen her this way before. His eyes widened as she greeted him with genuine warmth.

Had the Tripps taken on the role of hosts at Chellisbury, the new home of their niece? This was not yet clear to him. The captain waited and watched throughout their afternoon luncheon and into the early evening as he and the other guests dallied in the parlour. He hoped to gain insight soon.

Lieutenant Niles, too, was eager to understand the matter. More importantly for him, however, he had personal matters to discuss with Miss Reyne. He had last spoken with her two hours ago when a messenger had arrived from the mail service. Charlie had called both Lieutenant Niles and Captain Sand out of the parlour for a brief conversation.

'A heavy fog has settled over the roads in our district. Visibility is dreadfully poor,' she told them. 'The mail coach drivers are experienced, and the messenger feels they can handle these conditions. The company is sending another coach to pick up their passengers this evening and will transport them to the nearest inn. They are warning everyone else not to travel. For yourselves, I think it is better if you stay the night. We have rooms ready for you,' she told them. 'Captain Sand, if that is agreeable to you both, I can arrange for the coach messenger to deliver a letter to your family.'

'In that case,' he replied, 'I will accept your offer.'

They stepped outside to assess the changes in weather and chat directly with the messenger. Miss Reyne left them soon after, once again in the company of her aunt and uncle. She had not yet come back. Seated close to the fire, Niles watched the door, wondering when she would return. He wanted to speak to her in private but had not yet had the opportunity. He was glad when she eventually joined them for their evening meal.

'I hope you will excuse us for dining in this area, and so late,' said Lady Tripp apologetically. They had entered the recently constructed library where tables had been set up. 'Our niece wanted us to wait until the passengers from the mail coach departed. They pulled out ten minutes ago, except for one individual who will stay here for further care. Our dining room is filled with cots,' she informed them. 'We have set a table in here, instead, where we can eat.'

'I say, what a small collection this is,' said Mr Jack Weyburn in a loud voice. He directed his comment to his cousin Edwin Weyburn, who had been driving the phaeton when it overturned.

Mr Jack Weyburn observed the empty shelves along the panelled walls. 'My father's library is twice this size,' he announced to no one in particular.

Lord Tripp gave him a quelling look.

'I am glad your cousin has woken up, but I am sorry he is not feeling up to joining us for dinner,' said Lord Tripp. 'My niece advises that he should take rest here for several days.'

'Oh, I have no concerns at all. If he has a headache, it is more likely because he was into his cups last night,' laughed Mr Weyburn, elbowing his cousin in the ribs. 'Always having fun, that one.'

The Weyburn cousins were oblivious to the critical looks of the others present.

'Please, everyone, do be seated,' said Lord Tripp, exchanging glances with Gus.

Whether from his years of service in the army or perhaps the style of his upbringing, Gus was not one to mince words. Speaking loudly in German, he launched into a tirade of direct criticism of Mr Weyburn for his party's reckless escapade and overall lack of concern for the passengers.

'Saints preserve us,' said Wil in English, patting his brother on the back in a conciliatory fashion and offering a weak translation to the others. 'He says it is fortunate no one was killed.'

Wil looked beseechingly at Charlie, who reached over, as the lieutenant recalled her doing so for his sake in the past, and laid her hand on Gus's arm to calm him. Lieutenant Niles recalled the time when the man had levelled a sabre at his chest. He looked at Charlie with admiration on this occasion for her ability to quickly calm her friend.

Those without any understanding of German could only wonder at the man's use of English swear words, and in the presence of the ladies, sprinkled through his speech. Despite the language barrier, and except for the Weyburn cousins, who were conversing with each other and not minding anyone else, the others understood the gist of the remarks. Many suffered in the mishap and one individual might perhaps suffer lasting implications. They fell into a grim silence.

Lieutenant Niles, angered as they all were, looked in sympathy at Miss Reyne and Mrs Alvares. Both women appeared worn out from their efforts to care unexpectedly for so many people. Charlie, already exhausted from getting Chellisbury operational as a hospital, had dark circles under her eyes. Her posture reflected the fatigue she was feeling. Mrs Alvares, too, showed a general weariness.

Lord Tripp's voice broke the awkward silence. 'If you gentlemen would welcome a walk about the grounds, I will give you a tour of Chellisbury in the morning,' he offered.

'Yes, I would like that,' said Mr Weyburn before anyone else could speak. 'I am curious to see what you have got going on in the back of the manor here.'

'Going on? It is an infirmary, of course. Have not you seen the patients coming and going today? This is a military recovery centre.'

'Ah! So that is it!' said Mr Weyburn. 'Do you receive a payment for each patient? What an excellent source of income.'

'How very timely this is, Lord Tripp,' said Captain Sand.

'Portsmouth is overwhelmed with returning soldiers. What a godsend for those who are injured. Is this facility supported by a trust? How do you find yourself in the thick of it?'

'My brother-in-law provided the initial funding. The officers and soldiers from his regiment, and others as well, contributed what they could. Several of the general's friends contributed to support the initial costs for the short-term services being offered at Chellisbury. They planned for this years ago. My niece and her friends have provided the impetus and went about purchasing the land and renovating the premises, hiring staff, and so on. My wife and I mean to support their excellent efforts and do what we can. I am in the process of organising a foundation so we can provide operating capital over the long term. Lady Tripp has recruited some of her lady friends from hereabouts to form a new society,' he said, his voice dripping with pride. 'They are already active in organising meals once a day in Portsmouth for returning soldiers.'

'Their efforts are sorely needed,' said Lady Tripp passionately. 'The town lacks the wherewithal to feed everyone. A few of the hotel kitchens have set up soup stations where the soldiers can eat at affordable prices. The new arrivals require food and housing while they await transportation to their homes. Our society will help them to get what they need.'

'We have set up a team to help the patients coming to Chellisbury,' added Lord Tripp. 'We have men in town as I speak, checking our people off their lists as they arrive, and arranging to transport them here.'

Charlie and her friends sat quietly through these explanations. Charlie was overjoyed by her uncle's and aunt's involvement. She especially loved her uncle's support in setting up a foundation. It set her mind at ease, as well, to gain help finding a skilled director to run Chellisbury. She smiled warmly as her aunt spoke in excited tones about the work of her new society. She had not expected any of this. That her father's sister and brother-in-law, perpetually listless and disengaged from the world, would step forward at such a critical juncture and help the townspeople in Portsmouth cope with the flood of post-war arrivals astonished her. That they had enthusiastically joined in the efforts to get Chellisbury operational filled Charlie with gratitude.

'When I last went into town, wearing my blue apron over top of my white frock,' Charlie said, smiling happily and a little saucily at her aunt, 'people took one look at me and immediately asked me if I had come from Chellisbury. They said I must surely be the niece of Lady Tripp.' She winked at her aunt.

Inês reached over, squeezed Lady Tripp's hand, and whispered to her, 'She means it as the highest compliment, dear madam. Cannot you hear the pride in her voice?'

'Well,' said Captain Sand, choked with emotion and needing to clear his throat, 'I am most impressed by what you have already achieved here and are planning further to do. And it has all been done in such a short amount of time. That is quite something.'

'I can only imagine how reassuring it must feel for those who are returning to have a place like Chellisbury for care and support,' said Lieutenant Niles solemnly. 'What a tremendous project, and what an amazing place you have built.'

Mr Weyburn and his cousin were slow to understand the overall scope of what lay around them. More explanations and answers were required. It was well into the evening before they all rose from the table and bid their hosts good evening.

'Miss Reyne, may I speak with you?' asked Lieutenant Niles, pausing in the hallway before retiring to his room.

'I will go on ahead,' said Inês, understanding the lieutenant's desire for privacy and moving past them.

'I wanted to let you know that I have recently met with

Captain Sherrington,' said Lieutenant Niles once they were alone.

'Have you?' she asked, her voice trembling. 'And what of Captain Brantford? Is he well? And his sailors? I pray there has been no harm done to the *Pontus* on his recent trips.'

'They have had a few engagements of late. One was particularly challenging, but they came away victorious. I am sorry to tell you that our friend was wounded.'

'Wounded!'

'Fortunately, he is recovering. Captain Sherrington informs me that he has at last been granted shore leave.' Lieutenant Niles paused for a moment, letting her digest this news.

'You will have heard, I am sure, about the Grand Naval Review taking place in Portsmouth next month. Captain Brantford is expecting to participate in this event.'

'Yes, of course, everyone speaks of it,' confirmed Charlie. Her mind was racing. Surely what the lieutenant said was true, and the captain must be recovering well.

'The Grand Naval Review is in a month, in June. The exercises are to be at Spithead when all the sovereigns arrive in Portsmouth to celebrate the new peace. Afterwards, he is finally free to spend time with his family and friends. Both he and Captain Sherrington will be taking part in it. Sherrington is leading one of the other frigates from the convoy – do you recall the *Falcon*?'

Charlie nodded, remembering this news from earlier, and glad to hear it confirmed.

'I wanted to let you know,' he continued, searching for the right words, 'that Captain Sand shared other news with me, also of a disturbing sort.'

Concerned, Charlie waited breathlessly for him to continue.

'You will recall meeting the captain's brother, James Brantford, last October when we were all in Portsmouth at the inn. He has written to his brother on a delicate subject. It is a private family matter for my friends, but I am sharing this with you because you overheard our conversation when we discussed Captain Brantford's long-standing engagement. There has been an unexpected development. Much to everyone's distress, Captain Brantford's betrothed has married someone else. I must say, her choice is an appalling one in every respect. Breaking off the engagement to Captain Brantford is not, however, entirely unexpected. They have been apart for a long time.'

'Oh, my goodness. What dreadful news,' said Charlie, deeply upset. 'Poor Captain Brantford. How very heartbroken he must be. It must come as a great shock. I am sorry for them both.'

'We are all disturbed by how this has unfolded. It is a complicated situation, and I am not at liberty to say more. Perhaps you will learn of it one day. However, because the engagement was kept private, he is left to suffer the news in silence. I assure you, this is a blow that affects the entire family. They are most concerned for his happiness. They cannot be sure the captain has even heard about her marriage yet due to his recent schedule and her general lack of communication. His brother sent him a letter to inform him, in case she had not already done so. We shall find out soon. Captain Brantford is expected to arrive back in England this week.'

'This week! Oh, my! Thank you for letting me know, Lieutenant,' said Charlie, her voice breaking. 'I am so sorry for him.' Her eyes were bright and round. She scrunched her face. 'Oh, dear. This news has made me feel quite ill. I think I will bid you goodnight, and let you rest. If you are taking the tour around Chellisbury with my uncle in the morning, then I will see you at breakfast. We will be dining in the library again,' she reminded him. 'Come, let me show you to your room, so you do not wander in the halls all night.'

She led the way up the stairs and into a long gallery, stopping in front of his room.

'Do rest well, dear sir. And thank you for letting me know about the captain. I understand this is a highly private matter. You may rely on my discretion.'

Feeling worried for her, sad for himself, and anxious for his childhood friend, Lieutenant Niles placed his hands on her shoulders. To his own surprise, he leaned down and kissed the top of her head. Charlie stared up at him, astonished.

'You are rather special, Miss Charlotte Reyne. If you wish to marry someone who thinks highly of you and will look after you, laugh with you, and treat you like the queen you truly are, my offer still stands,' he said. 'I would be honoured if you would accept.'

He was uncertain who of the two of them was more shocked to hear him say this. Charlie stared up at him, wide-eyed.

'Sleep well, Miss Reyne.'

Niles opened the door to his chambers. He turned and watched the little woman whom he so deeply admired walk down the hall and disappear from his sight.

Charlie rounded the corner of the hallway and hurried to her room. She closed the bedroom door behind her and leaned against it, wrapping her arms across her chest.

She tried to comprehend the news the lieutenant had shared with her. Hearing that the captain had been injured upset her deeply. He was alive, though, and coming home. His engagement was at an end, whether fortunately or unfortunately for him she could only guess. A small part of her was sorry about that, for his sake, but her concern lasted perhaps half a minute. Her beloved captain was a free man. The war had ended. She would see him soon.

THIRTY

Several Surprises

FOR THE THIRD time, Charlie picked up the invitation card and studied the embossed seal below the elegant golden lettering.

'What a pretty little card,' said Charlie matter-of-factly, turning it over in her hands. 'We have all known about this for ages, of course, but shall I read what it says for you? At least the gist of it?'

'Ahem,' she cleared her throat and smiled sweetly. 'Aunt Lydia writes to cordially invite us to Greydon Hall to attend their Spring Ball on Thursday, the twenty-sixth of May, at eight o'clock in the evening. That is three weeks from now,' she said excitedly. 'Also, it is to be my formal "coming out" party, which is very strange since I have spent my entire youth in adult company. That is just an excuse for my aunt to dress me up so that I will finally look like her niece.'

Charlie looked utterly serious. Her friends could not help themselves. Inês broke down first, laughing so hard that she could barely catch her breath. Charlie gave a tiny smile. Gus snorted. Wil, not privy to their long-standing joke, stared at them all, bewildered, but enjoying their mirth. He crossed his arms and smiled.

'We are invited to arrive at Greydon Hall earlier in the week, on the Monday, and stay through the following weekend after the ball,' Charlie informed them. 'What a timely celebration now that the war has ended. How wonderful if both Father and Sofia could be home to celebrate! I am so excited! Do you think they might be here for the ball? Inês, do you think it possible? What did Sofia have to say in her letter? Has she written of her plans?'

'Only that she has gone home to Oporto and is tending to the vineyards and organising repairs to the buildings. She makes no mention of coming to England.'

'I wonder where Father can be. He has not written of late,' complained Charlie, worried. 'Well, regardless, we shall of course accept my aunt's and uncle's invitation. They have been planning this event for months. Lieutenant Niles will be attending, and the Sand family, and the Weyburns, and most of the families we have met in the neighbourhood.'

'Mr Weyburn's cousin, Mr Andrew Weyburn, will be there,' said Inês coyly. 'I never saw a man pay as much attention to you as he did while recovering at Chellisbury after the accident. It was good he finally went home. I wondered if he would ever leave.'

'He followed me around like a puppy dog. What a nuisance,' said Charlie, blushing. 'He is worse than any of the soldiers. Every other day, he asked me to marry him. Now that he is staying on at his uncle's place, he keeps inviting me to ride in his phaeton or walk about the family's properties.'

'That is not such a very bad thing, is it? Truthfully, he seems to be a nice enough young man.'

'Do you think so?' asked Charlie, genuinely surprised to hear Inês say this.

'He is the brother of the reckless fellow who drove the phaeton and caused the accident,' muttered Gus. 'How can he possibly be a nice young man?'

'His family connections are hardly his fault,' countered Inês.

'Your uncle told me that this Mr Andrew Weyburn has

petitioned for your hand,' said Gus, helping himself to another serving of poached eggs and fish. 'I told your uncle that you will not be interested in the slightest, but you will have to speak to him about it yourself. Wil, *bitte,* stop eating all the toast and pass me the little tray. Yes, that one, with the jam. I do think, Miss Charlotte Reyne, that you should anticipate a formal proposal soon. What will your answer be? Have you decided?'

'He is so very handsome, I hardly know.'

'I thought your interests lay elsewhere,' Gus replied.

'Well, that may be, but it was all I could do not to stare at Mr Weyburn throughout the day whilst he was recovering with us. It is a good thing he has gone away for a short spell,' said Charlie with a saucy smile. 'I am positively certain that I would not tire of looking at him for at least two more months. Wil, I have been meaning to tell you that Mr Weyburn has an older sister whom Aunty has invited to the ball. She will fall madly in love with you the first moment she sees you in your new London coat.'

'If not, your foreign accent will win her over,' added Inês. 'All you need to do is wish her good evening—"*Guten Abend, Fräulein Weyburn*"—and she will melt into your arms.'

'*Auf Wiedersehen,* more like,' said Wil.

Charlie looked up anxiously.

'What do you mean, goodbye?' she asked, catching his expression and the slight change in tone. For days, she had wondered if Wil and Gus had something secretive going on, some sort of plan they were keeping from her.

'Do you remember us talking about the *quadriga* that Napoleon Bonaparte took from Berlin at the start of the war? It has finally been found in storage near the Louvre,' said Gus. 'It is still packed in the same shipping crates used to bring it to Paris ten years ago.'

'Are you talking about that enormous statue, with the four

horses and a chariot and a goddess driving it?'

'Precisely that.'

'What does that have to do with you?' asked Charlie, looking from one brother to the other.

'We have enlisted with General von Blücher's special squadron to transport the *quadriga* back to Berlin. Once we arrive, it will be reinstalled on the Brandenburg Gate, where it belongs. Afterwards, we are going home to Hanover to try to locate our uncle and his family, if they are still alive, and return the sabres to the men's families.'

'Are you really going home?' gasped Charlie, examining their faces to see if they were serious. She scrunched her face tightly to hold back tears. 'Oh, my, that is wonderful.'

'It is beyond wonderful,' said Wil, watching Charlie's crestfallen face. 'It is a miracle.'

'I know it is,' she said, biting her lip. 'I am happy for you, truly, I am. But it is unexpected, and you will be away for months and months. It is too much for me to hear about in this way!'

'We plan to leave from Greydon Hall the day after the ball,' Gus carried on unapologetically.

Charlie fell silent. Her shoulders curled inward. Inês reached over and held one of her hands.

'What about Inês?' Charlie asked, accusingly, looking directly across the breakfast table at Gus. 'Are you going to leave her in England, all alone, just like that? When she is finally here with you, and we are all together?'

'Inês will stay here with you,' said Gus quietly.

Inês patted her hand. Charlie did not know where to look. Her heart ached for Inês. As well, she could not bear to be parted from her friends. She could not understand a single word Gus was saying by this point. Gus had loved Inês for years. How could he possibly go off with Wil, abandoning them? Charlie pushed her fists against her eyelids to stop her tears.

'We wanted to ask you,' said Gus, 'if foreigners need a special licence to get married in England. Also, we were hoping that you would let Inês and me have one of the cottages at Chellisbury to live in after we get married.'

'What?' Charlie clasped her hands in astonishment. 'Are the two of you getting married? Oh, my word! At last, you are finally going to marry! What wonderful news! But how could you tease me so? I should never forgive you, except that you have set my heart at ease with such happy news. And a trip home to Prussia! How good it will be for you to find your families again. Seven years, is it, or eight, now, since the KGL went on campaign to Hanover? And now you are returning! I am so happy for you! And that you and Inês are planning to wed—' Charlie pulled Inês towards her and gave her a long embrace, '—I could not be any happier, unless it was to hear that Wil has similar plans!'

'What, you would have us both marry the same woman? *Leider*, regretfully, I have not yet met my future wife,' he smiled nonchalantly. 'Perhaps I will, one day. If not, if you are still unwed, I will ask you to marry me, Miss Charlotte Reyne, to put an end to my solitary misery.'

Charlie rose from her chair and crumpled Wil's hair. He scolded her and tried to catch her hand as she darted away.

Gus and Inês smiled happily at one another, content in the knowledge that Wil and Charlie approved of their union. A time of separation was imminent for the couple, but it would not be their first time apart. This time, unlike their years spent in the Peninsula, there was no risk of war threatening them at every turn.

'I am going to my room. I need to write a letter to my Aunt Lydia and let her know our plans, and tell them of your engagement,' said Charlie breathlessly. 'I will tell her that we are of course all coming to her ball—we would not miss it for anything in the world—and I will let her know that it is to be an extra special occasion for a delightful reason. They will be so thrilled for the two of you. I will ask my uncle to investigate wedding regulations as they pertain to foreigners. Who knows? Publishing the banns might be all it takes. We should get that done right away. Perhaps we can even get you two married before Gus and Wil have to leave.'

'There is not time enough for that,' said Gus. 'We need to be in Paris by the first of June.'

'So soon?' Charlie sighed. 'Well, at least we have these next few weeks to enjoy each other's company. And then, my gosh, you are going to Paris, and on to Berlin! Take us with you! My aunt and uncle can take care of matters here. I beg of you! I always envied men their grand tours.'

'My dear girl, you have toured in parts of India and travelled for years throughout the Peninsula. You know a vast deal more about the world than any of the young men I have met around here,' said Gus. 'You had a grand tour all on your own.'

'Yes, but this is different. It will be a marvellous journey. But you are leaving so soon—right after the ball! Oh, my goodness, I miss you already!'

⌁

The sun shone brightly along the avenue in front of Greydon Hall. Lady Tripp handed Charlie and Inês each a pair of newly sharpened garden clippers along with a wide basket for collecting cut flowers.

'It is so very good of you to help out in this way,' said Lady Tripp. 'Everyone is busy with errands this morning and getting ready for our ball. I have no one at hand to collect the flowers. Now, remember, the vases are quite tall. We will need long stems on the lilacs. Be sure to cut from behind so that the avenue looks tidy when the carriages arrive for the ball on Thursday.'

'Yes, yes, we will cut everything perfectly,' muttered Charlie.

Charlie and Inês cheerfully went about their business cutting flowers to decorate the refreshment tables. Every few minutes, Charlie stopped and buried her face in the lilac blooms, breathing in the delicate fragrance. Adding to her pleasures, lily of the valley bloomed profusely under her feet around the shrubs. She crouched down and drew in a few deep breaths of the glorious scent.

'Charlie, there is a carriage coming through the gate,' Inês called out. She and Charlie leaned out from behind the shrubs to see who was arriving.

'Whose can it be, I wonder?' asked Charlie.

The front doors of the house swung open. Lord and Lady Tripp, alerted to the arrival of guests, came out to the front steps of Greydon Hall. They smiled happily while they waited for the carriage to pull up in front. From their position behind the shrubs, Charlie and Inês watched expectantly to see who had arrived.

'Oh, my word, it is Father!' exclaimed Charlie.

'Sofia is with him!' gasped Inês.

Tossing her basket aside, Charlie burst into a full run, leaving Inês to follow behind her. Charlie raced headlong into the outstretched arms of her father.

'My dear Father! I have missed you so much! I have not seen you since last July! You are looking fine and well! Thank goodness!' cried Charlie. Over seven months had passed since she and Inês had sailed on the convoy out of Oporto. It was nigh on eleven months since she had bid her father farewell in Vitoria.

'We have been so worried for you!' she scolded him. 'You have not written half as often as you ought!'

'My dearest Charlotte,' he said, embracing her, 'I have missed you greatly. How are you, my precious child? Look at you, in a pretty gown, and with your hair dressed in such a lovely way.

Your aunt has been a good influence, I see!'

'She has indeed, sir,' agreed Charlie, beaming. Charlie was just about to ask playfully if the gown made her look like Aunt Lydia's niece but Inês, shaking her head in consternation, laid her fingers across Charlie's lips.

'No more of that, I beg you,' she whispered.

Sofia was next to step out of the carriage amid a flurry of greetings and warm embraces.

Charlie's father turned to assist while another woman, a pretty lady, perhaps in her mid-twenties in age, stepped down from the carriage onto the gravel lane. A gentleman followed closely behind her.

'Captain Sherrington! Then this dear woman must be your wife!' cried Charlie, turning happily to greet the woman.

'None other,' he replied. 'When your uncle invited us when we all met in Portsmouth, I had no idea the timing would work for us to come. With the war over, we are free of duties for the time being. We are to stay within easy distance of Portsmouth until after the naval review, so we were able to accept this kind invitation to attend and stay on for a few extra days as guests.'

'We are delighted to see you, Captain Sherrington,' said Charlie's Uncle Tripp, coming forward to greet the captain and his wife. 'When we met that day, I had every hope of your coming. I am deeply pleased to see you, and to welcome your lovely wife.'

'We have one more traveller with us,' said the general, smiling broadly as a final passenger got out of the carriage. 'Captain Brantford has joined us as well.'

Charlie placed her hand over her chest.

'Heart, be still!' she mouthed the words without making any sound. She had stepped back to make room for those getting out of the carriage. Even Gus, Wil, and Mrs Alvares were before her in delivering their words of welcome. Now, being the furthest from him, she had to wait her turn to greet her favourite captain in all the world.

'My dear sir! Welcome to Greydon Hall,' she said shyly when her turn to greet him finally came. She examined him carefully. 'Is it true, what they say?' she asked him worriedly. 'Have you recovered well?' She searched him for signs of lingering injury. His hair was closely cropped. She could see signs of scarring across one side of his forehead. Was that grazing from the shot, or had he hit his head on the deck? She could not be sure. It seemed he had healed well. She looked into his eyes, concerned for him.

'When Uncle first invited you, I truly did not expect that you would be here. Who could have predicted that the war would be over, and you would be in England, and not at sea? And not with, well, not with other people. I am so glad you are safe! Can you hear my heart, how loud it is beating?'

'I am happy to see you, as always,' he said, taken aback by her candid remarks. He took a moment to take in her appearance, admiring her from head to toe. 'You look very lovely,' he said softly. 'Are you well?'

'I am, indeed. And you, kind sir?'

He nodded, smiling gently.

The others, chatting gayly amongst themselves, were moving up the stairs and into the entrance hall. Charlie laid her hand on the captain's arm to detain him.

'I wish to say, Captain, that I am sorry you are here.'

Captain Brantford, taken aback, stared at her.

'I trust your brother's letters have reached you. At least, I hope so,' she continued, uncertain of how to interpret his distressed looks. 'Truly, I never expected you to be here. It is a shame that you could come.'

He stopped moving, deeply puzzled by her remarks. He thought over her choice of words for a moment, trying to understand her, then turned to her and nodded appreciatively. 'Ah. You are speaking of my failed engagement. Did Lieutenant Niles inform you that I have been irrevocably rejected? I can say, in all honesty, I never expected I would be free to attend this ball. If all had gone as planned, I ought to have been in London by now and perhaps on my way to the altar. Truthfully, I am not sorry to be here, not in the least,' he said with utmost sincerity. 'My feelings have changed immensely over this past year. I mean no ill will to the lady, but I am grateful that my engagement is at an end,' he said to her quietly.

Charlie paused, studying his face. She patted him sympathetically on the arm.

'Do not dismay, Captain.'

'Indeed, I am not dismayed.'

'You will recover in time. I beg you, do not despair. We shall cheer you on. At least, I shall do so on my own since no one here knows about your engagement except for your own family. You must bear up. Your heart will mend one day.'

She looked so sad for him that he could not stop himself from smiling. He turned his face to hide this from her. Except for the news in April that Emperor Napoleon Bonaparte had abdicated, he had not found anything to cheer him in recent weeks while he recovered from his injury. Her candid expressions of concern made his heart feel light.

'You are beside yourself with grief,' she continued, filled with anguish for his trials. 'We will care for you here and help you to forget her. And if I were to meet her, I would have quite a few words to say to her! What could she be thinking, to let go of someone like you? You are far too thin. Have no worries. My aunt will see that you are well fed. If you stay a full three days, I can promise that we will fatten you immensely. You will soon begin to resemble my hog, Chica, in Oporto. Do you remember her?' Charlie beamed at him. 'And a festive spring ball this week—well, it is nearly summer now—is just the thing to lift your spirits. Music and dancing and the company of friends tomorrow evening will do your heart wonders. I must tell you; I have learnt to dance! Do you know the steps to the minuet? What about the cotillion? Perhaps, if you are not too tired from travelling, you will invite me to dance with you.' Charlie smiled up at him.

For the past weeks, travelling back and forth from the Peninsula to England, recovering from his wounds, escorting supply ships and troops and hospital ships over rough seas, he had felt almost despondent. When news arrived from his brother of the end to his engagement, he felt nothing much except perhaps surprise that the woman who professed to care for him had not the decency to write to him directly. He was almost ashamed of his own feelings of relief to be free again. Now, in front of him, stood this small embodiment of light, disbursing the clouds of weariness that had rested on his shoulders for so long. She seemed to glow. He felt blinded by her brightness.

Charlie escorted the captain inside Greydon Hall, chatting incessantly until they joined her uncle, who was almost as glad as Charlie to welcome the captain as his guest.

THIRTY-ONE

Guests at Greydon Hall

'COME IN, COME in. Follow me,' said Lord Tripp, welcoming the new arrivals to Greydon Hall. 'What a happy day! My dear brother-in-law,' he said to Charlie's father, 'how came you to be so thin? Let us offer you some light fare to tide you over until the dinner hour. We all long to hear news of your final campaigns. I heard you suffered terrible losses in the Pyrenees before word reached you that the war had ended. How terribly sad. But you are here, alive, with all your limbs, thank the Lord.'

'My dear brother,' said Aunt Lydia, her eyes misting, 'I confess, I never expected to see you again. And here you are, together with your lady friend. Well, we must get to know one another. Do you wish to make an introduction?'

'My apologies. This dear woman is Mrs Montalto,' said the general, tucking Sofia's arm into his.

Charlie stepped up on the other side of Sofia and wrapped her arm around the woman's slender waist.

'Mrs Montalto is like a mother to me,' she said firmly, in case anyone doubted Sofia's place in the family circle. 'She and Mrs Alvares are sisters. The two of them saved my life.'

'Nonsense, child,' chided Sofia. 'It is the other way around, several times over.'

'No, indeed, you did. You were my parent, my home, my

family, and my constant companion. I have missed you so! How glad I am to see you! Why did not you tell us you were coming?'

'Stop squeezing me. You are taking the breath out of me,' laughed Sofia. Her cheeks, bright with pleasure, belied her words. Sofia rested in the warmth of Charlie's embrace.

Lady Tripp tucked her arm into her husband's and the pair led their guests down the hallway. They were soon seated in the Tripp's front parlour. Captain Brantford tried to seat himself near Charlie, but the men had gravitated to the further end of the room. Seated some distance from her, he took satisfaction in gaining a clear view of her. To his surprise and pleasure, he found himself the object of her glances on several occasions.

'Captain Brantford, do tell us about this Grand Naval Review that everyone is talking about in town,' said the general, breaking into his thoughts.

'Which aspect, sir?' the captain asked.

'People speak of nothing else, but despite all the excitement and noise in general, I have heard very little detail. I take it you two gentlemen are both involved. My apologies—I have forgotten the name of your ship—but will you be part of the occasion and participating at Spithead?'

'Yes, we are both involved. I will be aboard the *Pontus*. Captain Sherrington has command of the *Falcon*,' said Brantford proudly, filled with pleasure for his friend's success.

'Notwithstanding the noise from the cannons,' commented the general, 'I am sure it will be preferable for you to be on the water that day. I expect there will be a mad crush of people in town arriving to see all the goings on. We shall have to book our hotel rooms at once, to have any hope of staying in town. I have never seen a naval review. I quite look forward to it.'

'If you would like to watch from a vessel rather than standing on shore, I can reserve a small boat for your family members and a few friends, to bring you out into the harbour, closer to the ships. There will be room for up to twelve guests.'

'I would enjoy that immensely!' responded General Reyne.

'In that case, I will hire some boatmen to bring you out,' the captain said, turning to be sure Lord Tripp and his wife knew the invitation included them. 'I hope Miss Reyne and her friends will join the party, as well as yourselves.'

'That would be delightful,' said the uncle, greatly pleased by the invitation. 'We are very happy to accept your offer.' Lord Tripp's eyes sparkled with excitement.

'Very good. I will share details later. It will be quite the event,' said the captain. 'May I ask that you bring Mrs Sherrington with you? We do not want to abandon her on shore by herself.'

'Yes, yes, of course!' agreed Uncle Tripp. 'We will take good care of Mrs Sherrington.'

'Have all the various sovereigns committed to attend this Grand Naval Review?' asked the general.

'That is our understanding,' said Captain Brantford. 'The Prince Regent is to arrive with the other royal princes, along with the Emperor of Russia and the King of Prussia. General von Blücher and General the Marquess of Wellington, Sir Arthur Wellesley—now the Duke of Wellington, so high has he risen—are attending, along with their various entourages. Our chief military and naval commanders will be present as well. Everyone will reach Portsmouth over a few days and on time for the review itself on the twenty-fourth and twenty-fifth of June.'

As the party dispersed to their rooms to change their attire for dinner, Captain Brantford seized the opportunity to speak again with Charlie.

'Miss Reyne, I am needing to stretch my land legs after sitting so long in the carriage. Perhaps you could point me in the direction of a path for a short walk about the grounds. I would value taking some brief exercise before I retire to my room,' he said.

'Certainly,' she replied, pleased by the suggestion. 'I will join you, in fact.'

Lady Tripp, appalled by her niece's intention to head out with the captain on a solitary walk, interceded. 'I am somewhat tired myself, but perhaps Mr Jaeger and Mrs Alvares would wish to accompany you.' She gratefully saw Mrs Alvares nod in agreement with this suggestion. 'Is anyone else wishing to take a little stroll?'

Captain and Mrs Sherrington welcomed the opportunity to join the others. Being familiar with the grounds, Gus and Inês took the lead in guiding the walk. The captain and Charlie lingered at the rear of the party.

'It is very good to see you again,' said the captain, holding aside a branch for Charlie to pass through a wooded section of the path. 'When your uncle first broached the idea, I had not thought it possible for me to be here.'

'Truly, I am sorry to see you.'

'No, do not misunderstand me. I have no regrets in being here.'

'How is that possible?' she asked, looking deeply into his eyes for any signs of dissembling. 'You need not keep up a pretence with me, sir,' she said. 'No one is listening to our conversation. You need not deny your feelings when you are in my company. You must acknowledge your pain and give vent to your feelings. That is how one heals.'

He smiled to himself at how she expressed her thoughts. 'You would have me rant and rave, I suppose, about a broken engagement that I had long wished to relinquish.'

She shook her head sadly. 'Denial and hope are powerful antidotes. I often found that soldiers would recover better, and more quickly, when they denied the circumstances in front of them and held on to hope, however faint.'

'I cannot convince you that I am not in pain. You are deter-mined that I am to be sad, and you insist that I pine over a broken relationship that I no longer cherish. So be it. I accept your condolences. But let me be clear on this point, Miss Reyne.' It took restraint not to call her "Little Charlie" or "sparrow", as he mostly thought of her. He cleared his cluttered thoughts.

'I am here by my own volition, and by your uncle's invitation, to attend a festive ball tomorrow,' said the captain. 'I am a man on leave from regular duties, home at last from the trials of war, free of responsibility, and granted an extended period of rest. I assure you; I do not intend to wallow in my supposed sorrow. I intend to claim my happiness and appreciate the company of friends as I have not been free to do in the past. Let us enjoy this time we have together. Do you understand me? I have not come to be pitied, Miss Reyne. Not in the slightest.'

'Then you will not mind dancing with me at the ball!' she said in delight. 'You may despise me when I misstep and tread on your toes, so pity you I must. Dancing is all very new to me. I am bound to turn left when everyone moves right.'

He laughed at this. He could tell that her thoughts were churning; that she needed time to think through what he had said about the end of his engagement. It was as close to a confession as he could make to her in the moment. She was convinced he was heartbroken. He needed to give her time to see that his affection for her was real and not a substitution for the loss of his engagement to another woman.

'Ah. Then I am to anticipate the unexpected once again,' he said, smiling at her. 'Has that not always been your pattern with me?'

It was Charlie's turn to laugh. 'Am I so unpredictable?'

'Delightfully so. Upon my word, do not you know this about yourself?' he asked, perplexed. 'It is your most endearing attribute.'

They had reached a makeshift bridge of stacked logs placed across a small brook. It required their attention to maintain balance. Captain Brantford went first, turning to assist Charlie as she stepped down from the stacked logs. He clasped her hand tightly and pulled her towards him as she slipped on the damp moss. Reluctant to let her go, he released her slowly.

They soon caught up to the others waiting for them in a nearby grove. Inês was standing apart, chatting with Mrs Sherrington. She gestured for Charlie to join her.

'I was attempting to let Mrs Sherrington know the names of some of the guests who will be attending the ball,' said Inês, 'but I am at a loss to remember all the neighbours and distant relatives.'

'You are so very lucky, Miss Reyne, to have such a large family gathering together in one place, with more guests arriving soon,' said Mrs Sherrington. 'I am an only child, and my family is not well connected. With my husband away at sea for long periods at a time, I have often felt very alone.'

'We are not so dissimilar,' Charlie said, smiling gently. 'We have only just reunited with our loved ones. I do not know many of my relatives here in England. I know I can speak for Mrs Alvares and myself in saying we shall treat you as part of our extended family, or dear friends at the very least if you will have us!'

Mrs Sherrington looked from one woman to another, her eyes glistening with gratitude for the quick and spontaneous offer of friendship.

'I would be honoured,' she said simply. 'It is not easy being the wife of a naval officer when the men are away at sea. This past year has been especially difficult. I once dissuaded a close friend of mine from marrying into the Navy. She could not have handled their periods of separation. Somehow, we have managed it, but it is not a role for everyone, you know. You are without your husband for months on end. I often yearned for the company of close friends whilst my husband was away. Fortunately, in the future, now that he has been made a captain, I will be able to travel with him from time to time. Thankfully, however, the men are now home. And I have the good fortune to find myself here. I will not let you change your mind, you know, about being friends. I will hold on to what you said.'

Charlie nodded, mulling over the woman's description of a life of marriage to a naval captain. Without knowing precisely what prompted this choice of topic, she nonetheless appreciated the woman's sincerity.

'I, too, have had to endure being separated from loved ones,' said Inês. 'Some have been away for a very long time; others are gone forever. My husband and young son died in the war during the first attack on Oporto. This is my family now,' said Inês. She seemed to don her grief like a cloak at times, being enveloped in it one moment, then lifting it and letting it slide off her shoulders. She gestured around her. 'My dear friend Charlotte, my sister Sofia, Miss Reyne's father, and our Prussian friends—these are the people I call family. They are truly precious to me.'

The women fell silent. It was not the awkward silence of strangers struggling to find some point of connection. Rather, it was a moment of embracing new friendships. Words were unnecessary. They understood one another. They shared common ground from similar experiences in life. Their bond was instant and genuine.

As they travelled along the pathways through the fields and woodland encircling Greydon Hall, their groupings shifted easily and comfortably. The bond of friendship and respect between Brantford and Sherrington was one of long-standing, and the men conversed readily with one another. Gus was the outsider, but Brantford welcomed him to join in their conversations. This was not difficult to achieve. Gus held Captain Brantford in high regard. He had witnessed the man's care and treatment of Charlie onboard the *Pontus* and he respected the actions of the two naval officers in holding their containers in storage until matters were clarified. As a military man, honouring rules and regulations was ingrained into his nature. Gus held no malice towards these men relating to past encounters.

As they returned to the house, Charlie manoeuvred to walk once again beside Captain Brantford.

'I have a favour to ask of you,' she said after a few moments in his company.

'I am at your command.'

'That I doubt very much,' she giggled. 'But your help would be invaluable. I would like to meet you tomorrow in secret somewhere to practise dancing. Will you assist me in this way?'

'Am I to understand that the indomitable Miss Reyne is worried about performing well before a crowd?'

'You are correct. Although the ball is a celebration of the end of the war, it is also, unofficially, my coming out party. Everyone is sure to stare at me. I do not mind looking odd, but I do not relish looking like a fool. If you will help me to practise my dancing, it will mean the world to me.'

'I shall be happy to oblige. There is no good reason, however, for you to meet a man in secret,' he scolded gently. 'I will speak to your father, or your uncle, whomever is best in this situation, and arrange a time. I will claim that I am the one in need of rehearsing. I can persuade Captain Sherrington to support my entreaty and make it a party of four. It has been some time since either of us has danced. Will that suit you, Miss Reyne?'

'That would be perfect,' she agreed happily. 'I shall place my trust in you to look after me.'

Captain Brantford felt his heart swell. He felt no small measure of grief for the young woman beside him. Miss Reyne was rapidly approaching twenty years of age. She was being presented in a community where women were out in society by the age of sixteen or seventeen and often married within a year afterwards. While her peers had been establishing their own homes and embarking on family life in England, Miss Charlotte Reyne had been marching behind the drums in Spain amid a violent war. This ball, ostensibly in her honour, had rapidly evolved into a celebratory event to mark the end of twenty years of fighting on the continent.

'I am glad to hear it,' he said sincerely. 'You may rely on me with confidence. My brother insists that, of the two of us, I am the better dancer,' confessed the captain. 'This should give you some assurance. It might surprise you, but whenever we land in some port or other, we officers are often invited to attend the local assemblies. You can be sure that I will claim your hand for two sets if you will accept me. I promise to guide you well. I swear that I will not laugh at your dancing skills. Do you trust me on this?'

'Of course, I do. It is Mr Weyburn and his cousins who have me worried.'

'And who might this Mr Weyburn be?' he asked, his interest piqued.

'Plural, the Misters Weyburn. There is a carriage-load of them, cousins close in age, who all go by the name of Mr or Miss Weyburn. Sir Reginald Weyburn is a close neighbour and friend of my uncle's. He lives to the north and east of here,' she replied. 'His son, Mr. Jack Weyburn, and a daughter, whom Lieutenant Sand has met, plus five or six of Sir Weyburn's nephews, are all attending. The men all go by the name of Mr Weyburn. They are sure to laugh at me if I misstep in the dances. Mr Andrew Weyburn, one of the cousins, is an exception. He is third in order of age among them but first in terms of charm. He has asked me to marry him, you see. I am quite determined he, at least, will admire my dancing.'

Shocked, the captain came to an abrupt stop.

'Marry you! And have you replied?' he asked, holding his breath.

'Not as yet,' she said, smiling sweetly. 'I am sorely tempted to accept. He is almost as handsome as you, and he seems genuinely fond of me. Since I happened to learn of your secret engagement, I felt you would wish to know about an offer that I received, which is also, at present, a secret.'

It took several moments for the captain to gain control of his emotions. He was a man who was finally free of an obligation that he had long outgrown. As a naval officer with a career that would take him away from his future wife for weeks and months at a time, he had spent many long nights debating whether he had any right to court the remarkable Miss Reyne. Many times had he stood lost in thought on the quarterdeck on the *Pontus*, leaning over the guard railing deep in thought, watching the waves, staring at the clouds and stars, and examining his miniature portrait of Miss Reyne, given to him those many months ago.

After much deliberation, Captain Henry Brantford had decided to offer for Miss Charlotte Reyne's hand in marriage and let her decide. His heart was filled with hope. He had just arrived after travelling eleven days at sea followed by three hours in a carriage with General Reyne, whose company he did not enjoy, on time to attend the Tripps' spring ball. He had come expressly to see Miss Reyne and to court her favour. How was he now to process the news that he had arrived too late?

Charlie turned to face the captain, her expression inscrutable. She tipped her head, raised her eyebrows, and graced him with a tiny smile.

'She is doing her silly sparrow imitation again,' he thought to himself. Normally, it would amuse him. In the past, he had often chuckled to see her hapless imitation at being coy. On occasion, he had even laughed outright at her imperfect attempts. Today, his humour deserted him. All he wanted to do was hold her. Or perhaps berate her.

'Mr Weyburn is quite persistent, which completely shocks me,' she said, raising her fan and flicking her hand to open it. The fan stayed shut. 'Dear me. This fan is supposed to open with a flick,' she pouted. She waved her wrist and attempted to open it again, deeply absorbed by the task. 'What I wanted to say is that Mr Andrew Weyburn is likely aware of my sizable dowry. No doubt the family determined that he is the best candidate to try for my hand. In any case, he is the first to express himself. In my estimation, he is far superior to all the other Mr Weyburns. What is your opinion on the matter? Do you suppose he might be sincere in his proclamations? One never knows, does one, how to interpret a situation like this.'

'Are you fond of him?' asked the captain, scowling.

'Ought I to be? I love that he has asked to marry me, that much I will confess.' Charlie's eyes twinkled. She turned her back to the captain, waved her little fan, still shut, and tripped merrily along the last stretch of path leading to Greydon Hall. 'Come, sir, you are dawdling. The others are at the door waiting for us to enter. Dinner is in one hour. I do hope you like venison pie. It is my uncle's favourite dish.'

THIRTY-TWO

Reunited

'I am terribly sorry. I did not mean to hit your ball so far into the shrubbery,' Charlie lied, unabashed. There was not a sliver of regret in her voice.

'Really? Was that necessary?' grumbled Inês. 'You had an entire lawn where you could send it and yet you chose the hedges.'

'I was temporarily distracted. I meant to hit it over the ha-ha,' laughed Charlie. She set down her mallet and pulled Inês with her to join Sofia and Mrs Sherrington under a canopy near the refreshments table.

'You can try to beat me later, once the men leave for Hanover,' she patted Inês on the hand. 'It will give you something to anticipate.'

'Charlotte, dearest,' came a piercing voice out of nowhere, 'where is your hat? Do please fetch it and be sure to sit in the shade.' Aunt Lydia emerged from behind a boxwood hedge in the nearby garden. 'We do not need you popping out any more freckles just before the ball this evening.'

Charlie waved at her aunt and scooted into the house to do as she was bid.

'Mrs Sherrington, here, move your chair in closer towards mine in the shade,' said Sofia. 'The sun is almost overhead, and it is feeling hot today.'

'Yes, thank you.' Mrs Sherrington studied the expressions of her new friends and peered after Charlie as she disappeared inside. 'You all seem very fond of one another. How did you come to meet? Was it in Portugal or in Spain?'

Sofia looked down and studied her hands. She lifted her chin for a moment and glanced at Inês. It was not a story she would normally divulge but her time spent in the company of Mrs Sherrington, whose character she had come to appreciate, tipped her decision.

'When the merchant ship Miss Reyne travelled on crashed during a storm in 1807, our town took in the survivors. Miss Reyne was still with us in 1809 when the French and Spanish invaded Oporto. Later, news reached us that General Wellesley's troops were pushing forward to Oporto. A small unit of enemy soldiers retreated through our property, which was off the path of the advancing allied troops. The men at our home were very young or very old. Anyone able to carry arms had been killed or sent to serve in Emperor Bonaparte's army on the continent. The soldiers who attacked us were mainly a ragtag group of deserters. Fortunately for us, the allied supply train and an escort of soldiers approached from the southeast near us. During the skirmish on our property, the deserters locked us in the stable and set it on fire. Charlie had managed to hide and was fortunately able to help us escape. Otherwise, we would have perished. I met Charlie's father soon after when he came to collect his daughter. We have been together as a family ever since.'

'It was one tragedy after another for all of you. I am sorry for all the lives lost,' Mrs Sherrington said simply.

Sofia nodded. 'Ours is just one of thousands of stories. Months earlier, four thousand people from Oporto died escaping from the enemy when a bridge collapsed, drowning everyone.' She looked sadly at Inês. 'Many more died on the battlefield. We all lost family and friends during the occupation. None of us are free of scars from the war.'

Tears rolled down Mrs Sherrington's cheeks as she observed the exchanged glances of grief between the women. She brushed her tears away as Charlie, unaware of their conversation, bounded cheerfully out of the house and re-joined them at their table.

'I wonder when the others are coming back,' said Inês, changing the topic. 'If the fish are biting well, I fear we shall not see the men for the entire afternoon. I have so little time left with Mr Jaeger,' she explained to Mrs Sherrington, 'that I am jealously guarding every moment.'

'I understand how you must be feeling,' nodded Mrs Sherrington. She had recently learnt of the engagement between Gus and Inês and the plans for the men to travel to the continent. 'My husband only just returned from a lengthy assignment in the Peninsula. I am loathe to let him out of my sight,' she said. 'Perhaps, whilst Mr Jaeger is away, you can come to visit me,' she suggested. 'You are all welcome to stay with me in Southampton, which is not so very far to come. My home is not a grand one, but it is spacious and comfortable. I can show you all my favourite places.'

Charlie watched the budding friendship between the three older women with a sense of pleasure. A difficult separation lay ahead for Gus and Inês and, as well, she would desperately miss the company of the Jaeger brothers. It warmed her heart to hear the invitation from Mrs Sherrington. The offer of support from a woman who had endured long separations herself was a clear signal of her caring nature. Charlie, who knew of Captain Sherrington's steadiness of character, could easily understand why Captain Brantford had become close friends with this couple.

'Captain Brantford has visited us a few times in the past. Perhaps we can entice him to join us as well, to do some sight-seeing together in the area and attend the local concerts,' Mrs Sherrington added, glancing at Charlie. She was not without her own thoughts on how matters lay between this young lady and her husband's closest colleague.

'Did I hear you mention concerts?' asked Captain Brantford, approaching from a nearby path. The other men followed him, returning from a most satisfying morning excursion. To the infinite delight of Gus and Wil, they had gone fly fishing for brown trout along a narrow river.

'My dear Lord Tripp,' came Lady Tripp's distinctive voice from nearby. 'I was afraid you errant gentlemen would miss the ball entirely. I am glad you have left enough time to scrub yourselves thoroughly for this evening's event. We will meet for a light dinner before our guests arrive for the ball. Let us all head indoors, shall we? Come, dearest,' she gestured to her husband, 'the water will be nicely hot for your bath. Do hurry along.'

'Coming, my sweet,' he replied in a pained voice, marching off behind her.

Charlie had hoped for at least a short visit with Captain Brantford but, under the circumstances, she had to satisfy herself with a rather brief exchange.

'Captain Sand assured us that he and your sister and Lieutenant Niles will all be coming to Greydon Hall this evening,' she told him as they walked towards the house. 'It will be your first time seeing them in months. You must be looking forward to it immensely.'

'I have already met with them since I returned. Did you think I had not? But yes, I am indeed happy they are attending.'

'But you came straight here from Portsmouth with my father.'

'They were in Portsmouth when we arrived,' said the captain.

'No, were they really?'

'Captain Sand had business matters there and Lieutenant Niles accompanied him. I have not seen my sister yet. She will box my ears when she sees me tonight. You can be sure she is annoyed I stayed here rather than coming directly to her home. It appeased her, but only slightly, when I sent word that I accompanied Captain and Mrs Sherrington, who were invited to stay here at your uncle's home.'

'How did it come about that you travelled here with my father?' asked Charlie. 'He has not said a word about it. Mind you,' her temper rose as she mulled over this point, 'he has barely spoken with me since he arrived.'

'We had dinner together with your father and Mrs Montalto the evening before we set out,' explained the captain. 'Since we were all coming to the same place, it made sense to travel together.'

Charlie nodded, sorting out her thoughts.

'You and my father have spent a fair bit of time together, then,' she said, digging for information.

He waited for her to continue.

She wanted to ask him outright about any conversations they had had, and if she had entered their discussions in some way, but her manners, rough as they could sometimes be, stopped her from taking this approach. She tried the indirect route.

'I imagine you are almost bosom friends by now.'

'That would make for an entertaining story,' he replied, almost smiling.

'Did not you speak to him about me at all?' she asked, whining a little.

The captain glanced around him. The general was walking twenty paces in front of them. The Sherringtons were behind them. Her family waited inside the house. There was so much the captain wanted to say to her, to ask, to discuss, that his frustration rose almost beyond what he could stand.

Charlie's sense of frustration was clearly at a similar level.

'I understand that you are a man of few words,' she said to the captain. 'You have spent so much time alone in your ship's cabin or talking about cannons and wind and waves with your sailor friends that you cannot put two sentences together to assure me that you are truly doing well and not suffering from all that has happened. And if you are well, as you profess, and still have nothing to say to me about anything at all, then I shall have to draw my own conclusions.'

After delivering this unexpected speech to her favourite captain in all the world, Charlie marched off to her bedroom. Slamming the door behind her, she threw herself on her bed and wept for at least a full minute. Recovering her senses, she patted her face dry and pulled out two of her two evening gowns and lay them across her bed.

'If you had enough flesh to fill this dress out,' Aunt Lydia had said just the other day, 'it would look fine to have it cut so low but, dear child, you have barely anything to show. And I prefer white or pale pink for an unmarried girl at her coming out. This dress, with the sheer white overlay and the pink satin underskirt, is perfect for you. This pretty layering of lace around the bodice suits you. Trust me, child, it is perfect for this special occasion.'

Charlie picked up the second dress, with its layers of sheer white muslin, and a green satin underdress to be worn beneath the gown. Simple and elegant, the gown featured very little lace and had an unadorned, low-cut neckline. She held the gown against herself and swirled defiantly in front of the long mirror in her dressing room. Charlie laid both dresses together again on the bed.

One of her aunt's maids knocked at her door. 'I have come to help you get ready,' announced the young girl.

Charlie went to her closet, rummaged through her shoes, and pulled out an elegant pair of slippers.

'I hope I can dance in these and not trip like some ridiculous fool,' she said to the maid.

'Yes, miss.'

'I will wear this gown to dinner,' Charlie informed the young lady, pointing to the pale pink one, 'and then I will need your help afterwards to change into this other gown.'

'Are you certain, miss? Everyone at dinner will already be dressed for the ball.'

'Yes, yes, but I will make some sort of reason to come back here and then change my gown after the meal. It will just create an endless argument with my aunt if I wear this second gown to dinner. I will need you to hurry back with me after we eat and help me change my clothes. Will you do so? Do not discuss this with anyone. Not a single word. Do you understand?'

Charlie picked up the leather sleeve where she kept her long knife and pulled it out, checking the blade with her finger. 'This badly needs to be sharpened. Do you mind taking this to the kitchen for me to get that done?' She slid the knife back into its sheath and passed it to the maid.

The little maid, scared witless, said that she agreed whole-heartedly with Charlie's plans for the evening. 'I will not say a word to your aunt,' she sputtered. Clutching Charlie's knife, the youngster scurried out of the room and darted away.

'Thank you! Hurry back!' Charlie called after her, chuckling to herself. 'I will need your help after my bath! Be quick!'

THIRTY-THREE

Presenting Miss Reyne

THE ARRIVING CARRIAGES rumbled along the gravel lane approaching the house. The family members, all elegantly attired, gathered in the large front entranceway at Greydon Hall to greet their guests. Lord and Lady Tripp, their daughter Mary, her husband George, and the general and his daughter stood in a neat row welcoming everyone as they entered the house.

'I am exhausted already, and I have not even danced once yet!' complained Charlie to Inês when she was finally able to step away from everyone. 'I am so thirsty! My aunty says I am not to have a sip of anything but lemonade this evening. She has threatened to watch me like a hawk. A hawk, of all things! Why not an owl, at least?'

'I almost suspect you of doing that on purpose!' was what her watchful aunt had uttered to Charlie just two hours earlier. They had been seated in the dining room at the time, enjoying a light repast with their house guests before the start of the ball, when Charlie suddenly squealed in horror.

'Oh, no!' she cried out. 'Good grief! Oh, dear! How can I be so clumsy? I have accidentally upset my glass. You must excuse me. I will change into another gown at once and return as soon as possible. I shan't be long!'

As Charlie rose from the table, everyone gasped at the stain of red wine splashed across the front of her pale pink ball gown. Captain Brantford, who had barely taken his eyes off her during their meal, was stunned. He had seen her knock the side of her own glass. Bewildered, he ran the images repeatedly through his mind, trying to convince himself she had not done it on purpose.

True to Charlie's promise, and to her aunt's dismay, Charlie returned shortly afterwards wearing the alternate gown with the low-cut neckline. The response to her change in outfit varied significantly among her family members.

'You look stunning!' said Inês immediately upon seeing her. 'At first, I thought you were some sort of enchantress coming from another world. Then I thought, heavens no, it is our own dear Charlie!' Inês ran her hands through the soft overlay, several layers thick, and admired the charming effect of the pale green underskirt. 'I love it. You have such a lithe figure. This looks delightful on you!'

Sofia, surveying Charlie from head to toe, took both of Charlie's hands in hers and winked. 'How very astute of you. What a perfect selection, darling. I could not have chosen better.'

'Where has my little girl gone?' lamented her father on seeing the sophisticated appearance of his daughter.

'Goodness, Charlotte,' her aunt said, coming close to speak privately to her. 'All of the men will be staring at you. Do you have a shawl you can wear? Worry not, dear, I will fetch one of mine for you later.'

That was when the clocks chimed. Carriages were arriving. The doors opened. The ball had begun.

Charlie's aunt had hastily pushed her niece to the end of the reception line beside her father. That is where Charlie stood for the next hour, meeting and greeting the crowd, and, in Captain Brantford's biased opinion, outshining every other woman who entered the room.

Lieutenant Niles was standing near the captain. The two

men had just returned to the front parlour, having already escorted Captain Sand, Mrs Sand, and the Sherringtons into the ballroom.

'I never imagined,' said Niles, 'after meeting Miss Reyne in Vitoria the way that I did, that she could ever look like this. Who would have thought it possible?' He leaned against the wall alongside Brantford and stared with him in admiration at Miss Reyne. 'She is quite the picture of beauty this evening,' he said. "It is really too bad she is not interested in me in the slightest.'

Brantford took a sip of his drink.

'Her hair looks most elegant,' Niles continued. 'I have not seen it this way before. She looks beautiful.' Niles had more to say on the subject. 'She is too short to describe as resembling some Grecian goddess,' he chatted on, 'but my word, in that style of gown, and seeing her from the side, her profile is simply exquisite.'

'Are you done?' asked Captain Brantford. His thoughts exactly mirrored those of his friend.

'Oh, saints preserve us, do you see those men over there? The Weyburn clan has arrived. There are thousands of them tonight.'

Brantford watched a group of young men coming into the room, crowding around Charlie.

'Do you know them by name?' he asked Niles.

'No. There are too many of them. It is not worth my time sorting them out. Just avoid the tallest one. Some weeks back, he was the one who rammed his phaeton into a carriage on the old road not far from Sand's place. Stupid, reckless driving was what it was. The impact injured some travellers. Miss Reyne and Mrs Alvares were on the scene when we arrived. They took everyone to Chellisbury to take care of them there. The driver's brother, Mr Andrew Weyburn, was injured and stayed on for a time at Chellisbury. He seems to have fallen in love with our Miss Reyne. Wait until you see the layout at Chellisbury. You will be mightily impressed. It is an amazing facility, I can tell you.'

Brantford had heard mention of the accident, but he knew very little about what happened. Not having seen Chellisbury yet and hearing only snippets about it from Charlie's father on their trip from Portsmouth and knowing only briefly from Charlie herself about the marriage proposal from Mr Andrew Weyburn, he was keen to learn more about the man.

'How long did they stay with her?' he asked.

'Most everyone left that evening. Your brother-in-law and I stayed on overnight, due to the weather, along with two of the Weyburns. They are dull company, I must say. The other Weyburn cousin, the one who has fallen for Miss Reyne, ended up staying for a week in the infirmary at Chellisbury to recover. Poor Miss Reyne, he never lets her out of his sight. That is him over there, the one standing next to Charlie on the near side— the good-looking one.'

Brantford studied the young man. Was this the Weyburn who had proposed to Miss Reyne, then? The fellow was certainly handsome enough to attract a bit of attention to himself.

'I ought to make time to speak to the general this evening,' said Niles, half to himself. 'I am certain he would not want that chap to ingratiate himself with Miss Reyne. He seems pleasant enough at first glance, but my friends in London say his looks are the best part about him. The more one gets to know him, the less attractive he becomes.'

'Is that so?' said Brantford.

'Can you hear it? The music has started up. I have asked Miss Reyne to honour me with two of the early dances. I wonder who she will dance with first? I assume you are going to dance a set with her. You had best reserve your spot. Otherwise, the Weyburns will fill up all the dances.'

Niles, bored with watching the Weyburns and eager to dance, gestured to Brantford. 'Follow me, old man. You need to get your legs moving so that people are not thinking that you just got off a boat.'

'It is not a boat,' said Brantford, highly annoyed.

'Whatever you call it, then.'

Niles marched ahead. Brantford followed. The room was hot and crowded. As some guests cut in front of them, Brantford separated from Niles and turned back to wait for Miss Reyne. She was still surrounded by the Weyburns.

'Captain Brantford!' she called out, waving to him. 'Excuse me, gentlemen, I must excuse myself. Duty calls! One of my uncle's house guests requires my attention. Do come and find me later if you wish to carry on our conversation.'

Handsome Mr Andrew Weyburn touched her arm to detain her. 'Dare I hope that you will save the last two dances for me, Miss Reyne?'

'Indeed, sir, I shall be delighted to do so.'

Satisfied, he released his hold on her arm and followed his cousins down the hall.

She said all this within the hearing of Captain Brantford and smiled sweetly as she reached him. Tucking her arm into his, she whispered, 'Come with me.'

Startled, he followed behind her.

'Well?' he asked, on entering the library with her. "What is all this about?'

'It is very simple. I needed to escape from all the Weyburn lads. Did you see the handsome one at my side earlier? That is Mr Andrew Weyburn, the gentleman who has asked for my hand. I plan to turn him down tomorrow, but I am going to tease him a little first. He is a grand schemer and I need to teach him a lesson.'

Completely befuddled by the woman in front of him, he could only stand and stare at her.

'Do you think I am pretty?' she asked him.

'I do,' he said quietly. 'I also think we ought not to stay in this room any longer, unless you are wanting to marry me in the near future.'

'Is that an offer?' she asked. 'I shall have to think about it.'

'I think you have gotten hold of some strange guidebook teaching women how to seduce young men,' he said.

'Not at all. You are not that young. These are, in fact, straight-forward war tactics,' she replied. 'Confuse and overwhelm until the party surrenders.'

He burst out laughing.

Charlie snorted through her nose.

'You must admit, I can be amusing sometimes,' she said, trying to keep a straight face. 'May I be entirely serious for a moment?' she asked, peering up at him. 'I must tell you, sir. You are so handsome; I cannot stop looking at you. Mr Weyburn is nothing in comparison.'

He became deadly serious.

'Stop what you are doing. Get out of here, right now,' he barked, pushing her gently towards the door. 'You are not going to do this, do you understand? This is your ball. Your aunt and uncle, your father, your friends, everyone is outside this room, waiting for you to appear, waiting for you to open the first dance. We are leaving this instant.'

'I only wanted to ask if you will dance the first set with me. It is a cotillion.'

'Yes. I promised you earlier that I would do so. You did not have to kidnap me. I am willing if you want me.'

'I do want you,' she said. 'Very much so.'

Her words flustered him. Clearly, he thought, this woman had mastered the class on war tactics.

Charlie suddenly stood on her tiptoes, leaned towards the captain, and kissed his cheek.

Using his foot, the captain pushed against the library door

to shut it. He pulled Charlie Reyne towards him, swung them both around, and embraced her.

'Miss Reyne,' he murmured.

'I heard you. I have a ball to attend. My family is waiting for me,' she said despondently.

The captain tilted Charlie's face towards him and kissed her gently on the lips.

'I adore you,' he said.

Charlie wrapped her arms around her captain and pulled him close.

⌒

'Where is that daughter of yours?' Lord Tripp muttered to his brother. 'Ah, finally, there she is. Charlotte! Hurry and take your place in the first grouping. Where did you get to? We have all been waiting for you. Is Captain Brantford opening the dance with you? Stand there, sir, at the top of the square. Quickly, the musicians are ready.'

Lord Tripp signalled to the ensemble to begin.

Everyone had their eyes on the dancers. Captain Brantford and Miss Charlotte Reyne had eyes for each other only. He was at her side, then separated from her, then back with her again, rotating through the steps, drawn away, drawn together, in an easy rhythm.

'It is like our time together over all these months, is it not?' she asked, seeming to read his mind.

'And for the foreseeable future,' he replied, looking longingly at the captivating woman beside him.

'Will you be gone again soon?' she asked him sadly.

'I leave tomorrow, in fact,' he replied, holding her hands tightly as they stepped around the other dancers.

'How long are you to be away?'

'Four weeks. I am going north to the Cotswolds to stay with my brother. My sister and Captain Sand will join us. Besides spending time with one another, which has been rare of late, we have family matters to address relating to our father's estate. I have not seen my brother James since last October,' he said, almost apologetically.

'Hmm,' she replied. 'And then you will be back for the Grand Naval Review, correct?'

'I must be back by then, yes. May I see you when I return?' he asked quietly.

'You may,' she said. Her cheeks were bright pink.

They fell silent for a time, dancing almost by rote as the couples performed the steps of the dance. Her heart fluttered each time they clasped hands. It would have done her good to know that his own heart was beating wildly. His response to her kiss in the other room told Charlie everything she needed to know. It was abundantly clear to her. Her dear captain, the man she cherished, was completely and utterly in love with her. She knew with equal certainty, though, that he did not believe he was the right match for her; that he felt his profession would be too hard on her. She had given that a great deal of thought herself.

'You deserve a man who can be with you all the time!' he had protested almost immediately after he kissed her, first holding her in a tight embrace, then just as suddenly releasing her and pushing her gently away.

'I deserve a man who can make me happy,' she replied.

They stepped back from one another. Soon after they marched into the ballroom together, each lost in thought, flustered by their emotions. They went through the motions of the dance, coming together, stepping apart. Charlie looked like she was about to cry. He saw her face and felt crushed by the hurt in her eyes.

'We will talk it through,' he told her. 'I am not going away for long. Let us think about things. I will see you as soon as I am back. We will take our time, and discuss everything, and decide together. Can you wait until then, for me to come back?'

She nodded and smiled through her tears at him. He had calmed her, uttering the words she needed to hear. She felt a surge of joy and seemed to float through the dance. Her head was telling her what the next step should be, but her feet, most unfortunately, went in another direction.

Miss Charlotte Reyne, the belle of her ball, suddenly tripped.

'Oh, my!' she said in disbelief. Astonished, she stared ahead, wide-eyed, as she fell to the floor face-first.

'Are you injured? Did you hurt yourself?' cried the captain, instantly crouching at her side.

The musicians had stopped. A crowd of dancers gathered around. Mortified, Charlie lay still on the floor.

'Close your eyes,' whispered the captain. 'Pretend you are ill.' He scooped Charlie into his arms and hurried from the room.

'Miss Reyne has fainted from the heat,' he called in a loud voice to Mrs Montalto, who came rushing over to assist. 'Can you bring some water and a cloth? I will take her to the library.'

He quickly left the ballroom, carried Charlie down the crowded hallway, and closed the door behind him in the library. He was loathe to set her down but released her finally onto the settee. He sat beside her, holding her tightly.

'You are squeezing me too much. It is hard to breathe,' she gasped at him.

'Oh, I am so sorry. Are you feeling a little better? The side of your face is red from your fall.'

'It is red because I am embarrassed.'

He picked up her hand and squeezed her fingers in consolation. He kissed her forehead just as the twin doors into the library swung open. Mrs Montalto entered the room with the general. Charlie's aunt and uncle and Inês followed closely on their heels. Gus and Wil hovered just beyond.

Suddenly, Mr Andrew Weyburn pushed his way into the room, speaking loudly for all to hear. 'Where has that man taken her? Is my future wife in here? Let me see her at once,' he demanded, catching a glimpse of the captain seated beside Miss Reyne. He scowled furiously at Captain Brantford. 'I thank you for your assistance, sir, but you are sitting far too close to my dear Miss Reyne. Move away, sir. I will stay with her now.'

Brantford stood up, still holding Charlie's hand.

'You are entirely mistaken, Mr Weyburn. You claim Miss Reyne is your betrothed. That is not possible. She is engaged to marry me. Is that not right, my dear?'

Charlie nodded shyly.

'We do not require your company,' said the captain. 'Let me see you to the door.'

The captain escorted the sputtering young man out into the hallway, closing the door on him. He turned to find everyone in the room staring at him.

'You say you are engaged to my daughter,' said the general, looking back and forth between the two of them.

'May I have a word in private, sir?' Brantford asked the general.

'I hardly see how that is possible right at this moment, with a house full of guests, unless we go upstairs to the privacy of my room and meet there. But this is hardly the time. Can it wait until tomorrow?' Rather than asking the captain this question, the general was looking directly at his daughter.

Charlie nodded again.

Perturbed by being ignored and seeing the private communication between the father and daughter with no acknowledgement of what he had just requested, the captain said, 'I am afraid it cannot wait. I leave Greydon Hall first thing in the morning and cannot postpone my stay. If I may impose upon your time, later this evening would do, sir, once the ball has ended.'

'Later it is, then. We will meet back here. Do not disappoint me.' The general opened the door and nodded his head for everyone to follow him out of the room.

'There is a latch here at the top that will let you secure the door,' said Lord Tripp on his way out. 'You ought to fasten it if you do not want Mr Weyburn, or his thousands of cousins, wandering in again.'

Sofia turned to speak to Charlie.

'Shall I stay with you, dearest?'

'I prefer that you go,' Charlie replied, not unkindly.

'I will expect you to bring her back to the ball within a few minutes,' Sofia instructed Captain Brantford.

'Yes, ma'am.'

It was certainly not the first time Captain Brantford and Charlie Reyne spent time alone together, but it was undoubtedly their most memorable. The captain seated himself on the couch beside his darling Charlie. He lifted her hand and kissed her wrist. She rested her head against his shoulder.

'You are far too thin,' he scolded. 'When I carried you from the ballroom, I was afraid I would break your ribs. You really ought to eat more than you do.'

She waited patiently while he composed himself.

'I said that we were to marry to rid you of an unwanted suitor. Look at what you caused, by wanting to tease him! I would not have claimed to be engaged, otherwise. Sadly, you and I are no further along in our decisions than before,' he said. 'I have thought about this every day, in every way, and cannot see how I am the right choice for you. I am sometimes away for half a year at a time. You need someone who can be by your side always, to protect you, care for you, and share every precious day that passes.'

'Would you let me sail with you?' she asked.

'I would,' he said without hesitation. 'But can you bear to abandon Chellisbury? Lieutenant Niles said it is an ambitious undertaking, a marvellous place, and mainly of your own doing. You have plans in place, projects to complete, and people about whom you care deeply and who all rely on you. How can I steal you away from everything you hold dear and important?'

'But how am I to stay behind when you are to go away again?' Charlie reached up and brushed the hair from his forehead. She traced the scar on his forehead with her fingertip then placed her hand flush against his cheek. 'Will you always sail? Must you sail?' she asked. 'Can you see a time when you would wish to do something else? The war is over now. Cannot you stay and rest here with me? I am not without resources. Could you leave the Navy, and do something completely different? You are at risk every time you step on board your ship.'

'Captain Sherrington sets sail next month to support our fleet in the war against the Americans. Our admiral will send me to join him at the end of my leave. There will always be another war, another port, another mission. I am a naval officer. I do not know if I could even survive on land. I would feel homeless here.'

Charlie, still dizzy from her fall, attempted to stand up. He rose to help her and pulled her close to him.

'Let us not talk about this anymore right now,' she said, struggling to remain composed. 'I understand your feelings. You are beginning to know mine.'

He fought hard not to pick her up and carry her upstairs in his arms.

'When I meet your father,' he said, 'I will say to him that you have agreed to marry me, though you have not done so. How could you? I have not even asked you properly. I will seek your father's permission. Under the circumstances, I cannot do otherwise. Then, you and I can reflect on our situation and see what is possible. I cannot bear for you to be unhappy, and

I cannot stand the idea of leaving you alone. I am torn with what to do.'

Tears ran freely down Charlie's cheeks.

Captain Brantford bent over and lightly kissed her. 'Are you ready, Miss Reyne? Your family is waiting for you.'

Charlie squeezed his hand. 'I am ready. And you?'

He unlatched the door and pulled it, holding it open for her to pass.

THIRTY-FOUR

The Grand Naval Review

CHARLIE STOOD EXCITEDLY on her tiptoes, holding on to Inês's arm. She craned her neck, attempting to get a better view of the royal barges below in the harbour. The two women had left their hotel room early in the day, intent on getting close to the loading pier where their boat awaited them. They had, for the moment, fortunately secured an ideal situation, and were well able to see the remarkable event unfolding in front of them.

'Can you see them? Is that the Russian Tsar? Is the Empress with him?' asked Inês, spying the royal guests on one of the large barges.

'I can see them all!' Charlie cried excitedly.

Charlie and Inês were making their way over to a small pier when they stopped to catch a glimpse of the sovereign entourages. Charlie had taken out her sketchbook and was happily drawing pictures of the harbour, with hundreds of ships within her view. Inês watched in admiration while her friend drew, enjoying the crowds and cheering all around them.

They planned to meet the family within the hour and sail out into the harbour to watch the Grand Naval Review. Her drawings done, Charlie took Inês's hand and pulled her up onto the low stone wall beside the pathway. People crowded all around them. Thousands upon thousands of spectators had come to

Portsmouth for the festivities and most especially to see the sovereigns as they arrived in town for the Grand Naval Review.

It was a spectacular celebration. None had witnessed anything like it in their lifetimes. Homes, shops, streetlamps, carriages, and fences were adorned with flowers, streamers, and ribbons. Fireworks were lit every evening. The allied sovereigns had arrived in Portsmouth two days ago.

'I wish Gus and Wil were here to see this with us,' Charlie said quietly.

Inês smiled tearfully and squeezed Charlie's hand.

It was the first time since the war began that the sovereigns and the military and naval champions of war gathered in one place. The celebration marked the defeat of Emperor Napoleon Bonaparte and his exile to the island of Elba. The world was at peace. Over two days in Portsmouth, the British Royal Navy would proudly raise its colours and man the yards in a ceremonial salute to England's Prince Regent and the gathered sovereigns. Charlie wondered if they would repeat their boarding of HMS *Impregnable* in today's events.

'Come, we had best get moving so we do not miss getting onto our boat,' said Charlie.

She and Inês pushed through the crowds and stepped along a narrow set of stone stairs descending to the water's edge. Her father was standing in the middle of the boat that the captain had provided for them, waving for them to hurry.

'What on earth has kept you?' asked the general. 'We are all here waiting. You are the last to arrive.'

'Are you meeting with Captain Brantford right after the review? You have decided, then, have you?' Sofia whispered to her as they took their seats.

Charlie nodded solemnly. 'We will meet once they come back from the harbour. He said he will still need at least an hour to come on land.'

Swaying gently in their seats on the boat as the oarsmen took them out into the harbour, Charlie looked around her, amazed by their surroundings. What a remarkable sight. Hundreds of ships of every rank lay beyond the harbour. Inside the harbour, countless fishing boats and small boats, filled with spectators, bobbed on the surface, hull against hull. Lords and ladies, townsfolk, fishermen, marines, soldiers and sailors, farmers and merchants, all turned out to watch the action. On land, thousands of spectators stood along the shoreline. Everyone cheered the progress of the Navy Board's barges and the royal barges, flying their huge standards, into the harbour in order of their seniority and status, as the Prince Regent and the sovereign imperial suites proceeded out to review the ships at Spithead. Flocks of gulls lifted off and floated alongside the boats, screeching constantly, as though caught up in the excitement of the moment.

'It will begin soon!' Charlie cried.

At last, the royal salute was underway from the platform. Charlie gasped and covered her ears as the cannon blasts from shore resounded across the harbour. She felt as though the whole world must be listening to the beating of her heart. She turned her eyes towards Spithead, out to the horizon where the man she loved so deeply was on his ship, where he belonged, leading his men. She watched as the ships held their formations.

They could not identify the *Pontus* and the *Falcon* from this distance, but she watched Mrs Sherrington cup her hands and blow a kiss towards the sea.

'Captain Sherrington's ship is the tenth frigate in the second line,' she informed them. 'The *Pontus* is the third after the ships of the line, on the near side.' She pointed out to sea. 'Do you see it?'

Charlie could not stop her eyes from welling with tears of pride. She clasped her hands tightly. She was no stranger to sea travel. She had sailed to India and back. She had been ship-wrecked with a merchant fleet off the shores of Portugal. She had sailed in a naval escort convoy and witnessed the pursuit and capture of an enemy prize aboard HMS *Pontus*. She had in that moment come as close to engaging in naval battle as she ever wished to be, and it had given her a glimpse of the courage and skill of the seamen aboard those ships. She felt an overwhelming sense of pride in their accomplishments.

Winds were picking up. Charlie watched with excitement as the ships pivoted and turned flawlessly, as though in a victory dance, much like Captain Brantford's convoy had done when assuming its battle formation on her return voyage to England.

At last, after the cannons on the platform and the ships fell silent, they watched the smoke from the final salute drift into the sky in thin strips of white. They could see the royal barges reversing direction and leaving the formation, sailing away from the warships.

'Take us back now, men,' said Uncle Tripp to the head oarsman. 'Let us get ashore before we are overtaken by all these other small boats. I say, brother, we have waited twenty years for all these wars to end. What a grand sight to see.'

'I only wish thousands upon thousands more of my men were watching from shore,' said the general solemnly. 'They will never see a day like this. They are not coming home.'

Charlie reached over and placed her small hand inside her father's. She sat quietly beside him, lifting her head occasionally to watch the birds soaring above and landing on the water.

'Look, Father, it is a little tern, come to visit us.'

'Is it now.'

She had his attention.

'Sir, I trust you have not forgotten, I am meeting with Captain Brantford in one hour's time and so I will not be returning with you to our hotel. Inês will stay with me, though I will be alone briefly, speaking to him by myself for a short while. It is not as though we will be out of sight. There are thousands of people everywhere.'

It struck the general that she had been alone for as long as he could remember. She had crossed the country in the dead of night with enemies to the left and right and never asked if anyone minded. It made his heart ill to think about it.

'I am not one to stand on ceremony as they do here in England. I have no objection to you meeting with him, provided Inês remains with you. You already know that I have given him permission to speak with you. The decision is yours, my dear daughter.'

Charlie made no reply. By now, they were standing on the pier. The family clambered out of the small boat, chatting excitedly about the marvellous exhibition they had witnessed. They climbed up the steps to the stone path on the bank above. Sofia kissed Charlie lightly on the cheek as she passed and squeezed her hand. Charlie held back to the last, letting everyone go in front of her, and then she and Inês quietly disappeared into the crowds gathered along the shoreline.

It was difficult at first to find their way through the dense groups of people moving along the walkway. Most people were headed towards the dockyard and the festivities in town whereas they wished to go the other way. Charlie and Inês soon found themselves in the middle of a group of townsmen, being swept along in their direction. The men had been drinking and they reeked of ale. The men relished having two ladies caught in their midst. They would not let them pass out of their circle.

A group of young soldiers looked on, disgusted by the behaviour of the men. Suddenly, one of them recognised Charlie.

'Men, look—it is Little Charlie!' a familiar-sounding voice yelled out. 'There, on the walkway!'

A dozen men in redcoats pushed their way towards Charlie and Inês, shoving aside the drunken townsmen who surrounded them. The soldiers formed two lines, with a front and rear guard, expanding their lines to protect the women from all sides.

'Sergeant Briggs! How good it is to see you!' cried Charlie.

'The pleasure is mine, miss! Are you headed to the Crown?' he asked.

'No. There is a small pier further to the east. We are headed there.'

'We will take you there.' Hearing of the need for a change in direction, the soldiers pushed their way through the advancing crowds and broke through to a calmer area along the embankment.

'The crowds are restless here today, ladies. We will stay with you until your party arrives.'

'Thank you, Sergeant. Gentlemen, how good it is to see you all. I have not seen you since the advance at Vitoria! I have missed your dear faces.'

The men nodded, smiling and greeting her in turn. An hour passed easily in their company while they waited for Captain Brantford to reach the shore. Sergeant Briggs looked out at the men approaching in a rowing boat.

'Good grief, it is that captain fellow. I know him. He paid a visit to your father when we were stationed on the coast, near San Sebastián. I brought him out to camp to meet with the general.'

Excited that her wait was at an end, Charlie watched as the captain's boat pulled up to the pier.

Once the small boat had dropped off the captain and pulled away, Sergeant Briggs jealously exchanged greetings with the captain. He and his men stood squarely at Charlie's back.

'We must ask your intention, sir, in meeting alone with our Miss Reyne in this location.'

'Mrs Alvares is with me. And if you have questions, you can simply ask me,' said Charlie petulantly. 'I have father's permission to be here.'

'That may be, Miss Reyne, but this is highly unusual.' Sergeant Briggs frowned.

'We are meeting to discuss personal matters and will join my father afterwards,' she told him.

'Is the general rooming at the Crown?' asked the sergeant.

Charlie nodded in reply.

'Sergeant Briggs, it is good to see you again,' said the captain, surveying the soldier. 'Did you escort Miss Reyne here? That was very good of you. I had not known it would be quite this crowded.'

'Miss Reyne advises that you have a personal matter to discuss,' said Sergeant Briggs, perturbed. 'My men and I, and Mrs Alvares, will wait for you atop the bank, on the pathway,' he said to Charlie. 'We can see you easily from there. Join us when you are done, and we will take you back to the general.' As he turned to march away, he saw the captain take Miss Reyne's hand in his and caress her fingertips.

'I say, sir,' he barked. 'That is forward of you!'

'You need not worry, Sergeant Briggs. We are engaged to be married,' explained Charlie in a conciliatory tone.

'Engaged!' His voice was heavy with regret. 'Well, if you say so, miss.'

Sergeant Briggs reluctantly marched up the stone steps to the pathway above, taking his men with him. 'Call if you need me for anything at all, miss!'

Charlie and the captain walked out onto the small pier and stood quietly together, waiting as the men finished climbing the steps to the top of the bank.

'I had not expected to speak to you with a dozen of the general's soldiers watching and listening to every word,' he said.

'Nor I.' She smiled at him. 'You are looking well, dear sir. The visit to your family has done you good.'

'Indeed, it was long overdue.'

'Have you sorted out what troubled you?'

'I have,' he said.

Charlie nodded.

Captain Brantford looked up the embankment at Mrs Alvares and the dozen soldiers staring curiously down at them. He took a breath and began to recite his rehearsed speech.

'Please, do not say it,' said Charlie.

He was holding both of her hands. He tipped his head, taken aback that she would not let him speak.

'You are going to tell me again that I deserve a man who will be by my side, and not someone who will be leaving me alone.'

The captain could not argue with this.

'You are going to say that I have an opportunity to start afresh in England and should not tie myself down to a man in the navy, who cannot predict where his next orders will take him.'

The captain lowered his gaze, holding on to the tips of her hands. Never had he felt as helpless as he did now, as though his lifeblood was seeping out through the tips of his fingers. What would she say next? His heart felt heavy.

'I want to ask you something,' she said to him, waiting for him to lift his eyes. Her own filled with tears. 'If you leave here today, without being engaged to marry, will you be happy? Is that what you want for yourself?'

'How can you even ask that?'

The men on the top of the bank could hear his angry tone. Sergeant Briggs placed his hand on his hip where he carried his army pistol.

'Do you wish to marry me, Captain Brantford?' she asked him.

He wanted to crush her to his chest.

'Miss Charlotte Reyne, daughter of a general, dedicated hospital aide, artist, wily interpreter, gorgeous young woman on the marriage market, if you were to marry me, I would be wild with joy,' he said, his voice breaking as he choked back his emotions. 'But who am I to deserve you? I am a second son, a man with a profession. My family's financial status has taken a heavy setback with my father's death. The navy is my livelihood and my career. Yes, I can be on land for a time, and I can make decisions later to mitigate the time away, but at this moment, I am a captain in the Royal Navy, with duties that take me back to sea. The risks of war at sea are my constant companion. You deserve someone who will stay by your side.'

'That is all very well, but I want to marry you,' she said to him. 'However,' she squeezed his hand, 'it is just that I do not want to marry you right away. I know you are not fond of long engagements and will be fearful that we might not make it to the altar, but a long engagement is best,' she said. 'It will not, cannot, be a secret one. You must promise to advertise it in *The Times* and tell the world that we are to marry.'

He shook his head in disbelief. 'What about Chellisbury?' he asked her. 'You have only just opened your facility, your new home. That is your dream. Your friends and family are all there.'

'I will stay at Chellisbury for at least another year until we get married. Then, if you are still staying at sea, I will come with you for part of the time. Mrs Sherrington says the captain is allowed to bring his wife when he sails. The rest of the time, I will stay at Chellisbury.'

'And you are willing to live like that, after all that you have endured. I cannot bear it if I make you unhappy.'

'And I cannot bear not to marry you, even if it means we must be separated at times,' replied Charlie. 'You are my darling captain. I loved you from the first moment I met you,' she confessed.

'No, no, no. Stop.' He cupped her face in hands and kissed her eyes, her nose, her chin, and her lips.

'Miss Charlotte Reyne, will you marry me?' he asked.

'I will,' she said, laughing and crying. 'I will be your wife.'

The captain picked her up and swirled her around. From the

bank above, eleven soldiers let out a cheer of congratulations for little Charlie Reyne. The twelfth, Sergeant Briggs, heartbroken to see the woman he adored in another man's arms, turned his head and looked away.

'We will sort out the details,' promised the captain. 'We have time to do so. But if I had my way, we would marry before I leave.'

'No, you are not listening to me. That is too soon. I still have much to do at Chellisbury, people to hire, and friends relying on me. I want to wait,' she said. 'Chellisbury must succeed. That is a promise I made to myself.'

He held her close, then took her hand as they looked out towards the ships anchored at Spithead. After a time, he said solemnly, 'While you want a long engagement, Miss Charlie Reyne, I do not. I have waited a lifetime to meet a woman like you. I wish we could be married tomorrow.'

'Tomorrow is not possible,' she said sensibly. 'I suppose we shall have to negotiate a few things.'

'That is my point exactly,' he said.

He looked up the bank at the soldiers who were stealing glances at the couple embracing on the pier below. 'Turn the other way!' he called to them. He waited as the men laughed and swung about.

Captain Brantford had never given much thought to soldiers. Now, he had good reason to dislike them immensely. He swore at them softly, then embraced Charlie and kissed her again. This time he barely noticed the loud cheers coming from the small army on the bank of Portsmouth Harbour.

A shout of cheers went up again but this time the sound came from the water. Turning about, Captain Brantford looked straight out at a boatload of sailors near the pier. The boat carried his own men from the *Pontus*, watching and cheering from one of the ship's tenders.

'Well done, Captain!' shouted one of his men. 'Congratulations to the little lady! When are you bringing her on board so we can meet her, sir?'

Charlie tipped back her head and smiled.

'Captain Brantford, do you hear what they are saying?' she asked him.

'I am not listening to a word from any of them.'

'They said they want you to kiss me again,' she said.

'Well, my darling, I suppose there is no point in disappointing them.'

To the great delight of the sailors in the boat and Charlie's dear friend and all the soldiers on the bank, and to the complete and utter satisfaction of his future wife, the captain gave Charlie Reyne a long, passionate, lingering kiss.

Separating at last, Charlie smiled dreamily at Captain Brantford while the soldiers and sailors watching them shouted and cheered in approval.

'Perhaps you are right,' she whispered to him, her heart beating wildly. 'A shorter engagement is the better plan.'

Acknowledgements

I AM THANKFUL to my husband Art who is my sounding board and companion, sharing my writing journey with me. My family and friends are a continual source of inspiration and encouragement.

I am grateful for the help of my launch team, returning after helping launch *The Brantford Wagers*, the first book in the Brantford Series. Evelyn Kampen Carrière, Ali Kampen, Bev Adam, and Nancy Dyck each inspire me with their qualities of perseverance and excellence.

My team of publishing professionals have shared their considerable talents with me throughout the production process. It is a pleasure to collaborate with such skilled partners. Thank you to Peter and Caroline O'Connor at *BespokeBookCovers.com* for designing the beautiful cover for *Charlie Reyne* and Sarah Peters at *GalleyCreativeCo.com* for interior book design for print formats. Many thanks as well to Nicky Galliers, whose technical editing savvy and understanding of differences in language usage between English-UK, CA, and US styles have been invaluable.

I offer my thanks and appreciation to the talented authors and bloggers who generously share insights and research on Georgian and Regency society through online posts and published materials.

To my readers, thank you for taking the time to connect on social media and to offer your reviews. I value your thoughtful comments and reflections.

About the Author

Charlie Reyne IS the author's second novel after *The Brantford Wagers* in the Brantford Series. The author Nadine Kampen immerses the reader in the fictional world of traditional historical romance, set in the memorable Regency England period. Embracing the heart-warming journeys of individuals open to the joys and challenges of love and romance, the author shares the hopes, schemes, and dreams of her characters.

Prior to her career as an author, Nadine served as a regional marketing manager with an international consulting firm and as a communications and marketing director on university campuses. Earlier in her career, she worked in public relations and journalism and was co-author and project lead for five non-fiction books comprising *The Canadian Breast Cancer Series.*

A resident of Winnipeg in Manitoba, Canada, Nadine loves relaxing with family and friends, gardening, and playing tunes on her 1905 Bell piano.

Readers are invited to connect with the author at NADINEKAMPEN.COM, on LinkedIn, and on Facebook and Instagram (Nadine Kampen Author).

9 781777 861636